JOE HILL
A Biographical Novel

Wallace Stegner

JOE HILL

A Biographical Novel

First published as
The Preacher and the Slave

University of Nebraska Press
Lincoln and London

First Bison Book printing: 1980
Most recent printing indicated by first digit below:
1   2   3   4   5   6   7   8   9   10

Library of Congress Cataloging in Publication Data

Stegner, Wallace Earle, 1909–
  Joe Hill, a biographical novel.

  First published under title: The preacher and the slave.
  1. Hillstrom, Joseph, 1879–1915—Fiction.   I.   Title.
PZ3.S818Jo   1980   [PS3537.T316]   813'.52   80–10760
ISBN 0–8032–4116–X
ISBN 0–8032–9115–9 pbk.

Published by arrangement with Doubleday & Company, Inc.
Manufactured in the United States of America

To My Wife and Son

Contents

Foreword

No thoroughly adequate history of the IWW exists. The standard histories are factual and doctrinal summaries, valuable for the record of the IWW's organization and activities but stopping short of the real climax of the movement just after World War I, and lacking in the kind of poetic understanding which should invest any history of a militant church.

From 1905 to the early twenties, the IWW was just that—a church which enlisted all the enthusiasm, idealism, rebelliousness, devotion, and selfless zeal of thousands of mainly young, mainly migrant workers. Its history is a chronicle of strikes, free-speech fights, riots, trials, frame-ups, and martyrdoms. It began in the industrial-union notions of Vincent St. John and Big Bill Haywood and the Western Federation of Miners. It was born of union and compromise in a national convention in 1905. It suffered its schisms and its withdrawals, especially when the Socialist Labor Party and the Socialists of De Leon and Debs withdrew in protest against IWW violence. It followed its own star of direct action, One Big Union, and the solidarity of all labor, applying its own industrial weapons of the strike, sabotage, free-speech fights. It won its great victories, as in the Lawrence strike when Joe Ettor and Arturo Giovannitti not only broke down the mill owners to the workers' demands, but won their legal fight against a murder charge in the Salem court. It had its magnetic leaders—St. John, Haywood, Ralph Chaplin, the Magon brothers, Frank Little, Elizabeth Gurley Flynn—and its areas of power, as in the lumberwoods of the Northwest and the harvest circle from Oklahoma to eastern Washington. It had its legendry, its lore, its songs. A singing union, volatile, mobile, "with more guts than good sense," it made itself in its short life the most militant and dramatic organization in the history of American labor.

It represented the very dissidence of dissent, the rebelliousness of rebellion, and it lived an increasingly violent life, battered at by all the power of industry and industry's local law, from 1905 to the series of anti-syndicalism trials that broke its back in the twenties. By the time its back was broken many of its founders and leaders were in jail, and had been since 1918, on charges of resisting the draft. Chaplin, Haywood, the Magons, dozens of others, shared the fate of Eugene Debs in those years. And others of the leaders were dead, like Frank Little, whose crippled lynched body swung from a Butte bridge a long time before anyone cut it down. Still others had drifted into the orbit of the newly formed Communist Party, headed for the sad manipulation and eventual disillusionment that awaited Haywood. Others hung on, and still hang on, belligerent as ever, dissenters to the end of a long resistant life, hating the ballotboxers as dupes, despising yellow socialists for their gradualism, loathing the Communists for the way they have taken over iww methods and twisted them to perverted uses. The iww now is an exclusive and somewhat mellowed club, but it can still rise up when it is stepped on, it can still muster pickets before the doors of the *New Republic* when it prints an article by me implying that Joe Hill, one of the great martyrs, could have been guilty. An injury to one is still an injury to all; the union doctrine has not changed by a hair's breadth. But now it is a church of old men.

They were militant in a period when militancy meant floggings, jail, bloodshed. They fought fire with fire, dynamite with dynamite. Police, newspapers, the middle-class citizenry, were all against them. Organizers disappeared, were run out of town, flogged through gauntlets, threatened with death. Towns passed laws against their speaking on street corners, and the word went out so that every loose Wobbly in five hundred miles grabbed the next freight, intent on climbing up on a soapbox long enough to get himself arrested. They jammed the jails, wore out the police, used up the city funds, and they kept on coming till the authorities buckled or they themselves were overwhelmed. And sometimes, as at Everett, they were mowed down by the guns of special deputies. Sometimes, as at Centralia, they were rushed by Armistice Day paraders, and out of that riot came another martyr, Wesley Everest, beaten and castrated and lynched and pumped full of bullets.

The iww was a fighting faith. It's members were the shock

troops of labor. Its weakness was that it really liked a fight better than it liked planning, negotiations, politicking. It won victories and attracted thousands of new members and let them drift away again for lack of a concrete program. Its ideas were vaguely the anarcho-syndicalist ideas that had stirred France a little earlier; its methods and shibboleths, even the "wooden shoe" symbol of sabotage, were the same. Its membership was an utterly American mixture, with a good percentage of the foreign-born because the foreign-born were often the most migrant, the most economically adrift, and also the most politically awakened. But in the best American tradition, it took its orders from no one, was ripped by internal quarrels of policy, and fought the battles that were most immediate and most concrete.

It was conflict of the bloodiest kind that kept the iww together. It existed for the prime purpose of making the first breaches in the resistance of entrenched industry so that later organizations could widen and deepen them. Its greatest single contribution was the production of martyrs.

The Preacher and the Slave is in no sense a history of the iww, even by implication. It is not history, though it deals here and there with historical episodes and sometimes incorporates historical documents; and it is not biography, though it deals with a life. It is fiction, with fiction's prerogatives and none of history's limiting obligations. I hope and believe it is after a kind of truth, but a different kind from that which historians follow.

For turning sometimes-historical people and sometimes-historical events to the purposes of fiction I have two justifications. One is that all fiction is made this way and cannot draw upon any other material than actual material. The other is that fact and fiction had already become so entangled around the controversial figure of Joe Hill that it seemed permissible to leave him as tangled as I found him. Innocent or guilty, he was already legend, thanks to his own flair for self-dramatization and to the campaign that built him into a martyr. Murderer or martyr, he was certain to resist absolute definition. So I contented myself with trying to make him a man, such a man as he might have been, with his legend at his feet like a lengthening shadow.

The people who have contributed to my knowledge of both the

JOE HILL
A Biographical Novel

May Day, 1916

Let me tell you.

In the Mount Pleasant Cemetery in Seattle there were three new graves in a row. They had been there since November but now on May first they were still new, still mounded with flowers, and there was a crowd of hundreds gathered under the spindling trees. From a knoll of lawn above the graves speakers talked one after another, and their talk was all of the martyrs.

We were rich in martyrs then. Their names were big in the speakers' mouths, even though this was before the lynching of Frank Little, before the Armistice Day riot in Centralia where Wesley Everest died, before the Department of Justice raids that sent so many IWW's to the pen. But even in 1916 we were rich in martyrs; the road militant labor had come was soaked with their blood from Lawrence to Ludlow. We heard about them all again that day, and especially about the three under the row of flower-heaped mounds.

John Looney, Felix Baran, Hugo Gerlot—Irishman, Frenchman, German, three young migratory workers, hardly more than boys. The speakers told their story and the story of the others who had stood on the deck of the steamer *Verona* when Sheriff MacRae's gunmen and the good citizens of the Commercial Club swept it with murderous rifle fire from their hiding places in the warehouses on the Everett dock. We heard it all: how MacRae tried for weeks to keep the IWW out of town, how he raided and closed the hall time after time only to have new organizers open it again, how he arrested street speakers, beat them up, exposed them to the saps and brass knuckles and "Robinson clubs" of special deputies,

how he led pickets of the striking shingle weavers into a trap on
the trestle, where they were ganged by scabs, how he ran forty-
one Wobblies through the gauntlet and the bloody cattleguard on
the tracks out by Beverly Park. We heard it all, though we knew
it already: how young Hugo Gerlot was up on the mast cheering
and waving as the *Verona* nosed into the Everett dock, yelling
greetings to the thousands who had assembled for an open-air meeting to protest MacRae's tyranny and the bloody oppression of
the lumber trust. Those thousands were watching from the hill
when the deputies opened fire. We heard again how at the first
volley young Gerlot threw his arms wide and plunged like a diver
from the mast. He was the youngest; there were tears among the
crowd to be reminded.

Four known dead, unknown others left in the bloody water of
the bay, more than forty wounded: that was the toll of martyrdom
MacRae's deputies took at Everett. And sixty still in the Seattle jail,
charged with everything from riot to murder.

The sober crowd stood quietly during the speeches, and it
watched in silence while two more martyrs were added to the
three already there. It watched the ashes of Jesse Lloyd and
Pat Brennan shaken into the air from the knoll, and a low murmur
grew as the two small dense clouds of white dust blew downward over the hill. But the murmur swelled and grew when it came
time to scatter the ashes of Joe Hill.

Not many in that crowd had known Joe Hill; all of them knew
about him. All knew that on that May Day, in every civilized country in the world and every state in the Union except one, tiny en-
velopes of Joe Hill's dust were being scattered. They were giving
him to the air from a ridge of the Coast Range south of San
Francisco, they were letting the mountain wind take him in
Colorado. All except Utah, where they killed him, where he did
not want to be found dead.

The sound of the crowd was a low, continuous murmur like
the sound of the sea on a quiet day; then it fell to silence so still
the tick of poplar leaves could be heard a long way. On the knoll
one of the speakers stood up again, a skinny man with a great
bush of hair, a high collar, a big nose. He read three verses, the
verses of Joe Hill's last will.

My will is easy to decide
For there is nothing to divide.
My kin don't need to fuss and moan—
"Moss does not cling to a rolling stone."

My body? Ah, if I could choose
I would to ashes it reduce
And let the merry breezes blow
My dust to where some flowers grow.

Perhaps some fading flower then
Would come to life and bloom again.
This is my last and final will.
Good luck to all of you. Joe Hill.

After the speaking of the last words, that name that was like a promise of final triumph for the workers of the world, and an assurance that even death could not prevent it or even slow it down, the speaker stood with his head back, his eyes far out over the crowd. The silence ticked away as he stood; it was so still we heard the bells of some steamer nosing into a slip on the sound—perhaps the very steamer *Verona* on which so many iww had died and shed blood.

Then the speaker raised his hand, tossed the envelope into the air. A sigh like a wind went through the hundreds watching, for as the envelope fluttered and began to fall, a puff of breeze came from nowhere and blew the thin pinch of dust outward and upward away from its container. It seemed to us that like the dust of a great volcano thrown high into the upper air, that pinch of white ash might blow all the way around the world.

The Bindle Stiff

1   Seattle, June, 1910

The two of them sat on the stern of the floathouse and looked across the water to the gasworks on the island. Worms of red and yellow light crawled on the lake surface, and the barge hull rocked softly and heavily in the ghost of a swell. Joe squinted his eyes, shutting out everything but the swimming, trembling rods of light. He had let the kid talk for a half-hour without himself saying a word. Now he said without lifting his chin off his chest, "You ever read *The Ancient Mariner?*"

The kid said doubtfully, "That the one about the old whaler from New Bedford?"

"No, it's a poem. I read it once when I was learning English."

"What about it?"

Joe did not answer. After a minute the kid said, still doubtfully, "I guess I never read it."

The silence spread out again, dark and circular, from the momentary disturbance of their speech. Joe squinted his eyes more narrowly, drowsily melancholy and dreaming, letting the light wriggle across the water and in between his lids. Lights on water. A thousand nights of his life there had been lights on water. The air was cool, with the dense moist texture of air near the sea, the kind of air you could feel between your fingers. But there was a strangeness about this air because there was not the salt smell of the sea in it. It had a brackish smell of mud.

"Ship coming in the canal," the kid said.

Now that his attention was called to it, Joe was aware that he had been hearing the engines for some time. Against the dark loom of the hill across the lake the ship's lights came on steadily, and the sound of the engines gained on the whisper of city noise that trembled on the air back on shore. The sound grew, the engines turning over slow, but there were no voices from the ship, even when she got within a few hundred yards. There was about her something mysterious and sad and dark; a wayfarer, a homeless wanderer, she slipped into a strange harbor by night. Then the high bow shoved across the lights of the gasworks, and just as it did so the gasworks opened a coke oven. The white-hot light flamed like a sun, outlining the freighter's stubby masts; the upraised spider arms of the booms stared like a hangman's tree against the light.

"I didn't know you'd been a sailor," the kid said.

As a matter of fact, he didn't know it now. Some connection his mind had made, hooking his companion up with the ancient mariner, with a freighter coming in the canal. Joe let his eyes follow the ship's bulk with the fading glare of the oven behind it as it slid smoothly into Lake Union. It seemed to him that a salt whiff came with her, a fresher breath than the flat damp air of the lake, and for a moment homesickness was an utterly unexpected knife between his ribs, and he smelled the bay and the wharves at Gefle and the stiff wind running between the islands in the Alandshaf.

The kid's uncertain, feeling voice groped out again. "You from Sweden?"

Vaguely irritated, Joe let the words run off him, and after a minute he heard the elaborate yawning and stretching of the legs that covered the momentary awkwardness. But there was talk in the kid, an eagerness to be liked and responded to. His chair squeaked as he tilted it back against the wall; his voice was fake-hearty, false-assured.

"Boy, this is all right," he said. "This is better'n rupturin' a gut on a crosscut and sleepin' in a stinkin' bunkhouse."

Joe made a low, indeterminate sound. The boy's voice ran on. "Bottles is a fine guy," he said. "You meet a lot of fine guys. Just boomin' around, you meet stiffs from all over, and all kinds of them are fine guys."

By turning his head a little Joe could see the boy's face with the last dying glow of the coke oven on it. It was a good-natured kid face. He had a lot to learn.

"Just for instance," the kid was saying, "who'd ever expect to light in a place like this? You blow in from somewhere, I blow in from the woods, we both know somebody that knows Bottles, and bingo, here we sit like millionaires on a private yacht." He laughed and stretched out flatter in the tilted chair with his arms locked over his head.

Joe said nothing. He watched the delayed coming of the freighter's wave. The gasworks lights bent like glowing rods in the water, and then the smooth wave reached the floathouse, shouldering it heavily upward and passing under and losing itself against the shore. The following waves rocked them, slapping under the flat hull.

"I'm sort of surprised," the kid said. "I expected to run into all kinds of rough stuff on the road. You know the kind of stories you hear. I thought I'd be runnin' into nothin' but a lot of stewbums and fruits. But Jesus, it's mainly nice guys you meet, just ordinary guys like you are yourself."

He yawned again, and the front legs of his chair hit the deck. "Well, it's a great life," he said, and yawned a third time, not so convincingly. "Always some'n new," he said. "You gonna ship out, or stick around Seattle, or what?"

It was only because he had been thinking about the same thing that Joe bothered to answer. "I don't know. Maybe I'll head south."

"Yeah," the kid said vaguely. He hung around, leaning against the wall. "The shark was signin' 'em up for a lumber camp over by Redmond the other day. You know anything about Redmond? That's the Snohomish outfit, I think." When Joe was silent he went on, "Hell, I don't know whether to go back to the woods or not. That's a rough god damn job. I walked out the last camp I was at." For a moment he waited, as if expecting Joe to say something or act surprised. His laugh was short, almost a giggle. "I told the boss to kiss me behind and I up and beat it." He labored to a halt, but then beat his way ahead again, fumbling and uncertain. "If I had my druthers I'd stay right here on Bottles' yacht and play jungle-buzzard all summer, but I don't s'pose Bottles'd want boarders that long."

Joe made the indeterminate sound again, wishing the kid didn't insist on being so important to himself. The people he met, the places he went, the plans he made, what he said to the boss. What difference did it make? He could get to be a pest, making adventures out of every two-bit thing that happened to him.

Now the kid yawned a last time, almost with determination; his feet shuffled determinedly on deck. "Well, guess I'll go see if Bottles has got paper and a pencil. I haven't wrote a letter to my Sis for six weeks."

"You better do that," Joe said.

"She takes an interest in what I do," the boy said. "She sits there in Akron, ironin' shirts in a laundry all day, and the places I get around to seem pretty exciting to her. If I know I'm gonna be someplace around a certain time I give her a general-delivery address, and she writes me these big long letters. If I let her, she'd quit tomorrow and hit the road out here. That old laundry stuff has got her goat pretty bad."

"Yeah," Joe said. "Well, you go write her."

Eventually the kid broke his embarrassed hanging around and went inside. After a minute the lamp bloomed yellow, pushing light through the window back of Joe and showing the worn deck planking, the unpainted stern rail, the broken armchair where the kid had sat. Across on the island the gasworks twinkled on, as remote as the stars, and as incomprehensibly conducted. The few lights that had shone high on the hill had gone out. The night air was growing chilly. For a long time Joe sat back in the dark by the window. Once he leaned to put his face against the pane and saw the kid at the table, still writing.

The tantalizing sea-smell that the freighter had trailed past was still in his nostrils. The past was in it, and pictures blew like smoke across his mind, the hills and the bay and the rivermouth and the ships, the schoolyard with the lush summer grass, the YMCA reading room where sailors had come, the smoke of boats coming down from the copper mines at Falum. He could have drawn every street and building in that seaport town, and yet when he tried to bring it closer, to put himself back in the cottage, to come in on some winter evening with the red muffler three times around his neck, and image his mother in the kitchen amid the warmth and the smell of food, something in him turned away and held it off. By an effort of will he could summon the house he had grown up in, but he couldn't hold it. It ran out of his mind like water from a leaky pail, and left him only an irritable, empty sense of loss.

Names wouldn't do it, either. He tried, softly and to himself, the singing Swedish sounds, naming every street of Gefle, stores and shops he remembered, people he knew. None of them meant what he kept trying to make them mean, and he felt himself watching and testing himself for the effect he wanted. He tried naming his mother's name, Berta Hillstrom, and waited for the emotion that had ground like hobnails through his childhood and youth. But his mother's wrongs and her skimped dejected life stirred in him only a vague unhappiness now. It was 1910 now; she was twelve years dead.

He walked around to the door and looked into the cabin. The kid hunched over the table, still writing. Behind him, against the wall, was the long bench jumbled with glass bottles, jars, beakers, racks of test tubes, that Bottles amused himself with when he was sober. There were chemical stains on bench and floor, a faint chemical stink in the air. One of the bare studs and part of the wall had been charred by fire.

"Got any more paper?" Joe said.

"Sure." The kid tore out three or four leaves of his tablet, and pawed among the mess on the table until he found a stub pencil. The point was broken, and he got out his knife to sharpen it. His forehead was pimpled, but he looked clean, curly-headed, healthy, not like the usual road punk. His hands were full of an eagerness to be helpful, and he smiled when he looked up from the sharpening and handed the pencil across.

Back in his chair in the stern Joe shifted to get light on the paper. On the top sheet he drew a quick cartoon of a lumber camp—stumps and drooping firs and a tall topped tree with a top-faller clinging in it, and down on the ground a donkey engine contorted and bucking, with a peavy handle sticking out of its insides and a lot of smoke and agitation and gear wheels going up in radiating explosive lines. Beside the donkey engine he drew a beefy man in a stag shirt facing a smaller, curly-headed figure. The curly-headed one was thumbing his nose. Below the drawing Joe printed neatly, "This is how I kissed my last boss goodbye."

When it was finished he took it inside and handed it to the kid. "Here," he said. "Put this in for your sister."

The kid looked at the picture and then up at Joe. The innocent awe in his face was pleasant to see. "Kee-rist, where'd you learn to draw like that?"

"Send it on," Joe said. "Give her my love."

Back in his chair again he sat and doodled aimlessly, producing a string of meticulous three-dimensional boxes, a string of sailing ships leaning in a wind. He spelled his own name, Joseph Hillstrom, in elaborate Old English lettering he had learned to make as a schoolboy from Salvation Army tracts. He turned the page over and drew a tophat with a shiny highlight up its length, and under the tophat he drew a pot-bellied man with a big watch chain. Across the page below this he sketched in the figure of a woman with a shawl over her head and one hand stretched out beseechingly. Then between the two his pencil made a tall severe figure with a pistol in its hand, aimed at the pot-bellied man, and out of the muzzle of the gun he drew a puff of smoke.

Just for an instant, when he moved the paper more into the faint light and studied what he had drawn, the old hatred leaped in him like the explosion of a match, but it went out as quickly as it had come to life, and he sat quietly with the paper in his hand. It was a long time since he had dreamed that murder-dream, a long time since he had even thought of the well-dressed stranger with the intent, half-puzzled eyes that he had once seen at a public meeting and known for the man rumor called his father. It seemed to him that he had spent months and years of his boyhood dreaming of how he would pay back that man, but the hatred was cold now. There was only a faint bitterness like quinine under the tongue, and a brief flare of anger that licked out not so much against the wrongs of his past as against the emptiness of the present. He felt as gutted as a codfish.

He brought his mind around to the kid inside, still writing his endless letter to the sister who worked in a laundry and dreamed of romantic adventures like her brother's. He imagined meeting a girl like that, one who had never been out of her home town, and thought of the things he might say to her and the places he might tell her about. She would love to hear of strange places and exciting things. She would have light curly hair like her brother's, and good teeth. Underpaid and poor, she would live in a boardinghouse, maybe, a single room in a house with mechanics and traveling men and clerks who parted their hair in the middle.

For a while, tall and quiet and strong, a man who had lived

a rough life but had stayed clean, he was her protector through a series of carefully composed scenes. He visited her greedy boss, a fat soft man in a peppermint-striped shirt, and cowed him into raising her wages. He destroyed several clerks with little mustaches, noting carefully how they fell when he hit them, working out the encounters detail by detail, varying a point here or there, going back and starting over, altering by a slight sneering word the contemptuous thing he said just before he swung. She was an unprotected working girl, at the mercy of bosses, mashers, white slavers. Indignation grew in him at the thought of the punk inside spending his time bumming on the road. He'd go bad, or get himself killed, and there would be no one to look after the girl.

Whistling abstractedly through his teeth, he stared out over the lake and imagined what might happen. The tune that passed between his lips was "Meet Me Tonight in Dreamland," and it got wound up in his speculations until it began to take them over and guide them. Suppose she got hard up and couldn't pay her rent, or lost her job, or got sick. There was only one way she could wind up. Her situation began to unravel as the words of a song, set to the tune he was whistling, and he let it unravel until he had a whole verse and a chorus that he could write out in a careful round hand.

> One little girl, fair as a pearl
> Worked every day in a laundry;
> All that she made for food she paid
> And she slept on a park bench so soundly.
> An old procuress spied her there,
> She came and whispered in her ear:

> CHORUS

> Come with me now, my girlie,
> Don't sleep out in the cold;
> Your face and tresses curly
> Will bring you fame and gold.
> Automobiles to ride in,
> Diamonds and silks to wear,
> You'll be a star bright
> Down in the red light,
> You'll make your fortune there.

Feet clomped on the deck, the floathouse moved a little, slug-glishly, something fell with a clatter and Bottles' voice, muffled with liquor, said "Sonofabitch!" His footsteps came along the deck to the door and stopped. There was a moment's silence before his voice said, "Night owl. What you doin', writin' a letter?"

"To my Sis," the kid's voice said. "We got on a regular letter-writin' bee. Joe's writin' one outside."

"Fella ought to write more letters," Bottles said. He came around the corner and stood in the misty dark beyond the window, a big-shouldered, big-headed drunken old buffalo of a man. Joe folded the paper with the song on it and creased it neatly with his thumbnail.

"God damn," Bottles said. "I'm glad to see you boys writin' letters. Guy never thinks how other people might feel. Selfish bastards, one little letter could make somebody happy as hell."

He loomed over Joe. "Hate to see anybody make my mistake," he said. "I ain't wrote home in ten-twelve years. Ain't that awful? How I know what they're doin'? How they know I ain't dead or in the bughouse or some'm? You take my advice and keep on writin' letters, then you won't wind up a bum like I am."

He lurched against the wall and felt his way around the corner. From inside Joe heard the kid say, "Well, it's me for that old soogan. Is it all right if I roll up out on deck, Bottles?"

"Anyplace you fuckin' please," Bottles said. "Sleep on the fuckin' roof if you want."

The light went out with a puff, and minutes later the faint stink of kerosene leaked out the window above Joe's head. With-out a light, there was no use trying to finish writing the song. It was no good anyway. The gauntness was back in him, the gutted feeling.

He folded the paper once again and put it away in the pocket of his flannel shirt. Writing a letter, he thought. Writing a letter! Who to?

He spit out a curse like a seed from between his teeth and felt his way around the deck to where his bindle was stuck on the sill of an open window. While he was unrolling the blanket the kid's shadow reared up briefly against the faintly luminous sky and then subsided again with a big sigh. "Boy, this is worth all the bunkhouses in Washington and all the straw stacks in Montana," he said. "Just like your own yacht."

Joe did not reply. He got the blanket under him and rolled his coat for a pillow and lay down on his back. There were stars across the sky, misty and remote, and he lay giving them back a bleak and savage stare. Tomorrow he would go south. There was nothing there that drew him, and it was no treat to hole up with John in the shack, and longshoring in San Pedro was no better as a job than logging in Washington. Worse, maybe, the way you sat around all day waiting for some snotty dock boss to point the finger and say, "You, and you, and you, and you." But he had been north ever since he had left the old *Sarah Cleghorn* at Victoria six months ago. Without wanting to go anywhere in particular he wanted to get out of here. He might as well head for Pedro as for anywhere else.

2   San Pedro, June, 1910

He traveled fast and light, with only a little bread and a couple of cans of beans in his balloon. Three days after he hooked a manifest out of Seattle he was soaking up steam in an Oakland Turkish bath. That night a strike of trainmen on the Southern Pacific stalled him in San Jose, but by the next evening, after talking with pickets and learning that the engineers and firemen had not yet voted to come out, he hung around the yards. There were so many railroad dicks around that there was no show to get aboard anything; he would have to snag one on the fly. Just at dark he started down the tracks out of town, through straggling shacks and Mexican *barrios*, until he was at the fringe of town, past where he estimated the yard dicks would have to drop off as the train gathered speed. Then he sat down by the trackside and waited, drowsing over his knees until a locomotive's light poked down the laddered track and roused him.

All the next morning he sat alone in a boxcar and dangled his heels out the open door, watching the picture-postcard ocean between San Luis Obispo and Santa Barbara twinkle and flow inward to the white beaches and break in big surf on the points. Outside of Santa Barbara he ditched the freight, walked clear through town, and picked it up again on the other side, clear out by Montecito, rising from his covert at a place where bums had jungled at the very edge of a big estate.

In Ventura a pair of shacks, going in pairs like nuns for protection, looked in one side of the car just as Joe went out the other. The train was still moving slowly. Before they could come through after him he had ducked through a ruck of rabbit hutches and chicken pens and littered backyards and out onto a dusty street. Again he walked through the town. This time he found a little jungle camp under some pepper trees, where about a dozen hoboes were lying around waiting for a stew. He chipped in a can of beans and ate with them, and after he had eaten he lay down with his hat over his face and slept. After dark he awoke, ate a tincup full of mulligan, washed the cup with sand and seawater down at the shore. There was a game of cooncan going on on a blanket by the fire; he sat off to one side, watching it.

After almost an hour word came down that a freight was coming. Joe stood up, and a man next to him said, "I'll be glad when their damn strike is over and the shacks are takin' bo money again. You really got to earn your ride, this way."

The bos were scattering along the grade. The headlight reached over them, the locomotive shook the ground as it passed in a moment of glare and steam and power. Back up the tracks Joe saw the lanterns of the yard dicks drop off, two of them, and bob and plunge and come to a stop. Figures were running desperately along the grade, but the chances were not good. The train was already rolling as fast as a man could run. The dark cars drew past him as he sprinted on the uneven footing, trying to keep his feet in the dark and still spot an open door. The man ahead of him swerved and gave it up, and in desperation Joe shifted his bindle over his back on the dead run and hooked a ladder with his right hand, jumping to get his feet clear as the train yanked him into the air. Panting, he clung to the throbbing rods, and then climbed carefully, his breath coming hard and his heart pounding, and made his way along the roof in the wind and

the rain of cinders until he found the propped hatch of an empty
reefer. His cautious call got no answer, but when he let himself
down he found two other bos already there. They shifted over
for him without a word.

At daylight the three of them ditched the freight together
as it began to jerk and crawl into the Los Angeles yards. By
nine o'clock Joe was riding the PE car down the Shoestring toward
San Pedro.

He had traveled without anticipation, for no reason except that
he was sick of what he had been doing and wanted to be
on the move, but as he stepped off the car he had a curious
momentary feeling of coming home. It was a morning of blowing
fog, with the sun breaking through and then driving under again.
He saw the footpath and the ragged shacks, the flats, the island,
and then the warming air chilled abruptly as a feeler of mist
blew inland. The footpath led blindly into a white, enclosed world.

Just off the blurred familiar path an old wheelless buggy swam
in and out of sight like the half-boat of a troll. The earth pitched
in sluggish waves, old Galway's pile of boards and rubbish crawled,
Sheehan's privy tilted, the bleat of Sheehan's goats was an other-
worldly sound in the mist. Then the fog thinned as suddenly as
it had thickened, the earth subsided, the buggy sank back into
the rank grass, the shacks emerged steady as islands, and the sun
mowed the flats like a scythe.

The rear end of John Alberg's shack dropped off by broken steps
to a tidal creek where a skiff lay aground in the mud of extreme
ebb. From the rusty stovepipe no smoke rose. Joe paused at the
door, fixing his face for greetings, but when he pushed inside
there was no one there, though the shack was warm and the
stove still hot to the touch.

The place was a pigpen, as usual, the brass bed and the bunk
along the front wall humped with dirty quilts, the table littered
with dirty dishes. The air smelled of sardines and coffee. Looking
around to see who was living with John now, Joe found a tin
suitcase under the bunk, and in the suitcase a letter addressed
to Otto Applequist. Otto, then. That guy.

Under the other bunk, in his old sea chest, he found his blue
serge suit, a suit of long drawers, a striped shirt, three stiff collars,
and a pair of yellow button shoes. Looking at them, he made

a soft sound of derision, but he wiped off the shoes and hung
the suit on a nail. In the piece of mirror stuck behind a stud
he examined his whiskery face, the flat cheeks rough with beard
except where the scar ran smoothly under his jawbone, the eyes
cold blue, the hair lank. A vision began to grow in his mind of
coming into Pedro all dressed up, greeting acquaintances, hearing
the gossip. After the momentary disappointment of finding no one
at John's, the vision was full of warm possibilities.

There was a bucket of water on the back of the stove. He
peeled off his flannel shirt and honed his razor on John's strap
and lathered up and shaved and washed himself to the waist.
In the high collar and yellow shoes and blue suit he looked unfamiliar to himself, a gaudy stranger. Counting his stake on John's
bed, he found that he had twenty-six dollars and some small
change. The change he dumped back into the snap purse, the
bills he buttoned down into his hip pocket. Then he pulled the
door shut behind him and cut across the flats toward where the
town curved on its higher ground against the hills.

San Pedro was the same as ever, Beacon Street was the same
as ever, the fog blowing like gray rags over the Pedro Hills was
the same as ever. The air was soft and cool, delusively like air
before a rain. Down the gray streets boxed in by stores, warehouses, saloons, eateries, hotels, he got glimpses of the two long
docks angling out into the harbor toward Dead Man's Island, and
of the breakwater far out, almost on the horizon. The sky flowed
restlessly landward, gray as the sea.

There were a good many people on the streets. Drays rumbled
on the cobbles, an automobile went barking off up Harbor Boule-
vard like a distracted dog, workmen stood outside cafes and picked
their teeth and talked. They watched Joe pass, but he did not
know one of them. The Harbor Cafe, where Joe had a sandwich
and a cup of coffee, was crowded, and though Pete Dimitrios, in
the kitchen, spotted Joe through his little window and shook a
hairy arm at him, Pete was obviously too busy to talk, and so
Joe went on.

At the next doorway he was almost run down by a young man
with red hair who fell out of a saloon, rubber-legged, feeling
with his feet for steps and dangers and manholes, a long way

from his feet but still conscious of them, and with an air of deadly seriousness and concentration wobbled off into a side street. A block further down a little man in a cap and a leather snapbow tie stood under a corner lamppost staring up into the moving clouds, talking quietly and with a kind of ecstasy to himself.

The same as ever. Half the people you saw either cracked or stewed. Pedro hadn't changed. It was still no different from the Bowery or West Madison in Chicago or the Seattle Skid Road or Third Street in Frisco or Burnside Street in Portland. Some of the gray of the day seeped into his spirits like a bilge that weighed him down. Turning down toward the wharves he felt again what he had felt on Bottles' floathouse in Seattle: the kind of despair a man feels when he is alone at the edge of water or among blank buildings, the little lost feeling that makes him want to scratch his name on a wall or the piling of a dock.

Along the Hammond Lumber Company dock two lumber schooners lay with hatches open, both riding high and light. Their cargoes were stacked in clean white piles on the dock. At the foot of the dock a handful of men were loafing. Nothing seemed to be going on. Gulls cried in the air, and sat on the ends of pilings, and two or three old men fished off the wharf in the oily water. Joe went past, and on past the Admiral Line dock further on, and did not see a soul he knew until a voice hailed him from behind and he turned to see Harry Piper, a longshoreman he had known in Frisco. He was so glad to see a known face that he had to harden his own face to keep from showing his pleasure.

"The old stranger himself," Piper said. "Ain't seen you for years. Where you been keepin' yourself?"

"Oh, around."

"Looks like you'd been good to yourself," Piper said, and his eyes touched the blue serge, the yellow shoes.

"Can't kick," Joe said. "How's it been with you?"

Piper spit on the planking. "Same old crap, work a day, sit on your ass a week." He jerked his head out along the dock. "s.p. strike's tied up things so we can't even move stuff that's right out here."

"Seen John?"

"He's around. Did you look out at the shack?"

"He wasn't there."

"I don't know," Piper said. "He's been playin' the guitar up at Tinetti's saloon nights. You might find him up there."

Joe drifted on, vaguely dissatisfied. Harry Piper didn't mean anything to him. He doubted if John did. It wasn't people he was looking for, but something else, some house to go to or some family he thought of as his. Maybe John, after all. John was at least his cousin.

The bartender at the Forecastle saloon had not seen John that day. Joe went out and got a haircut and came back. Still no John. He went out again and spent an hour in the hot suspension of a Turkish bath, sitting still and feeling the slow ooze and tickle of his own sweat, the cleansing immersion in the dense, drifting, drowsy, liquid room. But after his purification he came out into the cool street and returned to the Forecastle to find that John had still not come. Still alone, with the sluggish lost feeling stronger in him, he looked in disgust up and down Beacon Street and wondered what he might do. It was only then that he thought of Lund.

The door said antiquely, in ornate letters, "Scandinavian Seamen's Mission." The inside of the show windows flanking the door was painted gray, and the backed glass gave him back his own slim dandified figure and the glitter of his shoes. As his face moved in the glass, his hand reaching for the door handle, he saw his clean haircut, his tight mouth.

He opened the door on the smell of coffee and the sight of eight or ten men reading or playing checkers, all with thick white cups at their elbows. Like everything else in San Pedro, the room was unchanged. Above the piano the American flag hung limp as it had hung two years ago. The Danish, Swedish, and Norwegian flags on their staffs at the corner of the platform had not lifted to any stir of wind. You went in circles that took in the whole world from Hull to Durban, but you always came back to some dingy room like this.

While he stood there Gus Lund came in from the kitchen at the back, carrying a big granite coffeepot with a towel around the handle. Halfway up the room he paused, squinting toward the door, his face thrust forward and his pale mustaches drooping. His hand went sideways to set the pot on a stack of papers, and he came forward scowling, looking more like an irritated bartender than the director of a mission.

"What do you want here?"

"Gude dag," Joe said. "Ay yust like little cup coffee for Svedish sailor man."

Lund's scowl blackened. "No Swedes allowed in here."

"Val, holy Yee!" Joe said. "Ay tenk sign saying for Scandinavians."

The scowl dissolved in Lund's beautiful wide welcoming smile; Lund's hand grabbed for Joe's. "Joe, you scoundrel, where've you been? What've you been doing?"

"Val, Ay yust coom from voods," Joe droned. "Last year, Ay ban vorking on ship, taking gude look at Pacific Ocean."

"Come on back," Lund said, and led him back to the desk by the kitchen door. "Here, have a doughnut." Broad-headed, big-mustached, he sat and watched Joe with a face made for smiling, a big Dutch-uncle face. Warmth radiated from him; he was the friendliest man in San Pedro, so friendly that Joe looked at him and had to laugh.

"You look more like William Howard Taft every day."

"You look like Bill McAdoo," Lund retorted. "You could chop wood with your face. What've you been doing, starving?"

"Vorking," Joe said, and showed his yellow-calloused hands.

"Got a place to sleep?"

"Out at the shack."

Lund grunted disgustedly, but before he could say anything the door opened and two bewildered-looking young men came in. "I'll be back in a second," Lund said. Joe had another doughnut while he listened to the gargled and slurred sound of their talking. They spoke in Danish. When Lund returned, Joe said, "A Dane talks just like oatmeal cooking. He kind of bubbles."

"Bubble like a Dane or sing like a Swede, they're all square-heads," Lund said. "With a chance to sleep in a decent bed they'd rather hole up in a tideflat shack."

Joe grinned. "No preachers out there, only goats."

"Plus John and Applequist."

"What's wrong with John and Applequist?"

Comfortably Joe reached for a fourth doughnut. He felt more relaxed and at ease than he had felt in a long time, ready for an argument on anything. But Lund batted the air with his hand and laughed. "You invariably lead me into a moral scolding."

"*Lead* you!"

The wide mustaches parted in Lund's wide warm smile. "All right, exasperate me into it. You ought to be spending your time reading books and studying music instead of wasting it with a drunk like John and a piece of jail meat like Otto. What have you got talents for?"

"I often wonder," Joe said. He snorted, watching the missionary fill his pipe from a little tin barrel of tobacco. The warm humorous eyes met his; the smile widened.

"I see you've been in some more fights and improved your looks."

Touching his chin where the engineer's ring had ripped the skin, Joe said, "Got my jaw broke."

Lund waited. Joe touched the slick scar again, remembering that trip and that furious Scotchman and the heat of the stokehold. "Third engineer had a habit of knocking somebody down to start each watch. He knocked me down the fifth day out, broke my jaw. I had it set in Honolulu."

The smile had half died on Lund's face, but his eyes were still crinkled at the corners. His cheeks were ruddy knobs as he drew on his pipe. "You took this, I imagine. You turned the other jaw."

"Not exactly," Joe said. "When I got up I paralyzed him with a slice bar. He was in the hospital longer than I was."

The sound that Lund made did not commit him either to disapproval or amusement. He looked at his watch. "Just about time for the service. How about playing a couple of hymns for us?"

"I haven't touched a piano for six months."

"We're not particular."

But Joe was stiffening and hardening, resenting the way Lund tried to use him. "I am," he said shortly. He turned away because he did not want to look at Lund's Christian solicitude or Christian forgiveness. Talking about the engineer of the *Sarah Cleghorn* had made him mad. The sense of moral pressure behind Lund's friendliness made him mad. The feeling that he was being judged and good-naturedly forgiven made him mad. He flipped through a stack of papers on the desk—Swedish-language papers from Minneapolis and Chicago, frayed copies of *Midweek Pictorial* and *National Geographic,* stacks of Lutheran tracts. Buried in the pile was a red pamphlet, and when he turned it over he saw that it was entitled *Industrial Unionism* and that it was written by Joseph Ettor. It was so out of place on Lund's desk that Joe flapped it at him. "You organizing for the Wobblies now?"

Lund growled, threshing into his coat. "I forgot to throw that thing out. Somebody left it here."

"They've got the right idea."

Lund said, "If you think you can bait me into an argument you're mistaken. I'm a better union man than you are. I'm all for industrial unionism, for that matter. But the IWW isn't a union. It's a revolution. Read the Preamble."

"I have."

"'The working class and the employing class have nothing in common,'" Lund said. "'Between these two classes a struggle must go on until the workers of the world organize as a class,' and so on and so on, and abolish the wage system."

"You've been studying up," Joe said.

"And I haven't much cared for the lesson!" Lund shot back, and reached for the Bible in a desk pigeonhole.

Joe could not quite prevent the sneer. "That's the Christian in you."

"Yes," Lund said seriously. "It's the Christian in me."

"The Christian that turns the other cheek."

"Maybe the Christian that won't resort to evil even for his own good."

Joe stared at him, stammering with the rush of words that came out of his mouth. "Oh my goodness! Oh, holy smoke! Did you ever fork wheat off a bundle wagon for some Dakota rube that drove you till two hours after dark and fed you spoiled pork for your supper? Did you ever get knocked around a stokehold by some moron engineer? Did you ever watch the bulls go to work on a picket line?"

"You can resist. You can organize."

"That's what the Wobblies are doing."

"A union can win its battles without sabotage and dynamite."

"Oh sure," Joe said. "How many of 'em are winning? They're all getting just what they want, is that so? Sure they're getting it—right in the neck. All the craft unions are good for is to scab on each other. Look at this s.p. strike."

"Why not try organizing the scabs?" Lund said. "Every Wobbly I ever talked to wanted to beat every scab's brains out. Scabs are workers too. Why not get together?"

"Why not talk sense?" Joe said in disgust. "A scab is a scab just because he *won't* organize. And a scab isn't a worker, either. He's a worker from the neck down. From the neck up he's a capitalist."

They were nose to nose, and their voices had risen. Lund looked around quickly, made a disgusted sound under his mustache, shoved Joe's shoulder to take the unfriendliness out of anything he had said, and stepped up on the platform by the piano.

Joe found a magazine and sat down against the wall. He did not listen to Lund's short reading from the Bible, and when the others, lonesome sailors and derelicts, stood up dutifully to sing for their coffee and doughnuts, Joe remained in his chair, tilted back against the wall. But he laid aside his magazine and listened to Lund's closing remarks, because he saw that Lund was speaking directly at him.

". . . what it is that we are after in this life," the missionary said. "We carry around all our lives a load of bitterness and discontent, pretending that it's something else than what it is. We hate the rich, or hate the capitalistic system, or hate women, or hate politicians, or hate God. But I'll tell you what we really hate. We hate ourselves."

Heavy, his chest and shoulders bulky in his too-small coat, his face shining a little in the warmth of the close room, he leaned on the back of a chair and spoke at Joe, watching him steadily and crinkling the corners of his eyes slightly and speaking with an unpretentious dignity so that Joe was compelled to watch him and listen. "We hate ourselves," he said. "We hate our own failures and our own weaknesses. We hate ourselves because we cannot help comparing what we are with what we might be. Our discontent is the voice of God in us, prodding us to live up to ourselves. Until we recognize and admit this we will always turn savagely outward, destroying other things because ourselves are at fault."

His mustache twitched and his eyes crinkled more deeply. For a second he seemed to smile with some inward knowledge; his square teeth showed briefly. "Live up to the best that's in you and you'll stand all right with God and man," he said almost lamely, and picked up his Bible and stepped down.

The self-regulating life of the mission went on, ignoring Joe Hillstrom where he sat. Two men drifted outside. Two others came to Lund for paper and pencil and sat down to write letters. A checker game, interrupted by the services, started up again. The dead afternoon slid toward evening. Finally Joe stood up, wandered over to the piano, put out a finger and touched a key. The single pure note hung in the air, and he felt that everything in the room momentarily stopped. He half wished he had played the piano for Lund. What difference would it have made?

But he felt sullen and irritable now, and he did not turn toward Lund. For a little while there had been here the welcome he had hungered for—which was a sour thought when you pondered it, that you had no place to go except a mission or a YMCA. But he didn't belong here, really, he didn't want a lot of greasy preaching thrown at his head, he didn't want his soul saved. Lund was not his kind. The room was full of his kind, sailors and workingmen on the drift, but when he looked at them from the platform he saw no face that he knew and no one to whom he had anything to say. If he had been a user of tobacco he might have borrowed a match or a pinch of *snus*. If he had been a drinking man he might have said to one of them, "Let's go get a can of beer someplace." Out of the casual opiates of his kind he might have manufactured some bond, at least a temporary one, between himself and these others. But he didn't even have beer and tobacco in common with them.

He laid his hand again on the piano, tried a whole handful of keys, a jangling discord. Then he hooked the stool with his toe and pulled it over and sat down, swinging on the rotating seat until he faced the keyboard.

For a while he fooled around, building up chords and listening to the way they mounted. There was a pleasure in the sounds like the pleasure of being clean and in good clothes. He limbered his stiff fingers on scales, and from scales he wandered off into little hesitating tunes, feeling out the combinations with hands and ears. Across the piano's corner he could see Lund's big solid back, and he let his fingers work out on the keys the orderly pattern of Lund's beliefs. Live a Christian life and work hard and develop

your talents and stay away from bad companions and turn the
other cheek and organize in some good sound AFL union and make
well-bred demands and thank the bosses when they raise your
wages ten cents a day, or forgive them when they lay you off or
cut your pay envelope. Above all, take your licking philosophically
when they break your strikes with Pinkertons and gunmen. Be
polite and the plutocrats might toss you a bone. Maybe there'll
be a job scabbing on someone less polite. You might get to be
Casey Jones the Union Scab, and blow a whistle on the S.P. line.

The tune came to his fingers and he played it through. Casey
Jones the Union Scab. All the engineers and firemen who wouldn't
come out in support of the trainmen. All the boomers who jumped
up to form scab crews and beat the trainmen before their strike
got a start. All the scissorbills who were good and faithful to the
bosses, and got their reward in heaven, or in the neck. He could
prophesy the course of this strike from the earful he had got from
pickets in the San Jose yards.

His fingers were still working over the tune of "Casey Jones."
Words began to fit themselves to it, an ironic parody that made
him go without a word to Lund's desk and grab up a piece of
paper. He wrote the song almost as if from dictation, with very
little crossing out and thinking, and when he stopped to read them
over cold he had two verses and two choruses.

> The Workers on the S.P. line to strike sent out a call;
> But Casey Jones, the engineer, he wouldn't strike at all;
> His boiler it was leaking, and its drivers on the bum,
> And his engine and its bearings, they were all out of plumb.

> Casey Jone skept his junkpile running;
> Casey Jones was working double time;
> Casey Jones got a wooden medal,
> For being good and faithful on the S.P. line.

> The Workers said to Casey: "Won't you help us win this strike?"
> But Casey said: "Let me alone, you'd better take a hike."
> Then someone put a bunch of railroad ties across the track,
> And Casey hit the river with an awful crack.

> Casey Jones hit the river bottom;
> Casey Jones broke his blooming spine;
> Casey Jones was an Angeleno,
> He took a trip to heaven on the S.P. line

A line at a time he coaxed it along, juggling St. Peter, the Pearly Gates, harps, wings, angels, until they fell into place, erasing and changing until he had another verse:

When Casey got to heaven to the Pearly Gate,
He said: "I'm Casey Jones, the guy that pulled the s.p. freight."
"You're just the man," said Peter; "our musicians went on strike;
You can get a job a-scabbing any time you like."

Now Lund was looking over his shoulder. "Inspiration?"

Rotating on the stool, Joe passed him the sheet. "Communication to the Brotherhood of Railway Engineers." He swung gently, indifferently, but he kept Lund's face in the periphery of his vision, and the way Lund's smile widened as he read was a thing of importance. He waited for the laugh, and it came.

"Wonderful!" Lund said. "You've really got it coming. But why make poor St. Peter into the image of Collis P. Huntington?"

"Not Huntington," Joe said. "St. Pete isn't that big a bug. He's just a labor shark in heaven. He runs the hiring hall."

Still laughing, Lund beckoned to a man reading at one of the tables. The man came over, a short wiry man with an enormous Adam's apple. "This is something you'd like, Mac," the missionary said. "Sing it for him, Joe. This is Frank McGibbeney, he's a train-man himself."

McGibbeney shook hands, impassive, and listened with an expressionless face as Joe played and sang the first verse and chorus half under his breath. But by the fourth line he was grinning. At the end of the chorus his face was reddening and his eyes were half closed with a suspended guffaw and his mouth was hanging as he listened. When Joe finished the railroader was almost hopping up and down.

"Say!" he said. "Say, that's a daisy, Jack. That's really a peacherino."

Lund had put on his bartender scowl. "Are you going to leave that scab in heaven? Isn't there any solidarity among the angels?"

"All right," Joe said. "Let's get him out of there." Their eyes were on him as he leaned on his elbows and thought. His mind worked like a watch, little wheels turning, gears meshing, a controlled and triumphant mechanism. After no more than two or three minutes he spread the paper against the music rack and wrote:

The angels got together and they said it wasn't fair
For Casey Jones to go around a-scabbing everywhere.
The Angels' Union No. 23 they sure were there,
And they promptly fired Casey down the Golden Stair.

The abrupt laughter at his back inspired him, and he tossed off another chorus as fast as he could write.

Casey Jones went to Hell a-flying.
"Casey Jones," the Devil said, "Oh fine;
Casey Jones, get busy shoveling sulphur;
That's what you get for scabbing on the s.p. line."

McGibbeney was almost lyrical with admiration. "Oh, that's a pip," he kept saying. "Boy, that's really first class." For a marveling second he looked at Joe, but he spoke to Lund, as if one didn't quite talk to a man who could write such songs. "The boys over at the hall would like to hear that, they sure would."

"Take it along," Joe said, and thrust the paper at him.

"There's a meeting tonight," McGibbeney said. "You wouldn't feel like coming over and singing it, would you?"

His wandering, rather furtive eye held Joe's a second and then slipped away. A skinny little man with an exaggeratedly fierce face, he looked almost in embarrassment toward the front door.

"I can't sing," Joe said.

"It'd sure be appreciated," McGibbeney said.

Pulling his mouth down, Joe looked at Lund and said, "Gus here would have a right to be mad if I played and sang for a union right after I turned down a chance to play for Jesus."

But Lund only shrugged and smiled, refusing to bite. McGibbeney's urging voice said, "We can use all the help we can get."

Someone had opened the front door and was standing in it. Joe glanced up and saw who was there, and his cousin John's roar of welcome made people jump and turn around the whole length of the shuffling, repressed room. "By Yudas, har he is!" John said. "Yoe! By golly, Yoe!"

Big as a tree, square-hewn, a Terrible Swede, he came down the room waving his arms, and after him came Otto Applequist, sheep-faced, smiling his silly-looking, surprised smile. Still feeling good, feeling excitement and the anticipation of something good to come, Joe stood up and made a grinning pretense of getting ready to knock his cousin's block off. To McGibbeney he said, "Here's the man you want. He's a guitar player, and he can sing."

Then he was overpowered by John's welcome.

3   San Pedro, June, 1910

On a summer Saturday afternoon the Forecastle saloon is cool and dusky. There are no lights on yet, the Saturday night rumble has not yet begun out in the street. It is cool and the light is gray and the smoke of stogies and pipes rises and hangs under the high ceiling.

This is a quiet hour, an interim period. In a few minutes Tinetti will remove the greasy, crumbed-up empty plates from the free lunch counter and replace them with full ones. The crowd is thin now, and men who occasionally come through the swinging door stand a moment with an almost resigned air, as if looking for someone or something they know they will not see, before they turn to find a place at a table or the bar. Everything hangs in suspension like the smoke, everything waits, everything is a little tired and slack muscled, and the talk is quiet, unargumentative, relaxed.

". . . in Ohio," their talk goes. "His old man was stationmaster. Sure, I know him, known him since we were kids. What's ever become . . ."

". . . snowed three feet that one storm," they are saying. "I started to go out next morning and the door was snowed clean over. Finally I went out the second-story window and tunneled in to the door so's we could open it. That drift was fifteen feet high if it was an inch. Stayed there till after . . ."

". . . dead pigeon," their sad voices say. "Some'm just busted in his gut. We was setting in the kitchen and he looked kind of green and said he had this belly ache, and all of a sudden he grabs the basin off the washstand and bends over and *blurp*, he fills her with blood. It come out of his mouth in a stream big as a ball bat, and *black* . . ."

They coddle their beer, their broken shoes indifferent among the other feet on the rail, their elbows proprietary on the bar, their hands circling the glasses in wet rings on the wood, their eyes watchful for when Tinetti will renew the free lunch. They raised their elbows and pull their chest away from the bar as Emil the bartender swabs with his wet rag, and then belly back to the dark old walnut before the twilight mirrors.

". . . cold this summer," Emil says. "Logs of fog." His face is square and serious, with a pale curl stuck flat on his anxious forehead. His hands are clean and unhealthily white, like something pickled.

It is a lovely and restful thing to stand in a saloon in the late afternoon taking your time with a nickel glass of steam beer and hearing the quietness of the talk, nobody argumentative yet, nobody drunk and wanting a fight, everybody relaxed and waiting for the free lunch, the light gray across the tables and the mirrors shadowy and the bar shining with pale soft reflections. It is a good thing to cross your feet, leaning; or to put one foot on the rail and hunch over the bar's friendly solidity, just resting and taking it easy after a day's work or a day's hanging around or a day's walking on the picket line.

Across the bar, before the dusky mirrors, there are bright-colored punch boards painted all over with gold coins, and with shoulders comfortably touching the shoulders of the men on right and left you can study the things the boards will give you for nothing, for a nickel, if the luck happens to come your way: 90, 190, 290, 390, 490, 590, 690, 790, 890, and 990 all win a box of delicious assorted chocolates. The boxes are there in a stack, solid proof of the board's honesty. There are also the things the even hundreds will get you —a jackknife, a razor, a fishing reel, a varnished fish basket with a strap, a shaving mug. There is the grand prize for number 1000, a .12-gauge Marlin repeating shotgun worth twenty dollars. It slants there in the corner of the mirror, a satiny shine up its blue barrel, its stock seductive and smooth and curved.

You can get it for a nickel. Everybody's got a chance. If you miss the shotgun, you've still got a chance at the reel, or the fish basket, or the shaving mug, and if you miss those you can probably win some chocolates.

In the squares of little paper-covered cells where luck hides,

some of the holes are punched out and black. Someone has played
a system and punched out the corner cells of each square; one
whole square in the lower left hand corner is punched out.

". . . Anybody won anything on that board, Emil?"

"Just one knife and a box of chocolates. That's getting ripe."

He lays the board on the bar, and you say, "If it wasn't for
suckers like me, sharks like you would have to work as hard as I
do." But there are all those chances. You can pick off a twenty-dollar
prize for a nickel. Everybody's got the same chance.

You push at random with the little punch. "What the hell," you
say, "I'm shooting the wad." You unroll the little worm of paper,
596, and Emil slides your nickel off his edge and drops it in the
till.

The crowd is thickening at the bar, and you move down, making
room for more shoulders. "How about another beer, Emil?" Then
there is a difference in the room, as if a corner has been turned,
and here is Tinetti with the tray of mounded plates, the loaves
of thin-sliced rye, the pickles knobby as an alligator's back and
sweating cool brine, the sliced bologna and the salami with globules
of fat among the rich dark meat, the slices lying spiraled and
overlapping like the ripe coins painted on the punchboard.

As the plates slide out there is a perceptible drift, a gradual slow
surge, dignified but irresistible, toward the free lunch end. The
men who are closest say something to Tinetti, something friendly
and casual, and for a suitable interval Tinetti stands there dangling
the empty tray, talking. It is two or three minutes before one of
the beer drinkers, almost absentmindedly, reaches out and picks up
a slice of bologna. Still talking to Tinetti, he peels the gut off and
chews slowly. They are talking about the relative chances of Detroit
and Philadelphia in the American League race. A man on the left,
listening politely, covers a slice of rye with a slice of ham, and as
if by afterthought with a pickle. The first man moves away, getting
a slice of salami and a piece of bread as he goes, and the crowd
edges past a little at a time. There is a smell of garlic in the air,
and Emil refills many beers. Tinetti, moving away from the free-
lunch counter, lights the lamps back of the bar, and now another
phase has come, the warm phase.

After a second beer and a bologna sandwich and the lights, the
Forecastle is a place of warmth and comradeship and life. Now

everything is rich and gilded, the colors shine fatly, the pearl handle of the prize jackknife is fabulous, the razor is a princely instrument, the shotgun a weapon for King George in a Scottish shooting box.

There is more talk now, louder, more vehement.

". . . I matching you or you matching me?" the voices say.

". . . Ketchel?" they say. "He couldn't lick his weight in duck feathers. Over in Goldfield once he hired out as a fink, and one night a friend of mine laid him cold as a wedge with a ketchup bottle. You want to talk fighters, I'll talk to you, but not Ketchel. Not that dirty stool . . ."

". . . so when she'd been gone three or four days they finally find her in this hotel with the Greek, and I guess her old man was wild. He busted in the room, and her and the Greek was in bed, and the old man just grabbed the covers and yanked. Neither of them had a god damn thing on. Bert said she had hair on her like a man. How'd you like that, boy? Jesus, I'd like to have been there when they busted in that room. I guess the old man was really mad . . ."

". . . split you ten punches, Jack," says the man on the left.

You punch five apiece, and then another five, and win a box of chocolates and then match the man for them and lose. The expensive Marlin shines, blue-satin barrel and polished stock, against the mirror, and the pearl-handled jackknife and the razor and the reel and the mug and basket stay where they were. They shine there, a comfortable reassurance and a promise, and multiply themselves in the fecund deceptive glass.

There is usually music about this time of the evening, a big Swede who sings and plays the guitar with fingers so thick it is a miracle he manages to hit only one string at a time. Not a *j* or a *w* to his name. It's a riot to hear him when he gets a little stewed and starts off on "Yoost a song at tvilight." Maybe on Saturday nights he starts later.

But here he is now—Lord, what a moose!—between a couple of other men, a slim dressed-up fellow with a tight mouth, and a funny-paper Swede with a face like an old ewe. They crowd up behind the men at the bar, and the big Swede says, "Vot you got for soft drinks, Emil?"

The way Emil stops and stares, puckering his troubled forehead under the flat curl, gets a laugh.

The big Swede keeps insisting, laughing. "Sure, vot you got?"

"Lemon pop," Emil says, and they both look at the slim man in the blue serge. He smiles as if it hurt him. After the big Swede's, his voice is quiet and low. "Lemon pop'll do fine," he says.

They get the pop and a pint of whiskey and mix back into the crowd looking for a table. Every now and again the big Swede's laugh vibrates the glassware, but it seems that he is not going to sing. Maybe he will later.

After a while he does. The guitar starts to plink and hum, and men at the bar or around the room half cock their heads to listen. The Swede has pushed back his chair and slung the guitar around his neck and is picking aimlessly at the strings, saying something and laughing. Now there is a little hook-nosed man, McGibbeney, a railroader, sitting at the table between the man in the blue suit and the ewe-faced Swede.

The men who are listening grin a little and nod a little when the big Swede, Alberg is his name, starts off. "Halleluiah I'm a Bum." That's the one. The Swede has a voice like coal pouring down a tin chute, but his thick fingers are surprisingly nimble on the neck of the guitar. Voices join in from along the wall, among the tables:

> Oh why don't you work like the other men do?
> How the hell can I work when there's no work to do?
> Halleluiah I'm a bum,
> Hallelluiah bum again,
> Halleluiah give us a handout
> To revive us again.
>
> Oh why don't you save all the money you earn?
> Well if I didn't eat I'd have money to burn. . . .

The Swede's voice leads them and drowns them out and leads them again. The tune goes like a man who swings his elbows as he walks.

> I went to a house and I asked for some bread,
> And the lady said, "Bum bum, the baker is dead,"
> Halleluiah I'm a bum,
> Halleluiah bum again . . .

Warmth flows into the room from the lamps, the rich reflections along the bar, the glint and shine of glasses, the sound of singing. John Alberg's cousin and McGibbeney sit watching the singer, their lips turning up in the curl of a smile. He is a man that everybody likes, John Alberg, a big worthless good-natured man like a shaggy dog that wags its tail at everybody and hangs out its tongue and laughs. This is his theme song, the thing they expect of him, a kind of national anthem of the iww. You can tell the Wobs around the saloon: they are the ones who sing. Quite a lot of them, by their clothes, are also railroaders. The Wobblies have been organizing a lot among the trainmen, especially among the boomers.

Smoke rises toward the gaslights slowly, is sucked into the draft and streams upward above the jets. John Alberg hits the guitar a final lick and rolls out his big laugh. With that laugh on tap, he should play Santa Claus in department stores.

". . . it's the back muscles," a high argumentative voice says at the bar. "Hell, what're you givin' us? That's where you get your punch. Look at Bob Fitzsimmons, he had back muscles big as oranges. You can't hit just with your arm. Look at John L. . . ."

McGibbeney is leaning forward, saying something with his sharp fierce face thrust toward Alberg. Alberg pulls a paper from his pocket and spreads it on the table. He looks at the guitar, hunts some chords, taps with meaty fingertips on the soundbox.

"Dis is new song," he says confidentially to those nearest. "My cousin Yoe yust wrote it. You listen, dis is damn gude song. 'Casey Yones the Union Scab.'"

"Hey you guys," McGibbeney says. "Listen to this!"

As Alberg plays and sings, the blue-suited man sits almost uncomfortably in his chair, poker-faced. With his pale skin and his neat fair hair and his string tie he looks like a gambler. It is as if Alberg applauded him with eyebrows and lips, singing directly at him, but the cousin cracks no smile in reply. Once when two men edge closer behind him to hear he half turns and looks at them, but he is stiff in the face of the applause that comes when Alberg is through. The man next to him now is Herb Davis, the secretary of the iww local, and he is saying something into the cousin's ear. The cousin shakes his head, a quick, impatient motion.

McGibbeney is very excited. "By God, a thing like that can

win for us! Come on, Alberg, the meeting'll be on in ten minutes.
Come on down there and sing it once."

Other voices are saying the same thing. "It'll have 'em breaking
up chairs," Herb Davis says. A kind of delegation forms, and
McGibbeney carefully picks up and folds the paper with the song
on it. "They'll want you to take a bow," he says. "I didn't quite
get your name. Hill, was it? Joe Hill?"

"That'll do," the cousin says.

They go out, ten or a dozen of them working between the tables,
Herb Davis with his hand around the cousin's arm, talking seriously. Over their heads John Alberg shakes his guitar at Tinetti,
who has rolled down his cuffs and is adjusting a heavy gold cufflink.
"Dese boys vant me to do a little yob," Alberg says. "I be back
pretty qvick, Nino."

They go on out, and the doors they hold open as they pass let
in a brief breath of evening air, the lugubrious sound of a Salvation Army band down on the corner, and the sad ragged voices
singing "In the Sweet By and By."

The man called Joe Hill walks with the others, unsmiling, light
and easy on his feet but unbending, almost ill at ease. Under the
expressionless pale face lies another face, mercurial as an actor's,
eager-eyed and tugged at by responsive smiles; inside the erect
blue serge is another man, no laborer but an artist, fine-tendoned
and blue-veined and white-handed, a skinless man, avid for praise.

4   San Pedro, June, 1910

The shack was hot from the stove and the blaze of sun on the
tin roof, and full of the laundry-smell of boiling rice, the sweet-
sour fragrance of Chinese cookery. Joe Hillstrom, delegated cook,
an experienced hand who knew what he was about, watched over
the kettles, draining the gluey liquid from the rice, pouring dipper-
fuls of cold water in to separate the grains, draining that. Out
on the back platform above the tide creek the boys were kidding
Moe Dreyfuss and Moe was retorting in excited, staccato bursts.

A cool little wind blew through the shack and drew Joe to the back door, where he stood looking down.

He was amused at their variety: Pete Dimitrios, a black-browed Greek from Macedonia; Alberg and Applequist, Swedes; Art Manderich, an Austrian anarchist; Moe Dreyfuss, a philosophical Alsatian Jew; Herb Davis, indistinguishably American, with the kind of face that looked out from racing-driver's goggles on the cover of *Police Gazette*. The great American workingman, straight from Ellis Island.

"Sure," Herb Davis was saying. "So what do you want the boys to do when the company puts gun guards on the trains and fills the yards with finks?"

"Do?" Moe said. "Why do they have to do anything? Why do they put these guards on? To keep people from throwing coal at locomotives going by, isn't it? So don't throw any coal, that's easy."

"Just . . . let 'em ride over you, is that it? Let their scab trains go right on through."

"Moe," Dimitrios said, "start the jug."

Art Manderich, his eyes lidded and sardonic, spit over the edge of the platform into the mud. Like a fallen Goliath, John Alberg lay flat on his back, squinting vaguely into the air, making helpless motions with his arms.

"The yug!" he said, feeble and faint. "The yug!"

But Moe kept the jug protectively between his feet. Mongrel-smart, scarred by smallpox, he looked up at Joe and smiled a quiet, confidential grin even while his angry finger waved and his voice burst out at John and Dimitrios. "I should follow your advice!" he said. "Wine is for meals. You uncivilized Schlemiels would sour your stomachs for good food."

John groaned and rolled his head. Against the wall Otto was working at his nails with his knife. The argument started up again, nagging and unheeded. Davis said, with a wink at Joe, "I was reading in the *Industrial Worker* the other day, the Wobblies got a new slogan. 'A kick in time saves nine.'"

Like a dog stepped on Moe Dreyfuss' voice came up; his skewer-like finger stabbed the air straight upward. "You want vigilantes, eh? You want to bring out the mobbers and burners. A kick in time saves nothing, it is only a kick, it will get you back two for one. I leave it to Joe."

But Joe shrugged, grinning, keeping one eye on the kettle of chow yuke.

"I ask you!" Moe was yelling. "What good is chunks of coal at an engineer's head except to get a policeman shooting at you? What is to be gained by it, please explain this. What is the matter with argument, why do we have to have this force, force, force all the time? They have ten times as much force as you. This kick in time only raises hell."

Before anyone could answer his finger was trembling upright again. "Another thing. This stealing from freight cars and warehouses. This is something that you justify too, maybe. We are fighting the s.p. and so we are entitled to steal from them, is that it?"

Otto Applequist dug in his ear, interested but apart; Manderich spit over the rail again. Herb Davis said, "Everything the boss makes is stolen from labor anyway. Labor creates all wealth. What's wrong with taking a little of it back?"

"Show me an open boxcar some dark night and see how fast I equalize things," Dimitrios said, but he and Davis were drowned out by Moe's yelling. "Such logic! Such a way to think!"

"It sorts of depends on what you do it for, doesn't it?" Joe said.

"The yug!" John said from the tomb.

"Moe," Manderich's grating voice said, "you're just a yellow sheeny socialist. You remember v'en Alexander II vas assassinated? John Most wrote all over the front page of *Die Freiheit* how pleased he vas, and they t'rew him in jail. But he vas right, all the same. He knew it iss nezessary to fight. He said the same t'ing v'en McKinley vas shot."

"Sure, and they threw him in jail again."

"Does dot prove he vas wrong?" Manderich said.

With a wild gesture Moe raked his hair on end and gazed for a moment heavenward. The others were laughing, sprawling back on their hands.

"Listen!" Moe said. "Let me ask you something! You talk sabotage, you talk syndicalism, or anarchism, or whatever it is you talk. You talk like one of these assassinating people. You believe in dynamite under bridges and bombs at the policeman's ball. You are one of these kick in time saves nine fellows that think they can persuade the Southern Pacific with lumps of coal . . ."

"Vell, there iss vun t'ing . . ."

"Let me tell you! I do not believe in murder as a means of propaganda. I don't like stealing for a way of redistributing the wealth. I don't like my free speech protected by continuous riot. Direct action! I would not want the smell of it on my clothes!"

"Moe's a ballot-box boy," Davis said. "Vote us right into the millennium."

"There is more in it than ballot boxes," Moe said. "If a man cannot use any arguments but punches in the nose, those are the arguments he will have used against him. There is such a thing as honesty and dishonesty, and right and wrong, and keeping your own hands clean."

Manderich's heavy body heaved up. His face was warped with contempt. "Vot business has a vorkingman got vit right and wrong?" he demanded, standing over Moe. "Right and wrong has notting to do vit us, nor neffer did haff." His head swung at them, and with his lips clamped shut he clumped inside the shack and lay down on the brass bed and stared at the ceiling, breathing hard through his nose.

Moe Dreyfuss made a monkey gesture of dismissal, and they all laughed. "Old Art," Dimitrios said. "He'll blow some'm up yet."

"He is a foolish man," Moe said, almost quietly. "He is a person who would use sulphuric acid to cure a burn."

"What you don't make any allowance for is what *they* do," Davis said. "You pull this kind of stuff for yourself, you're just a hood and a strongarm man, but you do it in a fight, when they started it, and that's another thing. It's like Joe said, it depends on what you do it for."

"Well, how far do you go?" Moe said. "Sabotage? Stealings? Assassinations?"

Joe's eyes wandered to Otto, slumped against the wall, steering a bug with his finger as it crawled on the planks. His hand came up and he picked his nose lightly with his thumbnail. On either side of a center part his hair hung lank and limp. He was paying no attention to the talk.

"Do you see?" Moe said pityingly. "That is where you fool yourselves."

Quietly John had rolled over behind Moe. Now, on hands and knees, he motioned at Dimitrios, who rose. There was a rush, a squawk as Moe went over backward, and a pounce on the jug of red wine. Putting his hand over Moe's whole face to silence him, John said gently, "You vait for Moe or the s.p., you starve or die of t'irst. Sometimes you yust have to take t'ings avay."

The jug was already uncorked and being passed around, while Moe watched in puckered disgust. He bent his head while John took a swig, but when John held the jug toward him he refused.

"Two things you get from wine," he said. "Benefits or belly-aches. I am telling you this seriously. Benefits or belly-aches."

When he had jumped to stir the chow yuke, Joe came back to the doorway. He felt rested and at ease, warmly among friends. "What benefits?" he said.

Now Moe's inevitable finger was up again. "Ah," he said, "you speak as a non-drinker. How should I tell you? But I bet you something. I bet you never felt one hundred per cent good in the stomach yet in all your life." The finger dipped to jab at Moe's breastbone between the open flaps of his vest. "You know about ulcers? Stomach ulcers? You know what it means, stomach ulcers?" His hand made squeezing and relaxing motions, as if crumbling dry bread. "This is your stomach. Grinding, grinding, always grinding, day in and day out, grinding away. A hen has gravel in her gizzard to help her grind, but what have you got? Nothing. A stomach only, always grinding. No wonder are ulcers."

His look swept them all; his hand worked in the air. "Grinding, always grinding. No wonder are ulcers. Now! You put a little wine in your stomach when you eat. You oil up this grinding. What happens? Grinding, sure, but with lubrication. Ha? A little oil in the machinery. This is the benefits of wine."

The finger trembled upright in the air. "*With* meals."

"Art," Dimitrios called, "you want a swig of Moe's benefits?"

Manderich did not answer. With a winning, mischievous lifting and working of the eyebrows, Moe said, "Maybe he is afraid it is poisoned. That is what an anarchist would do. That is the anarchist way to win arguments, with strychnine."

The dishwashing crew made a game of it. Davis, back against the wall as far as he could get from the stove where Dimitrios had his pail of suds, smacked his fist in his hand and crouched, waiting for the throw. Like a shortstop pivoting in a double play he took a slippery, spinning plate, swabbed off the suds, and spun it toward John, who clutched it in meaty hands and slid it into the packing-box cupboard. "All right in there!" Davis said—a terrier, the pepperbox of an infield. "That's the way to go in there, boys! One away, two to go. Whaddyasay!"

In the open door Joe sprawled between Otto and Moe. He had a piece of paper stuck on the back of a broken washboard and he was sketching old Manderich, asleep against the house, his scowling face fallen half open, his breath sighing through loose lips. With his face lax in sleep he looked like a drunk. The lines from cheekbone to jaw were so deep they might have been made by a cleaver. He was an easy man to draw.

Crockery smashed inside, and Joe leaned in to see. Davis was stooping over the fragments of a cup. "Woops, error on the second baseman," he said. He threw the fragments in the slop bucket and turned just in time to see a whirling iron skillet coming. He sprang backward, grabbed, and miraculously caught it by the handle. "Jesus," he said, "take it easy!" Dimitrios, inspired, filled the air with knives and forks, and Davis fled, holding the skillet as a shield for his backside.

Joe looked back at his sketch, accenting the harsh sag of Manderich's cheeks. Otto's sleepy voice said, "You sticking around Pedro for a while?"

"Maybe."

"Longshoring?"

"Not as long as this strike's on."

"I mean afterwards."

"Maybe."

He looked at Otto for an explanation of the questions, but Otto was staring across the flats, faintly smiling, and when he caught Joe's eye the smile broadened.

"Ready to grease that lousy dock boss to get on his star gang?" Joe shrugged, going back to the sketch.

"Because that's the only way you'll get any work," Otto said.

Joe drew the hint of a wall behind Manderich's shoulder and sketched the crumpled coat. "All right," he said, at ease, among friends, not caring much, not paying much attention. "If there isn't anything here I can try the lumber schooners."

"Know any mates?" Otto said. "They're the same god damn breed."

"Listen!" Moe Dreyfuss exploded at Joe's shoulder. "What is that of dock bosses and lumber schooners?" His finger tapped the sketch, and the washboard under it thumped like a drum. "Look what you can do. What do you want of star gangs and drinks for the mates? What are you after, anyway, a fellow like you?"

For one odd minute, in the warm shade, it was as if he had been caught asleep, torpid and full-bellied, and propounded a question that he must answer for his life. He looked at Moe as he would have looked at a dwarf suddenly materialized from the earth, and he answered cautiously, stalling.

"Do I have to be after something?"

The dwarf's eyes were on him, bright as a bird's. "You know what I am talking about," Moe said. "Sometimes you remind me of a dog I had once. Did you ever know that dog? He was a foolish Chesapeake spaniel, and he had no brains, only energy."

"That sure describes Joe," Otto said.

"Only energy," Moe was saying. "This dog would run all day, and you know what he ran after? Bird shadows. Up and down the shore, running with his nose to the ground, chasing bird shadows."

A hand from behind pushed Joe's head down until his nose was on the washboard, and John's great feet went past. Dimitrios and Davis came after him, so that the odd importunity of Moe's question was relieved. Manderich awoke, clopping his jaws. "Here comes McGibbeney," Dimitrios said, and Joe looked across toward town and saw the railroader coming along the path through the salt grass.

Horsy and full of beans, John Alberg placed himself in McGibbeney's way and postured like a prize fighter, throwing out his butt and cocking his fists. McGibbeney, who came to his shoulder, thumped him hard on the chest, and when John reached for him in earnest, beat a nimble tattoo on the big Swede's arm and shoulder and skipped away.

"Oho!" John said. The railroader was grinning.

"You big hunk of beef," he said. "I warn you. Just try laying your dirty paws on me. I'll cut you up like stew . . ."

John lunged for him; there was a brief swift flurry of grunts and blows, the railroader ducking back out of reach, his hands light and fast against John's bulk. But as he ducked sideways his foot turned, and John's hand closed in the back of his jumper. As McGibbeney went up in the air he flipped nimbly and whipped a headlock around John's neck, but John pawed with one hand, broke loose the hold, and like a man trying to control a struggling cat, turned McGibbeney upside down and held him out by the ankles. Then he vibrated. There was no other word for it. His face red with effort, grinning back at the circle of men around him, he jiggled up and down so fast that McGibbeney was unable even to double back and get hold of a leg. He was vibrated out as stiff as clothing in a wind, and in a moment he began to disintegrate.

The laughter of the watching men exploded as McGibbeney's jumper shook down over his head and his fat watch came out and jerked and flipped on the end of its thick chain. Small change scattered out of his pockets; a smothered strangling yowl came from inside the dangling jumper; McGibbeney threshed, trying to twist and catch John's leg. With a final mighty effort, leaning far forward and jigging like a minstrel, John shook him loose. There was another squawk, and McGibbeney's upper teeth flew ten feet sideways and landed in the dust.

They collapsed on the ground and howled. Even Manderich was laughing so hard that Joe, wiping his suffused and streaming eyes, felt laughter weaken and melt his bones. John dropped McGibbeney on his shoulders in the dirt and staggered, purple-faced and helpless, to the shack wall.

When Joe could see again he wiped the backs of his hands across his eyes and watched McGibbeney getting himself assembled. McGibbeney was jerky with wrath as he stooped and hunted for dimes and quarters. With his teeth out his sharply hooked nose almost touched his chin, and as he bent to retrieve his teeth from the dirt he looked impossibly like a hen eyeing a bug just before pecking it. They died again with mirth.

"Big god damn ape!" McGibbeney said as he passed them.

They fell out of his way in mock terror as he stamped into the shack and washed off the teeth in a dipper of water.

"Laugh!" he said, coming out again. "Laugh your damn lunatic brains out! I'll take on anybody my weight here, and by God I'll make hash of him." He dusted off the shoulders of his jumper, slapping the stiff denim.

"Nobody here your weight," Herb Davis said. "You're in a class by yourself, Frank." His head perked sideward. "Unless maybe Moe . . ."

They yelled and shoved Moe forward into McGibbeney, who stood still with folded arms and shouldered him contemptuously away. Pushed at by half a dozen hands, Moe looked up under his eyebrows with little twinkling eyes, and then he put out his hand.

"Fellow worker," he said, "I am a man of peace. What about you?"

There was something so hilariously humble about him that they collapsed again, and laughing brought back the memory of McGibbeney dangling by the heels. John thumped Joe on the back, his arm falling with helpless weight. His eyes were red and full of tears. "Yesus God!" he gasped. "Oh, holy smoke! Did you see t'ings fall out of him? Pennies, and vatches, and store teet', oh Yudas Priest!"

Joe gave him a hard elbow in the solar plexus and he bent over, too weak to be resentful, and fell to the ground and rolled there. McGibbeney stood with dignity while the joy declined and eventually died, and he eyed John Alberg with disgust.

"Until you guys started your god damn Roman holiday, I had something I wanted to do over here," he said. He looked at Joe. "I came over here to get you."

"What for?"

"Got some'm to show you. You and Herb, especially."

"Why Herb and me?"

"Come on and you'll see."

"What's the hurry?"

"What I want to show you happens at five sharp."

"I should have been over at the hall a long time ago," Davis said. "Will this take long?"

"On'y a few minutes."

Finally they let McGibbeney herd them out across the flat, along the waterfront, across the web of tracks, and up to Beacon Street. He was triumphantly secretive until he stopped them in front of the Argosy Theater.

"What the hell is this?" Davis asked. "I haven't got time for a show, Mac, that's a fact. I got to get in and work for the trainmen even if you won't."

"You got time for this," McGibbeney said, and bought three tickets.

The entrance smells hotly of popcorn and butter. As the outside door sighs behind them they are pushed into the warm stink of bodies. The air seems as thick as glycerin, and they stand at the head of the aisle in a gloom of half-seen heads and shoulders until the seats grow slowly into vision. "Here," McGibbeney whispers. "Here's three."

On the lighted stage, strange and far away as something seen down a long tunnel, three acrobats slide and tumble down, bow, spring muscularly offstage to a spatter of clapping. But just as the last one, a girl, is disappearing, a hobo with big flapping shoes darts out of the wings and trips her with his cane. He ducks her indignant swing, saunters out onstage to meet a man in a derby who comes in from the other side.

At the moment of the encounter the one with the cane points upward and cringes, turning up his coat collar. "Duck!" he yells. Derby glances upward. "Duck hell, that's a gull." "Well b'y or gull, you better duck!" yells the hobo at the top of his voice, and grabs his knees and guffaws. Derby swings a mighty kick at the hobo's tempting backside, which twitches away just in time so that the kicker misses. His foot flies an incredible distance into the air and he crashes to the stage. From the audience comes a sharp, explosive bark of laughter.

The two come together again, rubbernecking the gallery, still talking in bellows. A white rope of light falls from the ceiling and nooses them there.

"You know," Derby bellows, "I had a terrible fright the other night. I was sitting out at the water tank waiting for a freight and a tarantula ran up my pants leg."

"That's nothing!" Hobo bellows back. "Yesterday I went to see my friend Cohen at his tailor shop and a sewing machine ran up the seam of my shirt."

He ducks a roundhouse swing with the indifference of a shooting-gallery duck and breaks into a big-footed, loose-soled tapdance. His baggy pants flop and fly around his legs, he cocks his smashed tophat over one eye and skates backward without moving from one spot, he holds up one leg and jumps over it, alighting with a splat of leather. One foot gets going in a continuous roll of taps and sticks there, so that he stands for a full minute with one uncontrollable leg flapping, his face contorted in anxiety and surprise. At last the leg locks stiffly. Pulling fails to budge it. He bends over and seizes it with both hands. Nothing happens. With all his weight he hauls backward; without warning the foot comes loose and he does a complete flip to light flat on his stomach. Somebody in the orchestra pit hits the bass drum as he lands, and the giggling murmur of laughter rises to a shout. Rising very slowly, a betrayed man, Hobo sees his friend Derby. He chases him furiously offstage, and the clapping begins.

"For the love of mike," Davis says, leaning across Joe. "Is this what you brought us over here to see?"

"Wait."

Now Hobo is back on the stage, pacing back and forth, and on his shoulder is a sign, UNFAIR. (Davis nudges Joe with a little grunting appreciative chuckle.) From the opposite wings comes Derby, now a railroader in a hogger's cap, carrying a big oil can. They confer in pantomime; Engineer keeps shaking his head, and goes around touching imaginary machinery with the spout of his oil can. They wave their arms at each other. Picket is insistent, Engineer angry. Finally he drives Picket away, climbs up into an imaginary cab, leans out an imaginary window, hoots long and mournful with his mouth, lets off steam with a sounding hiss. With nothing but his mouth and the shuffle of his feet he sounds amazingly like a locomotive starting to roll. Picket, defeated, sulks and thinks.

Then he is struck so hard by an idea that he is almost knocked down. He rushes offstage, and in a few moments appears at the other side lugging a railroad tie, which he lays in Engineer's path and tiptoes away. The shuffle and hiss and chug of the engine is coming along fast now; the Engineer is debonair in his cab window, waving at the audience as he pours by. Abruptly his neck stretches, he stares, he leaps for the brakes. There is an indescribable rush of sound with help from the cymbals in the pit as he falls twice his length and crashes. A moment of silence, then a weak hiss of escaping steam, then silence again.

Someone in the audience yips like a dog, McGibbeney punches Joe's shoulder and his eyes shine, Davis is laughing. On stage the actors are now standing arm in arm, looking with an expectant simper up into the floodlights. In the pit the pianist has started a rolling introduction to "Casey Jones."

Joe sits as still as if a quick move would bring the building down. To hide the tremor that is growing in his hands, he has folded his arms across his chest, but the palms of his hands are moist, and for an instant he is scared to death. He makes a curt shrugging acknowledgment of something Davis is saying. The theater is too quiet. The applause has been for the pantomime; the song, he knows, will fall flat. Then his ears pop as if from altitude, and he hears the vaudeville team, already on the third line:

His boiler it was leaking and his drivers on the bum,
And his engine and its bearings they were all out of plumb . . .

But now Joe is jerked out of the embarrassment that has held him stiffly, for like a chorus that has been rehearsed, a dozen people in the audience come in.

CASEY JONES kept his junkpile running,
CASEY JONES was working double time . . .

"See?" McGibbeney says in Joe's ear. "By God, I knew it the minute I heard it first!"

Davis roars out the second chorus. The whole theater is coming in, even Joe Hillstrom, having the song dragged out of him by the exuberant will of the people in the dark around him and the waving arms of the two vaudevillians.

But Joe is sweating, and almost before the last chorus he is standing, sidling his way to the aisle. Davis and McGibbeney are behind him, and out in the glare of the afternoon street they look at him curiously. "We should've stuck," McGibbeney says. "They encored those guys twice last night."

"How'd they get it?" Joe says.

But the railroader lifts his hands. "I guess they just picked it out of the air. These vaudeville boys are sympathizers, but they just been in town four days."

"Damnedest thing I ever heard of," Davis says. "You only wrote it a week ago." He looks at Joe quickly. "I s'pose you could sue, if you wanted."

But McGibbeney looks at Joe with a wrinkled forehead. "Jesus, then they'd stop singin' it. You don't want them to do that."

In the popcorn-smelling entrance, his back against the posters advertising the Three Alegrettis, he stands apart from his own presence and his own laughter and his own companions, and through slightly narrowed eyes looks at something else. Something had been stirring in him ever since last Sunday, when they whistled and gave him a hand at the trainmen's meeting. He knows perfectly what it is that he feels: pride, and a sense of power. There are things he can do and things he can be. He is already out in some current, and he can feel his bows swinging, his engines coming to life.

Davis has said something. Joe looks at him and McGibbeney, opening his eyes wide, and what he says surprises him with the way it rings. "I didn't write it for money," he says. "I wrote it for the good of the working class."

Davis has hold of his hand, shaking it. "All right!" he says belligerently. "All right now, by God! I been laying off of you, but I'm not laying off any more. It's just a bunch of god damn baloney that you ain't wearing a button and carrying a card. How about it?"

"I told you, I don't like jails well enough to join the Wobblies."

"Horseshit," Davis says. "You don't have to work in any free-speech fights. There's plenty of us that can't do nothing else. You can do more good staying home and writing songs."

"Look what this one's done in a week," McGibbeney says.

Davis is still shaking his hand. "The Wobblies are a singing outfit. You can stir up a hell of a lot of solidarity just with a good song, one with real militancy in it."

Joe is pretending to consider, but the current is already shoving him along. "Well, I've got no big objection," he says, and instantly they have hold of him, steering him. It is pleasant to him to see how they gloat over landing him; he is a prize, a triumph for them, somebody. The sense of being on the verge of something remarkable, and of being made for what is now to happen, is as palpable as the heat beating up from the sidewalk, but almost before he recognizes it for what it is he is hiding it, not to show it to the others. He walks quietly, smiling, and when Davis offers him the makings he makes a little foolish rhyme. He says,

> Smoke and snus I never use,
> I live on straight tobacco yuice,

and is rewarded by their soft snorts that pretend to indicate disgust but actually indicate their recognition of his superior powers, their unenvious admiration. They take him on to the Wobbly hall, something special.

It was late when he left the hall, and though he could have had a choice of companions he went alone. He did not go immediately back to the shack, but under the push of a vague restless desire to stretch his legs drifted off Beacon and into a side street that led up the hill. The night was dry, swept clean by a gusty wind, and the stars were like stars at sea, but there was none of the loneliness of the sea here. All around him as he walked under the steady night-sound of trees there was the sense of human crowding. It was a pleasure to him to walk quietly in the dark, past lighted houses and dark, and feel the people inside and know that he was utterly strange to all of them. Nevertheless, here he walked, with strength and speed and brains in him that they never suspected, and fingers that could play a piano or a violin, and a mind that could set words to rhyme and an eye and a hand that could make pictures. He felt like a lion that walks disdainfully through a sleeping camp of hunters.

At an intersection he paused, seeing the chip of moon through the leaves of a tall eucalyptus. It looked inexpressibly far-off, vanishing, and he was reminded of a time in his boyhood when he had carelessly left a skiff untied after he stepped out of it, and the tide had run it out, bobbing and dancing and hopelessly out of reach, into the bay.

What are you after, a fellow like you? he asked himself, and smiled to himself like an actor. He discussed himself with the wind, sitting on a gravel hill and looking down over the lights of the harbor. You are no usual Swede immigrant, no ordinary working-man, the night assured him. If you were, you'd be down at the Forecastle with John, or shooting pool in some joint, or sponging a bed and a cup of coffee down at the mission. People see something in you. What are you after, a fellow like you? Moe Dreyfuss asks. What have you got talents for? the missionary says, scolding you. You're one we really wanted, Davis says, pinning a button on you and making you out a card. That one song is better than the whole damn picket line, says McGibbeney.

The wind comes across the Pedro Hills and whines in the thin grass, and out over the harbor the channel lights and the starlike line along the breakwater are splintered by the wind.

It is a fine warm dream, this dream of the self. It moves as freely as the wind from triumph to triumph. There are shouts in it, and the respectful faces of workers and bosses and politicians. There is a kind of march in this dream, a slow purposeful surge, and an anger that like a fire loose in a city spreads over everything in its path.

And faces: the stiff-lipped Bible-reading captain of the first ship he ever worked on, between Stockholm and Hull; the suspicious, snoopy, County-Galway phiz of Joyce, the proprietor of the Bowery saloon where he first landed work in America; the furious twisted face—the face of a man with an unbearable pain inside him, or a fury that he cannot satisfy—of the third engineer on the *Sarah Cleghorn*. Others too: the worried, beet-red face of a Norske farmer in Dakota, a man who kept glancing at the fading day-light and loped like a clumsy bear, trying to get in another fifteen minutes, another fifty bundles, another ten sacks. Faceless figures of men in cutaway coats and big watch chains—they swim and swarm in his mind while the wind tugs at him and the lights of the harbor splinter and re-form and shine with diamond brilliance in the wind-split night. He feels his lean strength like a cat stretching; when he stands erect above the wind-tormented grass he is as tall as Moses lifting his hand over the Red Sea and crying for the waters to divide.

More than an hour later he came in the faint moon-and-star light along the path through the salt grass and up to the door of the shack. Somebody was home; he saw a shadow stoop and move against the light of the window. When he opened the door he found Otto at the table rolling something in a newspaper. For an instant he had the impression that Otto crouched, ready to fight or run, before the slight tension relaxed and Otto's face pulled up in the sleepy smile.

"Hello," he said. "What was Mac's big secret?"

"*Eniting*," Joe said. "Nothing special."

Otto's smile widened while he rolled the newspaper package and twisted one end. He had his hat and coat on as if ready to go out. "You're sure a talker," he said.

"I talk enough," Joe said, surprised.

"Never too much, eh?"

When they locked eyes, Otto's eyes did not fall. They wrinkled at the corners as if he were enjoying some private joke.

"Maybe I haven't got much to talk about," Joe said.

"Not as much as me, is that what you mean?"

"Maybe."

Into Otto's smile now had come something definitely knowing and amused. He picked up the package and rolled it gently between his palms. At last he said softly, "Who're you trying to fool?"

Puzzled by the concentrations and the air of knowingness in Otto's look, Joe felt the backs of his knees tensing as if before a fight. But he only said, "Not you, I guess."

"I got eyes," Otto said. "I wasn't born yesterday." Holding Joe's eyes, he tipped the package and jiggled it until a pair of wire cutters and a thin-bladed hacksaw slid out on the table. "I been watching you," he said. "I like the way you keep your mouth shut."

"I kind of like it too," Joe said.

Otto was loosely built, shorter than Joe, nondescript except for the sheep face and the silly-looking smile. Everything about him seemed limp and loose, hair and smile and clothes, even the way his arms hung from his shoulders. But his eyes had the unwavering reflecting brightness of a rat's. "How'd you like a build up your stake a little tonight?" he said.

But now Joe began to smile. He shook his head. "Don't tell me anything about it, Otto."

"You can't live forever without work," Otto said. "Even if

they break this strike, you're back on the dock bosses and the mates."

"That's all right."

Shrugging, Otto shook the hacksaw and wire cutters back into the package and retwisted the end. "You like to work alone, is that it?"

"Maybe I'm particular what I work at," Joe said. He returned Otto's mocking grin, and as Otto turned to the door he wagged his finger at Otto's coat lapel. "You wearing that button out tonight?"

Otto's eyes lighted on the button in Joe's own coat. He laughed aloud, shaking his head almost in admiration, and slipped the button from his lapel and into his pocket. "You're all right," he said. "We'll get along."

5   San Pedro, July, 1910

On ordinary days the waterfront is a blocks-long stage crisscrossed with railroad tracks, cluttered with stacks of poles, lumber, neatly layered ties, pyramids of coal. The two long wharves stretch out into the bay toward Dead Man's Island, each with its own pattern of tracks, stalled freight- and flatcars, piles of merchandise going or coming. Around the ends of the wharves small craft cluster like fruit flies around something sweet and sticky; along the other end lounge the longshoremen waiting for the dock boss's call.

This is a stage on which are enacted the tedious scenes of arrival and departure, of fetch and carry, more erratic than the tides but just as repetitive. Out along the docks the stagehands prepare the sets, warp in freighters and lumber schooners and colliers and coastwise passenger ships and an occasional old three- or four-master. Their work is complex with lines and bawled orders, but it comes quickly to a neatness, a readiness, and a waiting. At a certain point the dock gates are unlocked and at the window of his little office the stage manager selects his actors from the loungers on the proscenium. He selects them for various reasons:

because they are personal friends, because they have bought him drinks, because they have kicked back a folded bill out of their wages, because he is tired of seeing their faces around looking hopeful, because he needs every man he can lay hands on, sometimes even because he knows them for good workers and strong backs.

Then the antlike act, the drama of burdens.

If there are several schooners lying at the wharves, or if some collier is anxious to be under way, the ants may crawl under their loads for twelve or fifteen hours at a stretch, and take their pay and go home to sleep the clock around and return to hang around again waiting for the boss to swing the gates and pick another crew.

There are those who try, by bribes or good fellowship, or by tapping clerks and agents whom they know, to get advance information on sailings and dockings so as to be johnny-on-the-spot when the call comes. It generally happens that these wiseacres can never go anywhere, even under the dock to relieve themselves, without someone hopeful or suspicious at their heels.

Along this whole waterfront there is a suspicion and jealousy as restless as the lipping of water against the pilings. Every man's hand is against every other man. This is the way the bosses want it. If those who are passed over do not hate those who are picked, something has slipped in the system. A healthy competition for work is the best insurance against labor troubles.

But there are some, less eager, who will not shove and scramble and buy drinks and kick back out of their wages. They are not going to run up and slobber all over some petty Caesar like the dock boss. They do not stand up and take a look every time a ship's smoke shows beyond the breakwater or a switch engine backs a string of boxcars onto the dock. They go on pitching pennies, or arguing, or playing cards in the shade of a warehouse, until someone among the eager reports real action at one pier or the other. Then they walk over, maintaining the dignity of the American workingman. They do not need work bad enough to kiss anybody's foot for it. And some day they will strike this harbor and tie it up tight and get some decent conditions and decent wages and an eight-hour day on the longshore. When they get strong enough. Not yet.

These are the ones who will talk back to a slave driver, refuse to lift things too heavy for a man, holler for more handtrucks, more dollies, more manpower on a job. They read books and radical papers and attend meetings, and they make a sharp and contemptuous distinction between themselves and the scissorbills. The lumber companies and the stevedoring company keep a careful check on their numbers and activities, even when the waterfront is quiet. Now, with the trainmen striking, these are the ones who are out in sympathy, throwing a picket line across the foot of each dock. When a carload of scabs is backed through the line, protected by mounted police, the pickets give way reluctantly, beckoning and yelling. So far there has been no trouble, only words.

In ordinary times itinerant radical intellectuals and organizers hit the Pedro waterfront as if on a Lyceum circuit—ex-professors and ex-preachers, rebellious college boys, union delegates, professional revolutionaries preaching socialism, anarchism, syndicalism, bimetallism, the single tax. With faces like saints or madmen or prize fighters or farmers or clerks, but always with the eyes of believers, they come and go, leaving a little deposit of their eloquence and fervor and belief among the men who will listen. Now with the waterfront struck they come in greater numbers, and back from the picket lines in the temporary headquarters, and in the shade of sheds and warehouses, little meetings go on. Prominent among the men in the audiences are those with the red button of the Wobblies in their shirts.

One of them is the slim Swede with the scarred jaw. He can take a piece of chalk and draw a picture on a wall so anybody could recognize it. He is the one who wrote the song about Casey Jones the union scab. The other morning there was a Wobbly sticker on the dock boss's window: "Join the One Big Union." The Swede is supposed to have put it there. Not that he ever admitted he did. He hangs around with the boys, and when he talks they pay attention to him, but he doesn't talk much. A kind of a clam. And a strange smile, sometimes, almost as if there were nobody home.

The street that paralleled the tracks along the waterfront was a canal of fine gray dust that climbed the spokes of dray-wagon wheels and hung in the air for minutes, as if it had no weight at all. Anyone crossing the street stamped his feet hard on the loading platforms to shake off the clinging powder, but at noon not many were crossing the street. The picket line at the Hammond dock was down to a handful; the rest were over at the headquarters or sitting in the shade eating. There was a smell of hot planks, tar, fish. Anything metal in the sun was too hot to touch, but in the shade of the warehouse where Joe sat alone there was a cooling smelly breath wavering up from the water along with the wavering reflection of light. Nothing was coming in or out; the cops were out of sight in the dock boss's office.

In the nearly complete quiet hardly a gull cried. The tide was down, leaving the barnacled piles exposed like scabby legs. The water lipped around them oilily with a tiny wet sucking noise.

He was remembering the islands, and a time he had looked down into the lagoon through a glass-bottomed bucket and seen how the fishes hung among the watery coral gardens, and how at the shadow of a shark they all streamed off together across the sand, and how they came winnowing back when the danger was past. All the little fishes, rushing in one direction or another because of food or fear. And all the big fishes, some poisonous, some with stings, some with teeth.

With a sandwich half eaten in his hand he sat in the heat-stunned noon and thought about them, and as he sat he saw a rat come creeping in quick bursts of movement along a timber under the dock. It moved as if danger lay at every crossbeam; it tried the air with its nose, saw everything with bright bead eyes. Joe knew it saw and estimated him, though he had not moved the slightest muscle for two minutes. A big rat, big and smart and careful, it came in creeping bursts of movement that were somehow indicative of a curious boldness mixed with an overpowering caution.

For a moment it disappeared, then it was in sight again. When it chose to move fast its creep became a hop almost like a rabbit's. On the loading platform someone stamped his feet hard, and as the sound and vibration shook along the planks the rat froze, its whiskers twitching, its nose trying the air. After a pause it moved again, arrived at an angle in the beams, twisted and with one smooth movement was up on top in the sun.

Joe broke a piece off the sandwich and tossed it out onto the planks. For a long time the rat sat perfectly still, not even its whiskers moving: a big rat, big and smart, not to be baited into danger. Even at forty feet its protruding perfectly round eyes shone with an intense concentration of life.

Now, belly to the planks, its motion less like an animal's than like a snake's footless slide, it came toward him until it was within ten feet of the piece of bread. Joe sat very still, and when he heard footsteps coming along the platform he willed angrily that they go back. Some flatfoot would have to come along just at this minute.

The rat heard the steps too; it was still again, a gray hump on the planks. Joe cheeped softly with his lips, and without more hesitation the rat crossed the last few feet and took the bread between its paws and began to eat. The thing made Joe smile; he had been holding his breath.

Not so fast, Grandpa, he said. Look a little closer before you take things people offer you. There's always arsenic in the cheese and strychnine in the bread. Remember who you are. They wouldn't put it out there if it wasn't poisoned, would they? Why would anybody do *you* a favor?

The rat had finished the bread. Joe tossed out another piece, and the rat scuttled away, stopped, returned and fell on it. The dragging tail crept after it across the wood.

If you didn't have such a naked tail, Joe told it. If you just looked pretty, and learned to sit up and beg politely. If you didn't swarm in dump-grounds and sewers. Why don't you grow fur on your tail and learn to do tricks and quit hanging around wharves and living like an outcast?

When he threw a third piece of sandwich toward the rat there was no running away. That's the way it goes, Joe said. The minute anybody tosses out some food, you practically stand on your head. The biggest, toughest, smartest rat under the wharf, and all it takes to tame you is a scrap of sandwich. If you really got wise you could take over the town of San Pedro, did you know that? Just by going after what you really want and not being satisfied with a chunk of bread.

Steps came around the warehouse, close, and in one motion as smooth as water the rat was over the edge and gone. For a moment its snaky tail lay there, and then as if it had a life of its own it crawled out of sight. Joe looked up into the cocky, square face of Herb Davis.

Davis pulled down his mouth. "I guess I queered it."

"Queered what?"

"Weren't you trying to get him?"

"I was feeding him."

Davis stared, his tough red face contracted. Even on so hot a day he wore a snap-bow tie. His sleeves were puffed out above metal elastic armbands. "What the hell for?"

"Anything wrong with it?"

"Nothing except the city probably spends a hundred thousand a year exterminating 'em."

"That's why I was feeding him," Joe said. "What's new?"

"I come down to spread the word. Tom Barnabas is here."

"He is?" Joe stood up.

"Flying trip," Herb said. "He'll be around all afternoon and talk at a street meeting tonight. Also he wants to talk to you."

"Me?"

"I been telling him about you," Herb said. "What you get for being famous."

Since Sunday he had felt it—a kind of expectancy, and he believed implicitly that there would be a day like this when the waiting immobility of his life would be broken and something big would happen. Destined and dedicated, a man on a big errand, he had yet hung on the brink, uncertain, committed but not wholly involved; and his unprecipitated, uncorroborated myth of himself hung with him. There would have to be a moment or an event that would be crucial. He felt it coming now.

Dusting off the seat of his corduroy pants, he said carefully, "He at the hall?"

"Was when I left. You coming back now?"

"I want to stop off at the shack for a minute first. I'll see you in half an hour."

"He particularly wants to see you," Herb said. He went off along the platform, a hurrying man, an aggressive, thrusting-aside, doing man, and Joe started for the shack.

Barnabas was a member of the General Executive Board of the IWW, an intellectual and an orator, almost as big a figure

as Trautman or St. John or Haywood, and he represented something Joe wanted to see and know: a man high in the union,
a leader and an organizer, Barnabas also wanted to see him.
To be known and sought out—there was a satisfaction in that
that pulled his mouth upward in a smile. But he still felt what
he had felt when Davis told him—a little uncertainty, a little
fear. He was going to the shack to change his clothes and see
if John Alberg was around to go down with him.

The moment he came in the shack he gave up the second
notion. John had got himself tanked last night as usual. The
quilt and the shucked-off clothes were all over the floor. In
underwear and socks, John sat on the brass bed rubbing the back
of his neck, bleary-eyed and whiskery and with the corners of his
mouth brown from *snus*. Anger flew in Joe's face like a bird
caught in the room. Without a word he yanked the chest out
from under his bunk and got out the blue suit, the shirt and
collar, the yellow shoes.

John scrubbed at his swollen face, yawned, sank his head and
cautiously rolled it on his neck. "Holy yee!" he said vaguely but
with feeling. His toes curled in the holey socks, he watched Joe
change.

"Going somev'ere?"

"Tom Barnabas is in town."

For two or three minutes more John said nothing, but watched
stupidly. Then astonishment visibly broke the surface of his mind.
He said, "You dressing up to see *him?*"

Tying the string tie, Joe saw the image of his cousin in the
broken mirror, temples clutched between the heels of his hands,
dog-eyes bent upward.

"Maybe I should go around looking the way you look," Joe
said.

"You couldn't look as bad as I feel," John said. He rose, groaning
"Oh, holy smoke!" and shuffled to the stand and with one hand
poured a dipperful of water over his head. Dripping, with water
catching in his stubbled cheeks, he turned and groped among
his clothes on the floor, finally coming up with a pint bottle about
half full. Muttering to himself, his big foolish face stunned and
swollen, his big head wagging, he worked the cork out with his
thumb and finger while Joe watched.

"Are you going to start right in again?"

"Vell, holy yee," John said.

As if he carried a fifty-pound weight on his head he cautiously tipped the bottle, moving his head and the bottle together. Joe let the anger lick out again, realizing how much was there only when he let it go. He said, "When every man in the union ought to be down on the line or over at the hall hearing what Barnabas has got to say, you sit around here in your drawers starting another drunk."

The bottle came cautiously down. "Dis is har of dog."

"A souse!" Joe said. "A lousy dehorn!"

He slammed the door on the sight of John's opening, astonished face. Along the path he walked carefully, walking on grass instead of in the path, so as to avoid getting dust on his shoes. Without precisely admitting it to himself, he knew why he had jumped on John, why he had felt it necessary to dress up. He could even, in the layer of his mind which knew things without admitting them, discover an almost voluptuous appreciation of his own cunning.

Barnabas was for labor but not born in it. He was not a working stiff, but a college graduate, a leader. And to him now, ready to listen with attention but not in any way acknowledging any superiority in brains or value in the other, came Joe Hillstrom in good dressy clothes; also a leader, also a man who showed above the rest.

But he wished with a last flash of anger that John had been sober enough to come along. A man alone showed up more.

6 San Pedro, July, 1910

He came into the hall under the poster of the worker stripped to the waist, with the red letters IWW rising behind him like a red dawn, and saw Barnabas in the midst of a group—Davis and Manderich and some others, and a girl Joe did not know. The whole group turned as he came in, so that he entered alone and spotlighted. "Here he is now," Herb Davis said.

So he was expected, he had been named. Crossing the room was like an actor's entrance. Though he shook hands with Barnabas almost indifferently, he felt at once the man's magnetism. Something emanated from him, a glow of conviction and assurance that shriveled Joe's confidence instantly. Barnabas gave his undivided, friendly attention when he shook hands, his eyes were brown and warm, and his eyes and his hand and his voice all said the same thing. Glad to know you. Really glad.

"You wrote Casey Jones," he said.

"Yes."

"It's a great song. It really puts the finger on something."

Joe said nothing. His embarrassment and his pride made him look into Barnabas' open handsome face almost jeeringly. The brown eyes were warm and compelling on him. He knew that his unadmitted notion of being equal to this man was a pipedream. His challenge was defeated before it ever got made.

"Herb tells me you're working on some more."

"Yeah," Joe said. He felt in the group around him, in Herb especially, the unspoken urge: Go on, tell him about it, show your stuff, impress the visitor so the local boys can take pride. But something stiff and clumsy in his insides would not bend, his tongue was awkward in his mouth. To his own ears his voice sounded surly and resentful. On the broad freckled face of the girl in the circle he thought he saw amazement, and he leveled a glance of hatred at her.

Barnabas was pressing him, his warmth unchanged. "You're making a book of them, is that right?"

"I had a notion."

"Can I see it?"

"It isn't done."

"How many songs?"

"Only three really finished."

"That's all right. Where are they?"

"Over at the mission."

He felt his neck redden at how the words sounded and the things they implied, and added, "I write them there because there's a piano."

Barnabas was looking at his watch with one eye still on Joe. "I was just going over to the hotel. Can you bring them there? Regent Hotel, room seventeen?"

"How soon?"

"Right away."

"I guess so."

"Good!" Barnabas said. His voice boomed, a big commanding sound, and his actions got at once brisker, as if something now was settled and other things remained to be attacked. He put his hand on Joe's shoulder. "Sooner or later we've got to quit organizing to 'Halleluiah I'm a Bum.' I want to see your songs for a very particular reason."

Several of them went through the door together, and in the street Barnabas turned, apologizing. "You didn't meet Betty. This is Betty Spahn."

He looked at her sharply now, focusing on her for the first time. The hand she gave him was broad as a man's, her eyes were flecked with yellow, her mouth was flexible, wide, amused. So Barnabas traveled with a klootch. And this klootch! "Boxcar Betty?" he said.

She was known wherever migrants gathered, in boardinghouses and jungles and camps all up and down the West. Her father was an itinerant populist agitator, her mother the daughter of a country parson who had lived with a half-dozen workers in the labor movement. Mother Spahn's house in Aberdeen was still headquarters for harvest stiffs; in the yards at Aberdeen the girl had grown up with boxcars for playhouses. She had hit the road at sixteen, been for a while the girl of Dutch Weiss until he was killed in a battle with the Kansas City cops, and she had scratched her name on the walls of half a dozen jails where she had been thrown for her work in free-speech fights and walkouts. Once she had ridden from Seattle to the iww convention in Chicago with the Overall Brigade of Jack Walsh, hopping freights with the rest, jungling up with them, working at meetings and asking no favors, one girl among twenty-five men, as red a Wobbly as ever grew.

She had a neck as strong as a tree. Joe said in wonder, "So you're Boxcar Betty."

"Why, heard of me?"

"All over."

Her laugh was hoarse, big-chested, full of delight. He thought

as he left them and went on to the mission that there ought
to be a song about a girl like that, a real dyed-in-the-skein rebel.

The door to room seventeen was open. Tom Barnabas with his
suspenders dangling was shaving in front of the washstand mirror.
"Be with you in a second," he said over his shoulder, pulling the
skin of his throat to stretch it. Joe sat down. In a moment
Betty Spahn came in from across the hall and sprawled on
the bed.

"Got your songs?"

Joe tossed her the envelope with the sheets of verses and
drawings.

"How about the music? You write that too?"

"Not for any of these."

"Not for any of these," she said, raising her eyes to his face.
"Do you write it for some of them?"

"I've got one, 'Workers of the World Awaken' that I'm writing
a new tune for," Joe said. "I haven't got it worked out yet."
With a finger he scattered the sheets till the one he wanted was
showing:

> Workers of the world, awaken!
> Break your chains, demand your rights.
> All the wealth you make is taken
> By exploiting parasites.

As she read it he watched her, but Barnabas, clean and pink,
tenderly mopping with a towel, leaned to read over her shoulder
and obscured her face. He made no comment, but only said, "If
I have to shave once more in cold water I won't have any hide
left."

Betty Spahn's fingers picked up another sheet. "What's the tune
to this one?"

"Which one?"

"'Mr. Block.'"

"'It looks to Me like a Big Time Tonight.'"

She hummed it, reading through the lines, and now Barnabas
threw the towel on the stand and chuckled, swinging his alert
face toward Joe. "That's a good one—good as Casey Jones."

Joe was annoyed at how much the casual praise meant, and

he half hated Barnabas for putting him in this position of a menial who could be thrown a bone of commendation. Yet Barnabas was his ally, his friend, his fellow worker. Joe looked away from him into the yellow-flecked eyes of Boxcar Betty. She flapped another sheet at him. "How about this one? 'The White Slave'?"

"'Meet Me Tonight in Dreamland,'" Joe said. "I wrote that a while back, up in Seattle. It isn't exactly a labor song."

"It is at the end," Barnabas said, and put his finger on the last verse:

> Girls in this way fall every day
> And have been falling for ages.
> Who is to blame? You know his name,
> It's the boss that pays starvation wages.

"That's a tear-jerker," Betty said with her throaty laugh. Barnabas reached over her and gathered up the papers, leaning against the dresser with his suspenders down, his face expressionless as he read. Over at the window a blowfly buzzed and stopped and buzzed again, angrily trying to force a way through the curtains. The room was hot and airless. On the bed Boxcar Betty leaned back against her braced hands and catching Joe's eye inexplicably winked. Joe stirred, wanting to be gone.

Even when he was done, Barnabas said nothing, but reached into the suitcase on the chair and brought out a small bottle from which he poured a little lotion into his hand. The sharp cool odor of bay rum spread in the humid air. With both hands Barnabas worked the bay rum into his cheeks and jaws, and through his hands he said, "Those are absolutely wonderful, you know. They've got the real stuff in them, the real *feel*." His smile was so suddenly winning that it extorted a weak and unwilling smile from Joe in return. But as abruptly as he had turned on his charm Barnabas turned it off again, reached into the suitcase and started getting into a clean shirt.

"Any chance you could find a Chinaman to wash some shirts before we leave tonight?" he said to Betty. He had apparently forgotten Joe completely.

"I'll see," Betty said lazily. Barnabas was already tucking in the tails of the shirt, turning momentarily away from the girl. He pulled on a light alpaca coat and slapped the flat straw hat on his head.

For a second Joe thought he was going to leave without saying anything more about the songs. But at the last minute Barnabas sat down on the bed beside Betty and looked across at Joe with a widening smile, his eyes alert and filled with the clearest, most disciplined intelligence.

"You want to make a book of songs," he said. "How?"

Again Joe was put at a disadvantage by the unexpectedness of the question. He stumbled. "I don't know. Just make it. Have them printed and sew them together. I could do some drawings. We could sell them for a dime."

"Just locally, you mean."

"I guess so, yes."

Barnabas removed the hat and smoothed the leather band. In the heat the band had already left a slight mark around his forehead. "What if the union wanted to put out a book, distribute it all over the world, put in the 'Internationale' and some others besides yours. Would you be willing to give us your songs for a book like that?"

In their faces he saw their eagerness that he should do it, and he felt how his own vague plans had fitted into larger plans. "Why not?" he said.

The hat was back on Barnabas' smooth head, tipped over one eye, and Barnabas rose with the big booming, something-settled satisfaction in his voice. "Good! Good. Can I take them along?"

"These are the only copies I've got."

"Can you copy them for me?" He hesitated. "I'll be so wound up with Herb and the strike committee . . ."

"Sure," Joe said. His resentment of Barnabas' magnetism was gone. Now he was an accepted partner, not a local boy being patronized. "How soon do you want them?"

Barnabas was already pulling paper and pencils from the suitcase. "I'll have to see the stevedoring company with Herb, and later we're talking with the committee over at the brotherhood office. Do you talk at the street meeting tonight?"

"I'm no good on the talk."

The eyes were sharp and shrewd on him. "You ought to be organizing, with your knack for making songs."

"I'd make a bad soapboxer," Joe said. "Organizing, that's all right, but I haven't got the gift of gab like Herb and some of the others."

"Well, we'll talk about that later," Barnabas said on his way to the door. "Maybe Betty can help you copy them off now." He hung in the doorway, and Joe intercepted a curious quizzical look that passed between him and the girl. "You want to come along, or stay here, Betty?"

"It's too hot to be running around," she said. "I guess I'll stick here, unless you need me."

"No," Barnabas said. His eyebrows lifted, the corner of his mouth went down slightly, and with a fleeting, odd, half-humorous glance he went down, his heels sharp on the brass binding of the stair-treads.

Boxcar Betty stood up from the bed, felt in her hair as if she were used to having a pencil stuck there, and said, "Well, shall we get busy?"

Silently Joe passed her half the sheets. The room was stuffier than ever, and though the door into the hall stood open it seemed almost unbearably intimate for the two of them to be writing here. Joe's constraint had gone with Barnabas. Now every detail of the room, bed and pitcher and washstand and slop jar and the mirror in which he could see the top of Betty's head, was suggestive. His nostrils quivered with the belief that he could smell her. It took an effort to bend his head and copy "Mr. Block."

A movement of her arm made him lift his eyes alertly. She was lighting a cigarette. Across the exhaled smoke her eyes brushed his in the friendly, amused, comprehending look he had noticed several times before. But somehow her look was more intimate, less careful, than what she said.

"What got you started writing songs?"

"I don't know. I always liked to fool around that way."

"Hillstrom, that's Swedish, isn't it?"

"Yes."

"You've hardly got any accent at all."

Because he could think of nothing to say, he kept still, and she bent her head to the copying. He had just brought himself back to his careful round transcribing when she snorted with laughter and slapped the pencil on the suitcase she was using for a table.

"What is it?" he said.

"Nothing."

Half rising, he saw that she was copying "The White Slave."
"Is it as funny as all that?" he said.

She came twisting around on the chair toward him, and he
saw that in her face was an almost incredulous mirth. "I love
it. Don't you?"

Slow heat began to burn in his face. "I can't tell about
them," he said and returned to his copying.

He knew she watched him for a while; he heard the sound
her clothes made when she finally looked down. Once, when
their eyes met during a break in the writing, she pulled her arm
slowly up from the varnished surface of the suitcase, showing him
how the heat had stuck her skin down, but he was troubled by
her now, and he made no comment.

After another five minutes she stood up. "Well, that's it." At
the window she stood pulling back the limp curtains. "My God
it's hot."

Joe wrote on. In a moment she was beside him. "About done?
Want me to do some of these?"

"There's only this one left."

Now he could definitely smell her, a faint, exciting effluvium
of sweat and powder and starched shirtwaist.

"You write a nice hand," she said, and in a tone of definite
irony she added, "I used to read character from handwriting."

His hand paused, embarrassed to go on making letters under
her gaze. "I guess my character wouldn't stand much reading."

Then abruptly she seemed to lose interest. "I'm going in and
take a sponge bath," she said. "Stick around a few minutes and
I'll walk over to the hall with you."

"All right."

Her eyes met his, yellow-flecked, slightly narrowed in her smiling
face. He felt as if he could breathe only off the top of his
lungs, as if the lower parts were stuck together like sheets of
flypaper face to face. He watched her through the door and into
the open door opposite, and at precisely the right instant she turned
her head and gave him the narrow-eyed smile again.

The thought of Tom Barnabas kept him sitting still, writing
mechanically through the last chorus, but his ears were pricked

for sounds from the other room, and he had shifted his chair slightly so that without turning he had the open doorways in the corner of his eye. For several minutes he neither saw nor heard anything. Then her head appeared around the jamb.

"Has Tom got any clean towels in there?"

Joe looked. There were two rumpled face towels and a clean bath towel on the stand. "There's one, yes."

Her head had disappeared again, and he waited, expecting her to come and get the towel. The sticky constriction in his lungs almost deprived him of air. Abruptly, in three steps, he crossed the hall, hesitating in the doorway. Betty was standing with her back to him, near the washstand. The light-crazed green blind was drawn to the sill. She had taken off her blouse, and he saw her bare shoulders, the strong taper of her back. Her head was bent, her hands fussing with something at her waist. In the greenish humid twilight her skin looked waxen.

Finally she turned her head. Something leaped the arc of space between them, and he was against her, his arm circling her from behind. Her uncorseted ribs rose sharply as she drew in her breath; her face was provocatively twisted, her eyes close to his. Her breast was sticky in his hand.

"Nice," he said thickly, almost voiceless, and bent his lips to hers. As he fumbled with her clothes she turned toward him fully, but he was mindless by then. There was only one impatient lucid moment when he waited by the bed and she came toward him from the door where she had turned the key. He saw her then clearly, deep-chested and chunky, strong-armed, flat-bellied, a woman on a man's frame, but as female as a mare in heat.

Later, lying quietly, he felt her bodily heat beside him and moved a little to escape the stickiness of her skin. "The strategy meeting will be starting pretty quick," he said.

She laughed low and throatily at his shoulder, and nipped his arm. "We've already started the meeting with a song," she said. She nipped him again. "That's my favorite song."

Joe made an inarticulate sound, wanting to be up and gone. Against his back her breath was scalding hot. Her hand came across him, felt up his ribs, across his collarbone, under his jaw, over his chin and mouth, delicately tracing the outline of his lips, and down across his jaw again.

"You've got a hard mouth," she said. "Is it the scars?"

At first he had let her hands go over him, not knowing how to brush them away, but as they went on, crawling like insects over his closed eyes and his brows, he rolled his head to be free of them. She stood up without warning, yanking the sheet off him. In alarm he grabbed for it, but her own nakedness was so careless that he was ashamed to be more delicate of his own. Trapped, worrying about what might happen if Tom Barnabas came back, all at the same time furious with himself and fascinated by Betty Spahn's animal unconcern as she padded around the room, he lay and watched her while she bathed. With the wet towel she mopped face and neck and throat, and when she moved the towel over and around her breasts, pushing them into provocative unconscious distortions, he felt again the sticky closing of his lungs. He watched her, queerly moved by the revelation of the secret places under her breasts and the rough way she flopped herself around with the towel.

As if a blind had slipped and gone roaring to the top of the window, he was back in a scene from his boyhood, from the time when he was perhaps twelve or thirteen, when he had come home from school one afternoon and caught his mother bathing in the bedroom. He had seen her from the kitchen, through two open doors, not directly but reflected in the dresser mirror that tipped at just the right angle. She was completely out of sight, yet completely visible, and it had not occurred to him that mirror reflections went two ways, and that he was as visible to her as she to him. Stopped on the instant of calling for her, he had stood and watched, and had seen her all over. There was a moment when her face turned toward the mirror and she stood still, bending, but after a moment she straightened again and went on with her bath almost stiffly, almost ritually. She let the crooked eye of the mirror stare at her until she was done, and afterward he tiptoed off and in ten minutes came loudly back into the house, whistling and banging his books. When he reflected on it later he knew she had seen him and stood up to his peeping with a kind of proud modesty that made him crawl with shame whenever he remembered. Now Betty Spahn stood and stooped and mopped with the towel, giving him her whole body to study coolly, and it fascinated and half sickened him to see how the weight of her breast drooped over the secret fold precisely as his mother's breast had drooped, and how the nipple looked out like a stupid cocked eye.

Swinging his feet over the edge of the bed, he found his scattered clothes, but before he could put any of them on she came over to him and somehow willed him to his feet. Cool now from the sponging, her body moved against his, and he stood dull as a stump, embarrassed and helpless, while she stood against him searching his face. He could see no gold flecks in her eyes now; they seemed pure amber. She was not laughing, or even smiling, and what she was doing to him could not have come from unsatisfied desire. Quite seriously she said, "You're a funny one. It isn't women you want at all, is it?"

"Why should I when I've just had one?" Cupping his hands like the pans of a scale, he balanced her breasts, one against the other, but she paid no attention to what he was doing, and she was not fooled.

"And you never give a straight answer," she said. "You're as cautious as a rabbit in a foxfarm. But I'm right, it *isn't* women you want, is it? They don't mean anything to you. You want something else."

"What?"

"I don't know," she said, and pulled away as if irritated. "I thought I knew a hungry look when I saw one, and what a guy like you is generally hungry for, but the kind of hungry look you've got beats me." She turned and started dressing, and in the silence he disliked her sullenly.

But when she finished buttoning her blouse she kissed him and held his face between her hands. "Forget it," she said. "We had a nice time and nobody's hurt."

"How about Tom?" He knew what about Tom, but he wanted her to say it.

"Tom and I understand each other," she said. Unlocking the door, she poked out her head and pulled it in again, laughing. Across in Barnabas' room he gathered up the song sheets. "Leave the copies here," Betty said. "We're pulling out right after the meeting tonight."

"North?"

"Frisco, Portland, Seattle. We're trying to work where we've already got some strength. Tom thinks it's smart to concentrate your power. He'll be after you and everybody else to get up there and organize."

"That's all right with me. I've got no love for the lumber trust."

Before they went downstairs she touched his face again, gently, and her smile squeezed her eyes almost shut. "Sweet," she said, and then knocked her head raucously with her fist. "Why do I have to go on all my life playing second fiddle to the union?"

At the street door he paused. "I'll see you later."

"Aren't you coming to the hall?"

"I've got some business to tend to."

"All right," she said. "So long, kiddo."

As if by design he went up the street to Romberg's Turkish Baths and for three quarters of an hour sat in the breathless steam feeling the sweat start from his pores and his body open and grow slippery with sweat and the impurities drain from body and mind. Eventually the unrest created in him by Betty Spahn subsided and he knew who he was again.

Gradually, as he quieted in the lulling, thick-breathing cubicle, his feeling about the afternoon subtly altered. By the time he dressed and went out, headed for the Harbor Cafe and a hot beef sandwich, it had become a feeling very like triumph. At least when he met Tom Barnabas again there would be no uncomfortable inferiority. He could look Barnabas right straight in the eye.

7   San Pedro, July, 1910

Herb Davis had the usual iww style of oratory—direct, loud, emphatic, and profane. He pounded his hand and shook his fists and spread his arms, thrusting his face down close from the soapbox and bawling out what he had to say. But Tom Barnabas, who followed him, was a different kind of public speaker. His voice was deeper and richer; without effort he could make it carry twice as far as Herb's. He did not swear and he did not denounce, but broke the opposition on a wheel of irony. And he had one infallibly successful trick: at any moment the rich voice would drop until people leaned and strained to hear what he was saying with such profound and confidential feeling. And just as they lost the sense of his low murmur the big booming volume would burst out in their faces, rattling their wits. He was as soft and insinuating as an actor and as irresistible as a firehose. It made no difference what he said. The slightest triviality, bursting suddenly from the middle of a confidential and conversational discourse, sounded like the thunder from Sinai. At eight o'clock, in a doorway on Beacon Street, Joe and Art Manderich and Frank McGibbeney stood at the edge of a good crowd and listened.

"By damn," McGibbeney said, "if we only had him around here for a while we could lick the b'Jesus out of the s.p. I think he could convince even a scab."

"You t'ink he iss dot goot?" Manderich said.

"He's pretty good," Joe said. He had just caught himself leaning to catch the lowered voice, and now as he looked at his companions he saw that they were both leaning too. "See?"

". . . our mothers used to tell us," Barnabas was saying. ". . . taught us in Sunday School. Remember how it used to go? Honest toil . . . tell us. Labor is an honorable condition. In the sweat of thy brow shalt thou earn thy bread. Man's lot on earth. Sure, there were bosses, but the bosses were decent fellows, generally. So if you'd just do right by the boss he'd do right by you."

Big and well dressed and handsome, with eyes that were eloquent even in the broken dusk of the street, he stood above the crowd smiling, waiting for the laughter to die. His voice accepted them all as brothers to whom one could talk freely. "There are scissorbills all around us who go through a whole lifetime without knowing that stuff for what it is," he said. "You and I know what it is." He paused, broke contact with the crowd as if for a moment's thought. Almost to himself he added, "There's a lot of it in cow pastures as well as in Sunday Schools."

Then his voice went out over the spreading laughter, shouting it down, cracking over them like a whip. "I don't have to tell you these things, fellow workers! You don't have to come to a meeting and hear me talk to know these things! You know without me telling you that you can work till you get a hump on your back like the sacred ox of India, and when you can't work any more does the boss take care of you, that decent fellow? The cemeteries and charity hospitals in this land of liberty are full of workingmen who tried to do right by the boss!"

McGibbeney was shouting with the rest. He wet his lips and pounded his hands together and then held his applause to hear Barnabas' voice.

". . . our fellow workers the railway trainmen," it said. "The iww is behind this strike with everything it's got. You'll see us in the picket lines at the yards and the docks, not because the iww itself has got a thing to gain or a dollar to make out of this strike, BUT BECAUSE WE STAND FOR THE SOLIDARITY OF ALL LABOR! BECAUSE WE WON'T SCAB ON OUR FELLOW WORKERS!"

Joe kept himself back from the flow of the oratory, refusing to give his full acceptance to it, because he was busy appraising Barnabas, the smooth head dully shining under the light, the wide reassuring shoulders. But he felt no real envy, only curiosity, a watchfulness that might teach him something, and he was practicing in his mind how the words of a speech might go when the heckler broke out off to the left. "Shovel it somewheres else!" the voice bawled. At Joe's elbow old Manderich stiffened and half turned like a dog stopped by a sudden hot scent. Barnabas went on without interruption.

"I have one thing to say to you tonight, and only one. I can't give you the lowdown on this strike. I'll leave that to Herb Davis and the other local boys. But I can tell you this because I have lived it and worked for it and I know. This is the message of the One Big Union. There is only one way for the workingman to fight the bosses and obtain his rights. Industrial unionism, the solidarity of all labor . . ."

Granite-faced and stolid, Manderich took a step or two out of the doorway. Joe followed, alert for a repetition of the catcall. They moved smoothly among standing men, a sailor and his girl, a skirted, smiling, out-of-place priest, drifting toward the left where the voice had come from. They had to wait several minutes before the heckler opened his mouth again, and when he did, they were within ten feet of him. He looked like a workingman, young, hat on the back of his head, hands in his pockets, a big grin on his face, enjoying himself. The veins swelled in his neck with the strength of his bellow: "If you don't like it here why don't you go back where you come from?"

A look passed between Manderich and Joe. Manderich went right, Joe left. From the soapbox Barnabas' big laughing voice came back: "Because where I came from they teach this crap about honest toil!"

Laughter smothered whatever else Barnabas said, but the heckler, either drunk or stupid, bawled delightly, "Bullshit, fellow worker!" He squeezed his shoulders together and said it again. "Bullshit, fellow worker!"

A man close to him caught Joe's eye and stepped back. Manderich had come within arm's length of the heckler on the other side, and McGibbeney was behind. Laughter and angry muttering rumbled off in the crowd, but in this close pocket there was sudden quiet. The man who had caught Joe's eye backed up another step.

Across the heckler's shoulder Manderich looked at Joe, his face as expressionless as wood. Then he lurched awkwardly, shoving the heckler back into McGibbeney.

McGibbeney snarled, "Watch where you're going, for Christ sake!" and shoved him back. He turned with his hands up, ready for fight, but Joe swung silently from the side and the wind went out of the heckler with a grunt. His hands came down just as Manderich hit him, then Joe swung again, a hard bone-jarring blow to the head, and the man was down. The three of them stood in a little eddy in the crowd, Barnabas still speaking, everything done so smoothly that there was hardly a disturbance. Of the four involved, only McGibbeney had made a sound. Now Manderich stooped, got the heckler under the arms, and dragged him against the wall, where he propped him. In another minute the three of them had melted into the crowd and got across the street.

McGibbeney was so delighted he could hardly speak. He pounded Joe's shoulder and stared with respect at the iron-jawed, saturnine Manderich. "I never saw anything done so slick," he said. "You guys must have worked on goon squads before."

Manderich grunted. "We worked out that technique when Jack London was running for mayor of Oakland."

"Is that a fact? Do you know Jack London?"

Manderich winked at Joe and said heavily, "Frank iss like a liddle boy. He hass neffer been in a fight."

"Any old time you want anything!" McGibbeney said. He shadowboxed, doing fancy footwork on the sidewalk, ripping the air with jabs and hooks. The grim face of Manderich almost smiled. In the look he gave Joe there was something humorous and comradely, recognizing a bond that set the two of them apart from a magpie like Mac. As for Joe, he had always thought of himself as a reckless man; he had never doubted his own nerve. But old Art, he thought, had never backed up from anything in his life. If he started coming for you you would have to kill him to stop him.

Singing was spreading raggedly across the street—"Casey Jones hit the river bottom, Casey Jones broke his blooming spine . . ." The boys were already working through the crowd selling song cards for a dime each. One thrust a card into Joe's face, peered and saw who his customer was, and passed on laughing, saying, "What the hell!"

"So you are getting famous," Manderich said.

Herb Davis was making the pitch for relief funds for the striking trainmen, bellowing over the stir and break-up of the crowd. Joe dropped fifty cents in the hat as it went by. It was just-dark, the air misty and soft on his face. Standing back against the wall he saw how the dew settled and clung to metal and stone, how it condensed and ran down the tin sign tacked against the bricks.

The brief flurry with the heckler had left him aroused and unsatisfied; he waited like an actor for another cue that would bring him onstage, and as he waited beside McGibbeney and Manderich, Davis came by with Barnabas and Betty Spahn, hurrying them toward their hotel. Barnabas stopped long enough to shake hands.

"You'll hear from me soon as I get back to Chicago. If you write any more, shoot them on to headquarters."

To Manderich and McGibbeney, turning to them as if not to distinguish Joe above them, he said, "You boys down here are doing a fine job. Just keep on organizing, that's the ticket."

McGibbeney said, "How does it look to you? How do you think we'll come out?"

"This strike?"

"Yeah."

"We can win." It was in the tone of his voice that he already thought this strike lost. His voice rose on the oratorical boom. "Even if we don't, we'll use it to build with. We get stronger all the time. Just keep on bringing the boomers in."

He saluted them and turned away, Betty Spahn with him. She had not said a word, but as she turned she smiled at Joe in the dusk, and he nodded in return. That way, as casually as she had come into it, she went out of his life. He had a feeling that he would never see her again and that it would not matter if he didn't, but he bore her no ill will. He even liked her rather vaguely. She had taught him something. The hand he raised in answer to Tom Barnabas' salute was as casual and easy as Barnabas' own.

Their hands behind them against the bricks, they leaned back again. After a minute old Manderich growled, "Ve vill build! Gott damn, vy don't ve *fight?*"

"How?" Joe said. "It isn't really our strike."

"It iss alvays our strike," Manderich said. "It iss alvays our strike and a strike iss a fight. It iss all right for trainmen to valk up and down only. Trainmen are only fair vages for a fair day's vork people. But it iss not all right for iww's. The iww iss for fighting. Valking up and down, dot iss no way to beat the s.p."

McGibbeney said, "You should have got up there and soapboxed, Art," but Manderich brushed the irrelevant gabble aside. "Today I vas down on dot picket line. A big cop vas dere, a big bull-necked cop. He says to me, 'Vy all the time valking up and down? Don't you get tired? Vy don't you go home so ve can all take a rest?' I says to him, 'Efen valking iss better as kissing bosses' asses.'"

Joe laughed. McGibbeney, delighted, said, "What'd he say then? He get sore?"

"Vot should he say? He said, 'Probably you haff kissed enough so you know all aboudt it.'"

His great head ducked, and he spit. "So I said to him, 'I haff kissed plenty. Vunce I used to be a cop.' But dot cop vas right. Vot good iss valking up and down?"

The knuckles of Joe's right hand were still stiff from the blow he had landed on the scissorbill—a satisfying slight pain that kept him aware and awake. He was thinking how seldom you got a chance like that, a clear punch at a clear enemy. He knew the dissatisfaction that lay beneath old Art's grumbling. Solidarity, sure. Make speeches, organize, take up collections, strike, join the picket line, sit in smoky halls and plan strategy, meeting moves with countermoves, trying to make your little strength match everything that the bosses could bring to bear, writing protests and petitions, carrying placards and banners—the clear sense of a fight got lost in the machinery of labor tactics.

"What we need is a few tough old lumberjacks down here," he said.

"Shit," Manderich said in contempt. "Vot do ve need of lumberjacks? Vot iss the matter vit us?"

"They always roll out the paddy wagon," McGibbeney said. "That's what makes you sore. There's always a batch of coppers around, and the first move you make you land in jail."

"Let me tell you," Manderich said. "In such a system it iss a distinction to be in jail."

It seemed to Joe that they had been standing there indefinitely. He flexed his fingers; the itch to be doing something made him kick the brick wall. Up the street the electric sign above the Peerless Pool Parlor jerked into brightness, its hundreds of little globes glowing steadily for a few seconds before it took off on its mechanical night-long repetition of movement. First there was a pool table and a bending player outlined in white lights. Then a cue flashed on in the player's hand. Then the triangle of colored balls appeared at the far end of the table. Then the cue jerked backward, jerked forward. The cue ball blinked down an unerring line, the colored balls broke and ran in every direction and one after another blinked out in corner or side pockets. Then cue and table and bending player went black too, leaving only a single clicking light that crawled around the outline of the sign, unhurried and inevitable and purposeless as the days in a man's life.

Joe recognized the sign and everything it said. It said that in

the friendly surroundings of the Peerless Pool Parlor players of
unerring accuracy made mechanically perfect shots. It implied
that at the Peerless everything was arranged for a man's pleasure
and relaxation; friendly games of skill to pass the time. It intimated
that it must be a pretty good world if on a workingman's street
there could be palaces of pleasure like the Peerless, open to everyone, and that in these places the shot never missed, the ball never
kissed or rebounded, the cue never scratched, the cushions were
never dead or crooked. The sign said this to him three or four
times with a rigid, automaton inflexibility; on every break, every
ball ran unerringly toward a pocket. And all the time the little
clicking insinuating light crept around and around and around the
edge.

"I wonder what would happen if that guy missed sometime?"
he said. Manderich and McGibbeney looked, but he saw that they
had no idea what he was talking about. To break the inertia that
pressed too heavily upon him he said, "Let's go on down to the
docks and see if anything's stirring."

"Jeez, I don't know," said McGibbeney. "I was just thinkin' I
better be gettin' on home before the old lady throws a fit."

"They keep running scabs through there. The bigger we keep
that picket line the better."

"I did a trick down at the yards this morning," McGibbeney said.

"All right," Joe said. "You go on home." He half expected McGibbeney to follow as he and Manderich turned down the street, but
when he looked back from the corner the sidewalk was empty.
Contempt for McGibbeney tightened his mouth. A spare-time
milker, a milk-and-water rebel, a big bag of wind.

Crossing the web of tracks on the way to the waterfront they
were yelled at, and a man put a bull's-eye lantern on them.
"Where do you guys think you're going?"

"Down to the dock," Joe said.

"What for? What do you want?"

"Vot difference does it make?" said Manderich.

"Go on," the yard dick said. "Get on back where you come from.
You don't go across here."

They retreated. "Dot iss a sample," Manderich said. "Dey own
the gott damn vorld."

Circling, they crossed the tracks at an intersection. The watchman in the door of the switchman's shanty stared at them but made no move to stop them, and they came out on the dock side to see the glow of lanterns and the popping fizzle of the arc lights out on the dock. Evenly spaced along the horizon, the breakwater lights strung out beyond. Between lanterns hung on both sides of the dock gates, two policemen sat their horses and talked with the gatekeeper.

"Vorking overtime," Manderich said, and jerked a hand at the figures out along the dock. "How does a scap figure?"

Joe saw how it was arranged like a stage, how the shadows of the skeleton picket line moved back and forth in the street below the platform, how the dock stretched vaguely outward, spotted with lights and the small dark figures of men. He put his foot up on the edge of the platform, silently watching.

Then he felt the silence, and into the silence came the soft plop of hoofs. One of the cops was above them, leaning on his pommel. "What are you boys doing down here?"

"Standing," Manderich said. "It iss a public street."

"Ah, Dutchy," the cop said. "I didn't recognize you at first." For a considerable quiet time he looked them over. "You guys better move on," he said.

"Yes?" Manderich said. "Vy?"

"Want to argue it?" the cop said softly.

"We've got a perfect right to get into that picket line," Joe said.

The cop straightened up. "If you're getting into the line, get in it. You can't just hang around here."

Bringing his foot down from the platform edge, Manderich grunted, "I vould argue aboudt my rights to stand on a public street, but ve are not arguing now. Ve are valking only. So ve vill go valk."

They passed contemptuously close to the putteed calf, the swelling thigh, the uniformed wrist with the billy hanging loosely from it. Neither horse nor rider moved. Behind a shadow who turned out to be Whitey Blattner, a Wobbly trucker from a brewery warehouse, they shuffled into the line. Joe lagged, turning to see who else was on, and recognized Coscarart, a longshoreman, and Bill Sever, a sailor. The other two he did not know. Across the street the temporary headquarters shack was dark.

The man ahead made one circle and stopped, waiting for them. "Who're you guys? Wobblies? Yeah, okay."

"It looks to me as if this was more sympathy than strike," Joe said. "Where are all your trainmen?"

"Hell, I don't know," the man said. "This is all sort of on the spur of the moment. They run in this bunch of scabs about six, and we're sticking it out till they quit. I been here since four."

They started again, moving slowly, Joe and Manderich lagging until they opened a space between themselves and the other. "Holy smoke," Joe said. "This is a kind of sad strike." Art only grunted.

Around and around, shuffling and lag-footed, half asleep, a headless and tailless motion without destination, the line moved. Into darkness, around into murky light, into darkness again, stubborn and dull and ineffectual, seven men walking in protest before a locked gate to shame the scabs who labored on uninterrupted; a handful of impotent men trying to force concessions from an opponent who laughed at them and rode over them and held them off with the blue and brass of the law. To Joe, shuffling with the rest in and out of the light, it seemed as if he had got trapped in something immutable and interminable, without beginning or end, like the little blind light that crawled round and round the sign above the Peerless Pool Parlor.

Maybe it was always your strike, as Art said, but this was a bad strike, badly organized and already drying up, and it graveled him to sink himself in it and get muddied by its hopelessness. It was a meager satisfaction that being on the line was a defiance to the cop. The cop could run the whole bunch of them off the waterfront if he wanted to call out the wagon, and the s.p. and the newspapers and the law and public opinion would all justify him. Only because the bosses held it in contempt was the picket line permitted to operate at all.

And out on the dock the scabs were justifying themselves as free American workingmen who weren't going to be pushed around and told what to do by a bunch of radicals and foreigners.

Around and around and around, stubborn and shuffling and sullen and confused and too few, the pickets circled. Probably all of them wanted to sit down. Occasionally, for a while, one did, or two, to light a pipe and smoke a few minutes before coming back in again. There was no reason they should not all sit down except that if they did they would admit to the cops and gatekeeper and scabs that militancy had its limits and that rebellion could grow tired.

So they shuffled along their symbolic frontiers, and as they shuffled Joe with another part of his mind walked in other lines, not in pointless circles but directly and boldly toward a gate, a door, a goal. He walked ahead of multitudes like a troubadour or a pied piper, leading them with songs, scattering sarcasm like acid on the ones who held back and weakened the cause. These were the ones who prepared every defeat: the unconvincibles, the immovables, the Mr. Blocks, the scabs and the scissorbills.

He was making a song as he went:

You may ramble round the country anywhere you will,
You'll always run across the same old Scissor Bill.
He's found upon the desert, he is on the hill,
He's found in every mining camp and lumber mill.
He looks just like a human, he can eat and walk,
But you will find he isn't when he starts to talk . . .

Scissor Bill the foreigners is cussing,
Scissor Bill, he says "I hate a coon."
Scissor Bill is down on everybody,
The Hottentots, the bushmen, and the man in the moon.

Don't try to talk your union talk to Scissor Bill,
He says he never organized and never will. . . .

He bumped into Manderich, who had stopped. "Dey're coming oudt," Manderich said.

A stir moved among the shadowy figures of the pickets. Blattner and Coscarart had picked up placards from the platform and now had them on their shoulders: "Don't Scab on Your Fellow Workers—Join the One Big Union," and "Shoulder to Shoulder—Solidarity of All Labor." The line was not a line any longer, but a group, and there was more life in it when it stood still than there had been when it moved. A perceptible preparatory intentness had come over the gatekeeper and the cops too. The cops were sitting straight on their horses, the gatekeeper scraped his chair as he rose. The scabs were coming in a compact cluster.

Just as the gate swung open Manderich's harsh voice grated at Joe's ear. "Come oudt! Don't be a lousy scap! Come oudt and fight on the right side!"

Now they were all shouting. The cops moved over, holding their horses broadside so that the pickets had to yell across them at the scabs, who moved compactly across the platform and into the street. In the shifting light of lanterns the scabs' faces looked still and wooden. The further they moved the more furious Manderich's harsh bellow became.

"Vot are dey paying you to scap? Uh? Vot kind of dirty sonofa-pitching money do you get? How does it feel to be a scap? You know vot a scap iss? A scap iss a sonofapitch dot vould steal Christ off the cross for two bits!"

Someone in the tight group of scabs shouted back. In an instant Manderich had sprung around the shoulder of the protecting horse. "Vot do you say? You sonofapitching scap?"

The policeman rode him back among the pickets, and as the horse moved Joe saw Harry Piper in the crowd of scissorbills. He had been cool enough before, shouting with the others but not letting himself get mad. But to see someone he knew among the enemy filled him with a strangling fury.

"Hey, Harry!"

Piper's face jerked for a moment sideward, looking blindly into the murk, and turned back. "Come out!" Joe yelled. "You don't belong in there. Come out and join up!"

The policeman had pivoted his horse and was coming back, so close that Joe had to jump to avoid being trampled. A dab of saliva from the bit flew and landed wet on his cheek. The touch of it doubled his rage. He ducked, came up, saw that Manderich had again eluded the police and was blocking the way of the scabs, who veered left to go around him. That put them between Man-derich and the police, so that they couldn't ride him out of the way. The cop nearest Joe swore and kicked his horse, which leaped suddenly off to the right. And into the hole he left Joe dove like a ferret, intent on reaching Harry Piper and dragging him out. As he caught up with the retreating edge of the group one of the scabs turned with a thin almost whimpering cry and swung a dinner pail at his head.

The pail crashed against his shoulder and spilled open, and he leaped in punching with both hands in the midst of a sudden violent melee. At the last moment he saw the horse coming and sprang aside. Something struck him across nose and mouth with eye-watering violence, he was on his hands and knees, covering up, and the weight and power of the horse went past him, missing him by inches. When he shook his head clear and came up among struggling figures and the short grunting outcries of fighting, he saw Manderich holding off several men by swinging a lantern. Art rushed, driving the men back and giving Joe time to scramble in beside him. Then the two retreated slowly, back to back, across the street toward the warehouses and protecting darkness.

Manderich was wheezing with effort. He fumbled at his suspender and pressed something into Joe's hand. It was a four-inch hatpin. "The horse, if you get a chance," he said.

A man ran diagonally across the intersection pursued by one of the policemen. When the horse was almost on him he ducked, covering his head with his hands, but the cop anticipated him and clubbed him twice before the plunging horse carried him past. As he turned and came back past the puddled shadow of the picket's body the shadow of horse and man, cast by light from a spilled and broken lantern, leaped clear across the street and up the corrugated warehouse wall.

With the cops behind them, the scabs were pressing in again. Manderich kept them at arm's length with the swinging lantern, Joe held the hatpin ready for anyone who rushed. "Vatch him!" Manderich said.

Joe rose to his toes, ready to jump either way, as the cop came in from the side. He had a moment of absolute paralyzed panic when the hoofs roared in on him. He saw the flattened ears, the glaring eyes, the foaming mouth, a spark of metal on the martingale, and then he was leaping aside, the swinging club grazed his coattails, and he pivoted awkwardly and swung the hatpin at the passing haunches.

It went in sweetly, almost its full length. The screaming horse rose up, plunging out of control. He saw the arc of Manderich's lantern thrown at the faces of the scabs and the two of them were running, in almost total dark now. The black of a wall went past, they turned up a narrow alley between buildings, running cautiously with their hands outstretched, until the sky lightened above and they were in the enclosing walls of a court. Straining in the blackness, his eyes made out regular shapes that he recognized as parked dray wagons.

Following Manderich's heavy running shape across the court he put his hand up to his numb face. Cheek and lip and chin were dripping wet, and he tasted the metal taste of blood.

Manderich hissed over his shoulder and Joe followed him in pitch-blackness down what seemed to be another alley, following him by the crunch of his shoes in cinders. Back of them, apparently far away, he heard the faint noise of riot.

Now they came again into the open, and their feet felt rails. Over three tracks and around a string of boxcars, and they were headed toward town. But as they stepped out across another track a lantern burst from behind something and its light drove them backward, running again and hearing the pound of feet, the yells of pursuit. They dodged right, sprinted along a string of cars, dodged right again, working back toward the waterfront side. Looking back Joe saw two lights coming now instead of one, and when he turned his head there was a third light ahead.

Manderich swore. Yells converged upon them, and they ran, only to find themselves abruptly against a high wire fence with buildings beyond. "Left!" Joe said. They should be at the edge of the yards, and there should be a street crossing. If there weren't, they were done.

Blood was seeping down under his collar. Whatever had hit him had cut him pretty deep. Trying to run silently, he turned his ankle on loose rock or coal and almost fell. Panic came up in him, and he sprinted.

Manderich's soft grunt told him they had made it. The fence turned a right angle, they cut down a narrow street between buildings, crossed two sidings and were out of the yards. It was so black that they had to feel again, slowing to a walk. Ties of a spur track, gritty cinders underfoot, warehouse doors one after another, two feet above the ground. The noise of pursuit had stopped. Perhaps the yard dicks had stopped when they failed to pull the net against the fence. Along the door-broken wall they groped carefully, panting. Then both stopped at once. Ahead of them more wall, solid black. They were in a court, a pocket. If the dicks came in the other end they were trapped.

Before they had moved twenty feet along the wall, looking for an alley or outlet, the lantern appeared at the far end of the court.

The court was as bare as a field, no place to hide in, not even a platform to crawl under. There was not a chance to ambush and slug the pursuer. A short block away the light was coming toward them, unhurried and confident.

Manderich made a soft, furious sound of disgust, and stopped, but Joe leaped along the wall trying every warehouse door in a last deperate hope of escaping. Incredibly, the third door slid open a few inches with a light rumble and squeak. He hissed at Manderich, they slipped inside, Joe put his weight against the door and very carefully slid it shut again. He felt for bolt or hook, but there was none. Apparently some patent lock that had failed to catch. A watchman's bonehead was their good luck. But there was no way of locking the door against the dicks.

He whispered to Manderich. "What if he sticks his head in here?"

"Knock it off."

Leaning against the wall in total black, trying to breathe noiselessly through his mouth and hearing Manderich's asthmatic wheezing six feet away, Joe keyed his ears for sound outside, but he heard nothing. Under the handkerchief he held pressed against his face, his cuts bled steadily. His collar was soaked, and the handkerchief was a wet wad in his hand. Nose and lip had begun to sting and burn.

His hand, groping cautiously behind him in search of weapons, found nothing. Then he realized that he still held the hatpin. That, then. It ought to take the fight out of a dick as fast as anything else. He listened.

Abruptly Manderich's breathing stopped. Steps were coming closer, there was a rattle as a door was tried. Then steps were just outside, stopping. Moving an inch at a time, Joe slid the soaked handkerchief into his pocket and transferred the hatpin to his left hand. Flattened against the wall, he waited.

The door rattled, moved a little, slid. A crack of light split into the big gloom. Its diffused glow showed the shape of Manderich crouched beyond the opening, ready to spring. Joe gathered himself.

But in a moment the door slid softly shut again, the crack of light closed, the footsteps went on, and Joe heard the next door being tried, and the next, then a third, and then silence.

The letdown was worse than a fight would have been. For

unbearable minutes they stood rigid, waiting for something—the
return of the footsteps, the rush of a whole bunch of dicks
possibly gathered now outside, a flank attack from inside the
warehouse. Both front and back, the dark was ripe with danger.
Joe strained his ears until the faintest sound of a rat rustling
somewhere deep in the warehouse, or the tick of a metal door
contracting in the night chill, filled his whole head.

Why should a dick or a watchman, finding a warehouse door
unlocked, simply shut it up again and go on without even locking
it? It could only be that he was afraid to tackle the place alone,
even with a gun and a light. He must have gone back for help.

"We'd better get out of here!" he whispered to Manderich.

"Maybe he iss vatching outside."

"What'll we do, then?"

"Vait," Manderich whispered. "Vait and see. Maybe he aindt
coming back."

"He's bound to."

"Vait!"

In the dark there was no such thing as time. They might have
waited fifteen minutes or three hours. Joe sat, holding the soggy
handkerchief against his cuts, and felt how his face gradually
stiffened and how the wounds began to develop a crust of dried
blood. The blackness above and around was hollow and unending.
It pressed in and down, and suddenly instead of being infinite
it was close and smothering, so that he put out a hand half
expecting to touch a silently encroaching wall. He had a moment
of white-hot rage at whatever or whoever had hit him in the
scuffle by the dock. Once he thought of Betty Spahn and her
remark about his hard mouth. Was it the scars? He would have a
hard mouth for fair now.

In the blackness, a mile or a yard away, something stirred.
Old Art's whisper was like something that came across space on
a wire. "Dis is damn funny!"

"I'm for getting out."

"Nah," Manderich said. "Let's vait a little longer."

Joe heard him rustling and groping back into the depths of the
warehouse, sliding his feet a few inches at a time across the gritty
floor. After an indeterminable time his hissing whisper came back.

"What?" Joe whispered.

"Come on back here."

He made little *pst pst* sounds for Joe to guide himself by, until Joe's hands found bales of something—hemp, by the smell—stacked one on another, and Manderich's *pst* came from directly above him.

"Come up and take it easy," Art said.

"Don't you think we'd better get out?"

"I t'ink ve better vait."

Up on the tight bales they could stretch out. Some of the tenseness went out of the dark. When after a minute or two Joe felt the bales shaking under him, he realized that old Art was lying there laughing silently.

"That all happened kind of sudden," he said.

"Dirty scaps, it's a good t'ing," Manderich said. He growled with pleasure. "I vish it had been me got dot cop's horse. But by Gott you got him good. He vent up ten feet."

"Where'd you get the hatpin?"

"In Austria ve carried hatpins for the *Polizei*," Art said. "I learned dot from Johann Most. Alvays I carry it here, in my suspender. You still got it? Giff it back."

Joe handed him the pin and lay back on the bales, staring upward and gently working the stiffened lip and cheek. "What do you think will happen now there's been trouble on the docks?"

"More *Polizei*," Art said. "Pinkertons and gunmen for scaps."

"Then what do we do?"

"If ve don't know vot to do ven a fight breaks oudt, ve should haff our heads examined," Art said, and would have said more if Joe's hand had not leaped out to grab his arm.

They heard the warehouse door roll gently open, roll shut again. No light came with it this time; it opened and closed in utter darkness. There was an indistinguishable low noise, rustling or whispering, and then feet moved on the gritty floor. In a moment Joe heard clear whispers. At least two of them then.

Afraid to stir for fear of making a sound, Joe lay on his back and strained to hear. It was Art's fault. If they had cleared out when they had the chance they wouldn't be trapped here now. Holding his breath, willing that even the beating of his heart should stop, he waited for them to begin the organized search that would hunt him and Art down.

Metal clinked, a match flared hugely in the barnlike space, and the steadying glow of a lantern swelled out against the dark. He heard their whispers again.

Why, if these were dicks or watchmen come to hunt them, were there only two? And why did they light a lantern so casually, making targets of themselves in case the men they were hunting carried guns? And why did they come now so incautiously into the warehouse, moving without hesitation or stealth?

The glow came closer, blocks and angles of shadow moved among the stringers overhead. There was a sound of stumbling, and an unguarded voice said almost aloud, laughing, "Yudas priest, give us some light!"

Joe rolled his head rigidly toward old Art, and in the vague passing glow saw the Austrian's stiff face, the strained whites of his eyes. There was no mistaking the owner of that vaudeville-Swede accent and that laugh, and it did not take a very bright imagination to know who was with him.

As soon as the glow was well past, disappearing, blocked out by big heavy areas of solid dark, Manderich touched Joe and swung his legs and let himself down to the next layer and thence to the floor. Joe came after him, ready to laugh at the way they had cowered in the dark scared of every noise, in the very warehouse in all San Pedro where there was least chance a watchman would come that night.

They moved as cautiously as if the two ahead were police, creeping toward the faint glow. Joe imagined the look on Otto's face when they surprised him. He had everything arranged so neatly—a fix with the night watchman who left a door open and stayed away for a certain time, then maybe a dray outside, or a house somewhere nearby where the stuff could be temporarily stored until it was safe to move it. With everything arranged in advance, Otto was obviously not afraid of being seen or heard. He would jump out of his skin when they popped up from behind something.

From a barricade of crates he and Manderich watched Otto and John stoop and pull among long, cylindrical bales—rugs, by their look. The lantern threw their shadows wide and huge. Hoisting a bale on each shoulder, they carried them to the doorway, dumped them, and came back for more, working silently and fast.

"Look at the sonsofpitches!" Manderich whispered harshly in Joe's ear. "Union men!"

That was the first indication Joe had had that their spying from the darkness had any other object than a joke. But in the obscurity he could just see Art's face. It was set like cement.

John and Otto were stooping for a third load when Manderich stepped into the light, Joe just behind him. The thieves spun around, crouching. If it had been a joke it would have been very laughable to see how Otto's hands let go of the bale and how the right one jerked inside the breast of his coat, and how John stood stupidly with his mouth open, a bale hanging limply from his hands.

"Making qvite a haul," Manderich said. After the whispering and the dry cautious hisses his voice grated.

The momentary tableau relaxed, Otto straightened slowly, his face assuming the silly dangling grin that it habitually wore. Recognizing Art and Joe, John sat down on a bale and wiped his forehead.

"You scared the hell out of me," Otto said. "What are you guys doing down here?" As his eyes came over to Joe, his smile deepened as if he acknowledged and understood something.

Art's dry, unlubricated croak said, "Ve got a tip from headqvarters dere vas some shtealing going on."

Strolling past the lantern, he experimentally kicked the bale that John sat on, testing with his toe what it contained. John wagged his head, "Holy smoke . . ." he said.

With the speed of a cat springing Manderich was on Otto, bearhugging him, wrestling him down. Before Joe could move or John get his feet under him to rise, Art had stepped back with a flat black automatic in his hand. Otto rose slowly from one knee, watching him pull the clip and pump the shell from the chamber. Without turning Manderich passed gun and clip and shells back to Joe, who dropped them in his pocket.

"I vouldn't take a chance on you, Otto," Art said. "You are too crooked to trust."

The smile had not quite left Otto's face, but his eyes were narrowed almost shut and his lips were stiffly curved, like something modeled in wax. Confused and unsure, taken for an ally by Manderich but unwilling to put himself against John and Otto, Joe stayed back. He did not especially like Otto, but he half resented the way Manderich acted like the chief of police.

"What do you want?" Otto said slowly. "A cut? You didn't have to strongarm your way in. Four of us can pack out twice as much as two."

"Cut?" Art said. "Listen, you sonofapitch, vhile I tell you somet'ing. Effery time somebody lifts some cargo, who gets blamed? The iww, so? I do not like a sonofapitch who goes around shtealing t'ings vhile he hides behindt a union button."

Otto's stiff lips curved more deeply. Joe saw that they were rigid with anger, but Otto stayed quiet and loose, shoulders drooping, arms hanging. He said only, "When did you sprout wings?"

"I am not holy, by Gott," Manderich said. "I am only . . ."

"Or the union either?" Otto said. "Maybe you'd like me to list a few . . ."

"You shut your gott damned mout'!" Manderich said. On the bale John Alberg stirred, glanced almost desperately at Joe, opened his mouth and closed it again without speaking. Out behind the tense little lighted core Joe could hear the silence of the warehouse hum.

"Dere iss a difference between a revolutionary and a gott damn t'ief," Manderich said. "I am telling you somet'ing now. Vunce I knew a hood up in Tacoma like you, using the union to hid behindt. He vas found out along the tracks. A union hass no place for hoods. I vonder vot the boys vould say if I should tell aboudt you."

Joe moved, merely to make his presence felt, because for a moment he thought that Otto would be fool enough to tackle Manderich. What John would do if it came to a fight was hard to say. Probably nothing. He looked hangdog, like a shamed boy, on the edge of the argument.

But in a moment the tension relaxed slightly, and Joe saw that Otto had appraised his chances and given up the notion to fight. He stared steadily at Manderich, his hair hanging lank on both sides of his face.

"I t'ink it vould be smardt if you got oudt of San Pedro," Art said.

"Ya?" Otto said. "Suppose I didn't think it was smart to?"

"Ven you t'ink it ofer, you vill not be here any more," Art said. He picked up the lantern and motioned the two to walk. Joe fell in beside John.

"What are you mixed up in this for?"

"Holy yee, I don't know," John said. "I needed few bucks."

By the outside door Otto turned. "Don't be a damn fool, Art.

There's two or three hundred in this. I got a deal all fixed. We can lug it out of here and be gone in half an hour, and nobody is hurt but the s.p."

To Joe Art said, "Take a look outside vhile I muffle the light."

He wrapped the lantern in his coat, and Joe slid the door a few inches, holding his eye to the crack until it adjusted to the grayer dark outside. There was neither light nor step, sight nor sound. "Seems all clear."

Manderich's grunt had a heavy pleased finality. He held the lantern high and looked around. Back from the door was some crated machinery, and beyond that the bales of doormats where he and Joe had lain. The three watched him in silence while he dragged the rugs Otto and John had dumped by the door over to the foot of the bales.

"Are you damn fool enough to throw away two or three hundred dollars?" Otto said. His voice was shriller, somewhere between whisper and shout.

"You vatch me," Art said. "I vill giff you a lesson in how a revolutionary iss different from a t'ief."

They saw him twist the cap on the fuel tank and upend the lantern over the bales. The chimney shattered thinly as his heavy foot swung. One bright lick of flame climbed the side of the pile, and then Joe heard the door and turned to see Otto jump. John hesitated a moment, his big stunned face working, before he too plunged and was gone.

Joe leaped after him with Manderich just behind. The sliding door jolted to, and they were running again.

8   San Pedro, July, 1910

Not more than fifteen minutes later Joe came up the alley that paralleled Beacon Street. He was not running—had not run since he and Art had split at the edge of the yards. He walked casually, like a man with nothing on his mind, but because of his face he kept to the darker streets, and rather than come to the mission by the front door he slipped in behind. There was a light showing through the dirty kitchen window. He tried the door without knocking; it opened.

The moment he got inside it felt very late. He wondered if Lund were still up. A turned-down kerosene lamp was smoking as if forgotten on the table. But he had hardly taken a step toward the inner door when it opened and Lund looked through. A deep cleft appeared between his eyes. "What happened?"

Joe laughed. "Little fight."

"I'd hate to see you after a big fight," Lund said. "Sit down, let me look."

When he started to pull off Joe's coat, the automatic clunked solidly against the chair. The missionary's hand went down and felt through the cloth. He did not indicate by word or look what he thought, but turned up the lamp, filled a basin with warm water, and dabbed at the caked cheek and lip. His dry voice said, "What hit you?"

"I don't know. Dinner pail, lantern, something. I was looking somewhere else when I got it."

With the dried blood removed from his face Joe could feel the slashed lips of the cuts open when he moved the muscles of his mouth. He put his fingers up to feel, and Lund knocked them down sharply.

"How bad are they?" Joe said.

"Bad enough. One down from the corner of your mouth, one down around on your neck, the wing of your nose gone. You'll have to be sewed up."

"No, no doctor."

Lund scowled. His voice was as harsh as Manderich's. "Nobody asked you. I'm telling you. You sit still here."

The inner door swung after him and in a moment there was the noise of cranking as he wound the telephone. Another considerable pause, then words, then the click, and Lund came back. With hands on hips he stood and looked Joe over, and after a moment he undid the collar button and let the bloody collar spring open and pulled off the stiff string tie. Dumping the bloody water from the pan, he drew another panful and began sousing collar and tie in it. Watching him, Joe began to grin.

"No scolding?"

Lund said disgustedly, "If you didn't want a scolding, why did you come here?"

The question surprised Joe. For half a dozen reasons he had not headed for the shack, but why had he come here instead of to the hall? Since he had no answer, he gave none. After a while Lund shoved the big coffeepot onto the ring and lit the gas, and a few minutes later he went to the front door, locked for the night, to admit the doctor.

The doctor looked at Joe's cuts without comment, took off his coat and rolled up his sleeves and laid Joe on his back on the kitchen table. After the hand-scrubbing and the daubing of the wounds and the stink of carbolic there was the sewing. Holding himself relaxed by a rigid act of will, Joe lay staring upward through eyes veiled as if a membrane were drawn over them, and counted each stitch as it went in through the flaps of skin and was tied and cut. He despised the doctor for a clumsy fool, who sewed like a sailor mending a sail. The needle was dull, the thread pulled through as if resined, the doctor's hands smelled of carbolic and his breath was loud through his nose as he worked. But eventually he stood back, wiping his hands.

"You've got your nerve," he said. A statement, no more.

Almost gagged with bandages, Joe sat up and felt for his purse. "How much?"

"Two dollars."

Joe laid the bills in his hand.

"Come into the office in three days," the doctor said. He had bristly white hair and a close-clipped mustache, and as he closed his bag he lifted one side of his face in a grimace of controlled amusement. Then Lund let him out.

The coffee had filled the room with steam. Silently Lund came back, poured two cups, stood back against the sink blowing into the chipped white mug. Joe tried taking a sip past the clumsy bandages, but the heat hurt his cut lip. He looked at Lund, knowing that the missionary would not ask questions. It had been quite a day—so much of a day that he could tell Lund hardly any of it.

"We were down on the picket line at the Hammond dock,"

he said. "Scabs came off shift and a squabble started. First thing I knew somebody beaned me with something."

Lund's face wore an expression of polite attention, but he said nothing.

"All right," Joe said. "You don't believe me."

The sober regard of Lund's eyes did not change. "It's a little hard to imagine you an innocent bystander in a fight," he said. Then he leaned forward and significantly swung the blue serge coat until the gun knocked on the chair.

"That?" Joe said. "We took that away from a guy."

Still Lund said nothing, and Joe grew irritable in the face of the steady look. "That's all," he said. "We took it away from a guy."

"During the fight?"

"No, later."

He tried to pull the collarband together and hook the collar button, but the bandage came down over the cut in his neck and the collar would not meet. It made him mad to try to talk with his stiff mouth half muffled, and the carbolic smell spoiled the flavor of the coffee. It angered him to see the fatherly, troubled suspicion waver in Lund's eyes.

"If I wanted to carry a gun, would I carry it loose in my pocket with the clip out and a lot of loose cartridges around?" he said. He turned the pocket inside out, dumping gun and clip and shells on the table.

"All right, Joe," Lund said quietly, and rubbed his hands together. "It's none of my business. I have no right to put you through any third degree." His heavy mustaches parted in a brief, square-toothed smile, and he said in a different voice, "What were you doing down on the picket line?"

"We're supporting the trainmen."

"Who's we?"

"The IWW."

"That's quite a lot of support, to nearly get your throat cut in a riot."

"Any strike is our strike," Joe said.

For quite a while Lund leaned against the sink and watched him with a faint, puzzled smile. Finally he said, "You've really made a choice, then. You're really in it heart and soul."

There seemed so much weight in the question that Joe considered, holding the missionary's eyes. One thing had led to another since he had come back to Pedro, but he hadn't had to let himself be led. He could have turned at any point. He hadn't had to join up, or turn himself into a song-mill, or help bust the heckler at the meeting, or agree to Barnabas' proposition, or go down to walk the picket line, or reach for Harry Piper to knock sense into his scab head. He could have stopped anywhere, nobody had pushed him against his will.

"I guess so," he said. "Sure."

"Sure you know what you're doing?"

"Doing?"

"What's your life going to be like from now on?"

"Something better than it's been up to now," Joe said. "Organizing, writing songs, getting in the fight."

Lund studied him so long that Joe raised the cup again to break the look. The missionary turned and mopped at the sink, threw the rag down and turned again and said with a little laugh, "The devil of it is, it's probably admirable in a way."

Now would come the sermon.

"What can a man say against it?" Lund said. "It comes straight out of the most generous of impulses, concern for the downtrodden. Nothing personal about it—no anger at particular people, nothing that you expect to get for yourself. Pure abstract philosophical devotion to principle. You get your face all chewed up out of unselfish sympathy for the working class. You'll go out and eat black bread or none at all, starve and freeze and be in a dozen kinds of danger, all in the interest of economic justice."

Joe watched him very closely. "Anything wrong with that?"

"Nothing," Lund said. "Not one solitary thing. Except the way you'll think it has to be done."

Still Joe watched him, trying to follow the kinks of the missionary's Christian mind.

"It's one part of humanity against another," Lund said. His face was so serious it looked sad. "It's class against class, it's a dedication to war . . ."

"Justice," Joe said.

"Justice by way of war. You pledge yourself to violence, not as a last resort but as a deliberate policy."

"Every other policy has been tried, and look where the working class still is."

"Listen," Lund said. "You Wobblies started this fight tonight, didn't you?"

"No. But if we had, what of it? A scab won't learn any other way."

"That's it," Lund said, and spread his hands and blew up through his mustache. His mouth twitched; his eyes, almost whimsical now, were fixed on Joe's.

"We used to have the church militant," he said. "The church militant was just as bad as capitalism militant or unions militant. It's the militancy I hate. It's the way we choose up sides and bloody each other's noses and shoot each other, every warring gang among us shouting about human rights and all of them trying to get them with brass knuckles or a gun. Wouldn't it make more sense to work for some cause that pulled people together instead of had them flying at each other's throats?"

"Yes?" Joe said. "What?"

Lund shrugged, a hopeless, humorous little twitch of the shoulders. "I don't care what flag it marches under. But no class war. No crusades. No inquisition. No riots, no damnation threats, no hellfire. Something that probably sounds funny. Christian love. Human decency. The golden rule."

Joe felt sorry for Lund. As long as he lived he would never know what the world was about. He would go on living with his head in a bag.

"The golden rule like the one the lumber trust or the s.p. follows?" he said.

He stood up, finding himself unexpectedly wobbly in the knees. "I'd better get along."

"No, not yet," Lund said. He had taken up the rag again and was sponging at the bloody collar of Joe's coat, frowning down at his work with a concentrated, sober intentness. "You're so deep into it already," he said. "I wish you'd come in and talked to me."

"Why?"

"I might have made you a counterproposal," Lund said, and lifted his eyes directly. "I might have said . . . You speak Swedish, you can draw and play the piano. You're a man of clean habits. There's a room upstairs, next to mine. You're made to order for this kind of work, and there's room for you. How about staying and helping me with the mission?"

The suggestion was so comical that Joe stared in gathering incredulity. "Is this what you might have proposed, or are you proposing it now?"

"I'm proposing it now."

A missionary's helper? A soul-saver? "Why not the Starvation Army?" he said.

"It might be better than spending your time in fist fights down on the docks."

Joe was smiling, shaking his head, beginning to laugh. "You'd get stung, Gus," he said. "You need somebody with the gift of gab and a big bright smile."

Eventually Lund laughed too, threw up his hands, handed Joe his coat, and stood spraddle-legged looking at him.

"Well, don't say I didn't try. Only sailor that ever came in here who didn't drink and smoke and chase women, and he has to turn out an iww."

It was a way of saying that their friendship was unimpaired, Joe understood. He knocked Lund's shoulder lightly and dropped the gun and clip into his pocket. "I've got to go."

"Where?"

"The hall, I guess."

"If there was a riot, and the iww was involved, they may have raided that already," Lund said. "If you're going to be an agitator, at least be a smart one. Stay here."

And that, Joe knew, was the reason he had come to Lund in the first place. The preacher was sanctuary, a neutral corner. "Sure it's all right?"

"Any time," Lund said. "Any time, and as long as you like. If you won't come as a helper we'll have to take you as a guest."

Together they went through the darkened mission after Lund had stuck his head into the snores and sighs and faintly foul air of the dormitory where his night's catch of drifters slept. He locked the front door and they stood on the empty sidewalk sniffing the soft, moist air. It was almost perfectly still; only a few lights showed down the dark street. Joe glanced up toward the Peerless Pool Parlor sign, but it had melted into the black cliff of brick and stucco and stone. Not even the single unhurried light crawled around to show where it was, and the sumptuous parlors where workingmen could while away their leisure time in games of skill—rotation, callshot, bottle pool, snooker, billiards, monte and blackjack in the back room—were dark and vanished. Beacon Street's saloons were all closed, the windows of rooming houses and hotels blind and lost, the shooting galleries, shows, tintype booths, lunch stands, emptied for the night.

Lund said something that made Joe feel how close, momentarily, he and the preacher were, how somehow the last hour had given them similar words to say. He looked the length of Beacon and said, "What a street! I don't know whether it's more frightening when it's quiet or when it's going like a house afire."

He took Joe upstairs and unlocked a door and showed him a clean bare room, still stuffy from being closed up all day. "Goodnight," he said, and looked as if he might have said more but had decided not to.

Before he went to bed Joe stood at the open window by the slack unstirring curtains and looked out, down Beacon Street that stretched like a topless sewer between the buildings. A working-man's street, mean and cheap, crammed with all the cheap stores a workingman could patronize and all the cheap amusements a workingman could afford and all the cheap opiates to make a workingman forget who he was and how he created all the wealth in the world for others to enjoy. A sad, gray, unlovely street—but such a street as men could march up thirty abreast. He saw it suddenly smoky and red with torches, packed with people, like a print in an old school book showing the storming of the Bastille.

It had not occurred to him until Lund spoke of it, but he had unquestionably made a choice.

Yours for the OBU

The land goes grandly westward, a mighty sweep of plain, from the dividing-line rivers, from the Red, the Big Sioux, the Missouri. Wheat country mainly, so big there seems no end to it, it is pinpointed by clusters of sun-whitened buildings whose names are Hutchinson, Salina, Grand Island, Pierre, Bismarck, Minot, Aberdeen, and patched with rectangles and squares broken through the prairie sod and colored in the green, yellow, brown, or misty blue of grain or summer fallow or flax. In the fall, following a cycle of harvest from Oklahoma up through Kansas, Nebraska, the Dakotas, and on westward into Montana, threshing rigs lumber from ripening homestead to ripening homestead, wheat wagons draw up in lines at the scales of elevators, farm women work with a driven excitability to feed the crews of go-abouts dropped briefly among them. On the long freights that creep westward deeper into the land of promise the men who follow the harvests perch like cowbirds on the placid hipbones of pasturing cattle.

Westward the plains are broken, the horizon becomes uneasy with low buttes and the exposed even strata where creeks and rivers have cut down in. The line between land and sky is broken only by the glint of a far lonely windmill, and now abruptly the outliers of the mountains, the Little Rockies and the Bearpaws thrust up out of the plain, and the combining rivers come down over the Great Falls of the Missouri past the stacks of silver and copper smelters and the shacks and boardinghouses of the many-languaged workers who run them.

There are construction jobs in the mountains, bridges and trestles, spur tracks; the gulches are pitted with tunnels and drifts and shafts and prospect holes, the mountainsides staired with stamp mills and flotation plants. The migrants trickling into Butte and Anaconda may go to work as muckers or drillers or black-powder men, but more often they do not. The established workers look upon them with suspicion as potential strike-breakers, wage-level destroyers, flooders of the labor market. The companies and the police have convenient vagrancy laws to handle them unless some labor trouble brings on a temporary need for scabs.

They work or they move on, skinning mules in Idaho construction camps, fighting fires in the Cascades, picking apples in the Yakima Valley, wintering in the mildness of the Pacific slope, filling the skid roads of Seattle and Portland and Frisco and San Pedro, or catching on in the shingle mills and lumber camps along Puget Sound. Coxey's Army, Kelly's Army, the army of the dispossessed, the unskilled migrant perennially unemployed labor pool which is a stronger weapon than terror or police persuasion in the companies' fight against organized labor, these are the men who must be organized if workingmen are ever to be united in the strength and solidarity of the One Big Union.

And a man who is both dedicated and committed, who has made a decision and bent his life to a cause, is a man whose life is no longer his own. He is not his own man, but labor's; he speaks not for himself but for the One Big Union; he goes not where he wishes but where the fight draws him. An organizer is more wandering than the wanderers, more foot-loose than the migrant jobless. Neither bum nor hobo nor tramp, he lives as much as they in the atmosphere of insecurity and homelessness and accumulated grievance and wrong. He is a man who has been bidden to go forth out of Nazareth and preach in the towns of Galilee.

He began to be a face men knew, a thin face marked with scars from the mouth down over the jaw, the nose sharpened by a cut that had nicked away a flake of the right nostril. Some who had traveled with him said he could get on or off a faster-moving freight than any stiff on the road, and some who had met his stare when he was in anger remembered his eyes like blue ice. A cat on his feet, limber and tough, he traveled mainly alone and herded by himself, but when he talked he talked the OBU and the class struggle.

The Wobblies crammed half the jails from Everett to San Diego with belligerent workers fighting ordinances against free speech and street meetings, piling in until they jammed a town's whole system of law and order, pouring down from the woods and the camps, beating their way up from skid roads and winter boardinghouses, streaming in from the harvest country. If they did not like a jail's food they "built a battleship," pounding on the walls and floors until frantic police turned firehoses on them or gave up. They organized and kept their jails spotless, and they sang till townspeople gathered laughing outside to listen. But Joe Hill spent no time in jails; he had a horror of jails, he said, and he could do more good outside. He was no soapboxer, anyway, and it was the soapboxers who dared town authorities in the free-speech fights. He was another kind of organizer: a singer, a player of the piano at local meetings, a maker of catchy rhymes and drawer of cartoons. The name of Joe Hill was better known than the man, for it was signed to cartoons pinned up in almost every hall up and down the coast, and his songs in the Little Red Songbook were the kind that men in a crowd discovered they knew. Any time, at any season, he was likely to drop quietly into town, spend a day or two or three, help out with a meeting, get out and work the waterfront or the bunkhouses, and disappear again, leaving behind a cartoon on the back of a laundry ticket, or a song written in a round neat hand that would next year be printed in the songbook but would be known by hundreds of Wobblies before it ever appeared.

He was seen in Spokane, Seattle, Portland, Frisco, Fresno, San Pedro, San Diego, Tia Juana, out in the islands, a silent and almost diffident man. He looked like a man who nursed a grudge, but he was quiet, well spoken, a good jungle cook, full of un-expected sarcasms and humorous remarks. But a man who never led with his tongue; a counterpuncher strictly. At parties he sometimes seemed to want to mix and to be held back and stiffened by some incurable reserve. A singleton, a loner, a man with a hot temper and no really close friends. But a rebel from his skin inwards, with an absolute faith in the One Big Union and nerve enough for five. Though he had a scholarly streak, and spent a good deal of time in the public library when he was around town, he was no spittoon philosopher, no windy debater. What called him, speaking a language he understood perfectly, was trouble. Where trouble brewed, he appeared.

In a shoulder holster under his left arm he carried a Luger .30 automatic.

2   Seattle, November, 1912

As soon as the meeting was over, Joe left the hall and caught a streetcar across town, knowing precisely what would have to be done, what he would have to arrange. He did not hold their caution against McCandless and Taylor and the rest of the Seattle boys. They weren't scared of a fight; they just wouldn't become real fire-eaters till they were pushed.

The air was gray and close with rain so fine that it hardly seemed to fall, but drifted and hung. On the windows of the car it gathered secretly as mist, until the lurch and joggle crystalized it suddenly into big drops, that ran a clear streak down the glass. Through the streaks and the misted panes Joe caught glimpses of raw cuts through hills, the earth yellow in the rain, of tool shacks of construction crews, piles of sand and gravel, Fresno scrapers and steam shovels, disjointed lines of sewer pipe, bricks and lumber, skeleton studding of new houses, all the raw new forms of a city in boom.

He left the car at the end of the line, took a quick bearing in the mist, cut across a weedy field where children or animals had angled a path that lay now dully shining and slippery in the rain. Eventually he came out on a cindered road between a shingle mill and a straggling line of storage sheds, and so entered a lane he recognized, that ran down through big stumps to the shore of the lake. An old army houseboat lay moored with washing hanging limply in the rain, and a clutter of shacks spread out along the shore. Two hundred feet further down, its windows blurrily alight and its stovepipe leaking smoke that dove and hugged the water, was Bottles' floathouse.

This was a return, of a kind. Joe felt it, setting his feet on the sagging gangplank—a port he had once gone ashore at, a place he had seen and used briefly and left, one of the hundreds of places a man passed through, one of the few he ever saw again. The sense of completion and purpose, the feeling that now he knew what he had been looking for when he came here in the first place, was probably an illusion brought on by the warmth of Bottles' windows through the drifting rain, but the memory came back in a quick thrust that on that earlier visit he had been low-spirited and sour, sick of his aloneness and the purposeless drift of his life. He felt the difference between then and now; the very fist he raised to knock on Bottles' door was no longer a random instrument, but a purposeful one. He almost smiled, wondering what had ever become of the curly-headed green kid who had sat on Bottles' deck that night two years ago and talked about his sister in Akron. That sister was in the IWW *Songbook* now, one little girl fair as a pearl.

Bottles' thrusting shoulders and great buffalo head filled the door. There was a strong chemical stink about him. He had lost his teeth since Joe had last seen him, and his face looked shrunken, collapsed, too small for his tremendous skull. But his eyes were the hard little agate knobs Joe remembered, and his voice was a belligerent grunt. Joe saw him look at the button in his lapel, and then Bottles stepped back out of the doorway silently.

"Remember me?" Joe said. "Joe Hillstrom? I was here a couple years ago. Pat Hiskey from up at Sedro Woolley gave me the steer."

Bottles shook hands. "If I remembered ever'body that come through I'd be ash good ash Whathisname Mishter Brain on the Pantagesh. Where you in from?"

"San Pedro," Joe said. "I'm organizing, been down at Hoquiam."

Bottles grunted and smacked. His mouth, was its too-long wet lips and its caved cheeks, was troublesome to look at, like the naked display of some degenerative disease. "Thosh Shonshabitchesh," he said aimlessly, and swung an arm with sudden violence. The puckered lips gave an incongruous, old maid prissiness to the words.

"Shit down," Bottles said. An expression of impotent exasperation crossed his face, and he worked his rubber lips as if to bring them back into shape by muscular effort. "*Shit down!*" he mocked himself savagely, and pushed Joe toward a chair. "Been having trouble with my god damn teeth. Had to have ever fuckin' one yanked."

"That's bad luck," Joe said. He had a feeling that Bottles might have deteriorated too far, that he might not be good for anything any more, and he had to be good for something or they were wasting their time. "Can't you get some store teeth?" he said.

"Don't sheem to fit," Bottles said, and sprawled over a chair that creaked and sagged. "Whole god damn jawsh shot, sheems like." He waved his arm at the chemical bench against the wall. Beyond the bench he had made a kind of brick kiln, stove-size, with a blacksmith's bellows built in near the bottom. "I been fuckin' around too mush with that shtuff. Got myshelf god damn good and poishoned."

Joe said carefully, "You've been doing a whale of a job for the obu, though."

The agate eyes bored at him, no old man's eyes, no sick maunderer's, though his face was so fallen that the sag of his cheeks pulled even his lower eyelids into a droop. "I fuck around with that shtuff for fun," he said. "My own enjoyment." After a moment's challenging stare, he said. "Come here, show you shome'm."

From the bench he reached a glass jar about a third filled with what looked like ordinary blue clay. On top of the clay was about three inches of a liquid, colorless like water, and on the surface of the liquid was a thick silvery scum.

"Shee that? You know what that ish?"

"What?"

"*I* do' know," Bottles said. "What the hell, I jusht fuck around for the fun of it. You know how I got that?"

"How?"

"Tryin' to make glue. Out in the woodsh theresh theshe fernsh, you sheen 'em, shticky shap oozhin' out all the time. I collect thish shap, shee? Gonna make shome new kind of glue. But I get fuckin' around, mixshin' thish shtuff with one thing and another, and I throw it in with shome clay and ashids, and all of a sudden I get thish. What ish it? *I* do' know. Aluminum? Metallic shodium? Magneshium? I do' know. Sho I'll fuck around shome more and find out. Jusht for fun."

Joe finished looking at the jar and put it back on the bench. "What I came over for," he said, "I wanted to talk to you about doing another job for the union."

He watched Bottles' eyes, but the eyes told him nothing, and the rough voice ground out only a grunting, abrupt sound that could have meant anything from curiosity to fury. There was a long pause, until Bottles said, "What're you talkin' about, jobsh? I do' do any jobsh."

"I've been talking with the boys at the hall, McCandless and Call and Riordan."

Bottles' lips made smacking noises as he worked them into shape over his shrunken gums. He looked away and spit into a can, leaning carefully. When he straightened he said, "They're mish-taken. They think I do jobsh, whyn't they come down here them-shelves? I do' know what you mean, jobsh."

Joe watched the ruined face, the hard little pouched eyes, but he could see no sign that he was getting anywhere. "This is a job I want to do by myself," he said. "You know what's been going on down by Potlatch?"

Bottles continued to look at him.

"Seattle's sent organizers down there three times to open a hall and keep it open and hold meetings," Joe said. "The sheriff and his goons have run them out every time, and wrecked the hall as fast as they open it."

"Yeah?" Bottles said.

"They've worked over the crews till they've weeded our boys all out," Joe said. "What they've got now is a picked mob of gunmen and finks and scissorbills, and the union can't even hold a meeting."

"Yeah?" Bottles said.

"Well, I want to bust that up and get the boys organized. It's a lockout, see? There are fifty workers there that've just been kicked out. All they need is organization and some help."

"Yeah? What help?"

Now Joe held the pouchy eyes steadily. "What it takes. Stink bombs, maybe. Phosphorus maybe. Dynamite maybe, if it comes to that."

Bottles hawked with contempt, and his head wagged. "Shtink bombs and phoshphorush and dynamite! I told you, I jusht fuck around for fun."

"Just the same . . ."

"Where you from?" Bottles said violently. His face was suddenly very red. "How the hell I know who you are? You come in here and proposhition me thish way, I do' know you from a hole in the ground. You're in the wrong plashe."

"Here's my paid-up card, for one thing," Joe said.

Bottles shrugged, but looked.

"Ever hear of Joe Hill?" Joe said.

"Maybe sho, maybe not, I'm tellin you, mishter, you got the wrong coon."

"Well, I'm Joe Hill. I've been working all up and down the coast. You know George Reese in Portland, and McCandless and Riordan over here, and you know Frank Little, and know he just went up to Great Falls on an organizing trip. I've been working with all of them. You've heard of Joe Hill, so you know who I am. You don't have to act as if I was a stool."

"I thought you shaid your name wash Hillshtrom."

"Hill, Hillstrom, what difference does it make?" Joe said.

Bottles stared at him steadily, his heavy shoulders thrust forward a little. He grunted as if in surprise, and coughed. "All right," he said. "I heard of Joe Hill. Now tell me why Bert McCandlessh didn't come down here himshelf if the union needsh help."

"I told you," Joe said. "They think they have to calm the public down. Too much talk of iww dynamiters. They won't move unless the company kills a half-dozen men, then maybe they'll do something. They'll get voted down sooner or later, but meantime those boys are down there taking a beating."

Lifting the lid of the stove, Bottles spit in on the fire, and after he had spit his lips puckered into an ancient, helpless hole. "I shpose you're all right," he said. "I got to be careful. Beshidesh, I got a belly full of thish phoshphorush. I got me damn good and poishoned, shee? I damn near died. Hadn't had shome oil of turpentine handy, I would of. I been fuckin' around with thish stuff too long. Now I got thish phoshy jaw. Any day now I'll yawn and busht my god damn jaw right off. My jawbonesh rotting right in my head, shee? I bitched myshelf good with that phoshphorush shtuff."

Joe was silent. For a moment, as he looked at the degenerated and poisoned face of old Bottles, he hated him for a scissorbill. Just once more. He was already wrecked, what difference would it make?

"You come around here ashkin for shome'm imposhible anyway," Bottles said. "Chrish shake, you do' make that shtuff overnight. You got to treat bone ash with shulphuric, and filter off the calshium shulphate, and conshentrate it, and mixsh it with shawdusht, and dry it, and dishtill it, and then you have to shuck it up into tubesh. Jusht shlip oncesh, like I did, and you get a mouthful. Maybe you'd like to shuck up that shtuff into a tube with your mouth."

"I thought you might have some left around," Joe said.

"Yeah? You know what I'd get if any cop came in and found any of that around? I'd be shmart to leave it laying around, I sure would."

Joe shrugged. "Well, if you did have any, it might be smart to get rid of it." He threw up his open hands, letting the possibility go, but he was not quite ready to give up the whole thing. Any chemicals, any explosives, were too precious. Bought at a drugstore or hardware, they could be traced—unless a Pinkerton bought them to plant and frame the union. In a fire, you needed a backfire, and he said to old Bottles, holding his anger and disappointment in, "How about stink bombs?"

The agate eyes blinked, the mouth pursed. "Okay," Bottles said. "I can give you shome shtink bombsh."

From a brace under the bench he fished out a padded chocolate box with the picture of a girl under a parasol on it. Inside there were many little blown-glass bubbles with a plug of cooled glass at the bottom. They looked like crude base-loaded salt-shakers. Bottles stood silently counting them, his limber lips moving. "About four dozhen. That do you?"

"Fine."

Joe reached for them, and as he took them in his hand he saw that Bottles was watching him intently. Across Bottles' shoulder he could see that the rainy dusk had frayed off into dark, and that mist was thick on the inside of the windows. Bottles' shadow loomed and moved on the wall; the movement of the shadow arm as the old man reached into his pocket was like a threat. His hand came out with a jackknife in it, and Joe tensed, muscles and nerves tightening alertly. For a moment he expected Bottles to attack him. Then the old man grunted, turned aside, opened the knife and set the tip of the blade under the edge of a knot in one of the two-by-four studs. The knot slipped out like a cork to reveal a slanting augur hole. Feeling with a thick finger, Bottles pulled out a six-inch glass tube filled with a yellowish, cheesy solid.

Slowly Joe began to smile, but Bottles did not smile as he handed the tube over. He replaced the knot and pried out another one and took three tubes from a second hole. From a third he got two more, and finally he stood looking at Joe with his mouth pursed and helpless and old.

"Thash all of it," he said. "Thash the lasht, and I ain't makin' no more. I been poishoning myshelf for too damn long. I ushed to be a shtrong man, shtrong ash a bull, by God. Now I haven't got shtrength enough to pull your pecker out of a lard pail. Phosh-phorush poishoning, ever hear of it? Phoshy jaw. Itsh got my heart, too. Other night I woke up like shomebody'd drove a crowbar through my chesht." He threshed the violent arm outward. "Phosh-phorush! I'm really bitched for good. I'm not makin any more."

"That's all right," Joe said. "You've already done your share to help the cause along." He rolled the tubes in newspaper and packed them into the candy box along with the stink bombs, and wrapped the whole box in another newspaper. When he had it all done Bottles, who had watched every move, splatted his loose lips contemptuously.

"I never ashked to get rotted away in the god damn cause," he said.

"That's the way the luck goes sometimes."

"Shcrew it!" Bottles said.

Joe tapped the box under his arm. "Every working stiff on the coast will owe you for this. Every working stiff's behind you, too. We're all in it together till we win it."

"Only I'm in it a little deeper than mosht," Bottles said. "I washn't cut out to be a fuckin' martyr. Hell with it. Thish ish the lasht."

Joe smiled and shrugged. He eyed Bottles a moment—an old guy, washed up. There would be no help from him any more. He felt no sympathy for Bottles' troubles. Maybe he *was* poisoned, but he didn't have to cry about it. You took what came. If you weren't in the movement for keeps, you didn't belong in it.

"Well, take it easy," he said. Bottles did not shake hands. He followed Joe to the door, and looking back from the shore end of the gangplank toward the lighted door where the old man stood, Joe saw him big-shouldered and bushy-haired like one of the mountain giants of the fairy stories, one of the workers in metals, the livers in deep caves, the lonely and isolated and dangerous, made poisonous by the fumes of their own subterranean forges.

In the late afternoon of the next day he walked out of the wood-enclosed right of way to the cleared rim of a gorge. Ahead of him the narrow-gauge tracks ran out on a spidery trestle two hundred feet over tidewater. Across the gorge, spilled in wild confusion down the slope, an avalanche of logs had been dumped from flat-cars coasting around the upper edge, and had fallen in a tangle of red-brown plated pine and gray fir down to the orderly parquetry of wet logs choking the river behind the boom. Lower down, on the far bank, already in deep shade, were the mills and the one false-fronted street of the town. He saw four men stacking lumber, and steam drifted from the mill buildings, wisping away against the bluffs. The rain had all blown away inland; the sun was setting clear, and the crossties and timbers of the trestle were already dry, though the grass and ferns where he sat down were damp.

In the ferny quiet he sat with his back against a stump. After a while he heard the quitting whistle down below. The sun glared fierily through the needle-tops of the firs, and the air grew chillier. Joe checked the angle at which the sun was setting, and turned to see where it would rise in the morning. Straight up the gorge. Then the rays would hit the trestle by eight o'clock, at least, and by ten the protected angles of the timbers should be getting nice and warm.

Tomorrow was Sunday; there shouldn't be anyone crossing the trestle, and no work going on. The scabs would all be lying around the bunkhouses getting over a big Saturday night, probably, and it would be hard to rally a crew for an emergency. Maybe the whole thing would fizzle, but there was a chance it would work, or work at least enough to slow things down, break up the opera-tion of the company's plans.

It was almost time, almost dusk. Joe filled his pockets with dry needles from a protected spot under a tree, and from his bindle he took the chocolate box. Working very carefully, he cracked the tubes and with twigs and newspaper worked out the pliable sticks of phosphorus. The glass he covered with needles and dirt, and when the gone sun was only an area of intenser light behind the forest on the point beyond the rivermouth, he rose with his bindle across his back and the phosphorus held carefully in his hands and started across the trestle.

The earth fell away under him, he saw the slaty reflecting water, the matchstick crisscross of the floating logs, the smokes lifting toward him in windless feathers. Down below were the elements of his devoted life: a struck mill and a lockout, striking workers evicted from company houses and scabs installed in their places, a permanent deputy paid by the company and a crew of goons to "keep order" among the mill hands camped in tents and shanties out beyond the company street. In the straggling street paralleling the choked rivermouth, among the raw lumber and piles of slabs and corrugated iron sheds, oppressive capital and militant labor faced each other in one of the ten thousand battles of the revolution.

He saw it below him small and cluttered and shabby, pinched down under the shadow of the river bluffs, ringed by dark trees, one inconsequent battleground among ten thousand battlegrounds, but as important as any, as legitimate a place to fight in as any. It seemed to him as he looked down that he saw with great clarity, not in any new way but with a new freshness, the meaning of the words in the Preamble: "There can be no peace so long as hunger and want are found among millions of working people and the few who make up the employing class have all the good things of life. Between these two classes a struggle must go on until the workers of the world organize as a class, take possession of the earth and the machinery of production, and abolish the wage system . . ."

But as he walked along, his sight was blurred by the ties, the alternate solidity and empty space beneath his feet. A wind puffed down the gorge toward the sea; he felt the trestle strain the thin pressure of the air, and a second or two later saw the feathers of smoke rising from the town bend seaward like candleflames in a blown breath.

It was fantastic. Ordinarily he was as steady and sure-footed on a trestle or scaffolding as on solid ground, but now his knees tightened with the fear that something might break the strong rhythm of his walking, that his eyes might misjudge the blurring alternation of the ties, that he might step through and fall. He felt the trestle sway lightly, dangerously, and he stopped and stooped, almost grabbing for support.

Alone and high above the chicken yard where he would soon pounce, he did not feel like a hawk. He felt scared and queasy, and in anger at himself he stopped and stood straight until the uneasiness went away. Then he looked around.

He was almost in the middle. Swiftly he squatted, broke the waxy sticks of phosphorus into short pieces, and using the piece of newspaper like a glove, laid them along a six-foot stretch of the sheltered eastern angle of the truss beam. Over them he scattered the pocketfuls of fir needles he had gathered. He worked quickly and surely, with no more shakiness of the knees though he had to lean out to arrange the sticks as he wanted them. When he was through he stood up and slapped the needles from his clothes. The covered phosphorus sticks were entirely out of sight. At 83° Fahrenheit they would burst into flame.

As he walked on, steadily stepping across the open ties, his mind was working like a clock. He was in search of a black German named Schermerhorn and a Frenchy named Tisserand. Tonight, with any luck, the Wobbly hall would be open for a while at least and a certain number of the strikers would be signed up and wearing buttons. Still later, while selected people threw stink bombs and kept the deputies busy over across the river, there would be a street meeting. Even a half-hour would be enough. Contact would have been made, solidarity established, a core of the iww planted in the town so that the union could move in its heavy support.

This time tomorrow he might be in jail or on his way out of town with the marks of clubs on him, but by then there would have been a job done. And before this time tomorrow there was going to be a nice fire that would cripple the operation of the mill and go up above the firs at the rivermouth like a yell of defiance.

3   Sacramento Valley, August, 1913

The spot where they had unrolled their blankets was a long way from the ditch, and outside the edge of the old orchard whose sawed-off stumps were put to use as stools all through the camp.

They were on the fringe, a little higher, up where dry oatgrass and tarweed spread under the fence and up the first slope of the hills, and they could look down over the camp sprawling across the old orchard and bunched under the pepper trees along the ditch. The sun, which had poured down heat all day, was almost flat; they sat with their backs to it, waiting for it to go down.

"Yes," Joe said finally. "But how mad are they? Can we do anything with them, or are they like most of these stoop laborers?"

Fuzzy Llewellyn lifted his face and gave Joe a distorted look. One cheek wore a puffy discolored bruise, and the eye on that side was swollen nearly shut. He talked stiffly past a split lip. "I think there's a . . ."

His one good eye sharpened and focused, staring past Joe. Quite slowly and smoothly he folded back onto the ground, crawled into the shelter they had rigged from two bent strips of corrugated iron culvert hammered flat, and pulled a blanket clear up over him. "Keep on talkin'," he said from underneath.

With hands hanging at their knees they sat on, facing half away from a man in breeches and laced boots who came up from along the edge of the camp. Backs to the sun, drooping, they sat still. Without appearing to look, Joe saw the man giving their outfit a sharp once-over as he came.

Joe caught his eye when he was within thirty feet. He nodded. "Evenin'," the man said. The others lifted hands and let them fall again, not quite looking around.

"You're pretty far from water up here," the man said.

No one answered for a moment, until old Manderich said, "More preeze." Virtanen, a slow-headed Russian-Finn, smiled. Joe and the Kirkham twins hugged their knees.

"I guess you're right, at that," the man said. He laughed and drew his shirtsleeve across his forehead, replaced his hat. His feet had not quite stopped moving. Now he was almost past, walking a little sideways in order to watch them. "She's a hot son of a bitch, for fair," he said, and passed on. They watched him plod along the fence and eventually drift down into the edge of the camp again. Fuzzy waited a long time before he poked his bruised face out.

"Ve vould show up less if ve camped down in the crowd," Manderich said.

"It ain't safe," Fuzzy said. "I'm too easy to spot, with a tow head and a buggered-up face. They prowl this place like cops on a beat. There must be a dozen special deputies and finks around." He sat down among them again and ran a finger tenderly along his leaking eyelid.

"That doesn't seem so many for a camp this big," Joe said.

"It's enough to show they're jumpy. If they wasn't jumpy they wouldn't have taken the trouble to goon me out of camp."

"What'd you do, exactly?"

"I called a meetin'," Fuzzy said. "I come in here and I took one look and I called a meetin'." His lips pointed sharply, alertly, and like a bird pecking he spit between his feet. His bruises gave his grin a cocky, one-sided leer. "Troublemaker!" he said.

Joe watched him. "What'd you have in mind when you came back?"

"Call another meetin'!"

They laughed, a short, unanimous acknowledgment of Fuzzy's cockiness. "When?" Joe said. "Tomorrow?"

"That's what I figured. What do you think? Sunday mornin' they'll all be sittin' around smellin' the backhouses, or waitin' in line to get in one."

Joe kept watching him, trying to appraise this Llewellyn. He knew nothing of him except what he had learned in the last six hours, and it didn't pay to take chances. "How are you on the soapboxing? Can you start her off?"

"Listen!" Fuzzy said, "just let me up there and I'll soapbox the livin' Jesus out of 'em. I got somep'm to tell 'em about this dump. Only I won't dare show my mug around too much beforehand. You boys'll have to set it up."

"We'll set it up," Joe said. He rose, beating the dust from the seat of his corduroys. "Before we settle any strategy I'd like to take a look around. You feel like a walk, Art?"

"Come on," Manderich said. "I show you."

He led Joe down to the edge of the ditch that cut at an angle through the immense camp. All through the city of tents and shelters and tarp-covered wagons the sawed-off orchard stumps made a regular pattern. Along the ditch people had crowded in close to take advantage of the shade of the pepper trees, and their tent ropes stretched to the edge of the path.

Even at seven o'clock it was hot. The ground was beaten bare; the sun caught in a golden haze of dust among the tents. Children were wading at the edge of the ditch, but a man with a pail chased them out angrily and stood a moment, his mouth grim, waiting and looking for a clear spot, before he reached far out and hooked a pailful from deeper water. The mealtime smoke of many fires rose and mixed with the dust, and all over the tent city and over the crude shelters and the shelterless bedroll-camps that spread for a quarter of a mile there was a light, sun-dazzled haze. Men chopped wood, women stooped and squatted around campfires, there was a calling and yelling of children. All the sounds, in the last heat of the day, had a dragging, tired resonance, the shrillness taken out as distance takes the shrillness from a train whistle. In the evening the sounds that rose above the camp had an almost musical hum.

"Tventy-eight hundred peoples," Manderich said. "It iss a city."

"Some city," Joe said. "Some City Beautiful." It bothered him that the sounds the camp made were not more obviously unhappy sounds, the vocal anguish of the oppressed. There was no doubt that the pickers in this camp were beaten down like slaves, yet the sounds they made were light, almost hopeful. The chunk of an axe had a purposeful and solid ring; the noise of the children was full of laughter. If people didn't have such a capacity to take a beating, the revolution would come ten times faster. He looked across the ditch into the great hopfields, unbroken, apparently without end. As far as he could see southward the geometry of the frames angled and changed and set up rows and lines. It was incredible that one man should own so much, and incredible that by the mere fact of owning it he could acquire the use of twenty-eight hundred human farm animals, and incredible that twenty-eight hundred people would consent to be used like animals, or worse than animals. An animal you valued, you took care of.

A hundred feet away, left in the center of a small discreet open space, was a weathered privy. Three children hung around it, and as Manderich and Joe came along the welt of the ditch Manderich's elbow dug Joe's body. "Here iss one t'ing." Loitering, they watched.

From back among the camps a man came, walking fast, and when he saw the privy with no crowd around it he speeded up almost to a run. But the privy door was locked, and when he had rattled it impatiently once he turned away scowling. A cloud of flies, luminous in the sun-struck dust, lifted from the half-open flap behind and slowly settled again. The man walked a few yards away and sat down on a stump to which a camper had guyed his tent. On the other side of the privy the three children lingered. One of the girls wrapped her legs together and hopped, grimacing, and the three giggled. A man with a boy by the hand came along the ditch, saw the man waiting on the stump, and wordlessly fell in behind him, starting a line.

The privy door swung back and a gaunt woman stepped out. The waiting man rose smartly from his stump, but the children raced as if in a game and piled in and slammed the door before the man had taken three steps. He went back to the stump, and he and the gaunt woman exchanged looks of hatred as she passed.

Old Manderich's face was like brown worn rock. "It iss for pigs," he said. "In all dis camp, eight backhouses, all mixed up for men and vomen, no lime, everyt'ing oferflowing vit flies and cherms. Three, four hundred peoples to one backhouse, and plenty of dysentery. Iss it for human beings or iss it for pigs?"

They moved aside to let a woman and two children pass. The drawers of one child, a girl, hung down dirty and sopped, and her face was tear-streaked. As her mother yanked her and the little boy down the embankment toward the privy the man on the stump saw her coming, and raised his head with an expression of warning on his face. The woman, glancing aside from her concentrated dragging of the two children, saw him, and the man and boy behind him, clearly a forming line. Her mouth tightened; she hung indecisive, hesitating. At that instant the three other children swarmed out of the privy, whamming the door back against the wall, and before the door had swung halfway back into place the woman was running, dragging her girl and boy along. Her hair flew across her face as she yanked the girl inside, stood sideways to let the boy slide past her, and pulled the door shut.

The man had risen from his stump. Now he looked across at Joe and Manderich, shook his head, said something to the man behind him. His look of outrage had given way to amused disgust.

He sat down on the stump again and pinched his face together and shook his head and laughed. He said, "In about five minutes I'm going over and let fly right on old Hale's doorstep."

"Dot vould be a goot idea," Manderich said.

He touched Joe's elbow and they went on, out of the more orderly area of tents and in among the camps scattered across the open field. Huddles of quilts and blankets, a few leanto' shelters of stretched tarpaulins, some parked wagons and buckboards, smells of manure and smoke and rank fermented garbage and burning eggshells, and over it all the terrible dusty pressure of the heat. There were makeshift tables on packing boxes, overturned pails, stumps or rocks. Under one frame with a blanket thrown over it an old Mexican woman sat unmoving and stared into space with eyes of a startling blind blue. Hairs grew on her upper lip, and her hands lay like dark dry leaves in her lap.

Manderich said, "I haff been in some stinkholes, but neffer one like dis."

"What are they here for?" Joe said. "Why have they stood it this long?"

A family eating around a spread quilt watched them as Manderich kicked a tin can and sent it rolling. "It iss a bunch of foolish sheepy peoples," old Art said. "Plenty Mexicans, some Japanese and Chinese, some Puerto Ricans, plenty bums from skid road, quite a few riffraff, *Lumpenproletariat*. It iss a matter of not speaking English, of not knowing anyt'ing, of being mad one at a time. Dey haff no organization, it iss a helpless mob."

"Too many women and kids," Joe said. "A family man is a natural-born scab. The whole labor movement gets betrayed at the cook-stove."

"Vell, we shall see," Art said. "Ve haff you and me and Fuzzy and a few more."

They had moved through the whole camp and were at the edge of the highway leading northward. The sun was riding the low hills to the west; behind them over the great camp the smoke lay blue and still. But north of them, shining in the last gold light, was a grove of trees sheltering the white wings and green roofs of a house.

"That the Boss's castle?" Joe said.

"Dot's it."

It could have been only a dusty ranch house in a grove, but that was not the way his mind wanted to imagine it. He could see gleaming floors, thick carpets, carved furniture. A Chinese cook was in the kitchen and there were Japanese houseboys in white coats. Women would come down to dinner with jewels on neck and hands. Everything in that mansion pulled fastidiously back from the dusty highway and screened among its trees was subdued and quiet and rich. He saw the boss, the king, as plainly as some-one he knew, a man with careful eyes, a senatorial figure, a heavy gold chain across his vest—the pot-bellied Moneybags of the cartoons. He had drawn him plenty of times himself. To keep Hale in that style, twenty-eight hundred slaves labored in the killing sun and lived like animals.

Manderich stopped, grunted, and turned left along the fence to where a family sat eating around a fire. There were five of them, a man, a woman, a gangling daughter in runover high-heeled shoes that came halfway up her legs and showed dirty white stockings at the top, and two half-grown boys. The man stretched his wrinkled sunburned neck and lifted his tin plate to Manderich in recognition.

"Goot efening," Art said. The rest of the family watched silently until the father had swallowed his mouthful.

"Set down," he said, and waved his plate. "Pull up a rocker."

They sat down under the still watchfulness of wife and children.
"Hot," Art said.

"Ain't it? I don't know's I ever seen it any hotter. Well, maybe once down by Merced, down there in the fig country." He swabbed his plate with a piece of bread and chewed and swallowed. "You fellers ate?"

They nodded.

"Good thing, I guess," the man said, and cackled suddenly, thrusting his head forward and pulling it back. "Grub's about used up around here. Have a drink anyway."

He reached for the dipper in a tin pail. Joe shook his head, but the picker said, "You don't need to be afraid of this, I went way the hell and gone up the ditch, way up above camp, to get this just for drinkin'. Lots of folks drink her right out of the ditch down here, but that don't look healthy to me. It ain't had a chance to run long enough to purify itself. Here, you try this."

Joe took the dipper with a wink and a smile and drank. The water was tepid, weedy-tasting. As he handed the dipper back the gangling girl said unexpectedly, mewing and spitting the words, "It'd be a nickel for that much of a drink down in the field."

Her mother stuck a quick finger in the kettle of water steaming at the edge of the fire. She was flat-chested and bony, with hard repressed lines around her mouth, and she glanced up once, quickly, when Manderich said, "Oh no! You are mistaken. Vater does not cost at the stew-vagon. All you haff to do iss buy a lemonade first."

"Boy, ain't it a system!" the father said. "Tell me that stew-wagon guy is Hale's cousin."

Moving around among them, the mother gathered the plates and slid them into the kettle. Her husband took out a section of plug and sat contemplating it with a relaxed, abstracted smile. Remembering himself, he offered it first to Joe and then to Manderich, and then he set his teeth in the corner and wrenched and twisted it off. For a while he was busy getting the chew shaped and pocketed in his cheek. Joe sat quietly, content to leave this all in Art's hands, content for the moment to sit still and learn what he could.

"Now it's funny they wouldn't have any water at all down there," the father said gently after a while. "Folks get mighty dry workin' all day in the sun. I seen two women faint down by me. I expect there was others, too. Well, you was workin' right down there, you seen those two."

"It was 105," the girl's harsh voice said. Her eyes moved from Manderich to Joe, assertive and insistent. "I saw the thummometer inside the stew-wagon."

". . . if you had a canteen with a strap to it, that'd be good," her father said. "I took a pail down the second day, after we most boiled alive the first time, but a pail ain't good. There's no handy way to tote it with you, and you set it down dogs come drink out of it and it gets all full of dirt."

"You're supposed to drink lemonade," Joe said. He winked at the two boys, and they snickered. The daughter sniffed, standing close, ready at any time to contribute her share of the talk.

"Marian," her mother said, and wagged her head toward the rock where the washed dishes were piled. Marian moved sideways,

keeping her eyes on the men, and groped up a gray towel from
a stump and started wiping. The boys sat hugging their knees,
their thin wedged faces turned toward their father. The going-down
of the sun left a grateful even twilight restful to the eyes.

"Takes a pretty mean man to refuse a drink to a little old
dusty kid," the father said. "Lots of folks shell out and buy cracka-
jack or lemonade so's their kids can get a dipperful, but a man
can't afford that as often as it'd take."

Grunting, old Manderich shot a pebble across the fire with his
thumb and squinted and pulled his suspender. "It iss one big Fourt'
of Chuly picnic. Lots of peoples, a chance to make lots of money."

Joe kept watching the faces, hoping to read in them what response the camp might make to an organizer. The daughter's was
sharp with resentment—good; the mother's was tight and expressionless as if she had only strength enough for work, and could spare
none for anything else, as if she doled out her strength for daily
jobs, cooking, dishes, picking, shaking the blankets, and anything
else would be a leakage that would drain her dry. Not so good.
The father's was ruminative, mildly reproachful, the face of a good-
natured man confronted with things he didn't want to believe.
Good or bad, it was hard to tell.

All through the camp there were families like this, and if anything were done it would have to be done through them.

"Don't you enjoy the great out-of-doors?" he said. "It's worth a
little trouble and discomfort just to get the chance of camping
out here in the open and getting all this sun and air. People come
from all over the world to camp out in the California sunshine."

They stared at him. The girl snickered tentatively, but the others
only stared. There seemed nothing that any of them could think
of to say. Finally Manderich grated out, "By Gott, vy do ve stand
it?"

To Joe, alertly watching, it seemed that something hung in the
balance, as if a mixture of things had been stirred in a flask and
now out of the cloudy solution something new might appear. The
tin dishes clinked lightly as Marian laid one on another. The father
looked around. "Don't seem to be much a man can do."

"Not alone," Art said. "You vas here two days ago ven some
peoples sqvawked. Dot night come the finks, and out dey go. Now
Fuzzy Llewellyn vears knobs on his head from a beating."

"Not alone," Joe said. He picked up a stick and broke it between his fingers. "But suppose everybody squawked. Suppose twenty-eight hundred of us got together and squawked. You don't beat up twenty-eight hundred people, or throw them out of camp."

The picker's look was long and careful, not so much hesitant as deliberate. "You guys organizin' somethin'?"

"Efferybody iss organizing somet'ing," Manderich said. His look told Joe to hold back, let him handle it. "I haff talked to fifty peoples today. All are mad to pay a nickel for vater in the field, all are mad to see a camp so dirty, vit tents for only half and no place for garbage, and vater from a ditch. It does not make cheers to haff a man's daughters sleep on the ground or stand in line a half-hour to use a stinking backhouse. If dere iss a meeting tomorrow it vill be not organized but an uprising."

"While you're adding it up, don't forget the company store," the girl said, and her father said, shaking his head on his red neck, "Marian ain't so far off, at that. I figured with three of us pickin' we could gain a little, but I forgot there was five of us eatin'. I won't have nothin' to do with workin' little kids, but it's a fact we don't much more'n stay even with the grub bill. Peaches, now. This afternoon we bought a little old can of peaches . . ."

Old Art moved his eyebrows at Joe and stood up with a grunt. "So!" Abruptly, almost as if he were angry, he nodded all around. "Goot night, missus. Goot night, young lady."

Uncertainty was in all their faces now. The girl said, "*Is* there going to be a meeting?"

"Ve vill haff to vait and see," Art said.

Joe shot a pebble at the two boys and ducked away when they grabbed wildly around them for something to throw. "Boys," the woman said, "is that a way . . ."

They left the family all looking after them and went back along the ditch toward the central sheds and the tent camp. Art walked with his hands behind him, thrusting out his lower lip and watching the ground. "Dis iss a system I learned long ago," he said. "You must not be sore because I took it avay from you. Long ago I learned how you leaf peoples vondering. If we said come to a meeting, make a protest, raise some hell, many vould be scared and stay avay. If ve say *maybe* vill be a meeting, *maybe* peoples soon going to get mad and get togetter, anybody who sees fife peoples in one place will come running to see and find out."

"You know more about it than I do," Joe said. "I'm just out to learn the ropes before tomorrow." He was ashamed now of the pique that had touched him momentarily when Art had stopped his spiel. It didn't matter who made the spiel or did the work. Everybody had to do the work. The camp lay around them in the dusk, an enormous sprawling helpless mass awaiting only the brain to make it obey as one body. It was an army of slaves, but an army nevertheless. If Hale could move it as if it were one man, and do it only by reason of ownership and the power of the job, then men with an idea could do the same. Once you got control of it, an army was a single weapon, like an axe.

Stumbling in the dusk along the ditchbank, he thought of how men might rise up behind the right man or group of men, the leaders and organizers, and come on like a wave. How hesitating, good-natured people like the family they had just talked to might become one with the big general voice, the big irresistible mass movement, and how the Hales of the world would be nothing but matchsticks before such a wave as that.

Fires winked everywhere. The smell of eucalyptus wood was fragrant in the dark, and he could no longer smell the garbage or the privies. Off under the peppers someone was playing a guitar; there was a jangle of girls' laughter and a squeal. The camp might have been an immense picnic, some Sunday School outing settling down to marshmallows and romantic songs after a day of baseball and canoes. He hated them suddenly, every apathetic and good-natured and stupid and enduring man, woman, and child of them, for the way they stood anything, bore anything, took anything, and still were able to play guitars and make light laughter in the evenings. Why couldn't they see what they had to do? Why couldn't they get and hold the savage anger they ought to have and would have to have if they were ever to be anything but the slaves and animals they were now?

Along the ditch people were already stretching out in their blankets, there were movements as they spread their beds among the stumps. A woman's voice called ahead of them, and a child's answered. Joe saw the child come up on the ditchbank, a small obscure figure in the near-dark, standing spraddle-legged. The boy bent backward, thrusting out his stomach. In the quiet there was the silvery tinkle—night-sound, garden-sound, fountain-sound, a sound out of a Spanish love song, as he urinated in the ditch.

Hours later, long after the camp had all but quieted and he had lain a long time on his blanket watching the processional passage of the stars, it was cool. His old curse of sleeplessness was on him. Like an instrument into which all the sounds of the night and the camp were conducted, he lay vibrating, recording the individual breathing noises of the five men around him, the barking at various distances of the three separate dogs, and far off and higher in key the yapping of coyotes in the hills. He heard furtive splashings from the irrigation canal—swimmers or muskrat or coon or the gray rats that fed on the garbage heaps. Along the road west of camp an automobile passed, its motor sweet and purring in the night, and faded out and was gone, unknown and lonely, leaving his ears humming a little like wind-vibrated telegraph wires.

He sat up finally and looked. The camp was dark except for the red wink of two or three dying fires, perhaps in families where there was sickness. Still he felt it around him: he heard a thing like its collective breathing and felt the presence of the sleeping hundreds. In the mere congregation of so many people there was some feeling, threat or promise, possibly only a great sense of *weight*. He had never felt it quite this way before.

With a rustle and heave Manderich sat up beside him, a shadow. "Vot iss?"

"Nothing. I couldn't sleep."

Old Art grunted, fumbling softly for his shoes, and then stood up. Joe stood with him, and they stepped over to the boundary fence where Manderich relieved himself with many sighings and breathings. "Gott damn," he said at last, "I vould giff the whole labor mofement for a bladder dot vould keep all night."

"You?" Joe said. "You wouldn't trade the labor movement for a million a year."

Manderich did not reply. Looking past him, Joe saw that one of the fires down in the camp had blazed up, and that over farther west there were two or three more low red blinks. There must be

plenty of sickness; it would be a miracle if the ditch wasn't full
of typhoid.

From up where they stood, the not-quite-sleeping camp seemed
lonely and full of strangeness; he felt a kind of spasm shake his
pulse, a contraction as if from cold raised goose-pimples on his arms,
and there was an urge to do something, to thrust forward into
purposeful action. He said to Manderich, "It's like a camp before
a battle. As if at the crack of dawn they'd get up and start putting
on armor."

"Dot iss possible," Manderich said. Where he leaned on a fence-
post, his shirttails glimmered faintly, his shanks were white in long
drawers. More perhaps than he had ever wanted to make confidential and intimate talk with anyone, Joe wanted to make it now
with Manderich; he felt that he must know if Manderich felt as he
did, and if he had a sense of personal destiny involved in what
might happen tomorrow. But he could not quite make himself say
it. Instead, he said, "Have you got a feeling this might turn into
something big, Art?"

"Maybe."

They hung on their fenceposts in the blue starlight, and it came
over Joe that of all the men he had knocked around with, of all
the Wobblies he had worked with for three years, old Manderich
was the best. Remembering the night they had run from the
cops among the warehouses and yards along the Pedro waterfront
and stumbled into Otto Applequist's little warehouse-pilfering job,
he almost laughed. Art was a beauty in a fight, a slugger who
never backed up and never stopped to think.

Encouraged by the kind of intimacy that the recollection brought
him, and hidden comfortably in the cool dark, he edged closer
to the thing that lay in his mind. "I wonder how Ettor and Giovannitti felt when they came down to take over the Lawrence strike?"
he said. "You suppose they were scared, or afraid they couldn't
win, or worried what might happen next minute, or how they
might be able to swing things?"

"Dey had a strike to vork vit," Manderich said. "Dey vorked vit
it. Ve got vun to start. Ve start it."

Something passed, all but noiseless, in the air overhead; Joe hung
alertly, trying to make his ear define what it had been. Then the
short, doglike bark from further up the hill told him: a burrowing

owl out hunting. He thumbed a loose, deep hum from the barbed wire with his finger and said, "How's Fuzzy as a soapboxer?"

"Goot," Manderich said. "He iss a pounder and shouter." He pushed himself away from the post. "He iss not carrying a card any more, you know dot."

"Why?"

"Stockton local t'rew him out. Somet'ing about some dynamiting up around Placerville."

Suspicion had awakened in Joe as alertly as a sleeping cat wakes. "Is he all right?"

"I t'ink he iss all right. I haff schnooped around. I t'ink he iss all right."

"I don't like the sound of that dynamite."

Manderich made a quiet noise and spit on the ground and Joe heard him laughing. "I don't s'pose you effer used any dynamite."

"As a matter of fact, I never did."

"It iss a tegnicality," Manderich said, still laughing.

"But if he isn't on the level, if he's a Pinkerton trying to frame somebody, this would give him too fine a chance."

"Fuzzy iss all right," Manderich said. "You t'ink he got his eye blacked stooling to dose finks?"

Joe hunched his shoulders against a recurrence of the goose-pimpling chill and thrust his hands deep in his pockets, staring down over the camp and thinking how immovable, how stagnant a mass twenty-eight hundred human farm animals would be for six of them to move. "So much could happen tomorrow."

Old Art's voice was almost mild. He hawked again, and spit, and said, "It iss hard to tell. So many sheepy peoples. Maybe dis iss somet'ing big, maybe it fizzles. Maybe ve get a couple hundred out to a meeting tomorrow and ve get our heads knocked by Hale's finks but Hale gets a little more scared and builds four more backhouses. Dot iss about vot happens."

But the sense of weight, the little chills of apprehension, said to Joe that there would be more than that. "That isn't enough," he said to Manderich. "Sometime a thing like this has to blow up in the boss's face. Why not this time? What's to keep this from being another Lawrence?"

Art started back across the weedy stubble. "Maybe vit educated vorkers, or a few educated vuns. Maybe vit organization. But such a batch of *Lumpenproletariat,* such a little half-dozen as we are."

It seemed to Joe that old Art was not half as militant as he should have been, not half as ready for a fight, not made of the old gruff granite. He was only an old man with a weakening bladder and failing kidneys, somebody almost too tired for the kind of action they would need tomorrow. Irritation made his voice sharp as they stepped close to the huddle of the camp and groped for their blankets among the sleeping forms. "Who took the Bastille?" Joe said as he lay down, but Manderich made a little shushing sound as if to a child and hauled his blanket over his shoulders with a grunting sigh.

So Joe lay counting. He had no real fear of old Art if a fight came up. He had no fear of himself. The Kirkham boys were run-of-the-mill Wobblies, unknown quantities, but since they were Wobblies at all they were probably good for something in a strike or a fight. They had both made the Spokane jail in the free-speech fight three years ago. Virtanen had come in with Joe—the only man he could lay hands on when he got word that something was stirring. Again an unknown quantity, a lumber-schooner sailor, too good-natured, too hard to work up, but honest. And Fuzzy Llewellyn, a dehorn, just possibly a stool. Six little men to wield twenty-eight hundred. He wished he were good at the gab; he would have felt better if he could have depended on himself for the soapboxing.

The stars went processionally westward, and the vibration that was like the breathing of the great camp still came to his ears and nerves. He kept half sitting up, thinking he heard sounds, and all night he did not go to sleep at all, but lay planning, imagining how it would work out at the meeting. He could get Fuzzy up on the box, get the crowd around, see them coming through the tents under the pepper trees, but it disintegrated for him there. He couldn't see the people's faces or tell whether they took fire, and all his trying couldn't trick them into some action, some march on the mansion or some wrecking of the stew-wagon or some committee confronting the boss and the foremen with a set of demands. He could think these things but he could not imagine them, he couldn't make the pictures come.

Yet when the sky began to pale and the moving stars melted

back into it and a chilly little wind came through the stubble and crept into his neck under the snuggled blanket, he sat up and stretched with a shiver that came more from resolution than from the wind. He knew he had too much imagination to be a good organizer. He should have been made of brass and hickory like Frank Little; or he should have been a general, a planner, an indefatigable undiscourageable manipulator of men and events like Vincent St. John. An organizer should not think about what might be gained until after he had gained it; he should act first and think afterward.

Now, as he looked down over the ugly sprawl of tents and shelters in the cool shadowless morning it was as if his heart moved two inches, bracing itself against something that he felt would come.

4   Sacramento Valley, August, 1913

The sun came up over the brown hills, hot from the moment of its rising, and it grew hotter with every quarter-hour of its climb. By the time the six had finished breakfast and were scattering through the camp to line up every man they knew and could trust, even the dogs were hunting shade, and the first dense twittering of birds in the pepper trees had died away to an occasional cheep.

Art Manderich remained behind with Fuzzy, ostensibly to protect Fuzzy from Hale's finks, but also for the influence he would have in keeping Fuzzy from the temptation to stool if he were inclined that way. Manderich himself had thought the precaution unnecessary; it was Joe who insisted on it.

Now as he worked through the camp listening to the talk, waiting in backhouse lines, passing the time of day with men along the canal, there was none of the mystery that night had thrown over the tents and shelters and the red wink of fires. Under the unblinking sun the exposure of the camp's poverty was pitiless and complete. Blankets, quilts, discarded clothes, trailed over the tent ropes and stumps, or lay in the dust. In some camps there were

cots, and these stood up above the dust with a kind of arrogance.
Tent flaps were open, tent walls rolled up to let in air, and the
contents of the tents bulged and slid out into the dust outside—
water cans and jugs, baby buggies, lanterns, suitcases and telescope
bags. He saw lizards dart dust-colored across dust-colored bed-
clothes. And everywhere he found people jumpy, already irritable
from the heat. At the slightest noise or movement they looked up
as if expecting something. Without any of the mystery, without
any of the obscurely ominous air as of a sleeping army that it had
worn last night, the camp was still full of that sense of waiting.

Two Mexican boys broke into a fist fight: within a matter of seconds men, women, and children had thronged around to see what
was happening. Further down the camp, a picker's child fell into
the irrigation ditch: instantly there were two dozen hands there
to pull her out, and for ten minutes afterward people kept coming
to see what the excitement was. There was a good deal of talking,
a good deal of spanking of children. In the space of a half-hour
he heard a dozen different languages spoken. It was a slovenly,
heat-tired, irritable, hopelessly mixed crowd; whatever they made
of it—and he went carefully, making what he could—would have
to be made by pure will and determination, and held together
against all the disintegrative weaknesses of the mob. They would
take a lot of talking to.

And there were also the finks to think about.

He was up on the ditchbank, looking over the shelters and waiting for the Kirkhams and Virtanen to appear, when he saw the
little flurry over by the packing sheds. A man's bald pink head rose
up above a group, mainly women, and the noise that at first had
been only a gabble of voices paused and steadied and became singing. Under the big thin-leaved pepper, with the road's empty
width between him and the sheds, the pink-headed man bawled
above the thinner voices of the women. They were singing "From
Greenland's Icy Mountains." The baldheaded man rotated so that
his voice went off almost inaudibly in other directions and then bellowed like a megaphone. Between verses he made sweeping come-
all-ye motions with his arms, beckoning people in.

Joe's first reaction was a pulse of rage. The preaching fool would
block everything. He was right in the spot they had picked for
their own meeting, and he would probably go on for an hour or

two. He would use up all the restlessness and all the patience to stand in the sun and listen that the camp contained, and he would send them home with the promise of pie in the sky.

Or was the preacher a plant of the boss's? Nothing would suit the purposes of Hale better than a Jesus-meeting. It would pay him to hire a preacher at a hundred dollars a Sunday to bring the slaves the gifts of the spirit.

He swung around, furiously intent on rounding up the boys and breaking up the meeting, at whatever cost to their own plans, but as he turned he saw the fink who last night had cased their camp. The fink was leaning against a tree, his booted foot braced back of him against the trunk, and he was idly peeling a green twig with his thumbnail while he watched and listened. Joe hesitated. Already people were coming from every direction like workers streaming into a factory gate in the morning. They picked their way between tents and shelters, crossed the plank bridges across the ditch, stood up from their sloven campsites and craned to see and hear. They were thickening by the minute around the bald-headed preacher at the road's edge. And the fink was casually peeling a twig. It was that which made Joe's anger back up and make way for a plan. One of the best ways to get a big crowd together without trouble from the finks was to let this preacher do it.

It took him five minutes, pushing through a gathering crowd like the milling crowd on a circus ground, intent and eager and not quite sure where to go, but following the stream toward the main tent, before he spotted the red heads of the Kirkham twins. They came pushing against the stream, Virtanen behind them, all of them laughing and shaking their heads.

"Hell, we thought it was our own meeting starting ahead of time," Russ Kirkham said. "We sprained our ass getting in there, and it's only this bughouse preacher whooping it up."

"Enno," Joe said, "will you get Fuzzy and Art down here? On the fly."

Virtanen left. The preacher's bawling voice went out over the camp, was blurred for a moment with crowd-sound. "What's up?" Russ Kirkham asked.

"We're taking this meeting over, soon as the preacher has it going good. And once we take it over we may have to fight for it a little. How many men can you get together that you can really trust?"

They looked at each other, shrugged, pulled down their identical mouths. They were gangling, red-necked; in the heat their thin freckled skins looked as wet and red and chafed as an infant's. They looked exactly alike but it was always Russ who did the talking. "I don't know," he said. "Maybe a dozen. There just ain't many in this place that've ever . . ."

"All right," Joe said. "A dozen'll do. You better start right now to round them up. Get in toward the inside of the crowd and work by two's. Art and Enno and I will take care of the preacher, and we'll get Fuzzy up on the soapbox. It's up to you to keep anybody from pulling him off again."

The crowd had swelled so that it spread almost out to where they were. The preacher's words were indistinguishable over the noise people made talking and asking questions. Women moved through the dust and sun with babies on their hips, and stood on tiptoe to locate friends in the crowd. Under the peppers people were packed in close, seeking shade.

Between the tents now Manderich and Virtanen came hurrying with Fuzzy between them. They had their hands on his arms, and helped him along, and he came with a step and a hitch and a half-jump, his hat pulled far down over his ears to hide his cotton-top. His face seemed full of a white eagerness; his teeth showed like a squirrel's.

Joe watched him as he came, and he was reassured by the eagerness and by Fuzzy's instant comprehension of what would have to be done. Maybe he was all right. He'd better be.

They huddled only for two or three minutes before the Kirkhams hurried away. At the last moment Virtanen was sent with them. They needed more assured protection in the crowd. Joe and Art alone would have to handle the preacher.

Even while they talked fast, laying it out, Fuzzy Llewellyn's eyes roamed over the fringes of the crowd, which by now Joe thought must number many hundreds. His tongue touched his split lip, and he said softly, "Oh by Jesus, it's made to order, it's made to order!"

Smiling, Art Manderich looked at Joe, a significant, humorous, allusive look, and his thumb touched the head of the hatpin in his suspender. Until then Joe had not been conscious of the automatic under his own arm. He had worn it so long that it was like part of his clothes. But now as they started fighting their way into the press toward the increasing bellow of the preacher's voice he felt the gun every time he pressed against anyone. The dust was gritty on his lips. He went ahead, edging, touching people, moving them aside, saying "Excuse us, how about getting through here." So far as he could see, few were paying any attention to the preacher. They looked, and waited, and said things to those beside them, and shushed their children, and watched the faces of their neighbors as if for enlightenment, but they stayed. The shadows of the pepper trees, at the edge of the fierce sun, dappled them with blotches and freckles of light and dark.

Ahead of him, not very far now, the preacher was loud, and Joe listened consciously for the first time as he slid and wormed and worked his way forward, making a path for the others.

". . . If you haven't known Jesus! Oh, brothers and sisters, I can't possibly tell you the joy I felt in my heart when I first knew Jesus was my friend! I been carrying a millstone around my neck all my days and never knew it. I was weighted down with sin, oh I confess it, brothers and sisters, I confess it gladly, I've had my soul washed clean and that old burden of sin don't bother me any more. But I carried it around till I was bowlegged with it, I carried a pack of sin like a peddler's, brothers and sisters, and all because I didn't know Jesus was my friend, all because I didn't know where to go to get my burden lightened. Now I've laid it down, and I tell you one and all, I'm a new man. You'll never know what living can be until you come to Jesus and have those sins forgiven. You've all got 'em, brothers and sisters, everybody's got 'em. Just make up your mind to come in and lay that burden down . . ."

The three were near the heart of the crowd, where a little breathing space had been left around the preacher's backless chair on which he stood and shouted. Joe looked around. There were too many women; in close the crowd was two-thirds women, yet even they did not seem to be taking in what the preacher said. Some were Mexican women he was sure did not understand one word in ten.

Once more he looked carefully around, tiptoeing to see better, but he spotted no finks whose faces he knew. The heat of the crowd packed him in; he wanted to break away and fight himself free and into the open. The red-faced preacher roared on, streaming sweat. "*Jesus,* my friends. Keep that name in mind. When He first visited this sinful world, coming from the city of jasper and pearl and pure gold, He stepped down out of that glory just to save sufferin' humanity, just out of the pity of His great heart, and I want to say to you, brothers and sisters, He's still ready to save, He's still got His hand stretched out to the poor and needy . . ."

The eyes of the three met. In two smooth steps Joe and Manderich were beside the preacher's chair. Joe took hold of the preacher's pocket and yanked, tearing the seam so that the white lining showed; instantly the preacher's hand shot down to grab his wrist, the preacher's hot face turned down on him, glaring. Then Manderich reached, and together they yanked so that he had to hop off backward to keep from toppling. His hoarse roar of anger was chopped off short as he leaped, but he was threshing his arms free as soon as his feet hit the ground. Manderich's heavy clutch pinioned one arm, but he broke the other free from Joe's lighter weight, and as he did so Joe grabbed a handful of the man's wet shirt with his left hand. His right dove halfway under his own coat, and held it there on the gun butt, his eyes inches from the preacher's furious face, until the man's eyes chilled and understood and the furious threshing of his arms quieted. With a final cautious half-meant twist he freed himself and stood still. Joe slipped around behind him, next to Manderich, his eyes swooping in one comprehensive glance across the faces near at hand. They looked merely astonished. A couple of the women had begun to edge away. But no trouble, not a peep. Ahead of him the preacher stood, breathing hard, his blue shirt wet and dark. Sweat ran as Joe watched down the pink scalp under the thinning fringe of hair, a crooked drop crookedly running until it came to the roundly shaven neck, and then it skidded and disappeared under the wet collar. Art Manderich, breathing formally through his nose, his face set like the face of a hussar at inspection or an usher in a church, stood with his arms folded.

Up on the chair Fuzzy Llewellyn was shouting in the preacher's place—a sharper, more cutting voice, saw-edged and nasal and penetrating. "We're takin' over this meeting right now! Why are we takin' it over? I'll tell you. Because we all got more important things to meet about than the size of somebody's private pack of sin. We got a lot of grievances in this camp, and a lot of conditions have to be improved. How do you get a drink of water in this stinkhole? You've tried it down at the field. You've hit up the stew-wagon guy. What'd it get you? And how long did you stand in line by one of those backhouses this mornin'? There was a line of twenty-six people waitin' when I came down. Just put your mind for a minute on what you was linin' up for. Waitin' in line to use a thing like that. I don't know how yours was, but mine would've made a hyena throw his lunch. That's what we're takin' over this meeting for. To see if anybody here agrees with us something ought to be done about it."

The preacher's sweat was as strong as a horse's. He looked straight ahead and said nothing, but his breathing hissed and gurgled, and his neck was beet-red, shining wet.

"I want to ask you somep'm else," Fuzzy shouted. He turned his body, shouting for the far edges of the crowd. "I want to ask you is anybody sick around you. Everybody near you healthy?"

He waited. A mutter of sound, a growl, came from here and there in the crowd. Joe was not satisfied with it. It seemed too small, maybe only the noise made by the Kirkhams and their squads. He searched the faces near him, and saw that their attention was split between Fuzzy and himself; they listened to Fuzzy but they watched him and Manderich and the captive preacher. It was hard to tell whether they understood anything or not, whether Fuzzy could touch them at all with a catalogue of their wrongs. To quiet his own fear that they were a bunch of meek cattle, he whispered to Manderich, "Did you say two hundred? We got half the camp."

Manderich grunted unintelligibly. The preacher looked over his shoulder, and Joe seized his arm in warning. Under the man's fat he felt the bone and muscle of power, and in the cold blue eyes that swung on him he saw hatred and watchfulness but no fear. For a moment he let his eyes lock with the pale eyes. The pupils were mere dark pinheads in the glassy, marbled irises, and it was a long time before the eyes would let themselves be beaten down. It would not do to give this preacher any rope.

Listening past Fuzzy's shouting, his ears alert for sounds of trou-

ble in the crowd, he thought once he heard the beginnings of uproar, but Fuzzy let out his voice another notch, and by the time
he took breath the sound was not there. A baby began to squawl.
Again Fuzzy raised his voice, whipping and goading their apathy.

"... unless we do it together! You can see my face, some of you
can anyway. If you're close you can see my back." He yanked
his shirt out and whipped half around to display his back crisscrossed with dark bruises, welted and scabbed from blows. "All
right!" he shouted, whipping around again. "All right, you want
to know how I got it? I'll tell you. Two days ago three other
guys and I got sick of the filth in this camp and we squawked.
We went over to the super and we raised some hell. You know
what happens after that? Just by accident we all have callers that
night. They take us out on the south road and beat hell out of us
and make us run the gauntlet while a dozen of them whale away
at us with barrel staves. Just a great big Hallowe'en party. Then
they point us down the road and invite us not to come back."

He paused, his squirrel teeth exposed by the back-drawn lips.
For a moment it was so quiet Joe heard his breath hiss, and heard
the sound of a motor starting on the other side of the sheds. He
looked for anger in the sheep faces of the crowd and saw none,
only the alert, half-expectant listening look.

"But I come back!" Fuzzy shouted. "By God I doubled around
and I limped back in that same night, and I been here ever since.
You want to know why I came back? I'll tell you. I came back
because I knew if enough of us squawked it wouldn't be possible
to take care of us with barrel staves. Let just a hundred of us out
of this whole mob get together and stand together, and they ain't
goonin' us off the ranch. They ain't doin' nothin' then. They're
listenin', because they'll have to listen."

The last faint lingering suspicion that Joe had had of Fuzzy was
gone now. Fuzzy was going good. He was militant and he had
guts and he could pour it on from up on the box. And no matter
how his eyes and ears searched the crowd, he could catch no
premonition of trouble, no shouldering stir of deputies coming in,
no sound of heckling, no fighting. Nothing but this waiting.

"I want us to sing a little," Fuzzy was shouting. "Anybody that's
going to work together can start by singing together. I want us
to sing a song about a scissorbill that didn't know which side his

bread was buttered on. This is a song by Joe Hill, and it goes to the tune of 'It Looks to Me Like a Big Time Tonight.' I'm going to say over the words and when you get the idea how she goes, we'll sing her all together."

For a second Joe felt a twitch in his solar plexus, a spasm of jealous protest. Joe Hill himself should be up there bringing them on, forming them from a mob into a single weapon of power. But the preacher moved restively and Joe tightened his grip on the fat arm. Fuzzy was the soapboxer, he was the one who could do it best. He listened intently to the words as Fuzzy bellowed them out, halfway between speaking and singing.

> Please give me your attention and I'll introduce to you
> A man that is a credit to the red white and blue.
> His head is made of lumber and solid as a rock,
> He is a common worker and his name is Mr. Block.
> And Block he thinks he may
> Be President some day.

"Any day now," Fuzzy's can-opener voice confided to the crowd, "any day now I'll own this ranch." He stuck out his face. "Anybody got any doubts?"

That brought the first real response, a riffle of laughter that was lost as Fuzzy lifted his arms and started the singing. Joe sang, and old Art, tuneless as a sea lion, growled at his ear, but there was only a scattering of support through the crowd, a thin unconfident singing, a few voices singing loud and trying to sound like many, saying

> Oh, Mr. Block, you were born by mistake,
> You take the cake,
> You make me ache.
> Tie a rock to your block and then jump in the lake,
> Kindly do that for liberty's sake.

Joe thought it would die out altogether, but the few of them carried it to the end of the chorus, and then Fuzzy was shouting out the second verse, about Mr. Block and the job shark, and then waving his hands wide again, inviting the big chorus.

This time it came fuller, louder, wider-spread. Joe could see people near him trying to pick up the words as they sang. He bellowed at the uncompromising red neck of the preacher.

It grew with every verse. Mr. Block tried the great A.F. of L. and got stung; he tried the ballot box and elected a Socialist mayor and got rapped on the block by a big Socialist cop; he grew angry at Spain and joined the army and lost a leg in Cuba and went around afterward on his peg shouting "Remember the Maine! Hurrah, to hell with Spain!"; and at length he died and met St. Pete and expressed a wish: He'd like to meet the Astorbilts and John D. Rockefell.

> Old Peter said, "Is that so?
> You'll meet them down below."
>
> *Oh, Mr. Block, you were born by mistake,*
> *You take the cake,*
> *You make me ache . . .*

They were roaring it out by the end. When the center was finished it heard the delayed but enthusiastic fringes coming on in with the whole last line. It was only after the final trailing off of the song that Joe heard the peremptory voice shouting, and saw Henry Kirkham and another man slide toward the soapbox.

Fuzzy Llewellyn looked out over the heads, his arms still wide in the gesture of leading the singing. For one flicking instant his one good eye dropped to meet Joe's, then Manderich's. His mouth formed a sidelong word. "Law." Joe made a motion to Kirkham to come in closer, to help form a ring around the box.

Now Fuzzy let out his voice again, and the nasal, penetrating half-whine seemed twice as loud and twice as penetrating as before. "They're comin' in here right now!" he shouted. "What are they comin' for? To stop me from talkin'. To run me into the calaboose and stop my mouth, or knock it off. They don't want any meetin's like this, and you know why? Because they work you like horses and pay you starvation wages and don't give a good god damn whether you live or die. Because they want that last bloody nickel you sweat out for them out in the sun. They want that last nickel even if it comes to them red with the blood of your children! And if you squawk, here come the finks and the deputies with pick handles and barrel staves. HERE THEY COME RIGHT NOW!"

The peremptory authoritative voice shouted again. Joe could see the crowd buckling and swirling compactly out in the sun of the

road, and as the swirl came inward Joe saw the red head of Russ
Kirkham coming with it, backing before it. Other men, four or five,
seemed to be doing the same.

"They're comin' in right now!" Fuzzy yelled. "What I want to
know is what you're gonna do about it. Do they shut us up? Do
they bring out their dirty hired law and do we knuckle under?
Do we submit to their god damn gunmen OR DO WE STAND UP TO
THE SONSABITCHES? DO WE CLOSE RANKS AND FIGHT FOR OUR RIGHTS?
I'M ASKIN' YOU, FELLOW WORKERS, AND YOU AIN'T GOT LONG TO
DECIDE!"

Manderich looked at Joe, and they shoved the preacher forward
a step so as to be free. Joe made sure the automatic was loose
in the holster. Manderich's grim smile deepened the creases in his
face; for the first time Joe noticed that his hair was thin, that
in his neck there was the beginning of an old man's dewlap of
sagging skin. Pushing the preacher again, they moved out another
step or two to meet the incoming disturbance of the law. Women
were clearing out; there was a quick, hurried, anxious pressing-
away from the direction of the disturbance as Fuzzy, useless now
and unlistened to, kept shouting from the elevated chair.

The swirl of the in-pressing law was close now. Into the space
the women had left, Kirkham and four others were thrust suddenly,
retreating ahead of a solid group of more than a dozen. The deputies
were sweating, their shirts sticking to them, their nickeled badges
sagging the wet cloth. All had guns buckled around them. With
them was one dressed like themselves but wearing a tie and a
white stetson. Joe guessed him to be the sheriff. And behind the
sheriff was a man in a Panama hat and an alpaca coat, smooth-
faced, pink with heat—boss or lawyer, a different breed, and wearing no gun.

Kirkham's group fell back with Joe and Manderich and the others. A narrow lane formed itself between them and the tightly
grouped law. Back of him Joe felt the continuous stir of people
getting out of the way; what should have been a silence as the
men faced each other was full of a steady, ponderous rumble, a
heavy stir in the air like the sound of wagons crossing a plank
bridge.

The sweating deputies were looking at the sheriff, but they were
nervous and their heads kept turning and their hands stayed

close to the guns on their hips. They braced a little against the curious weight of the crowd.

"Llewellyn!" the sheriff said. "I've got a warrant for you. You're under arrest."

Joe was up on the balls of his feet. He watched the sheriff and the man in the Panama hat, and he heard the rumble of the crowd closing in like silence after the sheriff's words. Behind him Fuzzy Llewellyn screeched in a cracking voice, "WELL, FELLOW WORKERS, HERE THEY ARE! I'M UNDER ARREST, THE SHERIFF SAYS. OKAY, I'LL LET MYSELF GET PINCHED. I'LL GO WITH THIS BUNCH OF GOD DAMNED LAW WITH THEIR SAPS AND SIX SHOOTERS. THAT'S ALL I CAN DO, ALONE. BUT IF YOU'RE WITH ME I CAN DO SOMETHING ELSE. I CAN TELL THIS SHERIFF THERE ARE ALMOST THREE THOUSAND WORKERS HERE THAT WON'T . . ."

It came as both a sound and a thrust of movement, a slow crescendo coming inward from the far edges of the crowd. Joe heard it rising and growing; he saw it take hold on the clustered deputies and saw them brace against it. He saw fear leap into the face of the pink-faced man in the Panama and saw with sharp clarity how the deputies elbowed and hampered each other, half turning to resist the pushing from behind. They shouted; one drew his gun half out.

He had completely forgotten the preacher who stood beside him, and only the flickering impression he caught from the corner of his eye of some danger, some blow, kept him from being taken completely unaware. He ducked, crouching, so that something came over the top of him and bore him down with a mauling weight. But even as he went down he heard the three quick shots and the terrible cresting roar of the crowd.

For a minute he was utterly helpless, tossed under trampling feet, smothered and squashed under struggling bodies. A shoe came down on his hand and he rolled, trying to break free. Blows were landing on him, and he struck back and kicked and rolled again until the feet thinned and he made his feet, throwing the long hair out of his eyes as he came up, his right hand diving for the gun. A bullet went past his cheek so close that he felt the wind of it and heard the soggy *puk* it made as it hit something behind him. But as he turned the crowd picked him up like a chip and carried him along. His feet tangled in the yielding mass of a body so that he almost went down again. The noise of the crowd now was an unbearable tense continuous stream.

He was borne struggling against the trunk of one of the pepper trees, a tree where children had made a ladder out of the stubs of old branches. As the pressure swirled past on both sides he caught one of the stubs and pulled himself up out of the tumult, the gun ready in his hand.

But already the thing was over. He saw fierce-eyed men whirl in the choking dust, fearful of enemies, but there were no enemies, only pickers like themselves. They fell back warily, mistrustful of everyone else, many of them nursing hurts, away from the soapbox where miraculously Fuzzy Llewellyn still stood, and as they fell back and the dust cloud stilled and cleared Joe saw the bodies on the ground, the bloodied, dirtied white shirts patched with adhesive dust, the fallen hats, the darker curving figures of fallen men.

At the first opening below him he jumped and landed running, coming up beside Fuzzy. One of the Kirkhams was there, blood streaming from his nose. Twenty feet away, one across the other, lay the pink-faced man and the sheriff, and near them a picker. Joe could not see his face, but his hand was brown. Still beyond, doubled up with his face against his knees, was a deputy. The rest of the deputies, as well as the preacher, had disappeared. And close up against the backless chair where Fuzzy stood, his dead face trampled and smashed by the fury and panic of the crowd, lay old Manderich.

Kirkham's teeth were chattering. He looked at Joe and shook his head and wiped his streaming nose with the back of his hand.

Up on the chair Fuzzy stood with his hands at his sides, his squirrel teeth bared, looking out almost abstractedly across the road. The short, savage flare of mob anger had lasted only a matter of minutes, the surge inward upon the deputies had been a reaction as sudden and automatic as impulse and blow. Now men were sneaking away, retreating from both instigator and result of their fury. The few who stayed stayed with an awed, scared look on their faces. A hush was over the whole meeting place, the whole camp. Even yet the dust had not settled completely. Joe knelt by Manderich and felt the thick wrist, but he knew before he knelt that Manderich was dead. From the brutally battered face he looked up into Fuzzy's. He felt himself wet as a drenched dog with sweat. "Let's get out of here!" he said.

Fuzzy shook his head. His eyes were glassy. His voice stuck and he cleared it. "No."

"They'll be back with riot squads or the Guard. The crowd won't stand up to them again. Look at them!" He was excited himself. He heard the chattering of Kirkham's teeth and realized that his own hands were shaking.

"I know," Fuzzy said. "They're scared now. But I started this. I'll see it through."

"They'll hang you," Joe said. "They'll hang anybody they can catch."

Fuzzy looked down at the bodies in the white dust. Someone groaned, and Joe saw that the sheriff, under the body of the man in the Panama hat, was stirring and feebly moving his arms and legs. They watched him try to lift his head, and they saw how the weight of the other body bore on him. Finally Kirkham, still chattering, went and rolled the body off the sheriff and backed away again.

"You go, Joe," Fuzzy said. "There's no need of everybody sticking. One's enough. You go on."

Joe looked down again at the dead and trampled face of Art Manderich. His teeth ached clear to the roots of his jaw. The automatic was still in his hand, and he put it away. "You can't fight them in jail," he said.

"No," Fuzzy said. "You'll do more good outside. You go. All of you go. I'll stick here."

The sheriff was stirring again, rolling his head. Dust was in his black hair as if it had been rolled in flour. In a few minutes he might be awake enough to recognize people. Whatever Joe did he had better do it fast.

"You're crazy, Fuzzy. What good can you do letting them hang you?"

"Maybe they won't hang me," Fuzzy said. "We wanted to show up what went on at this ranch, didn't we?" His lips pulled back so that the long front teeth showed clear to the gums in a sick, starveling grin. "Maybe this is as good a way as any."

Joe's head had cleared. He could see now with perfect clearness the course that events would take. If Fuzzy wanted to fight them that way, by being their prisoner, it was his lookout. As for

Joe Hill, he had better ways. Only Manderich and Fuzzy Llewellyn had known who he was; to the others he was only "Swede." If Fuzzy kept his mouth shut, there was no reason for Joe Hill to be involved in this at all.

His eyes strayed again, a last time, to Manderich's bloody face. Somebody would have to get even for old Art. Somebody would have to be free to carry on and redouble the fight.

He reached up and shook Fuzzy's limp hand. "Maybe you won't hear from me directly," he said, "but you'll know I'm working."

There was no time to do more than cross past their camp and pick up his bindle, and then he was one of hundreds on their way. The camp was emptying, people everywhere were in flight. The road was already jammed. It was a fool notion people had that they could get away by the road. The riot squad would be coming in from both sides in a matter of an hour. If there was any chance of getting away, it was over the hills and in toward the old gold country. From there it might be possible, taking it easy and slow, to work on down the coast and out of reach of suspicion. For the moment, at least, he did not worry about Fuzzy, staying back there on the chair to wait for the cops. He had enough to think about, just getting away.

5   Gaviota, August, 1913

I don't see what you expect to gain by it, he said to Fuzzy many times. For a minute they were organized, you had them coming. They were full of the class war and they wanted their rights and they were ready to resist when the deputy went for his gun. But look what happens afterward. They get scared, they back off. They see a couple of their own people and two or three of the law dead in the melee and they wilt. So what is there to be gained by waiting for the law to come back with riot guns? What possible good can it do the movement or anybody else to have you rot in the Sacramento jail and maybe fry in San Quentin?

It was just a grandstand play, he told Fuzzy. You liked the look of yourself waiting there with your arms folded. You felt the way you feel in a free-speech fight when the bulls roll around, but you were wrong. You gain something by getting yourself pinched in a free-speech fight, but you don't gain anything here except to get all the hatred and fear of the bosses poured out on you alone. Maybe you like it that way.

Suppose I'd stuck too, he said to Fuzzy's insistent image. Suppose I'd stood up there with you. I had a gun on me. This preacher saw it, maybe others did too. I had it in my hand when I got down out of that tree. Plenty of people could have seen it on me, and even if they didn't a smart D.A. could make a dozen of them swear they did. So they're all at the trial to testify that I had a gun in my hand during the fight. I haven't even shot it off, but I'm guilty of murdering everybody that's dead there, even old Art. Probably nobody does any shooting but the deputies, they shoot each other in the uproar, but some Wobbly has to burn for it. Well, I can do more good out organizing somewhere else than I can giving Hale the satisfaction of executing me. Art was enough to lose in that fight.

Old Art. It seemed to him that he had liked Manderich better than any man he knew. The image of the smashed face kept rising into his thoughts and stopping them. Nobody would ever know how Art got it, whether from friend or enemy, deputy or picker. He was just smashed in the jam. Perhaps the bullet that had buzzed past Joe's face as he got to his feet. He had heard its wet *puk* as it hit something behind him. Or perhaps the treacherous preacher. From the moment the man jumped him and they went down under the struggling feet Joe had not seen the preacher at all. He could have risen up in the dust with a rock in his hand . . .

Joe picked a pebble from the sand between his feet and threw it angrily. His hands were shaking. If only there had been some triumph in it, if the crowd hadn't quit just when it began to get militant, if it had stayed together and they could all have faced the returning law coolly, with a set of demands and a clear irrefutable statement of how the trouble had started. If it were possible to say that Art died helping three thousand pickers to some of the decencies of life. But you couldn't say that. You couldn't say anything but that he got trampled in the mob, unable even to put up the kind of grim slugging battle he was capable of. A stray bullet, a stray rock, a stray blow, and a good man dead and

nothing gained. It seemed to Joe, sitting on the beach and thinking it over for the hundredth time, that inevitably the fight ended
up in running. He was always running, every strike and brawl and
revolution and mass meeting ended the same way, in a choice
between being a willing sacrifice for no real purpose, and running
like a scared animal when the law moved in.

Who pays for Art Manderich's death? he asked empty air. The
public howls for the blood of the Red agitators who killed the
deputies and the D.A., but who pays for the life of Art Manderich
and the Mexican or Puerto Rican kid who died there too?

He was all alone on the empty curve of beach. He said it again
aloud, like a curse: Who pays for Art Manderich? Who gets hanged
for putting a bullet in the Puerto Rican picker?

It was late afternoon. Through the low mist clinging to the sea
the sun was weak and pale on the water, the sand, the railroad
embankment behind him. Between two horns of rock that jutted
to enclose the beach the sand curved evenly, and the waves were
bent and came in in v-ing angles, trying to conform to the curve
of the shore. Though the tide was coming in, there was no stir
about anything. The surf was small and sad, the noise it made
was only a murmur and a hiss, with none of the boom that big
surf had.

Ahead of the soapy edges of the waves as they ran up the beach
the sand fleas hopped by millions, some of them more than an inch
long. The thin sun shone through their transparent lobster-like bodies. They hopped and fell and hopped again, as automatic as snapping mousetraps, all around him, and he caught one in his hand
and felt the strength of its leg-kick once before it hopped loose and
hit the sand. Almost instantly its powerful legs dug it in and covered it over. When he scraped the top off the loose damp sand he
exposed a half-dozen that hopped and burrowed out of his way.
They were all coming higher up the beach as the tide rose, and
he thought how there were two classes, the masters and the slaves,
and how the difference between them was power and only power,
and how the individual worker was as helpless as a sand flea
swept ahead of the incoming tide, but how together the workers
could organize, resist, defy. Yes, defy? Build a wall, maybe, to keep
out the sea? In a moment of hopelessness it seemed to him that
the working class had about as much chance of bucking the power

arrayed against it as the sand fleas had of making a sea wall with their frail transparent shells.

A wave licked up almost to his feet, wetting and darkening the sand in scallops, driving the frantic fleas before it, burying some so that they threshed and struggled in the wet sand. Standing up to give the tide room, Joe heard the sound of a train coming. As he had done all day when trains came by, he picked up his bindle and moved down the beach a few yards to where the culvert came through. Though he was several hundred miles in space and a week in time from the hop camp where Manderich had died, he was not taking chances. Moreover, the beach was too private and useful a place for jungling up to let every s.p. railroader in on it.

When the sound of the train was close above him he stepped inside the eight-foot cylinder, standing spraddle-legged to keep his feet out of the slimy trickle at the bottom. Inside the culvert the train's noise was instantly muted, almost shut out. It became indistinguishable from the sound of the surf, which inside here sounded louder and hollower. He knew when the train was past only by the passing of the slight tremor in the corrugated steel under his feet. From inside the culvert he looked out as through an enormous round eye. He could see to Japan, and it was lonely all the way.

For a minute he remained standing inside, facing a decision that he should have made long before. There was nothing but a little coffee left in his bindle. That meant getting out and rustling something, or beating his way on down the coast, or looking for a bunkhouse job at one of the ranches. He was not yet ready to go back to San Pedro; some dissatisfaction, some qualm, something unresolved in his mind, kept him from that. And with the dragnets out, probably, for hundreds of miles around because of the hop-camp riot, it would be safer to show himself as a picker looking for a job than as a bo bumming through, and it would be safer to come in as if from the south.

Slinging his bindle, he went through the culvert to the land side. From there the far end was smaller, mistier. It was like looking through a reversed telescope, and the sad noise of the surf beyond was the sound of a country he had left in a childhood dream. A little prickle of gooseflesh touched him again on leaving this sad and lonely and private place.

On the land side, tall eucalyptus trees grew beyond the right-of-way fence. From the edge of the grove he looked across disced ground and the neat sweet-smelling regular trees of a lemon orchard. Beyond that, across the top of the swale through which the trickle of water made its way to the culvert, he saw ranch houses and a red barn, and to the left a string of workers' shanties and a tar-papered building that he took for a bunkhouse. He might as well start here.

He walked a half-mile south along the tree-protected tracks before he plowed down the grade, cut through an orchard, and got onto the dusty stretch of the King's Highway leading from Santa Barbara to Gaviota. Nothing passed him, wagon or horseman or buggy or automobile, until he was almost to the line of palms that curved in along the road to the ranch. Then a car squawked behind him and he turned, hugging the shoulder of the road, to see a red Locomobile boring at him trailing a long funnel of dust. The car rushed by, and its wind and dust swallowed him so that he cursed, standing shut-eyed and shut-mouthed until the air partially cleared. When he could see again he saw the car almost in to the ranch up the side road.

Oh fine, he said. A boss a man can look up to and admire, a man who scorches around kicking dust in people's eyes and probably owns ten thousand acres of tomatoes or lemons or walnuts, and a docile herd of stoop laborers to pick them for him.

Mister, have you got some work for a man, you . . .

He spread his blanket on the bunk the Mexican foreman pointed out, slid onto a bench at mealtime, washed at the plank trough with the others, kept his mouth shut and did his work. There was a day of leaning from a ladder in among the sweet-smelling trees, cutting lemons. There was a day of hauling to the packing sheds in Goleta. There was a day with a pick and shovel grubbing out a sugar palm the boss's wife wanted removed to open her view of the far eucalyptus grove along the railroad, and the sea beyond.

No job had ever used him up as cutting out that tree did. For one thing, he worked under the eye of the boss and the boss's wife, who came out and cut roses while he hacked away at the rocklike adobe. He was all morning digging a trench around the tree so as to get at the roots, and in the hot afternoon, waist-deep

in the trench, he swung till his arms ached and went numb, swinging the axe at the thousands upon thousands of ropelike roots that
wilted before his blows but seldom would cut cleanly. And always,
when he had cut away a hundred, there were hundreds more.
He had to deepen the trench to get under them, and still the tree
stood, balancing upon more hundreds of intertwined roots he had
not yet cut. Two or three times he looked up out of the hole, his
arms dead, his shirt soaked with sweat, and saw the boss with a
cigar in his mouth watching. The boss was a ruddy-faced man
with a crisscross of tiny broken veins in each cheek, and he smiled
and took the cigar from his mouth and all clean, cool, unsweated,
made comments on how tough a thing a sugar palm was to root
out. Joe wiped his face and leaned on his shovel and took a considerable, deliberate rest under the boss's eyes.

McHugh watched him for another half-hour, interested as city
people are interested in construction jobs, and watch the drillers
and the hod carriers with an endless curiosity and patience. He
appraised objectively the strength of every blow Joe swung with
the double-bitted axe; he estimated the difficulties of new roots
that came in sight, and his eyes followed Joe's as Joe got down to
shovel away underneath and get a clear look. He smoked his cigar
and the fragrance blew over Joe as he sweated in the hole. Eventually, late in the afternoon, McHugh said suddenly, "Why don't I
get Pablo over here with a team and see if we can't pull that
sucker over?"

Joe straightened without answering, and watched McHugh walk
away. The boss affected shirts of fine French flannel: every time
Joe had seen him in three days he looked as if he had just put
on a fresh shirt. His collars were high and immaculate, his cuffs
bound with heavy gold links. He wore a belt, not suspenders, and
his pants were snug across his well-padded rump. Joe spit in the
hole, hating him.

He would quit tonight. His three days' work would give him
stake enough to make Pedro. And from sleeping on the beach
he had learned that every night about ten-thirty a southbound
passenger train waited five or ten minutes at a siding a half-mile
north of the culvert to let a northbound express go by. This far
out of town, there would be no dicks. He could ride the blinds
into Santa Barbara and hitch onto something else there, be in

Pedro tomorrow, hearing the news from Sacramento, getting busy around the hall: defense committee, fund-raising, enlisting sympathy and help for Fuzzy and anybody else the law might have collared. Tonight was Saturday, payday. After supper he would roll his bindle and be on his way.

As he thought about it, curiosity began to burn him. Up to now, running and keeping low, he had not even let himself learn much of what had happened up north, as if his own ignorance of what they had done to Fuzzy and the others were a kind of protection. But he wanted now with a great impatience to know where and how they had buried old Art, whether the Sacramento local had held any protest meetings, whether they might even have got up a parade for Art and the Puerto Rican, given them a big public funeral. Or had they carted old Art off to the boneyard without a mourner or a song?

He should have stayed. At least he could have . . . what? Or should have beat it right on back to Pedro and got the boys working.

Pablo, the foreman, came with a team from the big red barn, walking behind the dragging doubletree that clanked and sawed in the dust. Joe climbed out of the hole and threw the axe aside. Together they squinted, estimating the height of the tree and the length of chain they would have to use to keep the team clear of the top when it fell. Joe put his hand against the pineapple-like stubs of old fronds and pushed. The trunk seemed as solid as granite. The foreman grinned at him and shook his head, but he hooked a log chain around the trunk ten feet above the ground and drew his team off and hitched on. The boss's wife came out on the porch to watch, and two Mexican maids pulled the kitchen curtains aside. Pablo chirped to his horses.

The chain tightened and quivered, the team paused, then dug in again, snapping the chain tight as a fence wire. The palm shuddered. From the hole came a tearing and popping of little roots. Pablo shouted at his team, looking back over his shoulder. The tree shuddered more strongly, tilted suddenly a foot or two, strained with a dry clashing of its big fronds, and then slowly and reluctantly, its braided roots giving one by one and two by two, it came over. Even when it was almost flat its roots did not let go completely, but hung like rubber. Joe had to get down into the hole and swing the axe on them for another ten minutes, and when the last one snapped the heavy butt kicked back in the hole and almost caught him. He climbed out shaking with a blind, pointless fury, and when he saw McHugh pull out of the yard in the red Locomobile and head out toward Santa Barbara he contrasted the aching of his own muscles, the dead-tiredness of his back, the near-accident that might have squashed him like a bug down in the hole, with the red and brass of the automobile, the clean shirt, the cigar, the careless security of McHugh, and he felt that McHugh personally owed him something, some satisfaction he could not name. The Boss. The sonofabitching Boss.

"Aha," Pablo was saying, backing his team to loosen the chain. "Tomorrow we get this *cabron* sawed up and haul it away."

"Not me," Joe said. "I'm quitting tonight."

The foreman looked at him. "You can stay. I got no complaints."

"I have to be on my way," Joe said.

Pablo shrugged and drove back to the barn, the doubletree jingling and thumping and the chain a long curving snake behind him in the dust.

Joe put the shovel, axe, and pick away in the tool house and walked on down to the workers' shanties. He could not get out of his mind the curiosity about Art's burial. He should have stayed. If he could have done nothing else he could have seen that they didn't just throw the old man in a hole.

He wondered too about San Pedro. Would any of the boys there think he had run to save his hide? Anyone who chose to think so would very soon get straightened out. A fantasy grew in his mind. Somebody accused him of running. He said nothing, so that the man (some loud-mouthed dehorn, some hanger-on) gained confidence and shot off his mouth still louder, until suddenly he found Joe Hill's face an inch from his own, his eyes being devoured by the cold fury of Joe Hill's eyes. "Yes?" Joe Hill said softly. "Yes, you were saying . . . ?" The man never knew where the blow came from. It spun him around, his nose and lips smashed to a pulp . . .

The crew was not yet in. Stripped to the waist, Joe washed in the plank trough that smelled of old soap and wet redwood. He took his time letting the cool water run over hands and wrists and arms, splashing it over face and chest, bending to let the tap run on the back of his neck and over his hair. He was almost through when the crew came in; the late tired afternoon was full of their laughter. Saturday afternoon. Payday. A week ago he and Art had been walking through the hop camp, getting the lay of the land. He recalled that he had been angry at the pickers for the way they could laugh and pick a guitar even in a stinkhole like that one. That was it, that was always it—the way people could stand anything and take a little fun out of their slavery. Until dinner he went in and lay out on the bunk, not thinking of anything, just letting pictures flow through his mind, drift on a current of slow unfocused anger. The tin roof popped once or twice, contracting after the day's heat.

Immediately after supper he packed his bindle, but it was still more than two hours until he could pick up the train. In the cool of evening, brushed by the soft wind that came down from the hills toward the sea, he sat alone in the bunkhouse door with his pay in his pocket. Four days, four dollars. Not enough to pay for one of McHugh's shirts. Nevertheless McHugh thought of himself as generous to his help. Four dollars in his pocket, a loner by temperament and a rebel by dedication, a man on his way from something and to something, Joe sat in the evening's coolness in the fragrance of unknown flowers blooming along the bunkhouse wall, and as he sat there Gonzales, a big-mustached Mexican, one of the foreman's many cousins, came out of the bunkhouse carrying a violin case. He sighed very loud, a long relaxing sound, as he settled back against the wall, and opening the case he took out a violin wrapped in a red silk handkerchief.

Very carefully he turned it in his brown gnarly hands, holding it to the light to see its shine, shifting it to see the changing image of his face. He rubbed the edge against his nose the way a pipe smoker will rub the warm bowl of a pipe on his skin to brighten it.

"You play it?" Joe said.

Gonzales was a man of great dignity. He smiled as if conferring a favor, and said, "It is a present for my son, who studies with the brothers in Santa Barbara. Next week he has his eighteenth birthday."

"Let's see it a minute," Joe said. After a moment's hesitation Gonzales laid the violin in his reaching hand. It was new and shiny with varnish. He picked the strings and got flat untuneful sounds.

"Give us the bow."

Gonzales got it out of its little catch in the lid of the case.

There was a cake of resin in the green plush box. Somebody had sold him the works. Joe resined the bow and tuned the violin, looking at Gonzales over it as he fiddled with the keys and sawed in short strokes hunting the pure tone. Finally he drew the bow over all the strings, and they sang. Out of the corner of his eye he saw a young Mexican walking with his girl under the eucalyptus trees; the two stopped, ready to listen.

"Let us hear you play," Gonzales said.

"I can't play very well."

"We shall judge," Gonzales said, and lifted his shoulders and smiled.

Joe shifted his feet and body to give himself room. He felt the gun under his arm as he lifted the violin and settled his jaw over it. Out under the trees, a hundred feet away, the young Mexican said something in soft Spanish to his girl, and the sound of his voice in the cooling evening, the sight of Gonzales' brown hands, stopped Joe with a moment's sharp recollection of the brown hand of the picker in the dust, the dead sprawled across each other. Like a reflection one sees looking out from a lighted room just at dusk, when the near-dark outside is obscured and shadowed by the light within, he saw the faces—the dead deputy stooping over his knees, the sheriff with his black hair whitened by dust, the battered face of old Manderich.

Namelessly dead, unmarked and forgotten, carted off to the boneyard and dumped in a hole. Nameless and unregretted as a bug squashed, millions like them that he had never known, all of them nameless and forgotten, a checked seething in the earth. Joe Hillstrom too, Joe Hill, Swede, due to be knocked off sometime in some strike or riot and never missed. He hung with the violin against his collarbone and it seemed to him that nothing was worth the anguish and anger a man put into it. You were born on the flypaper, and for a while you buzzed and made a big noise, and in the end you settled down like the rest, sodden and wing-stuck and slimed with the glue.

The young Mexican and his girl laughed softly, standing expectant under the fabric of the great trees.

He searched his mind for something to play, something Spanish for Gonzales' sake, something sad for the sake of the defeat that was upon the whole vast army of the slaves, something passively melancholy for the sake of the plaintive wind sighing down from the cooling hills.

"La Golondrina." He let it come with a sick feeling that he might cry, and he hated the clumsy stiffness of his hands, lame from axe and shovel handle. He played it and then he played it again, hearing it as a thin little sound of melody in the dusk, a thing that bent like smoke and drifted down toward the empty beaches.

The young Mexican and his girl clapped and laughed and walked on. The hanging leaves of the eucalyptus trees clashed softly. Over at the cookshack a screen door squeaked and a panful of water hit the ground with a sound like a slap. It was getting almost too dark to see Gonzales' face, but when he spoke it was plain from the polite inflection of his voice that he was disappointed.

"That was very good. Have you taken lessons?"

"No," Joe said. "I just picked it up."

"It was very good," Gonzales said. "I intend that my son shall take lessons."

"I haven't touched a violin for two or three years," Joe said. "You get all out of practice." Instantly he was annoyed at himself for apologizing to a fat-headed Mexican who valued a violin by the shine of its varnish. The song had moved him more than he wanted to be moved; he had heard it frail and thin and sad as waves on a lonesome shore. He needed to strike out at something to restore himself, but there was nothing to strike at, only Gonzales going on foolishly in the dark.

"Many can play the guitar, but few the violin. The violin is a finer instrument. More soul."

"Yes," Joe said. "More soul." He stood up and handed the violin back, went in for his bindle, and came out to stand again in the doorway. Down at the shacks where several married hands lived there were already sounds of a party starting, though McHugh would not be around with the payroll until later. Joe had heard the men say that he always paid late on Saturday night, so late that a man could not get in to Santa Barbara, and must go instead on Sunday, when it became a thing to be confessed to the priest. No stars were visible anywhere in the whole sky. A creeping layer of cloud had come over, and it was already coalbin-dark. He would have to grope his way down to the siding like a blind man.

"Well, *adios*," he said to Gonzales.

"Leaving?" the old man said in surprise.

When Joe did not reply, Gonzales said, "The road will be very dark."

Joe had his bindle across his shoulder. Caution admonished him, and he said, "I was supposed to meet my brother in San Luis two days ago."

"It's no pleasure walking this late," Gonzales said. "Maybe you can catch a ride with someone hauling."

"I've got a blanket," Joe said.

He attended the sound of his own soft footsteps in the dust, listening as if they were the footsteps of another, and he were Gonzales sitting against the wall hearing Joe Hill depart. There was a long lane of eucalyptus, close to a quarter of a mile, before the road swung to meet the driveway from the big house and the two fused to go out together to the King's Highway.

At the Y of the roads, on his way toward circling back the way he had come in, Joe paused. It was almost impenetrably dark, with only the shine of the big house lights through the trees and shrubs that enclosed it, and an assassin's desire seized him. He wanted to look in on them, watch them moving about unaware, sit in some safe covert and feed his hatred with their casual unguarded lives.

The clashing of palm fronds on the circular drive was loud, and he looked up, realizing that the wind had switched and was coming straight down the coast. In the dark and the noise of threshing branches it would be easy to go unseen and unheard. His ears sharp, he left the drive and slipped around to the back of the house, wondering if in his four days on the ranch he could have missed a dog at the big house. But he heard nothing, only the sigh and rasp and dry clash of wind in the trees.

From beyond the hedge he looked in avidly and saw a Mexican girl working in the kitchen, but he saw no one else, so he drifted on around the angle of the hedge, hugging the dense shadows of the palms. All along the side of the house the blinds were drawn, but far back, on the back wing, a light fell over the white blooms of an oleander bush and reached in slices and streaks almost to the hedge where Joe stooped and peered.

What he saw stiffened him to iron attention. Things that had been suspended, even unsuspected, in his mind came down like an earthslide in the rains. With hardly a second's hesitation, with hardly a thought, he put his hands on the pickets embedded in the hedge and vaulted over. Creeping among bushes, he came up in the midst of another oleander, his body screened by leaves. Through the blur of the mosquito bar on the window he saw the Coleman lamp's white glare across the desk where McHugh sat doing something. Behind McHugh the office door was half open, and to the left, almost obscured by McHugh's body so that Joe had to bend and peer to make sure, the terraced door of the office safe stood ajar.

He made three swift moves in preparation, as swift and sure as if they had been planned. He carried his bindle to the corner of the wing where he could find it instantly in the dark, he flipped the bandanna out of his pocket and tied it across his face, and he pulled the automatic, its metal warmer than his hand, from the shoulder holster.

His movements were so noiseless that he found himself standing in the short hall leading to the office and looking at McHugh's unsuspecting back. The outside door he eased shut behind him. One step, then another, then another brought him almost to the inner door, but he held back against the wall because he did not want to expose himself to the window. Like a child in a game he found himself counting, one, two, three, and then he scraped his foot on the floor.

McHugh jerked around. For one flickering instant he looked straight into the gun before his eyes met Joe's. He did not move; only his florid face changed, mottling and hardening slowly like cooling glass.

"Pull the blind," Joe said.

The rancher's eyes did not leave Joe's as he reached and groped and pulled the shade. It took only the twitch of the muzzle to make him go back and pull it clear down, closing the two-inch slit he had tried to leave the first time. Still standing in the half shadow of the hall, Joe said, with a motion at the safe, "Unload it on the desk."

Never turning even sideward to the gun, McHugh stooped and brought up papers with rubber bands around them, three wooden drawers, a metal strong box. This he opened at Joe's gesture. Inside was a canvas sack.

"Turn around and face the wall," Joe said.

He stepped inside and opened the sack. Mostly silver, a small package of bills. He took only the bills. Patting the rancher's rump, he felt the wallet and pulled it out. There were some bills in it too, which he wadded into his pocket with the others, throwing the gutted wallet on the desk. For a moment he stood thinking.

The ticking of the alarm clock on top of the safe filled the whole room; he saw that the hands pointed to five minutes past ten. In twenty minutes or so the passenger would pull off on the siding. It would be touch and go: he had been a fool to leap into this without thinking ahead. He saw too that the color had come back to McHugh's face and neck. Standing with his back to Joe, his forehead against the wall, his hands half raised, he did not look frightened any more. There was a tension about his body that said he might try to make a fight. His neck was thick, his hair had thinned over a double crown, he was a boss and he drove a red Locomobile in to Santa Barbara, stirring up a mile of white dust on the King's Highway, and he housed his married pickers in a string of derailed boxcars and the unmarried ones in a buggy bunkhouse. He took pride in the fact that he had put in a water faucet and a plank trough for washing.

He was a boss like Hale, an owner of human farm animals. His vest hung open, and from behind Joe saw how the heavy watch sagged the right lower pocket. Standing very still, he saw McHugh begin to fidget and sweat, he saw the fear come back, and he prolonged the moment now when the tables were turned and the boss was just a little man up against a power he couldn't buck. This was a situation he remembered; he seemed to have lived it a hundred times, and the sharpest thing he remembered was the fat watch, the heavy sagging chain.

Deliberately and without heat he swung the clubbed gun and brought it down on McHugh's thinning hair. The blow made a dull meaty sound, like a pick in soft dirt, and as McHugh pitched sideways Joe caught him and eased him to the floor. With a swift stretch he reached the Coleman lamp and turned the valve. For the moment before the light began to fade he stood waiting above the rancher's body. The gold watch, he saw, had slid out of his pocket as McHugh fell, and lay face up on the floor, a Swiss watch, thick and heavy, that told the second, the minute, the hour, the day and month and year. Fat and rich, a prize worth a hundred dollars, it lay at Joe's feet.

As the lamp flared, dimmed, flared again yellowly, and dimmed to the reddening outline of the mantle, Joe set his heel on the face of the watch and ground down with all his weight on splintering crystal and metal. The instant the light flapped out he was through the outside door, reconnoitering, gathering up his bindle at the corner, and running.

His circling cautious run took him around the barns and along the edge of the orchard, and as he ran he hated the necessity for running, and knew that he had made a bonehead play. Even though McHugh had seen only his arm and his masked face, they would naturally pin the holdup on him. His description would be out; every bull on the coast would have his number.

Then as he turned with the gully, feeling his way from tree to tree, he heard the train, and saw the glow, moving slowly, as the passenger loafed into the switch. Any minute now the express would show from the south. There wasn't much time. And if he didn't make this and get out right away, McHugh would wake up, the bloodhounds would be out for fair. He was sweating lightly as he got through the eucalyptus grove, felt and climbed the right-of-way fence, and made his way down to where the culvert bored through the cliff of the high grade. Getting his breath, he stood listening to the big puff and whistle and dry sighing of the wind in the branches, and under it the boom and swash of the surf. On an impulse he stepped into the mouth of the culvert and peered through.

The darkness was so deep it could almost be felt. At its far end, apparently miles away, was a misty paleness, perhaps only an illusion, a widening of his pupils, a strain on his eyes. The noise of the surf was surprisingly loud—the toppling, running thunder, the boom, the long hiss, the boom again. He imagined the sand fleas hopping before the lick of water, dizzying the sand in the dark.

Now the thing that he felt was fear—fear and an overpowering thirst. As he stepped backward out of the culvert he went in over his ankles in muck, and the thought of footprints, giveaway tracks, flashed in his mind, so that he stooped and flapped the slime and mud with his hand, smoothing it out. Up the gully, where he had got his water while jungling-up on the beach, he lay down and dipped quick handfuls. The water tasted of ooze; the cress that grew in it was leggy and clinging on his hand and wrist.

Slipping in the loose gravel, clawing with hands and feet, he climbed the grade, thinking again with a kind of helpless anguish of incriminating tracks. He was panting when he made the top. A pulse in the air, a half-felt vibration, made him kneel and put his hand on the rail. It vibrated faintly under his palm. Gone as fast as it came, a faint glow swept over and past him, and he saw the far headlight coming.

He began to run, his stomach tight with anxiety. The siding was a good half-mile. He could see, as soon as he turned the gentle curve, how the headlight of the standing locomotive was diffused and broken beyond the trees. Already light was growing on the track behind him. Sprinting awkwardly under the bindle, holding the straight grade as long as he dared, he finally felt the light so close and revealing upon him that he leaped down the bank, where he scrambled on through high weeds and stubbly burned patches. Light grew, the tunnel between the eucalyptus trees grew in definition, a steep-walled passage lined by the geometrical rails. Not daring to duck or hide because it would lose him too much time, Joe stumbled ahead while the express came on behind him like a nightmare, like retribution, light growing, sound growing, a thunder and glare rushing up and then a hot blast and the red wink of the firebox and the furious pound of the drivers and darkness again, with the steady drumming clatter of the dark Pullmans pouring by.

He had jumped to the left because the siding lay on that side. Now he saw the headlight of the waiting passenger begin to grope and swing along the tall white-trunked trees as it came back onto the main line. The noise of the express was already small, almost gone.

Joe hit the ditch, lying flat while the weeds became black silhouettes before his eyes and the glare felt over him and went on. He was going to be lucky. The train would still be crawling when it passed him. He heard its slow, warning, heavy chuffs with a wonderful, panting exhilaration, and when the locomotive shoved past and the light was gone he stood up almost casually, waited for the tender to move by, and swung up into the blinds with ridiculous ease. With his back against the door he felt the motion of the train jiggle through him; the taste of coal smoke was bitter in his mouth. But he felt safe, and he knew he was going to be continuously lucky. By the time pursuit could be organized he would have ditched the train and got out on the road across San Marcos Pass. He could catch a stage if he wanted to, go inland and come way around. There were plenty of ways to change your looks; with money and half a chance, he could make himself look like a clerk or a theological student in a half-hour, as far from the description of the holdup man as McHugh was himself.

The thought of McHugh standing before the gun with his skin mottling sickly was a pleasant image, and he thought, There are ways and ways. If the slaves won't organize and fight for their rights, if they fold up just when they should hang together, then there will have to be other ways. The trouble with the soft-pedal wing of the union was that they never carried their logic to its conclusion. They believed in the class war, they swore by the Preamble, but they didn't admit it was really war. Strikes were okay, free-speech fights were okay, sabotage was fair in a really bitter fight like some of the fights up in the lumber woods, but they tried to stop there, halfway.

He would have liked to talk, and the man he wanted most to talk to was Manderich. Art had been all through it, he had been a rebel for thirty years and fought the Austrian cops and lain in Austrian and German and English jails. He spoke with the voice of authority and experience. Joe could hear him:

– Right and wrong haff notting to do vit us, and neffer did haff.

– But you were ready to slaughter Otto for pinching a few rugs from the S.P.

– Dot iss different. Dot sonofapitch vas stealing for himself, he vas using the union for a hiding place.

–Well, what about tonight? What do you make of what I just did?

But he couldn't get an answer out of old Art. All he got was another of the old man's maxims: It iss alvays our strike.

He sat alert, but his mind wandered erratically and somewhat warily among images and ideas and formulas. It iss alvays our strike. Right and wrong haff notting to do vit us. I vill show you the difference between a revolutionary and a gott damned t'ief.

Once more Manderich's bloody trampled face rose up in his mind, and the wariness with which he was poking among his thoughts was obliterated in a rush of anger. Who pays for old Art? Who pays for the Puerto Rican kid?

But one thing he kept returning to, one picture had the power to fill him with voluptuous satisfaction, one thing he knew for sure old Art would have approved: the splinter and crunch of expensive glass and gold as he ground McHugh's watch under his shoe.

For the first time he began to wonder how much money he had.

6   San Pedro, August, 1913

The Sunday morning class in reading and writing for illiterate members is over, the folding chairs are back on the dusty stack against the wall of the outer room. Most of the home guards, at least the married ones, have gone home for Sunday dinner, but in the inner room, which during big meetings is thrown together with the outer one, a half-dozen bindles are piled neatly under the windows, and from the stove rises a meaty, fragrant steam mingled with the syrupy sweetness of stewing prunes.

Eight or ten men, home guards and go-abouts, are sitting around waiting for the biscuits and mulligan to be done. There does not happen just now to be a spittoon philosopher among them; there is no talk of Lawrence and Patterson, the Black International, the Haymarket martyrs, the organizational strategy of Haywood and St. John and Barnabas, the perfidy of the A.F.L., the inevitability of industrial unionism. The talk is relaxed, unpolemical; they are more interested in biscuits and mulligan.

The cook is warm over the stove, his bare arms are tattooed to the shoulder, the cigarette between his lips is dead. He moves about the stove squinting and with puckered lips, slipping his hand in his pocket and using the pocket for a potholder, swinging his hip around sideways and standing on tiptoe to move things on or off the hot part of the fire. He is like a man unlocking a high door with a key chained to his belt.

– That's a hell of a goddam way to take hold of anything. Why don't you get a dishrag?

– Peace on you, fellow worker.

– Piss on you too, Judge.

– When are them biscuits gonna be done?

– Don't get your ass in an uproar.

He tips the lid of the stew kettle, stirs the bubbling stew, moves about the stove with jerky movements, stabbing his hand in his pocket, poising tiptoe over the stove to shove the coffeepot against the stovepipe where it is hottest. He opens the oven door and looks in upon the biscuits, and another fragrance is let out into the room. Though it is August, it is like fall, pleasant to be inside, with smells of good cooking. Outside a gray, foggy day.

– Hey, Doyle, let's see your tattoos.

The cook holds a match against the stovelid until it explodes, lights the broken cigarette in his mouth, lets his dangling arm be passed around like something amputated. He is indifferent but obliging, and he never takes the cigarette from between his lips and never seems to puff at it, so that he has to keep his head thrown back and his eyes squinted against the smoke. They pass him on down the line.

– Every tattoo a blind drunk. What a dehorn.

– Did anybody ever get tattooed when he was sober?

– Who's Bernice?

– Beatrice, you dumb bastard. Can't you read?

– Well, who is she?

– Girl I knew in Sydney.

– What'd she ever do for you?

– She stuck by him, that's a cinch. Good old Bernice.

– Beatrice, you ignorant patoot.

–That's one thing I could never figure out about guys that get tattooed. You can never get rid of the damn things. Guy gets himself all done up like wallpaper and he has to wear the same pictures all his life.

–Somebody told me once if you got yourself needled all over again with milk, right in the same dots, it'd . . .

–That's a lot of crap. you can't get it off.

–It is ineradicable. (This is a Frenchman, a kind of nutty intellectual, who keeps books for some company and lives in a furnished room and comes down on Sundays to give reading lessons at the hall. An eager, wet-lipped, bright-eyed little man.) Let me tell you a story about that. When I was younger I lived in Algiers . . .

–Well, Algiers, I guess yes. That's where you see the tattooing. Fella told me once he seen a French soldier that had a whole general's uniform done on him, clear up to his ears.

–Exactly, but let me tell you. In Algiers there was a famous prostitute—not a prostitute, really, a courtesan . . .

–What's that, a higher-priced name for the same thing?

–I never saw that the price made much difference, myself.

–A courtesan. And right between her breasts, right here, she had a motto tattooed, *pour la vie,* and under it the name of her lover. *Pour la vie,* for life.

(The cook goes back to the stove. For a moment he stands wiggling his fingers, staring at the flag on his forearm that waves with the movement of the tendons and muscles, and then he opens the oven door and looks in at the biscuits. The little Frenchman's voice hurries as if he is afraid it will be cut off.)

–Life, that is a long time for a courtesan—for anybody. Soon this lover is out of favor, he is unfaithful, she tires of him, something. He is out. But his name is indelible, here. (He clicks his tongue and snaps his fingers, stiffening to a kind of seated attention.) *Alors.* She is furious at herself. This name is an embarrassment in her business. Men see it and ask questions. It is worse than a last-year's election poster with a picture of someone who was not elected. What does she do? She takes a cigarette, lights it, crushes it out, here, on the name of her lover. Thus she erases him, *pouf.* He is a scar, nothing more.

–That's what I'm telling you, it's too hard to get rid of. This cigarette method ain't practical, except maybe for high-priced whores.

– Harder to get rid of than bedbugs. Everybody that gets needled wishes he hadn't, sometime or other. Ain't that so, Doyle? Ain't that why you all swear you was stiff as a plank when you done it?

– But wait, wait! There is more. Now this courtesan has a second lover's name tattooed below the scar of the first, under the same motto, *pour la vie*. Alas, in two months he is out with the first one, and again she has this embarrassing label on her bosom. Again she takes a cigarette, again she wipes him out.

– Fatima, the human ashtray.

– Wait, I am not finished! (The little Frenchman throws out his hands in an overboard gesture and cackles invitingly, looking around with bright eyes, his mouth hanging a little open.) She is a woman of mettle, this courtesan, and of an amazing optimism. When I live in Algiers she is famous, for on her bosom is still this motto, *pour la vie*, and under it like crossed-off items on a grocery list are thirty-two names.

– What number were you?

– Jesus. just like an apartment entrance with a row of mailboxes.

– Was she tattooed anywhere else?

– Where'd you learn all this story, respectable old bookkeeper like you?

– He got it out of the Algiers papers.

– It ain't practical. Would you put out a cigarette on Bernice, Doyle?

– The name is Beatrice. And I'd put out more'n a cigarette on her.

– I still think it's a foolish thing to do. It don't give you any chance to change your mind.

– How about having a union button tattooed on you? I heard of a guy in Spokane that had "One Big Union" in red across his chest.

– Gives you away to the town clowns too easy. These days, you'd spend your life working off vag raps on the bullgang.

– Even politically, it is sometimes a mistake. (It is the little Frenchman again.) Remember Bernadotte, Napoleon's general, who had "Death to All Kings" tattooed on his arm? When he becomes

King of Sweden later, this must be as embarrassing to him as the
courtesan's names.

–What do you mean by that? (Now there is a slight, puzzled
pause. The talk suspends itself while the little Frenchman squirms
for having suggested that faith in the One Big Union may be as
impermanent as a general's convictions or a whore's affections. By
a kind of subsidence they let him off, and someone picks up the
thread of talk again.)

–Well, I wouldn't have a button tattooed on me. I'll wear one,
any old time or place, town clowns or no town clowns, but no
tattoo. It disfigures a man. There ain't anything beautiful about
an anchor on a guy's arm, or a bleeding heart with a dame's name
under it. You think you're beautiful, with all that crap inked into
your hide, Doyle?

–The ladies like me.

–It's just a way for punks to brag they been to Singapore
or somewheres.

–Singapore, shit. Some skid road, you man. You can get tattooed ten places in this town.

–But they'll always tell you they got it in Burma.

–Yeah, and you can get a hell of a lot more'n pretty pictures,
too. My old man told me once about a guy name of Kelly, went
through the country tattooing dancing girls on guys. He was pretty
good, my old man said. He could make a man look like a walking
art gallery. But this Kelly bastard has syph, see? His mouth is
full of sores. And every time he dots some color into a sucker,
he wets the needle or the color with his tongue. My old man says
they finally caught up with him after he'd give about two hundred
guys a dose of Old Joe. That's the kind of crap this tattooing can
get you into.

–How about it, Doyle, you got syph?

–He walks kind of funny, ever notice it?

–I seen him pickin' a scab the other mornin'.

–Peace on you, fellow workers.

–DOYLE, WHEN THE HELL IS GRUB?

–Don't get your ass in an uproar.

–Maybe one little motto or picture or some'm, that's all right,
but my God the stuff some guys get themselves done up with! It's
a bunch of whorehouse crap. You ever see a guy had had the

snake job done on him? I knew a kind of fruity bird back in Chicago that used to travel with a sideshow, only by God if he showed all he had to show it was some sideshow. He had snakes all over him, around his arms and legs, around his neck, two great big goddam snakes on his chest with his tits for eyes, and the way his hair grew it looked like they both had a big bushy head of hair like a Fuzzy-wuzzy. Scare the hell out of you. And down in his belly button he had a little tiny blue snake all coiled up like it was crawlin' out, and on his ass two big red ones that was all ready to start *in*. But that ain't all he had . . .

– Don't tell it, I can't bear it.

– How did *you* find this out? Peekin' again.

– Right around his tallywhacker, by God, coiled round and round and lookin' out big as life. You could damn near see it squirm.

– I sh'd think that'd kind of fix his wagon. He'd scare off any woman in ten miles.

– Some women I bet'd go for a thing like that, damn if I don't think so.

– You better go get yourself prettied up.

– I get along all right the way I am. I don't need any needles down there. Holy Christ.

– A lot of guys have spurs tattooed on their peckers.

– A lot of guys? What the hell you talkin' about?

– This is a fine uplifting conversation.

– Yes, a lot of guys. I've seen two-three myself. Great big boot with a spur on it.

– What's the significance of that kind of a thing?

– Shows he's a rough rider, maybe. I don't know. *I* ain't got any spurs. I'm just tellin' you about interesting sights I've seen.

– I can imagine.

– There was another famous piece of tattooing in Algiers . . .

– Here we go again.

– The filthy French.

– Another high-priced piece, or was this one cheaper?

– This was a man, a zouave, a soldier of the Foreign Legion, which your probably know is full of rough specimens. This man, so I heard . . .

– So you heard.

—was killed in a fight, and the undertaker who embalmed him told at his club about the tattooing, so that it was spread around. He said that on this man's buttocks, one on each side . . .

—*That's* normal, anyway.

—on each side was a soldier with his bayoneted rifle held out so that the bayonets crossed in the middle, as at a gate, and up above he had a sign, like a road sign, saying *on n'entre pas*.

—Onnontray pa?

—No one enters.

—Jesus, the filthy French.

—Shows you what kind of people get tattooed, eh Doyle?

(Doyle does a realistic imitation of spitting in the stew. He looks apologetic and puts the lid back on with his crabwise pocket hold.) God damn sores in my mouth keep me spittin' all the time.

—I don't see anything wrong with havin' a union button tattooed on you, though. It ain't the same as havin' some dame that you forgot before you even sobered up. I've heard of outfits back in India or somewhere that had secret tattoo marks they could recognize each other by. That wouldn't be such a bad idea, with so many god damn stoolies and spies . . .

(What has briefly formed is beginning to disintegrate again. Restlessness for food breaks up the group. One goes to the window, another picks up a copy of the *Industrial Worker*. Two or three, reluctant to leave a good topic, carry it on.)

—You ever hear that "French Tattooed Lady" song?

—I don't know. How's it go?

—Hasn't got much of a tune. Let's see—(he begins to sing)

> I paid five bob to see
> The French tattooed lady.
> She was tattooed from head to knee,
> She was a sight to see.
> All up and down her spine
> The king's guard stood in line,
> And all around her hips
> Was a row of battleships,
> And just above her kidney
> Was a bird's-eye view of Sydney,
> But on her chest was what I like best

– GOD DAMN, DOYLE, WHEN ARE THEM BISCUITS GONNA BE DONE?

—was my home in Tennessee . . .

– Come and get it then, you damn wolves.

They have all but finished, and pipes are going. Somebody has suggested that somebody else go out for a Sunday paper. Then the outside door opens, and those in the inner room lean a little to see who has come in. Two or three stand up.

– Joe! How the hell are you?

– Just in time for grub. Grab a plate.

He stands before them, shaking their hands formally around; taller than most of them, slim as an adolescent, his hair a little lank, his smile diffident. His eyes are wide, gray-blue, and have a kind of stare in them, as if he is always looking beyond you. But when they level into yours there is a shock in them like ice water. Strange eyes. If it weren't for them he would look like any other stiff.

Without doing anything, without more than a bare word of greeting as he shakes hands, he has taken over the room. The moment you see his face and eyes clearly, and feel the leashed intensity, the indescribable cold eagerness of his face, you find yourself watching him. Even the ones who do not know him are watching him now. His face is scarred as if it has been whittled on with a broken bottle; the lines from the corner of his mouth to his nose are accented on the right side by a white welt of scar. His voice is neither loud nor soft, but even, rather toneless, with the merest suggestion of a Swede singsong, and there is in it something of the reined-in quality of his face, an effect of controlled impatience. He looks like a man who would blow straight up if he were crossed.

Almost the first thing he says is a challenge.

– What about the boys at Oatfield?

– They killed Art Manderich.

– I know that. But what about him? Where'd they bury him? What about the others? I've been out in the sticks, I haven't heard a thing.

– Llewellyn and three others are up for murder.

(His mouth twists and his eyes change subtly. For a moment

he looks blind.) What other three? Virtanen and the Kirkham boys?

– I thought you hadn't heard anything.

– I heard a little. Where'd they bury old Art? Some ditch?

– Not on your life. The boys from Sacramento gave him a bang-up funeral, marchers for five or six blocks. It's in the *Worker*, around here someplace. We got a lot of public support. The deputies got too god damn gay for once, and then pinching four of *us* on this phony murder charge. Probably they planned the whole thing. The pickers was gettin' pretty sore and Llewellyn had them all organized for a showdown when the bosses get scared and send down these gunmen to break it up . . .

– What are we doing about it? Got a defense committee?

– They organized one right away in Sacramento, soon as the boys were hauled in. We're just gettin' goin' down here.

(His eyes are restless around the room, on the walls where One Big Union pennants are tacked, the glass-fronted bookcase full of songbooks, pamphlets, books. His eyes stop momentarily at the row of pictures of May Day picnics, with men and women sitting and standing, some of them holding banners spread before them, their faces full of smiles and pride and zeal. Joe Hill's own face is lean as an axe blade.)

– We ought to have a poster up here to keep the boys reminded.

– I was gonna see Sanson about that in the next day or so. He's the only guy that can do anything like that.

– I'll do it, you won't have to see Sanson. (The sudden eyes, the leashed and baffled look.) You on the committee?

– I guess I'm chairman of it.

– Made any collections yet? They got lawyers hired up there in Sacramento? They'll need money.

– They got lawyers, sure. So far all we did was beat it up at a street meeting last night. Picked up eight-fifty.

– Eight-fifty! (His eyes are incredulous, his hard mouth twists.) How far will eight-fifty go to save four men's lives? What's the matter with you down here? You ought to be able to raise that much from every man in the local.

– I don't know. Things are tight. We been havin' trouble payin' the hall rent even. We're a month behind on that.

(The scorn in his face troubles the men in the room. They shift under his glare, and sit sullenly like children being scolded. The toneless voice does not rise, but there is a whip in it.)

– Twenty-two bucks a month. We could pay that with what any three of you spend for beer.

(They continue to sit quietly, waiting for some other one to speak. Through the window, across the Sunday quiet of the town, comes the snorting of a switch engine in the yards. Joe Hill's hand goes into his pocket and comes out with a roll of bills. The rubber band breaks as he takes it off, and flips across the floor. One of the men stoops quickly and retrieves it. The eyes are on Joe's hands. He smooths off bills one by one—a twenty, four tens, two fives, two ones. Seventy-two dollars. The roll is reduced to a flat little wad, only four or five bills in it. Joe's eyes change again, fill for a moment with the blind blue cataract look.)

– There's a month's hall rent, and fifty dollars for the defense fund.

– Jesus, Joe, that's nearly your whole stake . . .

– Don't waste your time worrying about me. Start thinking about those boys in Sacramento.

(They watch him closely but not too openly. He has come in upon them as something hard, alien, and compulsive, so that they cannot recapture the relaxed kidding tone of their conversation. The whole Sunday atmosphere of slow inconsequential talk, food, digestion, rumination, has been fractured by Joe Hill's coming. In the next few minutes several men sheepishly shell out fifty cents or a dollar for the defense fund. Others, broke, look pushed around and a little rebellious. They phrase their rebellion in their minds, arranging how they will tell it to other boys who may drift in during the afternoon. They find the words and the ideas for it as a couple of cribbage games and a game of cooncan start up. Seventy-two bucks, just like that, they put it to themselves. Just peels it off his roll. Where does a working stiff get that kind of dough?)

(But it was something to see, they admit. He gave away more than he kept. If the whole working class was in the One Big Union the way Joe Hill was in it, those instruments of production would be taken over already, and the workers would be beating up their chains into plowshares.)

7   San Pedro, September, 1913

Now when the mission doors are closed for the night and the last stew-bum steered off to a cot in the dormitory, protesting all the way his shame before Jesus for his unclean life, a preacher who has long since lost his illusions about his ability to reweave the unmeshed character of the defeated may relax in half-amused communion with himself, and in the bare clean kitchen may examine the justifications of a clean bare life.

There is a ritual to coffee at midnight, and whatever reflections Lund may have, however the day may have tried his patience or his faith, however his private catechism may run, it is a ritual that calms him. He is a Swede, one of those for whom coffee softens the stiff fibers of the mind. He drinks twenty cups a day, strong as lye and hot enough to crack tooth enamel, but this last cup of the day is the best, the most leisurely. In this hour of privacy and meditation his feet sound hollow and pleasantly lonely on the linoleum. The room contains nothing but himself; for a while there is no fretfulness in his mind. Though he may indulge his scepticism, he doubts without bitterness; though he may debate the premises of his whole existence, he confronts himself without heat or self-accusation. For this short while he can afford to be a puttery philosopher, as quiet within and without as trees dripping in the stillness after a rain.

Coffee at midnight is a Low Mass performed without deacon or incense: a ritualistic laying-out of mug, spoon, sugar bowl, milk can, with something like a genuflection and a wordless intonation as the big pot, never empty or cool through the long day, is pushed onto the gas ring. There are formal movings and stoopings as before an altar; the pouring, the measuring of milk and sugar, are liturgically deliberate; and when the mug is finally held between the hands, warming them, the lips approach it as if it might contain the Host. To move through the ritual itself is one sort of pleasure; to contemplate it in these mildly impious terms is another. A man

trained for the ministry acquires a respect for ritual; a man con-
ducting a mission on the waterfront has little enough opportunity to
practice it.

Into this compline service one night, coming after canonical
hours and tapping with his knuckles on the kitchen door that
opened on the alley, came Joe Hillstrom, sailor, longshoreman, common worker, IWW organizer and composer of labor songs. He wore
corduroys and a blue work shirt and a gray and red coat sweater,
and as Lund put out a surprised and inquiring head he slipped in
sideways to stand faintly smiling while Lund shut and bolted the
door.

"What's up?"

"Nothing. I saw your light still on."

"You'll get shot sometime, sliding up alleys like a burglar," Lund
said. He waved at the table and pulled out a chair. "I was just
having a cup of coffee."

Joe sat down at the oilcloth-covered table. He seemed to Lund
little changed by three years in the labor wars. A little tighter in
the mouth, perhaps—a little tighter in every way, as if an inner
tension strung the rather flat voice, sharpened the eyes, screwed
up the cords of the muscled neck, pulled and stretched the whole
face so that it looked older, colder, less responsive. He sat loosely,
slumping in the chair, and his big workman's hands were quiet
on the oilcloth. He sipped, and grinned, and for a second he was
boyish.

"You still haven't learned how to make coffee," he said.

"What's the matter with it?"

"I was just trying to make up my mind. Something you put in
it, or wash the pot in. Varnish, or turpentine, or something."

"Well, there's only a dash of turpentine," Lund said. "For flavor."

Joe emptied his cup into the sink. "I better make you some
fresh as an antidote."

"You're a fine Swede," Lund said. Amused, he watched Joe dump
and rinse the pot and fill it again with water and coffee. In the
midst of measuring the coffee Joe turned.

"You weren't planning to go to bed, were you?"

"What if I had been?"

"That'd be too bad," Joe said. He lighted the gas and stood

with the curling black match in his hand, listening for a moment, head bent, his attention far off. Then he snapped the match at the rubbish pail and stared with hard concentration at Lund.

"How many hours a day do you put in in this place?"

"I don't know," Lund said, surprised. "I live here. It's not like working on a job."

"Eight or nine in the morning till after midnight," Joe said. "Seven days a week."

"I tried once to get you as my helper," Lund said. "If I'm sweated, you're responsible."

But he could not catch and hold Joe's eye for the mutual amusement he intended. Joe tipped the coffeepot and looked in, went to the back door and stood spraddle-legged, his head tilted, looking the length of the kitchen at Lund. As if he had not intended to, he fell to listening again, and Lund watched him curiously, thinking that he had the air of not paying attention to what he himself said.

"Quiet," he said, and shook his head slightly and came back to sit down.

"The best time of the day," Lund said. "Souls all saved, sheep all brought into the fold, everything snug."

Including the whole mission with a circular jerk of the head, Joe asked, "Who pays for this?"

"The mission?"

"Yes."

"Mainly the synod. I get some help now and then from two churches in Los Angeles, and the one here. Once a year we get a contribution from the old country."

"Rich church members."

"No. Mostly just ordinary people giving a few dollars. We're always in the hole."

"Who makes up the deficit, you?"

"Why do you want to know?"

"I'm trying to figure out why you bury yourself in a place like this. It ties you down, it costs you money, and you don't really believe you're saving any souls. What are you in it for?"

The direct blue stare was challenging, the face sharp and intent as if much hinged on Lund's answer. The missionary said mildly,

"What are you in the iww for? Are you making your fortune out of that?"

"No," Joe said impatiently, and struck Lund's words away with his hand. "I'm asking you now."

Eventually Lund had to shrug. "A lot of people need a helping hand."

The coffee boiled over and put out the fire, filling the room with the stink of burning grounds. Joe pulled the pot off the ring, turned off the gas, reached to the sink and got a half-cup of cold water which he poured into the pot. After a half-minute's wait for the grounds to settle he filled Lund's cup and his own.

"That sounds kind of smug," he said unexpectedly.

Lund was stung. If there was one thing he feared it was the thing he had seen too often in his own profession, the self-righteousness that could creep up on a man like fat or baldness, greasing the mind and clouding the vision and making a good man over into something almost detestable. In an unappreciated profession it was so easy to take comfort and justification from one's own sense of blamelessness. A hot retort jumped into his mind, but he held it back, glaring across the table into Joe's narrowed eyes. He saw the amusement there, and after a moment he could laugh. He was being baited again, and by one who knew how to find the tender spot.

"Self-righteousness is the vice of the meek," Lund said. "I'm not that meek. I'd just rather do this than be pastor in some Minnesota town."

But oddly Joe seemed already to have lost interest in exploiting the advantage he had gained. The argument that Lund was now prepared for died away before it was begun, and Joe eyed Lund over the rim of his coffee mug. His Adam's apple moved as he swallowed. "You know you're an enemy of the working class, don't you, not really a helper?" he said, and set the cup down.

"I hadn't been informed," Lund said politely.

"Then I'll inform you."

Across from the missionary he sat and pursed his mouth, thinking —a complicated and difficult young man with a mind that could never quite be predicted. He was tough, ironical, sharp, intolerant, full of stereotypes and tired revolutionary clichés and yet prickly with unexpected observations and the echoes of unexpected books, sometimes soggy with sentimentality and self-pity and sometimes as unyielding and hostile as a row of bayonets. In the slight pause Lund shifted, mentally on his toes, trying to anticipate where the attack was coming and in what tone. For one clean instant, as Joe looked at him, he remembered something he had read as a boy in some book of western adventure. A white man and a Ute Indian, to settle a difficulty that had arisen between their respective groups, tied their left wrists together and fought with knives. He remembered now how unexpectedly that argument had been settled: instead of stabbing for his enemy's breast or throat the white man made one quick slash across the Ute's bound wrist, dropped his knife and seized the Ute's knife hand and held him until he bled to death. Lund was mentally protecting his wrists as well as his throat while he watched Joe and waited.

"All right," Joe said, "let me tell you about preachers. Preachers and politicians. You can't be either one and be on the side of the workingman. You can talk and preach and pray and say come to Jesus, but you're still part of the system, and the system is against the worker. It's made special just to keep him down, and there are a lot of ways. One is the way Engels talks about, the armed men. That's all the state is, a body of armed men hired by the bosses. It doesn't matter what armed men. Deputies, cops, National Guard, Pinkertons, they're all part of it. They slam it on the worker or the down-and-outer and they tip their hats to the boys in the high collars . . ."

"Now just a minute," Lund said.

"Or the politicians. They're part of the system too. They come around on Election Day with butter oozing out their pores, with their secret Australian ballot and their manhood suffrage and all the rest. Holy smoke! That's a pretty bum joke. You don't elect your representatives. You swap masters. Fire one and get another one just like him, and this should make you feel fine. What good is the ballot box? A workingman gets freedom from it just about the way he gets protection from the law."

Cramming his pipe while he watched the intent thin face, Lund saw that what he was talking about meant something to him. It was something he had thought about and wanted to say out. The vagueness, the wandering of his attention, were gone. He talked seriously and a little pompously, as if reciting a lesson.

"I don't own a single ballot box," Lund said, to give him the proper amount of irritating prod.

Joe did not smile. "You're part of the system, just the same. Armed men to hold the oppressed class down, politicians to promise them everything and pull wool over their eyes and make them think they're controlling their own business, and then preachers to make heaven so wonderful a man will stand for anything down below. It's a thimblerigger's game. The pea isn't under any of the shells."

"So I shouldn't feed a hungry man or give a bed to a bum?"

"I didn't say that," Joe said slowly. "But just the same, if you didn't the slaves might get mad quicker and rise up and take the rights they've been done out of."

"Let's be practical," said Lund. "These are down-and-outers, stew-bums, derelicts, a lot of them. If somebody doesn't take care of them they'll probably not live to rise up."

The wide stare was oddly hard to meet, pale and intense. "The down-and-outers are licked anyway," Joe said. "They're the casualties of the system, and they wind up scabbing on their real friends. Once they take the handout they're gone. It'd be better they had to die off than hang around taking scraps and licking the masters' hands and beating down wages with their scabbing. It's the handout that does it. In the old country they oppress labor with bayonets, but here we do it with handouts. That's where you come in."

"Is this part of some soapbox spiel?" Lund said, not really meaning the sneer.

Joe was abstracted, thinking. "I go down to the docks a lot when I'm in Pedro. I take down a piece of bread or something and sit on the dock and after a while the rats come out and start nosing around. In about two days I can have the toughest old rat on the waterfront eating out of my hand in broad daylight like a squirrel."

Lund was silent, sloshing his mug around on the oilcloth and studying the circles like a penmanship exercise that it made. He laughed. "Well, I'm sorry for all the souls I've bribed over onto the boss's side with coffee and doughnuts." He was disappointed in Joe. The power to discriminate was no longer there; the hard uncompromising arrogance of the self-righteous was in his voice and in the sterile doctrines he preached. It was as if he looked out on the world through a set of ideas as rigid as the bars on a jail window, and everything he saw was striped in the same pattern. For a moment Lund was tempted to toss back at him the word "smug," but just then Joe looked up slyly and smiled and pulled down his mouth.

"Bad coffee, too," he said. Somehow that one remark took the insistent pressure out of what he had been saying. Lund found himself thinking that Joe could be absurd, as the intelligent but under-educated could always be absurd, and he could perhaps be dangerous, a really deadly partisan, but he would also be something of a seeker always, and something of an artist.

He continued to look smilingly into Joe's face. Finally he said, "Life is a battleground to you."

"It's always been a battleground. It's taken the working class hundreds of years to get to the point where they can fight with a chance of winning."

"But you think they'll win."

"It's inevitable."

"And after they've won, then what? After they've thrown the bosses off their backs and broken up this system, what do they erect in its place?"

"Then the workers will own the instruments of production and will operate industry for the good of all. After the class war is won there is no more need for the state. The armed men and the ballot boxes and all the rest of it will wither away, and we get a classless and stateless society."

Lund knocked hot ash into his palm and held it there till it grew too hot to hold, when he dumped it in the trash bucket. The hope. The unshakable piety! He whistled a moment between his lips and then said, "And you attack me for being a Heaven-monger."

"What?"

"Let it go, let it go." He thought to himself ruefully that he had taken up the wrong mythology. His own had led him to scepticism and humanitarianism. Joe had a faith that would have shamed a Christian martyr, and it led him to crusades, blood-letting and head-knocking in lofty causes, an assurance that could let the whole lost world of down-and-outers go because their decline would be a mark of the coming millennium.

There was no reaching him, no communication possible between a sceptic and a zealot, a dubious Christian and a militant iww. The Wobbly program, what made it attractive to men like Joe Hillstrom, was that it was no program at all. It was as reflexive as a poke in the nose, and about as constructive. We are oppressed; fight back. The other side uses any means to hold us down; use any means to get up. There went the whole weary round, the new hatreds begotten on the bodies of the old. The master class has gobbled the earth; throw it out and put in its place a new master class of workers in the expectation that under its benign rule government and class struggle and injustice will wither away. Wonderful. All it needed was harps and wings.

– Suppose just once, he said to Joe Hillstrom's thick contentious skull, that men tried to *whittle* their world into change and progress instead of blasting it. Suppose we didn't try to blast them out and burn them and kill them but whittled at them, replacing evil with lesser evil, forcing a concession here and an improvement there and substituting for good a greater good. Suppose we tried overcoming the old sins that have been with us since Adam, and have never left us because we have always elected in our hostility and eagerness and ignorance to fight fire with fire, violence with violence, oppression with oppression? Suppose you fought evil and injustice with your whole might but refused to adopt their methods? Would any more, in the long run, die? Don't you know that violence is unslaked lime that burns the hands throwing it as well as the flesh it is thrown upon?

You apostle of hostility and rebellion, I could read you a sermon in brotherly interdependence, I could show you how you and I are both everybody's servant and everybody's master, I could demonstrate to you that your way of righting wrongs may cure these wrongs but will surely create others. I could be eloquent to show you that there is no way but the way of peace. You sneer at peace, but I could show you that peace is not quietude, not meekness, not weakness, not fear. It need no more accept current evils than you and your fellows in the violent crusade. It doesn't even demand what Christianity has been demanding for centuries. It doesn't demand love, necessarily. It demands only reasonable co-operation, for which men have a genius when they try.

All the arts are arts of peace. Don't give me your Jack London Darwinism and your philosophy of progress by class war. Talk to me about class peace and I'll talk to you. Come to me as a man and I'll talk to you. But don't come to me as a partisan with bloody hands and talk about the cleansing and purifying that arises from violence. A partisan is no man any more, he is a man whittled to a sharp point, every humane quality in him, all his compassion and talent and intelligence and common sense and sense of justice pared away in the interest of striking power. The partisan is hooded like a hawk, kept on the wrist at all times except when the quarry is flushed, except when there is enemy blood to let.

But he did not say this. Neither did he say what he had often thought, and what he thought, almost irrelevantly, now: that humanity moves both ways on a street with a double dead-end, and that Vengeance sits with an axe at one end and Mercy sits in weak tears at the other, and that only Justice, which sits in the middle and looks both ways, can really choose.

He said none of this, though he thought it with a kind of anguish, because he liked Joe Hillstrom and took him seriously both as a man and as a representative. Instead he said placidly, pulling his heavy mustache, "So here we sit cheek by jowl, the Preacher and the Slave."

It was wonderful to him how the lean face lighted up, the eyes warmed, the scarred mouth curled like the mouth of a thin eager boy. "You know that song of mine?"

"Pie in the Sky By and By," Lund said. "I sing it every night to my stew-bums to make them satisfied with the kind of coffee I serve here below."

"The songs says it all, I guess." Hesitating, Joe looked at Lund as if waiting for the answer to a question. His hand was in his pocket. "That isn't what I came down here for, though. I came to do something sort of funny." He pulled his hand out and dropped a crumpled ten-dollar bill on the oilcloth.

"What's that for?"

"Contribution."

"To the mission?"

"More to you than the mission," Joe said, and now for an instant

Lund saw in the eyes an evasive flicker of that odd feeling that kept them friends. It moved him tremendously. "You never peddle the angel food," Joe said. "You feed a man and don't ask questions. I'm ready to respect that."

"And I make a bad rebel out of him with my doughnuts," Lund said, beginning to smile. "I'm an enemy of the working class, remember?"

Joe's face had already darkened. He was not one who could be joked, though he sometimes joked others. The impatient hand swept the bill across the table. "Take it. I want to donate it."

"All right, Joe," Lund said. "All right, if you can spare it."

Joe's eyes now were hollow, dark with what could have been anger. "I want to tell you it's for you and not for Jesus," he said. "I met another kind of a preacher a while back. Out in a hop camp. There were nearly three thousand people having to live like hogs. Talk about your armed men to keep the workers down! They had 'em there by the dozen. Also there was this ranting preacher in camp, climbing up on stumps and hollering about Jesus. That was fine. That kept people thinking how sinful they were instead of how their bellies were growling."

"Yes?" Lund said, watching him.

"Big pack of sins," Joe said. "He was hump-backed with 'em. Poor shaking sinner. That's what the bosses wanted, that stool-pigeon preacher up there bringing the comforts of religion to people."

"And what happened?"

"You read the papers," Joe said. "Did you ever know Art Manderich?" His eyes were hard, his face pinched and tight.

"No."

"They killed him," Joe said. "Their dirty hired gunmen came in to break up our meeting and they killed him. And this preacher was right at my throat like a wolfhound. He knew what side Jesus was on."

Absently Lund began to fill his pipe again. He had a feeling that he should speak with great quiet and caution. "This was at Oatfield?"

"I didn't say," Joe said. "Yes, as a matter of fact, it was, but you won't tell that to anybody unless you want me in jail with the others."

"That's right," Lund said. "Some of your friends are in jail."

"And some are dead," Joe said. He stood up, his fists on the table, so angered by his own words and his recollection that his lips were white. "You run a good mission, if there is such a thing. You've been a friend of mine. There isn't another preacher in Kingdom Come I'd give a nickel to."

There was a sound behind him, at the alley door. Joe spun to face it, his eyes touching Lund's. Across his shoulder Lund saw the knob turn and heard the thump as someone put his shoulder against the panels. Then the hard, peremptory hammering.

Joe's hand stabbed into his pocket, and he threw a loose handful of bills across at Lund, who automatically gathered them up and thrust them into his own pocket. In one motion Joe stripped off his sweater, exposing the holster snugged under his left arm and the flat butt of the automatic. A flip of the chest-strap buckle and the gun was off, in Lund's hands, and Lund, looking frantically around for a hiding place, was raising his voice and saying to the hard insistent hammering, "Yes? What is it? Who's there?"

"Police," a voice said. "Open up."

Lund moved swiftly to the breadbox, thrust gun and holster and strap inside, pulled a loaf of bread over it, shut the lid. Joe was slumped over with his coffee mug in his hands, his sweater buttoned halfway up. Their eyes met again before Lund stepped to unbolt the door, but Lund could read nothing in Joe's face. He had it fixed like wood to receive the police.

That night Lund went to bed late and troubled, taking with him Joe Hill's forty-two dollars and Joe Hill's Luger automatic to hide them in a bureau drawer. He did not believe that Joe had anything to do with holding up a Point Fermin streetcar, as the police had indicated. The instant unloading of gun and money could as easily be interpreted another way: any organizer was likely to be picked up in any dragnet, and police were not above twisting or even fixing evidence on occasion to put a Wobbly agitator behind bars. Any organizer moreover could feel it necessary to carry a gun for his own protection, but carrying the gun automatically made him a criminal to the police. And Joe was jumpy about the Oatfield riot, where he had evidently been. It was natural that he should have thrust the things at Lund.

He did not believe Joe guilty, but he did not sleep well, and he was extravagantly relieved next morning to read that a dozen suspects, including Joseph Hillstrom, unemployed stevedore, had been questioned and released for lack of evidence in the Point Fermin holdup case.

For a good many days he expected Joe to appear and claim his money and his gun. It was more than a week before he finally made up his mind that Joe was not coming, at least not now.

Well, he would be along sometime. He blew around like tumbleweed, but he always came back sooner or later. Gun and money remained in the drawer waiting for some night when knuckles would tap late at the door, interrupting the ritual of the compline coffee, and the singsong Swede voice would say, "Ay yoost like cop coffee, mister."

He was quite a man, Joe Hillstrom, and getting to be almost a legend. His name was heard on Beacon Street, and echoes of his movements up and down the coast came in with casual go-abouts, and songs he had written filled the street when the soapboxers stopped for breath—songs set to hymn tunes and sung by devout men who often bawled extra loud in order to drown out the trombones and trumpets and drums of the Salvation Army working the same street.

Lund shook his head over him: A John the Baptist with a hard mouth, a lowborn Maccabeus, an inarticulate Paul, a dark Christ migrant for his gospel's sake. The feeling he had about Joe Hillstrom was almost a yearning, an emotional insistence, as if Joe were a son going stubbornly wrong, and Lund a father helpless to prevent him. Absalom, oh my son, he said, and stood ruefully looking into the bureau drawer at the envelope of obscurely got money and the gun in its worn leather. More than once it struck him, and always as a wry joke, that here was one soul he really wanted to save.

The Singing Union

1 Salt Lake City, September, 1913

There is a city ringed on the east by mountains and on the west by deserts and barren ranges and a dead sea. A city hewed from the wilderness, it is green in the midst of wastelands, and between its barrier deserts and its rampart mountains it lies like sanctuary, extending along its incoming roads the invitation of trees. It wears an inland remoteness, a continental isolation, on its face, and over it yet is some of the aura of belief with which its zealot founders endowed it. It is the appointed city in the valleys of the mountains, the city of the Saints, the New Jerusalem.

Into it Joe Hill came as a stranger and a pilgrim, weary from riding a freight across the desert, hot and dirty and embittered, all but broke, with a few belongings in a straw suitcase, but without the automatic that for three years had ridden under his arm, and without a clear destination or a clear purpose except the restless and never-satisfied purpose of striking a blow, keeping a promise, exacting a partial vengeance.

Stripped of the marks and symbols by which he recognized himself, he stood at the trackside in a blaze of white heat and saw a tree-shaded avenue begin at the foot of the mountains and angle upward between the brick and stone and neat paint of houses. Beyond that he saw the granite dome of the new state capitol building, still crated in scaffoldings, thrusting upward from a bench of land; and beyond that, rocky and spruce-darkened, the peaks that went southward to rim the valley.

Also he saw, just across the highway from him, a low concrete building huddled under the hill, with a sign that said "Warm Springs." As if this were something appointed and planned he crossed the highway and entered. For a quarter a toothpick-chew-ing attendant gave him a towel, a gray cotton bathing suit, and a key on an elastic ring, and with these in his hands he went along a corridor and into a dressing room with sweaty cement floors and a pervasive, blurred odor of sulphur water.

At a numbered door his key fitted a lock; there were hooks for his clothes and a bench to sit on. When he came out he hunted past the deserted showers, past the doorway that opened into a swimming pool hollow with the yelling of boys, until finally he saw a door with a sign over it: "Steam Room."

Like the dressing room and the showers, the room was empty. It smelled faintly rotten, and its walls were clammy as a cave, with great drops congealed on them. For a moment he was afraid the place was out of order, or closed because of the hot weather, but then he saw the big valve on the wall, and turned it.

There was a hissing, an internal bubbling and rumbling; a few drops of water trembled from the vent and were overtaken by a white gush of steam. As he stepped back he felt pleasure in merely watching how it came, a jet as big as his wrist rolling in clouds to the ceiling and spreading, moving, filling the corners and eddying lower, reaching out tendrils, sinking and billowing and driving the cold air downward and mixing with it until the whole room was murky, so thick with steam that the door swam and vanished. The smell of the steam was strong, a living, meaty, half-foetid, rotten-egg smell that was like many bad smells, offensive until it had been breathed awhile, and then almost pleasant. Like the smells of his own body, this steam seemed a part of him.

He was in the midst of a deep hot cloud, and as the steam hissed steadily into the room the heat grew. The goose-pimples that the damp had raised on his legs and arms were smoothed away; his scalp began to prickle with the first sweat. At a certain stage of heat he took off the bathing suit and threw it on the bench; stooping, he rubbed gently at his ankles, black with travel. Under his fingers the warm moist skin gave up its dirt, the black rubbed off and the skin was white. Without haste he rubbed himself all over, and finally he stretched out on the bench with his head on his arms. For a time the bench was cool against his skin, but before long even that sensation melted away and he became one with the enduring lubricative warmth. He stretched his arms, as supple as rubber.

The prickling of scalp and skin had passed. Every pore in his body was open and breathing. The drops that rolled down his body were sweat or steam or both, the inward and outward waters merging, impurities gently washing out of him, warmth washing in. His mind was stunned. In a long time, his only movement was to pull himself up from the bench, which was growing hard against his belly and hipbones, and draw himself up with his arms clasped around his shins, his forehead on his knees. There, watching with half-open eyes how the vapor changed and rolled, he felt his lungs softened and moistened and warmed until it seemed that he breathed with gills like a fish. The angular corners of the room were gone. As flexible as rubber, he sat folded together, and the steamy room enclosed him like a sheath.

He all but slept. Lulled, protected, sluiced in and out with moisture and warmth, his lungs working evenly like gills, his heavy head drooping against his knees, he drifted for an indefinite time without a conscious sensation, a thought, or a memory.

A bang and clatter and outcry shocked him awake. The door slammed open, a draught of cold air rushed across him bringing tension and resistance and anger. He sat as he had been, but stiffly now, and willed the intruders to go away, while his mind yearned backward and downward toward the comfort and safety from which he had been aroused. But the makers of the racket stayed in the door, shouting for someone else to come. They came in coughing and choking and one bumped against Joe and startled himself into an exclamation. Joe twisted away from the touch, hating the way they coughed and laughed and spatted each other with wet hands.

The sheath was ripped, the hammock broken, the light let in, the cold admitted, the spell gone. After a minute of rebellion, Joe took his suit and went out of the steam room to stand under the hard insistence of a cold shower. The shower drove the dream deeper and washed away the anger. He was feeling good, clean, awake, when he passed again through the corridor and threw his towel in the hamper and slid suit and key across the metal counter top toward the attendant.

Now he stood purged and clean on the outskirts of the city, most of which was cut off from his view by trees and by the benchland on which the capitol stood. There was something hidden and contained about the city that pricked his curiosity; he wanted to get up on some high place and get a good look at this pious Mormon burg he had alighted in. Also, the steam and the cold shower had sharpened and multiplied his perceptions. He felt like a person with second sight. Something hovered ahead of him in the tree-shrouded city, and he saw himself as a small, clean, shriven figure approaching the city under the hot dome of afternoon. Something about this town made him move alertly. He sniffed, searching for familiar smells, and when he met people on the slanting street going up toward the capitol he glanced sharply into their faces, half expecting to recognize them.

The bench brought him out above a wide panorama of the valley. Below him he recognized the turtle-backed tabernacle and the six gray spires of the Mormon temple, a view almost exactly like one he had seen on a stereopticon slide. Back of him the capitol, massive and dome-topped, spoke to him of the power and strut of the law as the temple spoke of the power of the church. And far across the valley, beyond all the streets and past the last straggle of trees and miles across the arid flats south-westward, the stacks of smelters fumed slowly at the foot of the next range. Power again, the Copper Trust, the silver magnates.

The homes of Salt Lake City were humble, buried in trees, only the occasional glint of their roofs showing how they lined the trenches of the streets. But the homes of power were tall. Banks and business buildings leaped up tall at the foot of the hill, the temple spired upward to its gilded angel, the tall stacks of the mining bosses smoked across the valley. Above them all, lordly on its eminence, was the home of the law.

Sitting in the shade of a spindling new tree, he remembered a story a carpenter had told him in San Pedro. The carpenter and two other men had been working in the new office of the governor on a Saturday afternoon, fitting baseboard and trim. Taking advantage of the quiet, the carpenter brought a pint back with him from lunch. They had all taken a pull at it and corked it up when the governor came in to show his quarters to friends. The carpenter hastily shoved the pint in against a stud and went on working. But the governor's party stayed so long that he eventually had to case the bottle in. It was there yet in the wall back of the governor's desk.

For a moment Joe told himself that it was a good and laughable thing that the secret whiskey was there. It was a flaw in the imposing perfection, an expression of a workingman's right to be himself. But he couldn't stay amused. For one thing, the worker had lost his bottle, and that was the way it always went. For another, he shouldn't have been the slave of the bottle in the first place. The system made a drinker out of him and then beat him out of his drinks. The secret pint in the wall didn't mean anything after all. He wished it were a bomb.

But the feeling that something impended, that soon now he would remember what errand had brought him here to the heart of the sticks, remained with him. He was on the run, yes. It seemed that he was always on the run from something. But he was coming toward something, too. This town felt ominous with meaning, as if there had been a forgotten reason and a destined meeting. Yet the only things he could see from the hill that might have relevance to his life were the arrogant triple symbols of the system's power.

In his room that night, in the boardinghouse run by Mother Wynn on North Temple Street under the shadow of the gilded angel, he sat and wondered if he should not go out and hunt up the hall. But after the close call in San Pedro he felt the need of caution. It wouldn't hurt to smell around Salt Lake a little before making himself known. Besides, he felt languid, drained by the heat, and though he heard voices down on the porch where it was cooler, he did not move. Tomorrow he might find friends among them, good union men, or workers who might be talked into taking out a card, but he would not exert himself to know them now.

Idly he reached over and picked up the Gideon Bible that lay on the washstand. Inside he read the little message from the Gideon Society, and on the flyleaf the neat inscription: "Mother Wynn—Please accept as a token of gratitude this little book I just dashed off—with. Jesus H. O'Dwyer."

Turning the page, he read from the beginning of Genesis, and he had got as far as the generations of Adam when he looked up to see that the window was no longer giving him enough light, and that he was straining his eyes in the dusk reading a thing in which he no longer had even the interest of contempt. But when he started to toss the book back on the stand he hesitated and held it more to the light to read a little further. There was a terrible, uncompromising sadness about the monotonous verses of begats:

And Adam lived an hundred and thirty years, and begat a son in his own likeness . . . and called his name Seth. . . . And the days of Seth were nine hundred and twelve years, and he died. . . . And Enos lived ninety years, and begat Cainan . . . and Cainan lived seventy years, and begat Mahalaleel. . . . And Mahalaleel lived after he begat Jared eight hundred and thirty years, and begat sons and daughters. . . . And all the days of Jared were nine hundred sixty and two years, and he died . . .

Like grains of sand pouring between his fingers the generations came and passed, and centuries after they had passed the dry husks of their names made a forlorn sound in the world in which they and all their works were as grass.

This was the stuff millions of good Christians read for gospel. This was the way they built up patience in themselves to accept what they were given and bear the yoke they bore. And one generation of workers worked and got nothing and bore children and died, and another generation labored and was cheated and begot children and died, and all the days of every generation were sixty or seventy years of sweat and sickness and wage slavery, and they died.

He threw the Bible on the floor and looked out the window. Across a narrow court was the brick back of a shop, with two windows shedding light across the littered court. What went on behind the windows was so apt to his mood that it might have been staged for his benefit alone.

A baker in a white hat and short-sleeved underwear worked at a big table. His motions were jerky and precise, reduced to an inflexible routine. From a tub he reached a pillow of dough, slashed once with his knife, slapped the dough on the table, kneaded and flopped and kneaded and stretched and flopped, and tucked the wad in one of a string of pans. Another slice, and again the slap knead flop stretch flop. A row of filled pans grew along the table, magically moving ahead of the magical mechanical motions of the baker.

Watching him, Joe was reminded of the sign above the Peerless Pool Parlor in San Pedro. Both baker and sign had the mechanical perfection, the rigid regularity, of a string of begats. This was the way life was arranged. They sliced you off and slapped you in a pan and smeared you with lard and shoved you into the ovens, and after a while out you came, one more loaf of bread. Or maybe they had you scheduled for something fancy. Maybe you were due to be coffee cake, and then they ran you through a different mill and sprinkled raisins and chopped nuts around on you and baked you a little less or a little more.

What good does it do to fight it? a treacherous little voice said in his mind. You're on a treadmill, you just waste your strength. But he put the voice down, and he assured himself that even though Marx said the domination of the proletariat was inevitable, and that capitalism would ultimately destroy itself, yet there had to be agents and workers and fighters to bring the destruction about, and maybe hurry it.

But it was really unfair the way they mixed life up for a man. They carelessly dropped nuts and raisins around in ordinary dough and produced something like himself, neither bread nor coffee cake. The whole futile cloud of his ambitions rose up before his eyes and offended his sight. A poet. An artist. A musician. Akh!

He stayed at the window a long time, watching the jerky unalterable motions of the baker, until the baker pitched three tubs one inside the other and slid them down the table and the light clicked off to leave only a vague interior glow in which shadows of movement went on, incomprehensible for all his peering and staring and straining to penetrate the smeared light-struck glass.

2

The morning newspaper told him that the cornerstone had been laid at a new Mormon ward house, and showed him the faces of the men and women who had participated in the ceremonies. It informed him of a controversy between a Better Government committee and the sheriff about conditions at the county jail, and of the death of a tramp who had been found along the Western

Pacific tracks between Salt Lake and Black Rock, and of a family stabbing in Bingham. It gave him the information that ore shipments from the Silver King, Daly-Judge, and Apex mines were up thirteen per cent above the same period of the preceding year, and that the Second International was meeting in Switzerland and denouncing nationalism and war. But it told him nothing about what was happening in Sacramento, and he looked carefully among strange names and strange faces up and down the columns of the whole paper without finding any clue to the expectancy he felt. It was as if he had come here to meet someone and could not remember who.

At noon he ate in a workingmen's eatery on Second South, and came out afterward to pick his teeth and lean against the wall, watching people pass. A bum panhandled him for a cup of coffee, and Joe gave him a nickel. Another bum struck him for a match, but Joe didn't have any. He leaned comfortably against the wall, watching faces.

Along the sidewalk came a dapper young man with a mustache, his legs encased in peg-topped riding breeches, his calves booted in glistening British boots. In his hand he carried a crop with which he tapped the side of his leg as he walked. His heels were crisp and confident on the sidewalk.

Looking at him come, Joe was moved by ribald amusement. He was astonished that such a dude would have the nerve to appear on the street. With the corner of his mouth he chirped twice, sharply, as if to a horse.

The dude looked sideways, startled, his crisp walking uninterrupted but his hand forgetting to tap the crop against his boot. He had large soft brown eyes and his mustache was brown and luxuriant. As his eyes met Joe's they went angry and hard, and his mouth stiffened. Joe gave him a still, intent look, one the poor prune couldn't misunderstand.

"Giddap!" he said, and removed the toothpick from his mouth.

For a hopeful instant he thought the dude was going to take the challenge, and he shoved his shoulders away from the wall eagerly. But the dude's face, a face like a girl's with an artificial mustache pasted on it, turned ahead again, reddening, and the crisp bootheels clicked on. Two men standing across the doorway looked at Joe and shook their heads and laughed.

Joe let himself back against the wall, taking advantage of the narrow ledge of shade. As he leaned, his eye caught a glimpse of a man who passed and hesitated, turning; a man with loose shoulders and loosely hanging arms, and a face that took on a hanging, sheeplike grin.

Otto Applequist.

As they shook hands he felt Otto's eyes all over him, like the slapping hands of a cop, slapping the corduroy pants, the worn shoes, the shirt that he had washed himself at Mother Wynn's. Otto himself looked prosperous. His shoes were new and shiny, he wore a collar and tie and a straw skimmer.

"Well, well, well, well, well!" Otto said. He pumped Joe's hand and studied Joe with a secret smile. What he saw seemed to tickle him. His smile broadened. "I heard you was in jail."

"It's a fright what stories get around," Joe said.

"How'd you get out?"

"You can't get out unless you're in."

Otto's smile widened until his eyes almost closed. "Same old Joe. Still keeping the mouth shut."

"Same old Otto, still trying to get something on somebody."

That brought a burst of coughing laughter from Otto. For a moment, still laughing, he watched two girls go by. Turning back, he said, "How's old Manderich?"

"He's dead."

"Dead!"

"You hear all the stories," Joe said. "You should have heard that one. They killed him at Oatfield."

"Well I'll be damned." Otto's loose shoulders moved. "That old gorilla," he said. "He was all right, I guess, but he sure took his politics hard."

Joe said nothing. Otto, working his genial white eyebrows, looked him over again. "You been in Zion long?"

"Just got in."

"Damnedest place you ever saw," Otto said. "Town's full of Swedes. The Mormon missionaries must've cleaned out the old country. I'm forgetting how to talk English."

They moved back into the shade against the wall of a drugstore, putting their hands behind them on the wall. Joe was glad enough to see Otto. He was a petty-larceny thief, and he liked to snoop

out every scrap of information about anything, but if he had no
hard feelings about that night in Pedro there was no reason Joe
should. And he was somebody familiar; he took the edge of
strangeness off this town.

"Doing anything?" Joe said.

"Murray smelter."

"Honest working stiff, uh?"

"Want to see my letters of recommendation?"

"I'm afraid I'd recognize the handwriting."

They laughed together, two old acquaintances gabbing in the
street.

"Where you staying at?" Otto said. "Wobbly hall?"

"Mother Wynn's. You know it?"

"I heard of it. Bughouse rest home. Whenever the cops want
an agitator they look there."

"They do?"

"What do you care?" Otto said with a laugh. "The cops aren't
nothing to you."

Joe shrugged.

"You got quite a rep since I saw you last," Otto said. "You're
the kind of an agitator the cops'd really be interested in. You still
writing songs?"

"Not lately."

"Sticking around long?"

"I don't know."

"Bound anywhere special?"

"Nowhere special."

"Jesus, you don't know the answer to anything, do you?" Otto
said.

"My father was a Pismo clam," Joe said.

"I wouldn't be suprised." Otto crossed his feet and raised his
hat to cool his forehead. With his hat still off he turned, as if a
thought had surprised him, and said, "Say, you know who I met
here?"

"Who?"

"Woman that used to know you in Sweden. Anna Olson."

Alertness awoke in Joe. He felt in the pit of his stomach the
kind of paralyzed expectancy that had come in childhood games
when his hiding place was discovered, the moment of staring ex-

posure before the screaming race for the goal. "Sweden?" he said
carefully. "That'd sure be a freak. You sure it was me?"

"Joe Hillstrom. She said you went away to be a sailor when
your mother died."

"I don't remember any Anna Olson."

"Well, she remembers you. She was a friend of your mother's."

Joe raised his shoulders vaguely. The street lay hot and sun-
drowned before him, and it was suddenly as strange as a street in
a dream. Beyond it, over the flat roof of a building, he saw the
slopes of the mountain rising. It was a strange place, and he the
strangest thing in it, with the past washing in on him. "Maybe
she's changed her name," he said. But he remembered Anna Olson
all right, in her house and his own, summer afternoons on the streets
of Gefle. His mother's friend, one of the few.

"She lives right near where I'm boarding, out in Murray," Otto
said. He shoved Joe's shoulder. "Say, you know what you could do?
There's a kind of a potlatch of Mormon Swedes out at my place
tonight. You could come on out."

"That'd be a treat."

"Do you good," Otto said. "Stick around by yourself too long,
you'll begin to smell your own breath."

"Yeah," Joe said. He rubbed the scar at the corner of his
mouth, and from under his hand said, "What kind of a potlatch?"

"Whist," Otto said. "Coffee and cake. Just a bunch of good Mormons getting together to talk Swedish."

"What'll you be doing at this party?"

"Why not? I can talk Swedish."

They laughed together again. With an appropriate and calculated carelessness Joe said, "All right, I haven't got anything to do.
I might come along. You sure it's all right?"

"All right? You're a Swede, that's enough. For that matter, I
can introduce you as the big rww song writer."

"I guess we can get along without that."

"Plain Joe Hillstrom, uh?"

"That's my name."

"Okay," Otto said. He took out his wallet and found a scrap of
paper in it and scribbled an address. "This'll be a new experience for you," he said, and the sly grin spread and curled his lips.
"Respectable churchgoing people to associate with."

"I guess I can stand it," Joe said. "What time?"

"Seven-thirty maybe."

"Vell," Joe said, "Ay see you dar."

"Plenty of *Svenska flikas*," Otto said. "All these Mormons got twelve pretty daughters."

He crossed the street, natty in his straw hat, and Joe turned back toward Mother Wynn's. It was hard to figure what Otto was up to, or whether he was up to anything. It could be that he had found out something about Joe from Anna Olson and thought he could use it. But what could he use it for? Plenty of people had no fathers. It made no difference who knew where Joe Hillstrom came from.

But the cold expectancy, like the sensation of cold against a decayed tooth, was still with him. This whole town was prickly with the sense of something due to happen.

In store windows he examined himself as he walked, trying to label himself, looking himself over as if he were Anna Olson seeing the son of her old friend for the first time in sixteen years. He observed what thirteen years of knocking around and three years in the labor wars had done to Joseph Hillstrom of Gefle, Sweden. With the eyes of these Mormon Swedes he gave himself the once-over: a pretty glum customer, long-haired, bag-kneed, with an intent scarred face.

The moving arms of a taffy-pulling machine in a candy store window stopped him momentarily, and watching his own image in the glass he cracked his face just to see if he could look human. Ghostly among trays of panoche and peanut brittle, a reflected stranger smiled at him.

3

_____

He knew Anna Olson the moment he came in with Otto from the porch and saw her talking with other women in the hall. Plain, faded, comfortable, she meant Gefle so strongly that even though he had been anticipating the meeting he was stopped dead inside the door by the intense familiarity of her face. Quiet mouth, plain flat hair, the hands that worked on a half-knitted gray wool sock even while she talked: they leaped out of his mother's kitchen over the gap of years, and voices with them like voices that he knew, women's voices talking Swedish.

When her eyes moved casually to brush his, he waited expectantly, but she looked on past him, and her nod was for Otto. She didn't know him. If he wanted to, he could still walk out of here without speaking to her. In the other room someone was pumping a player piano. The party hadn't begun yet. He could beat it out and drop the hatch cover on all this past.

But Otto was at his elbow, shoving him forward, and he stood with Otto's hand pinching around his muscle and endured the questioning eyes of Anna Olson and two younger women.

"You know who this is?" Otto said, and he shook Joe slightly, holding him like something he had captured.

Anna Olson's eyes searched his face. He felt that her eyes were soft and her brows arched with a question. "Do I know you?" she said.

"I guess not," Joe said. "Not any more."

"Did I once?"

"A long time ago."

"A long time ago. In the old country?"

"Yes."

"Gefle?"

"Yes."

Half smiling, she searched his face again. He was conscious of his scars.

"I don't. . . . How long ago?"

"I left there in '98."

"Before we did," she said. Her forehead was scored by a frown. "It's so long, I can't. . . . You're not Olaus Berger?"

"No."

"There's something familiar," she said. "Your eyes, especially."

"Come on," Otto said. "You're a punk guesser."

Then suddenly her hand came out and touched Joe's arm, and her eyes were warm with recognition and surprise. "Why of course!" she said. "Of course, I know you now. But you've changed. You were just a young boy the last . . ."

"I have to have proof," Otto said. "Who is he?"

The look Anna Olson gave Joe was almost eloquently friendly. She ignored Otto. "You used to be such a funny solemn little boy," she said. Her hand with the gray sock in it reached and pulled one of the younger women over, a woman Joe vaguely noticed as tall, neither quite pretty nor quite plain, with eyes of a placid temperate blue like Anna Olson's, and with long strong white hands. "Ingrid," Anna Olson said, "just imagine. This is Joseph Hillstrom. You two went to school together."

Ill at ease and feeling that a dozen people were listening to the talk, Joe shook the young woman's hand with a vague impression of quick eyes and a confused pink blush before the girl stepped back. There were other hands to shake, and a string of names: Andreen, Strand, Carlson, Erickson. It seemed to him that the parlor and hall were as noisy as a tree full of blackbirds, and he was astonished at these people that Otto had fallen among, who welcomed him just because he was a Swede and a friend of Anna Olson's. They were already, in the way they accepted Otto, like sheep sheltering a fox. Now here they were admitting a kind of wolf, a revolutionary and rebel. By the time the first awkwardness wore off he began to be amused. He let himself be dragged into the parlor and seated at a table opposite Anna Olson, where he played clumsy whist for two hours, listening, keeping his mouth shut except to answer the questions Mrs. Olson put to him: What had he been doing, what was he doing now, was he working in Salt Lake, what brought him here, did he hear from anyone in Gefle.

This last question she asked him a second time, as if she hadn't heard or didn't believe his first answer, and her mild blue eyes probed him with a sort of insistence as if she expected some cryptic information that the others would not catch. He told her what he had told her before, what was true. He had not heard from a single soul in Gefle since he left, except his cousin John Alberg.

And where was John?

That one he could not quite answer straight, for the last he had heard of John, he was shacked up on the beach at Hilo, bucking sugar bags on the wharf when he had to, and indulging in a continuous *luau* between jobs. A dehorn, one of the casualties.

He said that John had apparently settled down in Hawaii.

"You left about the same time," Anna said. "Pretty soon after Berta died."

"Yes."

"She had such hopes for you," the woman said, with her look which invited all sorts of personal details, and held her head ready to listen, but he moved his lips and his eyebrows and said nothing. She took a trick and stacked it neatly and put her enlarged knuckles down on it while she studied her hand. "Do you still draw?"

"A little."

"Play the piano or violin?"

"Both, a little."

He saw her eyes stop, almost absently, on the scars that marked his face and neck. Then she led out the remaining tricks swiftly and triumphantly and pawed them in toward her and said, "Ingrid plays the piano too. She gives lessons. We're all proud of Ingrid."

Joe nodded to register politeness. Across at the round dining-room table where the girl sat he saw her flick a sideward look and knew she was aware they were talking about her. She brought her cards close to her face and consulted them seriously, rearranging them in a neat fan. At the third table Otto was being jovial, slamming his cards down on tricks with force enough to drive a stake. There was a lot of laughing going on.

Joe grinned to himself. Such hopes for you, he said. Now look at you. Scars all over your map, rough clothes. It's a cinch you haven't done so well. But we're all proud of Ingrid. She gives music lessons to runny-nosed kids and can play marches as good as the player piano, almost.

In the midst of his abstraction, poking in like a stick into a smug rat's nest, there came to him without warning or reason Moe Dreyfuss' question: Where are you going, a fellow like you? What are you after? In what he suddenly perceived to be this stuffy middle-class parlor he sat and cathechized himself in old Moe's excitable voice, and with the whole batch of good Mormons in front of his nose he did not have to look far for an answer.

Look what you might have done with your knack for music and drawing, he said. You could have been Professor Hillstrom with long hair and a violin case under your arm and given lessons to ten-year-olds and made almost enough to live on if you didn't bother with breakfast. You could have taught drawing in some grammar school and been a man who was asked to whist parties by a lot of pious Swedes like these. You could have played the organ in church, or sung in the choir.

They were talking to him. Their eyes were all on him.

"What?" he said.

"Your deal," Anna Olson told him.

The whist broke up about ten-thirty, and he found himself back in a corner with a plate and a coffee cup awkwardly balanced on his knees, listening to some woman whose name he did not know. She was telling him about her conversion and about how she was frightened to death when she first heard that Mormon missionaries were in town, as though they might have been gypsies—such stories you heard about the Mormons—until one night she was coming home and heard one of them speak on a street corner, and he seemed such an upright, clean young man, and he tried so hard in bad Swedish, falling all over himself so everybody laughed. But they were friendly, he was so obviously sincere, and she was struck by something he said. He said . . .

Trapped and getting desperate, Joe moved the plate and crowded the coffee cup in among the crumbs of his cake. He was hemmed in. The two Erickson boys, sons of Otto's landlady, looked at him, and one of them nudged Otto and they laughed. It made him sore to have been brought into this henyard and now to be stuck here.

On the other side of the room somebody said clearly, "Play something, Ingrid," and here was the girl standing up and working her way over to the piano. People backed up a little and arranged their chairs as she sat on the stool rubbing her fingers and smiling a little and blushing with the quick, passing surge of pink. Two people moved their chairs directly in front of Joe so that now there was not a chance in the world of getting away. He found a table-edge for plate and cup and hooked his hands around one knee and leaned back, resigning himself. At least the woman next to him couldn't go on any further about her conversion while the piano was going.

Ingrid Olson bent her head and touched the keys. Her face grew serious, almost strained, a tight cord appeared in her neck

and her lips pursed. He watched her curiously, a girl he had
gone to school with and did not remember at all. Not a girl,
actually, only a couple of years younger than he was, and he
was thirty-one. He kept his eye on her, this old-maid music
teacher who blushed at everything and was his contemporary,
from his home town. She was supposed to be one of the smart
ones, one everybody was proud of, and what had she arrived
at, with her respectable start as the daughter of a shipwright? As
she started to play he said to himself, Well, somebody's been
spared a good Christian wife.

The high jabber that had been raucous in the room since he
came fell away to a hush, and she played. The thing she played
was quiet and grave, as sedate as this whole roomful of people.
At first he listened with mild contempt for the formlessness and
vague posturing ornamentation of the piece, but after a while
he found himself listening harder, and he thought that there was
something like a subdued excitement either in the piece itself
or the way she played it. The song didn't repeat itself like an
ordinary song, but ran along like water.

When she was finished she dropped her hands in her lap and
blushed, and looking around the room Joe saw in the way they
clapped and called for more that they really were proud of her.
She gave them reason to think well of themselves as immigrants,
Mormons, Swedes. Through a fringe of ferns he met Anna Olson's
proud eyes and he clapped with the others. All right, he admitted,
she's pretty good. Why shouldn't she be? She's a music teacher.

They were still calling for more. "Maybe I'll play a Chopin
nocturne," Ingrid said, and massaged her fingers and bent her
head to the piano with the concentrated tightening look. This too
was music of a kind he did not know, highbrow stuff. No Salvation Army tunes here, no Sunday band-concert marches. Something
dreamy and fey, full of minors. What was a nocturne, exactly?
Nighttime music?

He watched her precise hands with the realization that she
was miles ahead of him, that by comparison he was no musician
at all but an uneducated amateur fit only to play on street
corners with a tin cup strapped to his shin, or in some waterfront
saloon.

The realization made him coldly mad. When they started clapping again he left his hands clasped around his raised knee. Then with a feeling like the feeling of being grazed by danger he felt a group turn to look toward him, and as the clapping spattered away to nothing he heard Otto say, "Sure, on the piano. He's a composer, he's written dozens of songs."

Full of respect, ready to be edified, their faces stared at him. Otto was grinning as if he had pulled off a good joke, and Ingrid Olson had half risen, clearing her skirts from the piano stool. "Come on, Joe," Otto said. "Take your turn. This is a home-talent show."

Joe let his foot down to the floor. "Not after that."

"Oh come on!" they said. "Play some of your songs."

Beyond the ferns Anna Olson's motherly accusing eyes were on him fondly. "You didn't tell me, Joseph," she said.

Shaking his head, Joe smiled at them and waved them off, but he got in one sharp look at Otto warning him to stop it at this, not to go on with any spiel about Joe Hill the Wobbly Troubadour. "Pie in the Sky" would sound pretty crummy after this highbrow nocturne stuff.

"Otto's just making a big joke," he said. "I can't play the piano." His eyes met the questioning eyes of Ingrid Olson and he said, "You play some more."

"Everybody'd rather hear you."

"Come on!" they said. They were full of laughter again, the chummiest, good-naturedest bunch of people he had ever seen. "He wants to be coaxed!" they said, and laid hands on him to pull him from his chair. Embarrassed and angry, he held back, a ridiculous object in a ridiculous position. "I can't play," he kept telling them. "No, you're mistaken. Otto's fooling you."

"Don't let him fool you," Otto said. "He can play the fiddle too. Make him get up there."

Joe jerked away from their coaxing hands, really angry now. He saw them leave off their urging and their good nature at the same time. Their faces were hurt and offended, and in the silence he sat furiously, knowing that he looked sulky and not caring a damn. The hell with them, the bunch of Christers, what were they to him? What business had any of them to yank and pull on him and try to make him do what he didn't want to do? Finally he heard the quiet voice of Anna Olson. "I guess

Joseph's bashful," she said. "Ingrid, why don't you play some songs people can sing?"

To walk out now, while they gathered around the piano, was perfectly possible, but he resisted the impulse out of a stubborn intention not to show that he was bothered or in any way aware of the huffiness that had come into their looks toward him. He picked up a magazine and read it while they sang. Once Otto went by with a girl and leaned to grin and whisper, "Say, I didn't mean to get you in a jam."

"No," Joe said. "Oh holy smoke, no!"

Stubbornly he sat until the singing dwindled and people began to shake hands all around and start home. They shook hands with him too; their concerned eyes looked him over, and he saw conversion in their looks and wondered why a Christian couldn't be content with his own slice of heaven but always had to be yanking some sinner up beside him. Eventually he got into the hall on his way out, and then he heard his name in the familiar: "*Du,* Joseph." Anna and Ingrid Olson were behind him. "Are you in a hurry?"

For a moment he hesitated, but his anger had worn away and only his ironic amusement was left. "Not especially," he said.

"We never had a chance to talk. Why don't you walk home with us? We live just down the street."

"Getting pretty late."

"Oh, come along," she said, and hooked one hand through his arm and the other through Ingrid's, keeping the grip on his arm even when the path narrowed and he had to walk along in the weeds.

"I've been thinking all night," she said. "I can remember when you were born."

"Yes?" He meant the tone to imply that he was not particularly anxious to have all the details.

"It seems so long ago and so far away," the woman said. Her fingers dug into his arm, and she pushed him along, leaning a little forward and walking heavily. "I can hardly think Gefle is real, any more. You said you never heard from anybody there."

"No."

"And you've never been back."

"No."

"I keep thinking it might be nice," she said. Her sigh was a comfortable, wistful noise in the dark. "Maybe I'd just be disappointed. We've been here fourteen years. The old country might not seem the same."

Joe said nothing, walking beside the two women up the path along the wide unpaved street; in the night air the weeds were aromatic and brittle; somewhere, when Anna Olson's voice paused, he heard the grassy low mutter of water in a ditch.

"You're not a Latter-day Saint," Anna said. "You wouldn't know what I mean, probably, but this is more than home to us now. Arne and I came here partly so we could be married in the temple for all eternity and be reunited in the last days."

Joe coughed, feeling about as appropriate as a billy goat at a picnic. They were passing open weedy lots, and he saw the faint outline of the mountains in the starlight, a high black continuous rim beyond the shapes of houses and trees. He asked himself sarcastically if it wasn't about time he got baptized; about all he had done all evening was listen to faith-promoting discourses.

The pause lengthened until he found himself absently counting their steps. Anna Olson finally said, "Your mother would have been glad about the music. Have you written lots of songs?"

"Only a few," he said. "Otto was trying to get my goat."

This time, as she sighed, he heard her corset creak. He kept on walking beside her because she had been a friend of his mother's and because she was the kind of woman his mother might have been now if she had lived. Quite suddenly he remembered a night when Anna had sat in the kitchen with her arm around his mother while his mother cried.

The shadowy shapes of trees uprose on their left. Untrimmed shrubs hung over a fence and forced the sidewalk-path to bend outward toward the road. The women stopped at a gate, and Joe stopped with them. He could see the glint of Anna's eyes as she looked up at him with her hand on the gatepost.

"I always thought your father should have done something for you."

"Why should he?"

"But if he had the slightest feeling . . ."

"He never showed any signs of it," Joe said, and tried to see

Anna Olson's face by the faint starlight, and added, "How do you even know for sure who my father is?"

While they stared at each other the girl moved restlessly across the gate from them.

"Don't you?" Anna said.

"I've heard tales, that's all."

"She never told anybody," Anna said. "At least she never told me. But it was plain enough. She was working there before, for a year. And your looks, too. After I'd looked at you for a minute tonight it was very plain. Your eyes."

"Well, it's a comfort to look like a small-town baron," Joe said.

"Not so small-town any more. Hadn't you heard about him?"

"Yes," Joe said, "I heard about him, but I'm not very interested."

Ingrid pushed at the gate, interrupting something her mother had started to say. "Come on in for a while."

"No, I'd better be getting back."

"Come on, we'll make some coffee."

"Isn't it terrible?" Anna said. "I'm a good Saint otherwise, but I just can't give up coffee. I tried and tried, and so did Arne."

"No Swede would want to go to heaven if they didn't have coffee there," Ingrid said. Her mother clucked at her.

With a shrug Joe followed them up the overgrown walk, mentally adding this to his other astonishments of the evening. You had to be pretty hard up for sins before you could begin to bullyrag yourself about coffee-drinking. But he came along because his curiosity was growing. If his mother had lived she might have been just like this, even to the coffee. Suppose the Mormon missionaries had converted her—and they might easily have done so; she was a sucker for salvation, and neither the state church nor the Mission Church was too friendly to fallen girls. Suppose she had been converted and had lived and had brought him to Utah as Anna Olson had brought her family. He might now be a returned missionary himself, worrying about his corrupt taste for Postum.

On the narrow porch hidden behind the vines it was utterly black. A bird rustled, alarmed, in the curtain of creeper. From some stooping place Anna fumbled up the key and found the lock with it.

"Shall we sit out?" Ingrid said. "It's so nice outside."

"Find Joseph a chair there," her mother said. "I'll go get the coffee on."

Bumping around finding chairs, Joe could smell the girl, like Castile soap. Then a lamp flickered and steadied through the window and he saw three chairs, the hanging surfaces of leaves, the almost-buried porch rail.

"Shall I bring the light out?" Anna said from inside.

"We don't need it. It would just draw bugs."

Joe eased himself into one of the chairs. Inside there was the sound of a stove being shaken down and kindling being broken. "I ought to beat it," he said. "She's having to build up the fire."

"Don't go," Ingrid said. "She gets lonesome for home since Dad died. She loves having you."

She spoke in English, as she had spoken from the beginning to him. It was as if she wanted to emphasize a difference between herself and her mother. Her voice was low, a little husky. Probably she sang alto in the church choir. But she seemed a pleasant enough girl. With the lamplight striking it obliquely, her face was cleanly outlined; he noticed that her eyes were rather deeply set, and that there was a long shadowy curve at her throat like a drawing that only suggested neck and shoulders by a hint of line and a touch of shadow. He could see none of the self-consciousness that he had observed earlier. At least if she blushed over every word now it was too dark for him to see her.

"What was that first piece you played tonight?" he said.

"Sinding's 'Rustle of Spring.'"

Having asked and having been answered, he found himself with no ready thing to say. She sat with her hands in her lap and watched him.

"How long did you have to take piano lessons before you could play a thing like that?"

"I don't know. A long time, I guess. I started when I was seven."

"And you're twenty-eight or nine now."

He was surprised at how easily and naturally she laughed. "That's something we don't say out loud."

"Twenty years, say," he said, and stared at her speculatively in the diffused lamplight. Twenty years while somebody else paid the bills. That was the difference. Without much more than dutiful-

ness, probably, with no more than average talents, she spent twenty
years learning to play pieces that would impress a lot of churchgoing Swedes at a whist party. He thought of himself and how
he had followed organ grinders and street singers with violins and
accordions, and of the hunger that had driven him to hang around
fairs and festivals as a boy. As palpable as a wind came the
memory of the YMCA piano and the Scotch sailor who had taught
him his first chords and his awe at his own accomplishments
when he first chorded out one of Luther's hymns by ear. There
had once been an itinerant merry-go-round with a calliope and
little painted horses, all of it run by the leg-power of town boys,
and he had spent whole afternoons behind the screen working
like a galley slave and listening happily to the wheeze and whine
of the music and taking his pay in free rides on lions and giraffes
and spotted ponies. He remembered himself in one powerful mul-
tiple rush of collection as he had been at ten, eleven, twelve,
and the duskiness of the porch moved and flowed around him as
the duskiness of his cottage bedroom had flowed around him in
boyhood. He felt like knives the innocence and futility of the
dreams he had dreamed. The bastard son of a sickly seamstress, to
lie in his bed and imagine splendors and triumphs.

Suddenly he wanted very much that this girl should know the
man who sat beside her as Joe Hill, the maker of cartoons and
writer of songs. He wanted to say, "Go into the lumber woods
or any construction camp or any Wobbly hall up and down the
coast and ask if they know Joe Hill. Start up one of the songs
and see if they know it. Maybe it isn't highbrow stuff like your
Chopin and Sinding, but it helps bring on the worker's world.
Once, let me tell you, I saw men sing a song I wrote and come
right on into the deputies' guns . . ."

As if she read his mind she said, "I wish you'd played."

"I told you the truth," he said. "I can't play. I'm good enough
to pound a piano in some saloon, that's about how good I am.
I never had the books. Nobody ever taught me."

"But Mr. What's-His-Name, Applequist, said you'd written a lot
of songs."

"Labor songs," Joe said. "Most of them set to Salvation Army
tunes."

"Didn't you ever try to write music yourself?"

"Once or twice. I never got anywhere. I don't know enough."

There was a momentary hesitation. "I should think you could," she said.

Her face was turned out of the light so that he could not see her expression. "Why?" he said. "What makes you think that?"

"I don't know. You look as if you'd thought a lot. You look like a sensitive person."

Interested, he sat back in the chair. "Yee!" he said. "That's a new one. How do you figure out I'm a sensitive person?"

"I was watching you tonight."

A late scrap of moon had climbed over the mountain wall and its light came through the leaves in flits and flashes. Anna Olson came and leaned in the door.

"You must have had a lot of exciting times," she said. "Where have you been to, you sailor?"

"Just about everywhere," Joe said. "I started out on a passenger steamer between Stockholm and Hull. After that freighters, mostly —tramps. Around the Cape of Good Hope one voyage, and out through the Indian Ocean and Australia, and back to the States. Across the Pacific three or four times, down through the canal. Just around, generally."

"Imagine!" she said, without any real interest. Then she added, "I'm sorry the coffee is slow. The fire was clear out."

"You shouldn't have bothered."

"It's no trouble. Just a minute now."

After a minute she went back in, and Joe said to Ingrid, "Most people that look at my face get the idea I'm some kind of hard guy. I'm supposed to have a poker face."

"You've got a poker face all right," she said seriously. "But it's not like some poker faces. Some people just don't have any expression because they're dull people, but some freeze their faces so they won't show anything. That's the kind you are."

He was staring at her hard, surprised at her. Propping his knees on his elbows, he leaned forward, rubbing his hands together with a dry calloused rustle. "If I'm such a frozen-face, how can you read my character like a fortune teller? What did my sensitive face give away?"

Ingrid stood up as if she had thought of something. "You can't freeze your eyes," she said accusingly. "You were seeing everything that went on tonight, all around that whole room!"

She went inside and brought out a little table, and in a minute her mother came bringing coffee and cake. There was no chance to pursue the interesting conversation with Ingrid. He praised the cake and then they were back in Gefle, recalling the dancing and fiddling contests on Midsummer Eve, and Pastor Eklund's unlucky series of wives, and the fish peddler who sometimes got drunk and destructive and kicked his cart apart in the street and scattered herrings over half a block.

The moon had climbed a long way, clear above the high eaves of the porch, when Joe stood up. "How late do the streetcars run?"

"Oh my goodness!" Anna said, and clapped her hands together. "I forgot you have to go into town." She hurried in to look at the clock. "It's after one," she said, returning. "The owl car will be gone. I just got so interested I didn't think."

"How far is it in to North Temple?"

"Oh, you couldn't walk. It's seven miles. Maybe we could . . ."

"What about Mrs. Erickson?" Ingrid said. "She's got a spare room for rent. He might get that for tonight."

"She wouldn't be up," Joe said.

"The boys would be. They never go to bed, or Mr. Applequist either."

"All right," Joe said. "I'll try there."

"I feel responsible," Anna Olson said. "I'll go over with you."

"No," he said. "I can make out. If I have to walk in, it won't kill me."

"If you took that room," Ingrid said, "you'd get a lot of chances to play the piano for them."

She was laughing; after a moment he laughed too. "I'd be right handy for music lessons, at least."

"Why sure," she said. "Any time."

"You mean that?"

"Of course."

"Could you teach me about harmony?"

"What are you talking about, you two?" Anna said. "Teach you music?"

"Sure," Ingrid said.

"If I brought over a song sometime, could you try out the arrangement and maybe take the kinks out?"

"I should think so."

"You got a new pupil," he said. "When's the best time?"

"I don't have any pupils after five any day."

"Expect me sometime after five."

For a step or two she followed him along the path. "Any particular day?"

"I don't know yet," he said. "I have to write the song first."

Their goodnights and their invitations to come again went with him through the overgrown gate. He walked two blocks back to the Erickson house and found Otto and the two Erickson boys drinking beer on the high front porch. When he asked about a room Otto was all over him, urging him to move out for good.

"Listen," Otto said. "You're right next to the smelter, practically. We could maybe get you on the bullgang, at least. You better move out. You know the kind of grub Ma Erickson spreads? Herrings, the only place in Salt Lake, and coffee cake and fruit soup. You live out here a week you'll start putting some meat on your bones. You could stick round all winter and organize the smelter. We'll all join the One Big Union and wear buttons and damn the boss."

"It wouldn't do you any harm," Joe said.

Karl Erickson said, "You an organizer?"

"Listen!" Otto said, and put his arm around Joe's shoulders. "I've known this guy a long time. He'd never tell you who he was. He gave you that deaf-and-dumb act about the piano, but you know who he is? You ever hear of Joe Hill?" He mauled Joe around. "These guys are no scissorbills, they know the score."

The Erickson brothers peered at him. There was respect in the way they leaned in the shadows. "Joe Hill?" they said. "My God, are you Joe Hill? You better stay."

That was something, at least, after the beating he had taken from Chopin. He let them lead him upstairs, and in the end he let Otto talk him into sharing his room. In the morning he could decide whether or not he would stay.

4

He awoke sharply and alertly, instantly aware of the strange room, instantly taking it in and understanding it. He saw the white-enameled iron bed, the washbowl and pitcher and slop jar, the Boston rocker, the dresser. He saw his own and Otto's clothes on floor and chairback. His recognition of them was like a renewed recognition of himself: the vague expectancy that had haunted him ever since his arrival in Salt Lake did not make of these things the sources or keys of future events. They existed for themselves, and so did he.

Otto was sleeping heavily with his face to the wall, taking advantage of Sunday morning. Lightly Joe got out of the bed; bending and stooping and exercising himself for a moment, he felt as limber and tough as a whip. There was no doubt in his mind that he would stay here. It was clean, it had none of the notoriety of Mother Wynn's. And there was a piano a couple blocks away, and Ingrid Olson for a schoolteacher. He had not written a song for a long time.

In the kitchen he found Mrs. Erickson slapping around in old felt slippers. With her teeth out and her hair tied up in a dustcap she gave him flapjacks and coffee, and before ten o'clock he caught a streetcar up the long straight reach of State Street toward the scaffolded dome of the capitol. A half-hour later he was at the Wobbly hall.

This too was a strange place of the utmost familiarity. There was a class in socialism going on. When it broke up he eased into the conversation—an old song, both words and music—about the proper conduct of a union hall.

—Yes, but that's just the point. A union hall isn't a flophouse, even if you do organize migrants. The minute you make it a flophouse you start getting in bums that join up just for the free flop and the mulligan.

—What harm does that do? You got a house committee, the

place can be kept clean. Go on in there now, it's clean. What harm does it do to let stiffs roll a blanket on the floor and maybe boil up a pot of java?

– I told you. It brings in the wrong kind of members.

– Since when did we get so choosy? I thought we wanted everybody in.

– Maybe we do, but not to flop in the hall.

– Like me? I flop in the hall.

– No, not like you. What the hell! But I've seen some guys come through here and spend a week that I'd sure hate to count on as union men. And I know plenty of home guards that stay away from here just because it's always full of hoboes with their socks and undershirts hung out to dry.

– That's too damn bad about the home guards. They got wives to wash their socks. Let me tell you, if it wasn't for the hall sometimes . . .

– What it seems to me, the hall is the surest way of maintaining solidarity. If a worker knows that wherever he goes he can find friends and fellow workers and a place to put up in for a few days while he hunts a job, he's going to think a lot more about the union, because it *does* something for him.

– I agree, I agree! But he doesn't have to sleep in it and hang out his socks in it. There are plenty of workers right here in town that would bring their wives to meetings—and that's something we want too, isn't it? But they won't bring them because they're never sure what kind of guys they'll find around.

– So the only thing to do is what I've always said. Have two halls, one for business and social meetings and one for a union-run boardinghouse.

They worried the argument back and forth in a desultory, Sunday-morning way while Joe listened. Through an open door he saw a massive man with a head like a block of granite come into the next room and sit down at a desk. That ought to be Jud Ricket, the secretary. Joe rose and went in.

The secretary looked at him across the littered rolltop desk with eyes of a startling, polished black. He bulged with life; a look from him was as intense as a stab. Joe knew him a little, by reputation. A manager, a comer. He put out his hand.

"Ricket?"

"Yes."

"Joe Hill."

Without taking his eyes from Joe's, Ricket reached out a big blucher-cut shoe and hooked a chair within reach. While Joe sat down Ricket studied him with curiosity, a jerky tic like a smile moving one corner of his mouth.

"Nobody told me you were coming," he said.

"Nobody knew."

"On your way somewhere?"

"I thought I might eventually get over to Colorado."

"Look in on Mr. Rockfeller, uh?" Ricket said. "Don't let anybody fool you, that can get bad."

"Lately I've spent a lot of my time raising money for the Oatfield defense committee," Joe said. "You doing anything about that?"

"Usual thing. Collection, street meeting. We've sent in a couple of contributions. But I don't know, I just can't get excited about that case."

"You can't? Why not?"

The fleeting wide smile touched Ricket's lips, held for a moment, and snapped off. "Fuzzy Llewellyn was a member in bad standing, for one thing. He'd been blacklisted out of the Stockton local."

"Art Manderich was in good standing."

"I know," Ricket said. "I ought to be in there pitching, but I just can't get my heart in that one the way I can in some others."

"An injury to one is an injury to all," Joe said.

"That's a fact," Ricket said solemnly. "That's a fact, sure enough. But some injuries just advertise better than others. Who's this Hale? Just some little punk rancher. If those boys had been used up by the lumber trust, or the copper trust, or John D., then the case would advertise better."

"Maybe they didn't go in there and get killed for the advertising."

They were looking hard into each other's eyes. The twitch moved Ricket's mouth again and he flapped his hand on the desk. "Well," he said, and shrugged. "We've sent what we could. It's a little far away from us here. We're sort of in a backwater."

"Anything doing at all?"

"Mainly on-the-job organizing. We've got to lay a foundation in this state before we can get anywhere. Haywood tried Bingham last year. You know how far he got. They busted his strike with Mexican scabs. But he left a lot of buttons behind. We're trying to spread it in the smelters and up in Park City and down in the coal camps. Next time we pull a big strike we want support."

There was a question in his black eyes, but Joe shook his head. "I don't want to waste my time working on some smelter bullgang when I could be doing something important. Do you know how many dollars it takes to keep a crew of lawyers working? How much does it cost to save a man from the chair?"

"Yeah," Ricket said, not as an answer but as an acknowledgment of the force of the argument. He rubbed his hands circularly one upon the other and then reached for a big brass-ended advertising pencil and twirled it between his palms. "This is a bad town for raising money in," he said.

"No town's much different."

"I don't know," Ricket said, "maybe these Mormons tithe away all they got. I should think for the Oatfield boys you might do better down on the coast."

"I just came from the coast," Joe said. He knew what was the matter with Ricket. Ricket liked the organizing and he liked a fight, but he didn't like dispersing himself in a dozen directions helping defend every organizer that got thrown in jail.

"I had a hunch when I came into this town," Joe said. "I can do something here, but not at any penny-ante organizing in some smelter."

Ricket tossed and caught the pencil. "That was a suggestion, that's all."

Looking restlessly around the jamb of the door, Joe nodded at the old flatbed press in the main room. "I see you've got a press."

Ricket nodded.

"A song printed on cards will double or triple your take at a street meeting," Joe said. "A really good song can make you fifteen or twenty dollars."

Ricket nodded again. "Now I see where you come in. You got a song?"

"I can write one."

"Then you'd be a sucker to go to work organizing in a smelter," Ricket said, and hitched himself forward to hump over the desk.

He gave Joe a glance of almost winsome friendliness. "I got a single-track mind, I try to drag everybody I see into what I'm interested in at any special time. I want you to know we're glad to have you in town. You got a place to live?"

"I'm at a boardinghouse down in Murray."

"There's a cot up at my place."

"Thanks, I'm fixed."

"About food," Ricket said, and smiled his phantasmal smile. "If you go broke, there's a Chink on First South will give you credit any time on the strength of your card."

Joe stood up, and the swivel chair shot backward against the wall as Ricket struggled to his feet.

"Any time you get a song ready," Ricket said. He shook hands with Joe and watched him go—Ricket, a great black bear of a man with an odd manner, and a smile that came and went like the play of muscles when a man grits his teeth. Maybe he was getting everything that the traffic would bear out of Salt Lake and maybe he wasn't. They would see what a Joe Hill song would do. Maybe it would wake this burg up a little.

One song. One more song. Joe went out into the morning heat with his mind already beginning to churn out scraps of rhyme, sort among the old familiar tunes. One song, we will sing one song . . . and there was the tune. The words came thronging to pair with it, and he went up a strange street wrapped in his inner swathings of contemplation, working at the verses. My Old Kentucky home sold for taxes, gobbled by the landlord, raided by the cops, taken over by the bank, sold by the sheriff at public sale. There was plenty you could do with the idea. He walked a street in Salt Lake City, in the bright stare and clarity, the barren brilliant light of a September morning, with words moving in his head, and he inquired the way to the public library and turned left out of the sun.

As he turned, he saw something out of the corner of his eye. Inside a pawnshop window, ringed by harmonicas and banjos and watches with thick chains, was an automatic in a worn holster. Pressing his arm against his ribs, he felt the emptiness where the Luger had used to ride, and he thought of how once in their talk Jud Ricket's shiny black eyes had dropped to the place where a hidden gun would be. In that flick of Ricket's glance he had seen a reflection of his own legend: Joe Hill, an ice-eyed stiff with a rod under his arm, a maker of songs and a hunter of trouble, an uncompromising enemy of the master class but maybe dangerous, maybe hard to handle.

With hardly a break in his stride he turned into the pawnshop, and five minutes later he came out with the gun in a package in his pocket. Now he went full stature again, veritably Joe Hill, wearing the things that completed and uttered him: an empty purse, a gun, the forming words of a song.

By the time he reached the stone library below the spread wings of the Eagle Gate he had arranged the easily alternated counters of his belief into a stanza.

> We will sing one song of the meek and humble slave,
> The horny-handed son of the soil,
> He's toiling hard from the cradle to the grave,
> But his master reaps the profits of his toil.

Other stanzas were clamoring at the gate, half seen. One song of the politician, one song of the children in the mills, one song of the girl below the line, one song of the poor and ragged tramp, one song

> . . . of the preacher, fat and sleek,
> He tells you of homes in the sky.
> He says "Be generous, be lowly and be meek,
> If you don't you'll sure get roasted when you die."

At the circulation desk he waited impatiently for the girl to come from sorting cards at a file. "I'd like to borrow a pencil for a few minutes," he said.

The girl's eyes behind round windows of glass jumped to meet his. He saw her mouth pop open. Two words came out: "We don't . . ." Her tongue touched her lip quickly, something moved in her throat. Without a word and without taking her eyes from his face she reached sideways and groped up a long sharply pointed pencil and laid it in his hand.

5

"I guess I don't quite understand what it is you do," she said.

It was the third time he had been to the Olson house. On the music rack of the piano sat the scribbled and erased music notebook they had been working on: a song he had begun long ago, in San Pedro, and had never been able to finish. Between the lines of music Joe had copied out the first verse, to see how the words matched with the notation.

> Workers of the world, awaken!
> Break your chains! Demand your rights!
> All the wealth you make is taken
> By exploiting parasites.

"I'm an organizer," he said.

He heard Anna Olson at the dishes in the kitchen. Through the open window he saw a man and two little girls setting up a ladder under an apple tree red with fruit. The dirt street lay lulled and quiet in the evening. There was a smell of mown alfalfa. Eastward the Wasatch showed between poplar trees, its slopes bronze and pink with the late sun and the first beginnings of autumn. He had momentary perception of how peaceful it was, and he thought of a little shanty somewhere in the hills.

"You don't work in any particular place," Ingrid said.

He let himself look at her serious, interested face, into her eyes that held his a moment and then dropped. She had nice skin and a faint clean smell, and sitting next to her was still an unfamiliar and faintly disturbing experience. He remembered having been bumped by her arm as she leaned to pencil something into the music notebook.

"Haven't you heard about the IWW?" he said. "I go someplace and stay long enough to plant a few sticks of dynamite, and then I clear out and go blow something up somewhere else."

"No, seriously. Do you make speeches?"

"I've made a few. I'm no good at it."

"How do you organize, then?"

"Talking to the men. Generally there's dissatisfaction, maybe some trouble. I get them to pull together, form a committee. At meetings, I'm generally the guy that thumps the piano. Sometimes I draw cartoons just to get people laughing, you know, promote solidarity. People fight a lot better when they can sing, or when they've got something to laugh at."

"Who tells you what to do? Do you get paid by the locals where you go, or by a national office, or what?"

He stiffened a little at that, delicately touched in his pride. "I never took a dollar from the union."

Her face went pink with the easy blush, and he saw that she felt rebuked. Watching her reach up self-consciously to smooth the pages of the music notebook, he thought of how much he could tell her that would shock her pious ignorance, and felt magnanimous for keeping still. "I guess I don't quite understand what it is you do." I guess not. The struggle of labor against the bosses was more than she ever would understand.

"You have to live *somehow*, though," she said.

He laughed. "A man can live quite a while on what he can mooch from free-lunch counters in saloons."

That brought her eyes up, testing him to see if he were joking. In a careful voice she said, "I see. Where do you sleep?"

"Under bridges, out in the jungles, on park benches. Or I can always unroll a blanket on the floor of the local hall."

Just when he expected her to smile she gave him her direct, serious look. "It's your whole life, isn't it?"

Somehow he felt the question as an accusation, and he stood up, tired of this conversation. He had taken a lot of satisfaction in doing for the past week what he had been doing, but he did not want to sit and justify himself and his life to Ingrid Olson.

"Let's go down and take in a show," he said.

A little smile of malice curled her mouth. "Can you get tickets at a free-lunch counter?"

Joe shrugged. "You gave me my supper. Why should you kick at buying me tickets to a show?"

First she laughed, and then she touched four black keys on the piano, and then she looked up at him with the pink washing again into her face. He saw that she would take him to the show if he asked it. Holy smoke! he said to himself. Aloud he said, "Quit worrying how I live. It's been two or three years since I even thought about it. Right now, as a matter of fact, I've got five dollars that I borrowed from Otto."

"You'll have to pay it back sometime."

"That's Otto's worry."

"You're a shiftless man, Mr. Hillstrom," she said, but he jingled the change in his pocket and smiled at her.

"I can afford to be shiftless. The world owes me a living. My labor has created enough wealth already so I could retire on my fair share of it."

"If you could get it."

"Yeah, if I could get it."

That night late, standing under the dark vines, he kissed her and found her lips warm, her body willing. For half a minute his hands were all over her, his mouth hot on hers, but then she strained backward, pushing him away. He reached for her again, his blood thick in his ears and his breath fast, and felt how the thin stuff of her dress slipped on her shoulders.

"No, no Joe, please!"

The hot fit passed, and he saw her coolly: a middle-class, conventional, pious, proper woman, a believer in marriage and property and children and cottages with vines on the porch and a husband with a regular pay enevelope, a Swede girl from Gefle who knew too much about him and didn't half understand what she knew.

"Okay, no," he said.

"Joe . . ."

"What?"

With her hands on his arms she turned him so that the vague glow of the lamp inside the parlor fell across his face. Her eyes looked into his so long that he began to wonder what she was up to. It was as if she hunted for something, her eyes pried at him. But she said nothing. At last she shivered suddenly and crowded against him, pressing her face into his shoulder, and broke away and ran inside.

Walking home, he spoke ironically and with some astonishment to himself. He said, Joe, look what you've just had offered to you on a platter. This is the chance of a lifetime. You can marry this girl and get a house and a couple of acres of land thrown in. All the rest of your life you can sit around the house in carpet slippers and spit off the porch or weed around in the flower beds while your wife earns the bread and butter giving music lessons. You even get a mother-in-law to boot for cook and bottle-washer. You can settle down on Forty-Eighth South Street in the middle of the Salt Lake Valley and to hell with the workers' revolution. To hell with the troubles of miners in Colorado or gyppo men down on the D & RG or stoop-crop pickers in the San Joaquin Valley. To hell with the radicals in the capitalistic jails. You can sit around the rest of your life eating apples and playing whist with a lot of Swedes and talking about the old country.

That's a fact, he said to himself—more and more astonished, more and more ironical. All you have to do is reach out your hand.

And be good, he said. You'll have to promise to be good. You couldn't be kept around the house unless you were house-broke.

The Erickson house was dark. So was every other house on the thinly built-up street. On the porch he sat down, too restless for sleep, and heard the dry unwearied noise of the cottonwood leaves like the rustling of thoughts in his mind. The loneliness that always lived with him, and especially late at night, came out of the dark and hobnobbed with him on the empty porch: a melancholy nighttime yearning washed in on the barely moving night air. He put his feet on the rail and pushed his chair back against the wall and closed his eyes. After a while he found himself in the midst of people he admired, the uncompromising enemies of the system, men and women he would have gone a long way to see and would have used for the models of his own life.

As if he had been there, he saw Frank Little parading back and forth in the street, up in the Mesabi, his tough, one-sided mouth distorted in jeers and his tongue going in a steady stream of profane catcalls, daring the finks inside their headquarters to come out and get him. *You think I'm afraid of you, you*

*scabby sons of bitches? I'm a cripple, I couldn't even run away.
What's holding you back? You hired out to beat up workingmen.
Why don't you start on me? I'm a red, red Wobbly, I'm a radical
agitator, and I hate the guts of every scabby fink of you. Why
don't you come out and start to work?* He saw Frank Little throw
his crutch fifty feet out in the dust and hobble along without it
between silent, watching miners and the company headquarters
full of finks. A human flame, a fire of hatred and protest, he dared
the whole wage system and its gunmen single-handed.

And Frank Little faded and the picture of Gurley Flynn's red
mane came in. He saw the veritable twist of her lips as she
spoke from a soapbox, and felt the electricity she gave off. Another
flame. And The Flynn faded into Katie Phar, the kid Katie with
her child's eyes and her child's silvery voice, a kind of saint,
an innocent homely Joan of Arc, no torch like The Flynn but
with just as much courage. And behind Katie as she sang outside
the Spokane jail came the other faces—the grim creased mask of
Art Manderich, the gopher teeth of Fuzzy Llewellyn bared in a
still grin, Herb Davis' cocked jaw, the serious, intellectual intentness
of Tom Barnabas, the rocky immovable face of Big Bill Haywood.
They came like a parade, the fighters, the devoted and dedicated
and incorruptible. They came in crowds—the free-speech fighters
in San Diego driven back by the white blasts of firehoses, washed
away like chips, and re-forming and coming back to be blasted
again, and re-form again, and come on. He heard them singing
in the Fresno jail, and opened his eyes on the darkness of this
sleeping street, the blotted shadows of trees and houses, the high
crestline of the Wasatch cutting off the stars. He remembered
himself kissing Ingrid Olson at her front gate, and the way her eyes
searched and pried at his for some assurance, and said to himself,
No, my God, what are you getting into? You don't want to wear
that collar.

Then what was he doing hanging around Salt Lake? He ought
to get out of here and hike for Colorado where he could do some
good. What he had told Jud Ricket was strict truth. He didn't
want to spend his time in the routine slow groundwork organizing
in preparation for something a year or two years away. He was a
trouble-shooter and he ought to be where trouble was brewing.
Yet there were Fuzzy and the others in the Sacramento jail.

He knew precisely why Fuzzy had stuck to his soapbox in that fracas. As definitely as if Fuzzy had told him he knew that Fuzzy stuck because he wanted to prove he was no dehorn. The Stockton local that had blacklisted him had to be shown that Fuzzy was as true-blue a rebel as lived.

And Joe Hillstrom? Why was Joe Hillstrom breaking his neck to raise money for Fuzzy's defense? Oh yes, he said to himself, that's a good question—and saw himself cutting through the clutter of tents, running like a rabbit while Fuzzy stood fast.

His mind ducked and bent, reaching out for the thought of the songs. Down at the hall the cards with "My Old Kentucky Home" still drying on them; over at Ingrid Olson's the notebook with the half-completed "Workers of the World." As if talking with some questioner or critic, he framed an orderly plan: I want to stay in Salt Lake long enough to get a lot of songs done. I can always have the use of a piano, and this Olson girl can help me with the harmony when I bugger it up. Maybe I'll try a popular song or two, waltzes or two-steps, not labor songs at all. If I could get one or two of those published and sold I could turn over the royalties to the defense fund. There's a lot more money in that kind than in a labor song printed on a card, and besides, the money for a popular song comes out of good bourgeois pockets, not out of workingmen. I could make the system contribute to the revolution that will overturn it . . .

A vaudeville singer in a straw hat, leaning on a cocky cane, sang from a brilliant stage, and a face, unrecognized but unmistakable, looked at Joe Hill with admiration and said distinctly, "I hear your song all over, everybody's singing it" singing what turkey trot singing what and he bent his head at the post office window and said "I want a money order for five hundred dollars make it to the General Defense Fund, Industrial Workers of the World." I can't get all that on one line, the face inside the window said, and turned his pad, too bad, and Joe said, "Make it IWW, that won't trouble you." He fell back from the window as Ingrid Olson put her head out, serious, with her hair in thick braids, and she said, "You're so shiftless, Mr. Hillstrom," but he held the blue slip of the money order up in front of her nose.

Holy smoke, he said, think what it would mean to the union to have just one rich bird in it. Everybody in the whole IWW is a working stiff without a cartwheel to his name, or an intellectual with shiny pants. Suppose just once some old Moneybags died and left a million to the union. Just suppose there was a really fat defense fund, plenty of money for strike relief. What if we had the money to fight them in the courts and in the press and everywhere where money gives them every advantage.

Out of the darkness beyond the porch came Joe Hill, walking erectly in a good blue suit. As he passed along a picket line, men spoke to him in friendship and admiration. He went into a hall and saw a strike committee sitting at a table and he said, "How much of a strike fund do you need to keep from being starved back to work?" The checkbook unfolded before their astonished faces.

Angrily, shaking himself, he stood up in the dark and the silence. The noise of the cottonwood leaves seemed to pause while he listened; then it began again, a dry, clicking whisper. He leaned out to see if he could detect any sign of light down toward the Olson house, but saw none. All alone, he felt how his thoughts and desires warred in him, how much remained to do, how everything he did was not enough. A man could go sleepless for a hundred years, and work like a horse the whole time, and complete not one tenth of what he wanted to do. He thought of Thor, trying to drink the ocean dry and tear up the roots of the Midgard Serpent.

Hell, he said, and let himself in. The house was still, the dining-room clock a loudness in the enclosed dark. He walked along the edge of the stairs, off the carpet, to avoid the squeaks. In the room he scratched a match, found the lamp on the dresser, and touched flame to wick, so that the room brightened around him into enameled bedstead and pottery pitcher and the shine of varnish on the chair arms. The bed was empty; Otto still catting around somewhere.

His pleasure at finding the room empty gave a shove to the vague intention that had brought him upstairs. As if he had planned just this, he got paper and pencil and sat under the lamp with a magazine on his knees for a writing pad. A popular song. Something for lovers and kids in high schools, some tune for bands to play on Sunday afternoons in a thousand parks. A waltz, maybe, some joyride song, something to sweep the country like *Ta-ra-ra-boom-de-ay*, some song that every good middle-class housewife would have to have on her piano, something every music teacher would give her pupils.

Thoughtfully he opened the magazine, turning its pages, looking among its words and pictures for inspiration, for a starter, an idea that would set him off.

Much later the sound of someone coming in made him look up from his paper with its scratched lines and its tentative annotations for a tune. He looked across at Otto's alarm clock. Two-twenty. Steps came up the stairs carefully, were muffled for a moment in the hall carpet. Then the door opened and Otto looked in.

For an instant he hung in the doorway. His grin was turned on; in the shadow he looked hare-lipped. Then he closed the door carefully and quietly and crossed to the bed and sat down. He did not look as if he had been out with a girl, or at a show. He wore corduroy pants that were streaked with mud. A patch of white cobweb like cheesecloth clung to the shoulder of his coat. Around his neck he wore a red bandanna handkerchief loosely tied. Joe glanced down at the pockets of Otto's coat and saw that they sagged heavily as if full of apples.

"You're up late," Otto said.

"So are you."

Continuing to smile, Otto untied the bandanna and threw it on the dresser. He yawned and shook his head with a doglike shudder. "You don't have to make that whistle in the morning. How's it feel to be a plutocrat and live without working?"

Joe folded his papers and put them in a drawer. When he scratched himself he felt the lean bars of his ribs. "I'm thinking of making it permanent," he said. "I can always borrow from you when I need a few bucks."

Otto turned his back and slipped out of the coat and hung it up on a wall hook. It sagged heavily, and Joe speculated on what it contained. Silverware, maybe. Something compact and heavy and valuable. Or maybe just Otto's second-story tools. Interested but not especially curious, he watched Otto undress, and thought of Ingrid's question, "But how do you *live?*" It amused him to think what she might say if she knew how that jolly whist-playing Mr. Applequist managed to get along.

Or Joe Hillstrom either, for that matter, though he kept himself carefully in another category. At that, he would probably have to do something about a job. He couldn't coast all winter without a stake of some kind.

"For a while," Otto said, answering so long after the conversation had stopped that Joe had to hunt back for what he had said. Otto pulled down the striped police suspenders. "Up to a certain point," he said, and grinned widely, full of slyness, pleased at something he knew, and yawned so cavernously that deep in his mouth the lamplight discovered the spark of a gold tooth.

6

The weather in Salt Lake City in late September is likely to be even, temperate, so balmy that the mind sinks into it as the body might sink into a featherbed. There are no dramatics to mark the transitional season: the earth tilts gently, day by day, away from summer and into fall: the oakbrush on the mountain slopes goes dull bronze, and then red-copper; in the gullies the sumac flames, and on the high slopes, among the winter-darkening spruce, the aspens are groves of gold. The morning sun lifts over the Wasatch crest into a faint haze that fills the valley, and as September draws on and the smoke of many fires thickens and mixes with the valley haze, it sets like a bulbous orange. In the wake of the year the poplars yellow along ditchbanks and lanes.

It is weather for parables of the grasshopper and the ant. The industrious glean and gather and preserve and store, bins and barrels are full, the storehouses of the Mormon bishops bulge with the accumulated tithes in produce. Along West Second South the stiffs with a winter stake begin thinking of California, or settle in against the coming cold in boardinghouses and the rooms of small hotels. In Europe the nations eye one another and hurry the preparations for war; in San Francisco Kelly's Army is being assembled to beat its way across the continent to storm Washington in protest against unemployment.

In the reading room of the Carnegie Public Library, which he uses scornfully and of right as a meager compensation for what Carnegie has taken from the pockets of workingmen, Joe Hill sits almost every morning with paper before him, working on verses, or putting into six-by-six drawings the acid of his discontent.

His pencil is fond of showing a fat man with a big watch chain hiding behind a corner near which lies a wallet labeled "Fair Wages." Stooping to pick up the wallet is a worker in overalls, but leading from the wallet to the fat man's hand is a string with many little tags on it. Of the three which can be read, one says "Premium holdback," another says "Company store," and a third says "Company boardinghouse."

Or many men with strong faces are marching toward a dawn called "Industrial Freedom."

Or a man is sweeping a littered street with a big broom entitled "Industrial Unionism," and the broom is heaping into a trash cart assorted debris named "Starvation Wages," "Lousy Bunkhouses," "The Ten-Hour Day," "Company Spies." Already in the cart is a dead horse with all four feet in the air, and tied to one ankle a label: "Exploitation of Labor."

Or four men press their faces against the bars of a jail window, looking out to a gallows with four dangling nooses. The caption says, "They fought for you. Will you let them die for you?"

He makes these drawings, or awaits the inspiration of a rhyme, and at noon he goes out for a sandwich and coffee. After that he drops off at the hall what he has ready for Jack Carpenter, the printer, or leaves with Jud Ricket a cartoon to be sent to the *Industrial Worker*. For reasons that he does not thoroughly phrase even to himself, he does not spend much time at the hall. Sooner or later someone he knows is bound to come through, and he does not want to see anyone he knows. There is the unfinished business at Gaviota, and the near recollection of the police at Lund's door. He tells himself that he is scrupulous about getting the union involved in anything, and he is honest in this belief.

His expenses are for carfare and the noon sandwich. The newspapers that he reads religiously he gets in the library or picks up on the street. Though his rent is already a week in arrears, he is not troubled. He does not drink or smoke, and his relations with the only women he knows in Salt Lake are such that they expect to feed him any time he shows up at their door. His musical handmaiden will sit with him at the piano for hours any afternoon or evening. They have finished the "Workers of the World" song; "My Old Kentucky Home" has so far earned eighteen dollars at street meetings. And by himself, secretly, wanting this to be entirely his own, Joe has written words and music of a popular song called "Come Joyride with Me in My Aeroplane," and begun a waltz to which as yet he has put no name.

One after another the days pour westward into the dead lake, windless days without stir or commotion or portent. And yet sometimes, looking up at the enigmatic wall of mountains, he feels how close to something these days may be. In this lotused interlude he sometimes thinks of winter, not so much afraid of its coming as sure it will come.

Until one day he came out onto the library steps in the hazy heat of afternoon and shook the change in his pocket, brought it out to count it in his palm. A quarter, two dimes, two pennies. The quarter would go for lunch, a nickel for carfare. Tonight he would arrive back at the boardinghouse with seventeen cents in his pocket.

The day was placid, cloudless, a little warmer than usual. On the exposed east side of the street it felt like hot summer. The trees drooped with heat; in the opposite gutter he caught the hurrying gleam of water. Aimlessly he pocketed the change. When he started walking he took the direction that he had taken every day for more than a week, turning right on First South and moseying along under the awnings on the north side.

Midway in the block he stopped, as he had several times stopped before, and looked in the window. There was a piano there, a new grand piano sleek with varnish, rich with polishing. Its cover was propped up on a stick so that he could see its gilded strings like a harp laid sideways inside the curved wood. He had never played a grand piano; he wondered how it would feel, how it would sound. A chaste card propped against one leg of the instrument told him what it would cost to find out: $984.

A reverie held him there at the window. A thousand dollars for one musical instrument, and in plenty of homes that he could suppose and imagine, a piano like this one would be standard equipment, as much taken for granted as dishes or beds. There were people in the world who could buy a piano like this as offhandedly as he would buy a hot pork sandwich.

As he stood looking, his fingers felt the coins in his pocket, sorted them, slid them one over the other. On the carpet between the piano and the plate glass, sheet music was spread in a carefully careless fan so that titles showed, and sometimes the partial face of a man or woman who introduced or sang or played or wrote the music. As far as Joe could see, the faces of these ornately successful people were alike, with oiled hair and little mustaches, except one who wore a derby cocked over one eye. That one was George M. Cohan.

He supposed that if a song came into the hands of George M. Cohan, and he liked it and sang it, a hundred thousand people would automatically buy the sheet music. If Cohan sang it on a gramophone record, everyone who had a gramophone would want that record, and for every record bought there would be a fee or royalty to the man who wrote the song. Say one cent a record, just to be conservative. A hundred thousand records would mean a thousand dollars to the author. And say two cents on each piece of sheet music, where no George M. Cohan would be involved except as a picture on the cover. That would be two thousand more. Three thousand dollars for one song.

As gingerly as a man exploring the dangerous surface of a glacier, testing it with axe and alpenstock, his imagination went over the song he had been carrying around in his pocket for a week, neatly copied into sheets from one of Ingrid's music note-books. He tried to summarize and catalogue what a song had to have. Sentiment, sure, some talk about sweethearts and how much a lover missed or loved or would do for his girl. And everything had to be like the Garden of Eden, all moonlight and weeping willows, made for spooning. It seemed to him too that there ought to be some twist, some new and catchy note. His aeroplane song had them all, and it had a dancy two-step tune. The slight bulge in his coat pocket might be worth three thousand dollars. The men who wrote the songs that George M. Cohan sang made that much from a song, and they would write a dozen, two dozen songs a year.

His impulse was to go in, but he hesitated, wondering if maybe he ought to get Ingrid to do this. She knew a lot more about it. But the song was his own, she had never seen it. And a glance at himself in the reflecting window showed him the blue suit and the high collar: he had dressed up that morning because his corduroy pants were in Mrs. Erickson's washtub.

Well, why not? What could he lose? If a song had to be sent somewhere, New York maybe, to get it published, then someone in here ought to know. And if there was any chance of publishing it here in town, this ought to be as good a place to find it out as any. He went in.

Among pianos, spinets, parlor organs, sets of drums, tables of songbooks and sheet music, he stood waiting in the abrupt dark coolness of the store. The place was empty except for two young clerks talking confidentially back at the rear, where the office was. Now one of them came forward, snapping his fingers lightly as he came, his head a little sideways in an inquiring sort of way. He was a dapper, somewhat pudgy young man. His trousers had a crease fit to carve a roast. On his shirt front he wore a rectangular black pin with a single diamond set off-center in it—a lodge pin of some sort, apparently—and on his plump left hand a big black and silver ring of the same design.

"Yes, sir?" he said. He had the air of a trained seal waiting for a thrown fish. He was deferential, suave, polite; he wore none of that superiority that Joe had instinctively tightened in preparation for.

Reassured, Joe said, "I want to see somebody about a song."

The salesman pivoted as neatly as if executing a dance step and laid one hand on the stacked music table. "Something new? Ragtime? Waltz? Here's the latest Castle tune, what they call a foxtrot. Everybody's buying this one. We can't keep it in stock." He whipped the music from the stack and held it in his hand, his head bent. "Play it over for you?"

"No," Joe said, feeling foolish, standing still. "I don't want to buy a song. I've got one I wrote, I wanted to ask somebody about publishing it."

Absently the salesman reached the sheet music back on the pile.

Touched by thought, he stood eyeing Joe, and now Joe felt the
inspection that took in clothes, shoes, face.

"I see," the salesman said. "Well, that's something a little different. You wrote it, you say."

"Words and music," Joe said. "I've written songs before, but
never the tunes. This is the first time . . ."

The large gray eyes of the salesman remained on him con-
templatively. "Who published the others?"

"You wouldn't know them," Joe said impatiently. "They're in a
songbook, eight or ten of them."

"Uh," the salesman said. "I'd like to see them. Happen to have
them with you?"

"Just the new one. I wanted to ask somebody . . ."

"Let's see it."

Joe handed it over. He was beginning to feel like a fathead,
being quizzed by this dude salesman, but he told himself that
if he wanted the song published he would certainly have to show
it to somebody. "Maybe that's not your line," he said. "Maybe I
ought to send it to New York."

"Um," the salesman said. Without raising his bent head or interrupting his study of the notebook sheets he called out, "Eddie,
come on up here."

The other young man came up, a tall thin young man with
pimples, and looked from Joe to the plump salesman. He was
one who wore boredom as some people wear loud socks. "What's
up?"

"Man has a song he wrote," the plump one said. He smiled
at his companion and said, "I want you to listen to this," and
then his smile moved over and included Joe. Weaving among
instruments, he went to the grand piano fronting the window and
slid onto the bench. His soft white hand with the black ring on
it touched a note or two, surely and nimbly, and skipped through
the verse tune. His beaming good-natured face turned back to
the others. "Man wants to get it published. Listen to it, Eddie,
give it your critical attention."

He propped the notebook sheets on the rack and his hands
leaped into the tune, putting into it a lot of fancy frills and
variations. Weaving a little on the bench, he leaned toward them
like a cabaret entertainer and sang as he played.

> If you will be my sweetheart I'll take you for a ride
> Among the silv'ry clouds up in the sky.
> Then far away from sorrows like eagles we will glide
> And no one will be there but you and I.
> Say, darling, if you'll be my little honey dove
> We'll fly above and coo and love.
> I'll take you from this dusty earth to where the air
> Is pure and crystal clear and there
> I'll give you my promise to be true
> While gliding among the silv'ry clouds with you.

His smile covered his whole face. "Say, that's all right!" he said, and bent against the light from the window, leaning to read the notes. He tinkled out the tune with his right hand. Joe watched him, uncertain and frowning. As the salesman played, he had heard a couple of sour chords, had even had a feeling that the salesman emphasized them and bore down hard on the words at those points. It was possible that he had played the whole piece to make it sound jingly and cheap. Joe set his teeth. A slow heat began to burn in him, something like shame. He looked at the pimpled youth and marked his sidelong smile.

"This is wonderful! This ought to sweep the country!" the plump one said, and with nimble hands picked up the chorus. He sang again, looking soulfully upward, slightly knitting his brows like a man tasting a rare and delicate wine.

> Come and take a joy ride in my aeroplane tonight
> Way beyond the clouds where all the stars are shining bright.
> There I'd like to look into your loving eyes of blue
> And if I should fall, then I know I'd fall in love with you.

"It'll be a bombshell," he said dreamily, still playing softly, and shook his head back and forth. "'Say, darling, if you'll be my little honey dove . . .'"

Joe moved toward him, so hot inside that he felt his own eyes like burning coals in their sockets. He did not say a word. An organ that stood between him and the piano player he went around or past or through—it was behind him. The plump one stood up.

"Say, listen," the pimpled one said shakily behind Joe's shoulder. The piano player slipped two steps around the piano, almost into the window. Joe moved after him, calculating which way the youth might jump, trying to anticipate him. A half-second would do it, one punch, one smash on the smart alec's mouth. That mouth was no longer smiling. The punk was scared.

He said something in his throat, but it never became words, and he did not know what it was he had tried to say. He feinted around the keyboard, then the other way. The plump salesman, slow and clumsy, jerked first one way and then the other. He was pale; he had begun to sweat; he wet his lips.

Behind him Joe heard the other salesman's frantic voice. "Say, listen! You get out of here! You can't start a row in here!"

"Did I start it?" Joe said softly, holding the plump one fixed. "I came in to ask a civil question."

He did not take his eyes by the merest fraction from the fat one's face. It shook him with fierce pleasure to see the sweat beading the white lip.

"I guess you like a little joke," he said, and put his hands on the piano's velvet wood, gathering himself.

A shadow darkened the window. Across the upraised fat arm Joe saw the blue, the badge, the sauntering ponderous weight. His tight diaphragm relaxed in caution and disappointment, and then, balked and explosive with fury, he grabbed the song off the rack. The pimpled salesman scrambled back between a spinet and a stand of drums to let him pass, and the whole seething top of Joe's mind as he went out onto the sidewalk was full of the picture of how he would look knocked end over end into that tangle of brass and rawhide.

The son of bitches! The dirty superior mocking sons of bitches!

Anger drove him at a plunging walk around many blocks. Every time the crumpled music sheets in his hand brushed his clothes or caught his eye his blood surged in him hot enough for murder. He felt as if he had swallowed a stone, and at every corner drinking fountain he stopped and stooped, drinking slowly, letting the cold water bubble against his lips and teeth.

Eventually he cooled his anger to the point where he could think, but even then he could think nothing but curses. He was not a swearing man: some finicky-ness of language ordinarily kept his talk pure, but now only obscenities came close to expressing what he felt. Every time he thought of himself standing there

like a rube while those two played their little insolent game he
felt his eyes bulging from his head with rage. Like city slickers
playing with a hick they had swallowed their smiles, led him
along, looked upward and rolled their eyes while they clowned
the singing of his words, and played the tune on that thousand-
dollar piano till it sounded like some organ grinder's wornout
cranking.

Oh, the sons of bitches, the dirty sons of bitches! The punks
in their classy clothes, doing their little slave jobs and leaning
elegantly to spit on anybody who didn't tie his tie the latest
way. The piddling little salesmen lording it around with diamonds
on their fingers. The lame-brained, fat-muscled pimps of the
System, the dirt, the lower than dirt, the slave-shit that they were.

He should have known better than to take any song of his
to a place like that. If anyone published Joe Hill's songs it
ought to be the union. If he wrote songs he ought to write songs
that a union could sing, not the kind some dribble-chinned punk
could snicker at. You didn't get any help from the System, even
indirectly. No song written by a workingman and a union man
would ever have a chance to make ten cents in the world where
Cohan coined money for Tin Pan Alley hacks. You fought the
System every waking minute or it gelded you. There was no halfway method.

Leaning against a wall staring slit-eyed across the glaring afternoon street he was visited by the words of the Preamble, those
words written by an unfrocked priest and memorized by working
stiffs and fighters for freedom everywhere. He said them to himself
as in his childhood, kneeling in the cold by the unwarmed bed,
he had said the Lord's Prayer:

*The working class and the employing class have nothing in
common . . . Between these two classes a struggle must go on
until the workers of the world organize. . . . We must inscribe on
our banners the revolutionary watchword 'Abolition of the wage
system' . . . we are forming the new society within the shell
of the old.*

Amen. Amen, and God curse the trade-union compromisers and
the shopkeepers and the salesmen and the fat-assed clerks and
the housewives and all those who wanted security at any price.
God curse all the slaves who didn't know they were slaves, all

those who licked the boss's shoes and put on the boss's swagger when only the janitor was around. God curse every smart alec working for ten dollars a week and thinking he'd be president some day. Curse their stupidity and their insolence and their arrogance and their dirty sniveling lickspittle cowardice. Curse the whole gelded tethered lot of them, and all the uniforms that walked up and down and protected them from getting what they deserved, or pulled up in the paddy wagon every time honest workers walked out of a hell-hole and peacefully picketed on a street that by rights they owned. Curse them and give them fits and visit them with diarrhea and give them dreams every night that will make them wet their secure little beds with fear.

He looked at the sheets in his hand, folded and smoothed them and replaced them in his coat pocket. His jaws were lame from being clamped together; the stone in his stomach gave him a sensation like hunger.

At the entrance to the cigar store against which he leaned there was a glass globe filled with colored jawbreakers. The urge for something sweet flooded his mouth, and he reached a penny from his pocket and put it in the slot. But when he turned the lever to release the ball of candy the machine jammed, and no jerking or yanking or pounding would free it. It seemed to him that even the candy machines were part of the general conspiracy, and only by forcing himself to stand over the water fountain on the corner for a full minute could he get himself calm. Just as he stood up, a Murray car pulled down State Street, and on impulse he jumped aboard.

7

At supper he took pains to make it clear he did not want to be talked to. Karl Erickson was rounding up people to take in a show, but when he tried Joe he got only a short shake of the head. Otto tried joking him about having had a fight with his girl, and got a look that made him move his eyebrows and shut up. When they all gathered in the parlor after supper to pump the player piano Joe deliberately broke his custom and went straight upstairs to the room.

For a while he lay on the bed with his hands locked at the back of his head, and stared upward and thought and burned slowly with continuing anger. After a while he got the music out of his coat and studied it, searching for the reasons why the salesman had laughed, but the whole attempt made him so sore that he put the music away. Finally, just to be doing something besides think, he got out of the dresser drawer the package that contained the automatic. It had never even been unwrapped since the day he bought it. Now he found a rawhide bootlace and started rigging the holster into a shoulder scabbard.

Somehow and somewhere he had been betrayed. His hunch that Salt Lake City would turn up something big had not panned out, yet he had felt it strong, as strong as he had ever felt a hunch in his life. From the time when he had first walked up and looked over the town, coming baby-clean from the steam room at the springs, he had had the feeling that he was looking for something: a house he would know, a familiar face, a thing he had planned. And then meeting Otto on the street, and after that Anna and Ingrid Olson, as if his past had crowded up to form a ring around what might happen here and now.

And what did happen? He wrote a couple of songs, drew a few pictures, lay around like someone on a vacation, tried to crash the System and got himself laughed at by a couple of punk clerks.

With his knife he cut the buckle off an old belt, trimmed the belt to the proper length, and bored holes in both ends. With pieces of the bootlace he laced the belt into the holster flap so that it made a loop; before lacing the second end snug he stood up and put the loop over his left shoulder, trying the fit. He was standing up fiddling with the strings when Otto opened the door.

Because Joe had not heard him at all, he was sure Otto had come on tiptoe, trying to catch sight of something private. A born snoop. But after a twitch of irritation he went on adjusting the strap, saying nothing. Otto sat on the bed and leaned back on his hands and watched.

Taking off the holster, Joe cut two slits in the part that housed the barrel of the gun. Through these he threaded the rest of the rawhide lace, and stood up to the mirror again to pull the lace around him. With the thong pulled snug around his chest, the holster fitted flat against his ribs. He slipped the automatic in it, pushed it back an inch or two, put on his coat to see if the bulge showed. It was all right.

"Going somewhere?" Otto said.

Glancing up into Otto's intent, feeding stare, Joe noticed that the grin was on Otto's mouth, but it was hardly a grin at all, only an habitual set of the muscles.

"Nowhere in particular."

From his sweater pocket Otto fished up a flat can of snuff. As if absent-mindedly he dipped himself a pinch between thumb and finger and tucked it into his cheek. The metal lid caught a dull flash from the darkening windows as he put the can away.

"Whatever happened to that little Luger you and Manderich took away from me that night?"

Joe paused at the job of cleaning up shavings and scraps of leather. He allowed himself a little smile. "I donated it to a church."

"You what?"

"Donated it to a church."

"In the collection plate, I suppose."

"No, in the breadbox."

He watched Otto's curiosity come out and nibble around at that one, trying to make sense of it. Finally Otto said, "You really got a lot of nerve, you know that? I don't know what the hell you're talking about, donating it to a church, but that was my gun."

Joe bent and brushed up the last scraps from the rug, saying nothing.

"Also," Otto said, "you owe me five bucks."

He was watching Joe with an intentness that seemed to carry some special unsaid meaning. In the dusk his eyes were steady and small and bright like the eyes of a watchful rat.

"You'll get it," Joe said.

"When?"

"When I get it."

"When'll that be? You ain't been hunting a job."

"No," Joe said. "Anybody with money enough to pay me wages is somebody I wouldn't work for."

"I been seeing about this trouble in Colorado," Otto said. "Just so you don't beat it over there and leave me holding the bag for my five."

"Quit worrying," Joe said. He got up and went out, and Otto came after him down the stairs, tonguing his cud of *snus*. Mrs. Erickson and her two sons were just leaving for the show.

"Sure you don't want to come along?" she said.

"No thanks."

"Otto?"

"I guess not."

Joe went into the parlor and sat down at the scuffed piano. A player roll of "Over the Waves" was on the spindle, and he pumped it through. The music, of an incredible mechanical nimbleness and regularity, beat in his face. He kept his feet going until it ended and then flipped the reroll button and pumped it silently back to its beginning. For a minute he tried playing the same piece himself, trying to make his fingers perform as faultlessly as the player roll. But he didn't really feel like playing, and the mechanical perfection of the player reminded him of the plump clerk and what he had done to the aeroplane song. In a pause he swung around on the stool, and found Otto still watching him.

"By God I wish I could figure you out," Otto said.

"Don't strain yourself," Joe said. Sitting half sideways, he put his fingers on the keys and played very softly the tune of "Workers of the World." The thought occurred to him that he might wander over to Ingrid's for the evening, but he decided immediately that he didn't want that either. He didn't want to sit around and talk old country. He wasn't sure what he wanted. He wanted to kick chairs across the room.

"You're one of these organizers that works for nothing," Otto said.

Joe said nothing.

"But when you get a chance to take a little contribution from the other side, you pretend you're too pure for that."

Still Joe said nothing. The glow from the big round-wicked lamp carved deep shadows from Otto's long upper lip to the corners of his mouth, and his ordinarily pale, rather protruding eyes looked deeply socketed. For an instant he looked like Manderich.

"Listen," he said, and dropped his voice. Holding Joe's eyes, he got up to lean on the piano. "I know a way you can make enough in one night, tonight, to keep you organizing for two months."

"Yes?" Joe said. But he did not say it in a way to stop Otto. He wanted to hear what Otto would say.

Otto's eyes were mottled like marbles in the lamplight. They opened wider, bringing back the silly-looking dangling grin.

"I know a bird runs a little joint," he said. "Every night this guy closes up his place and takes the day's cash home with him in a paper bag. He walks two blocks with it, all by himself. It's as easy as swatting flies."

"You can go pull it by yourself then."

"It's easier with two. One can keep him quiet while the other goes through him." Stooping until his rump stuck far out behind and his chin was on his stacked hands, he watched Joe steadily as a dog waiting for something to drop from a table. He looked ridiculous in that position, like the rear end of one of the masquerade donkeys in a political parade. "I always thought you'd be a good one to hook up with," he said. "You never fooled me, not for a minute. But you got a talent for keeping your mouth shut."

In front of Joe the player roll was punched with dots and dashes and staggered lines of holes like some intricate code. He felt as if he leaned back against some strong pressure from behind. The last thing he wanted was to get mixed up with Otto. If he took what the world owed him as a workingman, he would take it alone.

But he sat silent, and Otto said, "This guy's somebody I've had my eye on for a couple weeks. He don't vary by ten minutes from one night to the next. He walks those two blocks like he was walking a beat."

Joe rotated gently on the stool, pushing himself clear around until he was back facing Otto's mottled intent eyes. "How do you know all this?"

"I keep my eyes open," Otto said.

Joe's foot had started him around again. "What time does he close his joint?"

"Nine-thirty."

The Captive

1   Salt Lake City, June, 1914

The first thing Lund did when he got off the train in Salt Lake City was to call the county jail. An asthmatic voice told him, between coughing spells, that visiting hours were three to four Tuesday and Friday. Today was Tuesday. He was lucky. But court would be in session until three-thirty. There was only the half-hour opportunity, and unless he wanted to go to the courtroom first he had more than six hours to kill. He told himself that he did not want to go to court knowing as little as he did. Maybe he didn't want to go to court at all.

Eight years of uninterrupted work in the mission had made a provincial of him. The baggage carts and the redcaps and the news-stand girl and the big waiting-room mural that showed the driving of the golden spike were strangenesses, almost dangers, to his senses. He felt clumsy in the cool vault of the station, and when he stepped outside he got stranded on the sidewalk under a blast of white sun.

The newspaper item that had pulled him off the train was torn out and folded into his breast pocket. He had to know more, but where would he go for information? Not the sheriff's office, where there would probably be nothing but official indifference. Not the IWW hall, which would be dispensing partisan hysteria. A helplessness weighed upon him; when he put down his bag to think a moment, a bellhop captured it and led him to a big yellow hotel bus.

His room at the hotel held him only ten minutes. In another ten he was standing before the semicircular desk in the public library. A librarian came up and looked at him.

"Do you keep back files of the Salt Lake papers?"

"How far back?"

He consulted the scrap of newspaper in his pocket. "Beginning January 9, this year."

"The whole file from then to now?"

"If it's not too much trouble, please."

"It may be at the bindery," she said. "If you'll wait a minute I'll see. This month's are all on the rack over there."

Against the wall where she pointed, the papers hung in their wooden holders. But he didn't want to get the story backwards; he wanted to follow it as it had unfolded. It was important to him to know, and to know straight.

In five minutes the girl was back, sliding two ponderous volumes in new red binding across the desk. "Just came back," she said pertly, smiling. She shoved a card at him, and he signed, took the volumes in his arms, found an unoccupied table, sat down. The new binding opened stiffly; he pressed it down, turning the pages until he found the date he wanted: January 9, 1914.

The front page showed him nothing that he was looking for, and he had hunted through two more pages before he realized that January 9 was the night it had happened. It wouldn't have been reported until the next day.

In the January 10 paper there was no need to hunt. It was there in black headlines, a two-column story clear down the page, and more over on page 4. He read it through carefully, and on to the next day, and so on, hunting up every item. At noon he was still reading. When the reading room emptied he went obediently too, found a lunchroom on the corner, spent fifteen minutes there, and came back to read again. It was nearly one o'clock when he finished.

For a considerable still time he sat thinking. Around him was a dry rustle as readers turned pages. He saw, out of his abstraction, the faces of strangers, strange windows in a strange room, strange light through the windows from a strange city outside. In this foreign place he sat like a parent brought to hear accusations against his son, and though he willed disbelief he was forced to admit that there were puzzles, ambiguities, qualities of Joe Hillstrom's character and fragments of Joe Hillstrom's history, that lent some credibility to the charges. Even the story Joe told about the woman: anyone who knew Joe Hillstrom would instantly doubt it. Yet it was his only defense.

Things he did not want to remember came to the surface of his mind like corks that could not be held under. Except for stretches of longshoring, he did not know of a job that Joe had held in three years. In spite of his apparent idleness, there were those forty dollars in crumpled bills that he had thrust on Lund in the kitchen of the mission. There was the gun he had thrown him for hiding at the same time. There was that earlier time when he had come in with his face cut and the gun in his pocket. There was the long schooling in violence, the whiplash temper, the fights that had marked his face and jaw.

He thought of the way Joe could look sometimes when he was interested and animated, chasing down an idea, how his eyes could widen in the innocent stare while his lips twisted with irony. With that image sharp in his mind he turned again to the picture of Joe in the clipping he had torn from the paper on the train. Before he looked at it again he had repudiated the implications of that face.

Joe's cheeks were emaciated, blackened with a week's beard. The lips were drawn back wolfishly. Out of hollow sockets the eyes smoldered half-lidded and contemptuous. Joe must have known when the picture was taken that he had a face to scare babies, yet he had turned it straight into the camera in bitterness and contempt. It was the face of a desperado—or of an El Greco martyr before suffering or art or both had refined the passion and defiance out of the eyes and mouth. He tried to read it, to see behind it, but he could not for his life have said whether it was the face of a guilty man showing his teeth or that of an innocent one bitter at injustice. If it had not had a caption under it he would never have known it for the face of Joe Hillstrom.

There was more to be learned—there had to be—but not here. He closed the volumes and carried them back to the desk, where the librarian stood up to receive them, an anonymous young woman in a green eyeshade and glasses. She looked at him and smiled an indistinguishable smile. "Did you find what you wanted?"

"Yes. Yes, thanks." Looking at the notes in his hand, he said, "I wonder if you can direct me to a couple of places? Is the county jail somewhere near here?"

The girl's glasses flashed up. "The jail?"

"Yes."

"That's down on Second East, between Fourth and Fifth South. You'd go four blocks down and one left."

"Good. Now how would I get to Eighth South and West Temple?" She drew him a little map on the back of the sign-out card. Eight blocks south, two west. "But the blocks here are long," she said. "You'd better catch a streetcar down on the next corner and ride as far as Eighth South. Either a 6 car or a 12."

She was a pleasant and helpful young woman, and he thanked her. It occurred to him that Joe had probably, during his stay in Salt Lake, used the library. He was tempted to describe him, or show his picture, and ask the librarian if she had ever noticed him around, but that seemed a fruitless sort of investigation, and he thanked her again and left, to emerge from the strange reading room into the strangely brassy and unmisted sun. A sprinkler was going on the library's lawn, badly gone to plantain weeds. Somewhere chimes rang the half-hour. He had still two hours before he could see Joe in the jail. Down the steep sidewalk, under the freckled shade of trees, he walked to the corner and waited for a car.

Eighth South was wide and dusty. In vacant lots the weeds were head high, with a strong pulpy smell. Big cottonwoods grew along the parking strip, shading the whole street. Their leaves were an intense, varnished green; June cotton blew from their opening pods and drifted the street like snow. Sprinklers going on the lawns made erratic pools of cool air that he walked through.

Crossing Main Street, he passed three boys hunting sparrows with slingshots. Ahead he could see that the street dwindled off after a couple of blocks, and across the end he saw the smoke of a switch engine. The telephone wires were beaded with blackbirds that suddenly darted up in a cloud and left the looped wires swinging.

It was a calm, quiet, neighborly street. West Temple, when he came to it and stopped to fix it in his mind, was another of the same. But he saw the butcher shop and grocery on the corner. Cowan's Market, Morrison's Grocery, two neighborhood shops side by side under the same roof, and he walked up West Temple on the opposite side, trying to visualize how this block and these stores might have looked on the night of January 9. The newspaper reports had been detailed. He knew a good deal about the outward events of that night, and they built up for him now like something played on a stage:

The night was mild for winter, with the temperature on the edge between thaw and freeze. The streets were muddy, the slush at the sidewalk-edges just crusting the slightest bit. Except in the shelter of bushes and houses the snow was all melted off. Overhead the sky was opaque, without moon or stars, low and shut in by smoke. The winter smoke cloud was an acrid bite in the nostrils, a taste in the mouth like a railroad tunnel.

Up this street, coming from the west under tight poplars that even leafless would throw solid pillars of shadows, walkers would have come out of the winter murk like characters out of a story by Poe. First the footsteps, hard to locate; then the shadows, darker than the dark and smoke, more fluid than the poplars, emerging and taking shape. They came toward the corner, a tall man and a shorter one, and near the intersection, within the glow of the arc light, they met a couple returning from a show. Neither man made a move to step aside. They came straight on, crowding the woman off into the slush. As she swung indignantly she saw the taller one for a moment plain: a thin face and a sharp nose, a soft felt hat, no overcoat, a red bandanna tied loosely around the throat.

Lund walked in the tracks of the two men to the corner, turned with them up West Temple toward the store. When he stopped before the entrance he saw that the store had been closed for some time. Putting his nose against the window he shaded his eyes and looked in upon two dusty counters, empty vegetable bins, bare shelves, the cash register with its drawer hanging open, the icebox with its door ajar. His imagination peopled the stage as the news reports and the testimony of witnesses directed: front left, Morrison trundling a sack of potatoes toward the bins. Back, left, his seventeen-year-old son Arlin sweeping the floor in front of the icebox. Back, right, the younger son, Merlin, at the entrance to the stock room.

Experimentally he put his thumb on the latch and depressed it, feeling how it might have been for the burglar the moment before the act, this moment with the cold latch under the left hand, the right hand pulling the handkerchief up over his face and then going under the coat for the gun.

He felt how it might have been to enter the store swiftly, gun in hand, breath hot under the handkerchief, and to shout the words that young Merlin Morrison heard: "We're got you this time!" How Morrison would have started up from his stooping position, his hands still around the ears of the potato sack; how Arlin and his brother would freeze at their cleaning-up jobs at the rear of the store.

He felt it as vividly as something remembered, but at that point of confrontation his imagination balked. The story that Merlin Morrison had told in court didn't contain enough of the essential details. A terrified boy of thirteen, he had dilated some points and totally missed others. And even if he had seen everything that happened, there was nothing in what he would have seen to tell Lund or anyone else *why* the two men had come to this dusty little store at nine forty-five on a winter night with guns in their hands and bandanna masks over their faces. To Lund, at least, that *why* was everything.

Revenge, as the newspapers assumed? A deliberate murder— the quick step in the door, the shout, the shots, the getaway? Morrison had been a policeman, and had made enemies. Also, since leaving the force to open his grocery, he had twice stood off holdup men with a gun, wounding one of them in the second encounter last September. Revenge, quite possibly. And if revenge, and if Joe Hillstrom had really been involved, then Joe might be guilty of a double murder, premeditated, in cold blood.

Or robbery? Merlin Morrison had not seen who fired the first shot. He had fled, and turned running to see the taller robber fire the second shot into his father's body, and as he stumbled into the stockroom in panic he had heard a fusillade. But who fired first, the robber or Arlin Morrison, who grabbed his father's gun from the open icebox and died with it in his hand, one cartridge exploded?

For some time Lund stood looking through the window into the abandoned store, trying to make the pattern come clear, but failing. There was no pattern, only the shout and the shots and the two slumped bodies and the slam of the door as the murderers fled. He turned and looked down to the corner, the way they had run, and he saw how they had looked in the dark to the women, neighbors, who had hurried to their doors and looked out. He saw the shorter man sprint from the shadow of the trees across the dim intersection and disappear in the murk down Eighth South, and after him he saw the taller man run stooping, his hands to his chest, and heard him call that he was shot.

Like a second-rate melodrama—except that real death had been died in the store, and except that Joe Hillstrom might have been the man who ran with his hands pressed against his chest. Lund tried to think how it would be to run hard, along slippery sidewalks and through slushy alleys, with a .38 bullet through the lung, and he tried to imagine what might have been in the mind of someone who had just killed a man and his son, but he could not get his mind around either. It seemed to him only that in the chest there would be a desperate burning, and in the mind a pounding of fear.

Everything in the quiet, closed-up scene of murder led him farther from what he was after. He could not get Joe Hillstrom into it; the tall thin-faced man who took Arlin Morrison's bullet in the chest remained a stranger, the villain of a thriller.

Across the street a man came out of his driveway and stood in his shirtsleeves, watching Lund so that he swerved away from the window with guilty suddenness. The place was saturated with guilt. He did not want to stay around it. With his mind groping among contradictions, trying to fit the Joe Hillstrom he knew to the Joe Hillstrom who might have run from this corner five months ago coughing blood from a punctured lung, and repudiating the whole case the law made as preposterous, unbelievable, out of character, Lund started walking north toward his hotel.

The man who might have been Otto Applequist (and *that* part of the case was convincing enough, considering what Lund knew of Otto) was lost in the black alleys, separating from his wounded companion, abandoning him, making a clean getaway. The man who just possibly could have been Joe Hillstrom also disappeared in the alleys below Eighth South. He might have hidden away somewhere, he might have made the tracks and crawled into a boxcar and lived, or got away to die somewhere else.

But the real Joe Hillstrom appeared just before midnight on the porch of a Dr. McHugh in Murray, several miles from the scene of the crime, and asked to be treated for a bullet wound in the chest. He was weak, but holding himself stiffly. When he took off his coat to expose the wound, an automatic fell from a shoulder holster. The doctor did not examine it to see whether it was loaded or empty; he dressed the wound and said nothing to Joe Hillstrom's request that the whole affair be kept private. There was a woman involved, Joe said. There had been a quarrel over a woman. He was as much to blame as the other fellow, and he did not want to make any complaint against the man who had shot him. Neither did he want the woman to be dragged into any unpleasantness.

That was all that anybody really knew—the fact of his wound and the unwavering consistency of his story, or of his refusal to tell a story. The gun he threw away when a colleague of McHugh's drove him home, and it was never found. In pain, weak from loss of blood, he whistled twice, sharply, on his fingers as they approached the house where he boarded, and then the doctor helped him in.

He was half dead of his wound three days later when McHugh told his story and the police came down to get him.

2

At three-fifteen Lund was at the door of the county jail. The door let him into a little vestibule with an office on the right and closed doors on the left and a grilled steel gate straight ahead. A man and a woman were waiting in the office. Behind the gate a fat police-man in an office chair looked him over with puffy yellow eyes.

"I'd like to see Joseph Hillstrom, if he's back from court."

The jailer's eyes went over him in silence, and Lund stood them as he might have stood a crawling yellow-jacket. Living at the mission and working with sailors and hoboes and the drift that washed up and down Beacon Street had made him jumpy around police. If you were on the bottom you were at the mercy of every grafter and sadist and petty exerciser of power. But no matter how steadily he looked back into the jailer's dead eyes, the eyes did not change. A fat freckled hand shoved out a book like a hotel register, and Lund signed.

"Fifteen minutes," the jailer said. "Couple ahead of you. Wait in there."

He yawned, his yellowish eyeballs swam with sudden water, he looked past Lund as if he had already forgotten him.

As Lund sat down the woman on the next chair drew her knees together, holding her pocketbook on top of them primly. Her consciousness of him had in it a wan echo of coquettishness; her eyes fixed themselves in a businesslike way upon the opposite wall, strayed, touched him again, jumped back to the wall. Beside her on the other side a chinless little man smoked the fierce stump of a cigar. Behind the desk a deputy read a magazine. There was a noise of flies at the high windows.

Somewhere a bell rang, and after a couple of minutes a man came out of the door on the left. The man and woman in the office stood up uncertainly. From the chair in the hall the fat jailer said something, and the man and woman crossed the hall and closed the door behind them. The deputy turned a page, rolling half the magazine under in his left hand.

No more sure of what he would find, or of what he hoped to find, than he had been on the train in the morning, Lund sat on. The papers had given him details but no explanations; the visit to Eighth South and West Temple had done no more than upset him and accentuate his doubt. He was unable to visualize what Joe would look like: like himself, or like the bearded desperado of the morning paper? And what would they say to each other? No moral lectures, he said to himself. Above all, no moral lectures.

And yet there were questions he must ask, things he felt he must know.

After a long time the bell rang again. Though he had found the waiting tedious, marked only by the swish of the deputy's pages, it seemed now that the fifteen minutes allowed visitors would not be enough even for a greeting. As he stood up and looked to the jailer for a sign, the left-hand door opened and the couple came out. The woman was crying, her eyes puffy. She held her handkerchief against her mouth, and in passing looked for a moment full at Lund with an expression of brave suffering. Her tears were for herself and for spectators; she savored herself as sufferer. "You see?" her upturned eyes said. Her husband went with his arm across her shoulders, his weak little pucker of mouth clenched on the dead stump of cigar.

Oh Lord, Lund thought, and wondered why self-consciousness made even real anguish look like a pose, and went through the door at the jailer's nod feeling furtive and brittle. Inside a chair was pulled close to a barred wicket like a ticket window in the wall. A policeman leaning against the far wall nodded him to the chair. After a few seconds there was a scraping beyond the wicket.

His first emotion was relief that the face did not look like the face in the paper, and the instantaneous explanation came to him: that picture had been taken while Joe was still sick from his wound. Now, though his face looked pale and so sharp that the slight bulge of his teeth showed under the drawn mouth, he was clean-shaven and his hair was cut so short that he looked like a boy. His eyes were wide and surprised; Lund thought they were pleased.

"Well, holy smoke! What are you doing in this burg?"

"I was on my way east," Lund said. "I read about your trial in the paper I got in Ogden. It was the first I knew."

His face a little in shadow, his eyebrows lifted quizzically, Joe watched him. Their position was a little like that of priest and penitent in a confessional, though which was priest and which penitent, which hoped for comfort from the other, was a question. Joe tapped the steel screen between them and smiled. "It'd be nice to shake hands, but they don't seem to approve of that here."

He laughed, but Lund did not laugh. The screen was too unavoidable a reminder that Joe was cut off where friendship and good will could do little for him. Because he could think of nothing to say, he filled his pipe, and when it was full he offered it to Joe. Joe shook his head.

"Still a good Christian," Lund said.

"All the virtues."

Frowning at the suck and blaze, Lund got the pipe going and waved out the match. He was full of balked rebellion at having to sit here and talk through bars, with a guard listening twenty feet away and Joe's face so shadowed that he could not see it clearly. He wanted to study Joe's face, and he wanted the long interrupted unhurried talk they had had in San Pedro. But he would have no better chance than this.

"Joe, what can I do?"

"Nothing to do."

"I've still got that money of yours."

Beyond the wicket he saw the slow white smile. "You'd better use that to save souls."

"I guess they'll have to stay unsaved," Lund said. "I'm out of the mission."

"Out? Why?"

"You're entitled to your laugh," Lund said ruefully. "Political shift of power in the synod. Evangelicals went out, fundamentalists came in. I was a little too latitudinarian for them."

There was a pause while they eyed each other. Joe's face twisted with disgust. "My God, what a bunch of bolt-heads. You ran the only respectable mission on the coast."

"Not enough Augsburg Confession," Lund said. "Not enough Apostles' Creed. They want a nice tight denominational mission, and they knew I wasn't the one to run it." But it warmed him to hear Joe's praise. It was praise he valued.

"What are you going to do?"

"Back to the farm."

"In Minnesota?"

"Yes."

"No more soul-saving at all?"

"There doesn't seem to be much place for a latitudinarian Christian," Lund said.

"You ought to get into the union battle," Joe said speculatively. "You're educated, you can talk. Get yourself whipped up a little more and you'd make a soapboxer."

The thought made them both laugh." I told you," Lund said. "No soul-saving. Not even for the heaven-on-earth."

Their laughter ebbed and left them with the necessity of finding a new tack. At least five of their few minutes had passed.

"I do have that money, though," Lund said. "You'll need it for your defense."

"My defense!" Joe spat the words out so bitterly that Lund leaned, frowning, to see him better.

"Isn't the rww defending you?"

"I told them to lay off."

"But the papers said . . ."

"They go right on wasting money," Joe said. "They're crazy. The union shouldn't bleed its treasury defending me. One man isn't worth it."

Lund straightened a little. "Now you're talking nonsense."

"No," Joe said. "I'm not talking nonsense."

His hard stare was difficult to face; his mouth was set like a stubborn boy's. Lund looked down at the warm bowl of the pipe in his hand, looked up again to see Joe's mouth move as if tasting something. Rather than force a clash, he let the talk edge away.

"How does it look, really?"

"You've seen the papers."

"Anything critical happen in court today?"

Joe shrugged.

"What I can't understand," Lund said, "is why you don't prove where you were that night, and settle this quick."

With the crossed shadows of the wires on it, Joe's face was changeable and hard to read, but now his eyes were dark, his mouth harshly pinched, the long scar white along jaw and neck. "Why should I prove an alibi? I'm innocent till they prove I'm guilty, that's what the law books say. If there's any proving to be done, let them do it."

"But if it means saving your life!"

"You sound like my lawyers," Joe said. "I don't have to prove anything. That's the D.A.'s job."

"What if they ever catch Otto? Can he clear you?"

"If they catch Otto he'll be right where I am, charged with the same thing," Joe said. "He was smart to take it on the lam. But even if they caught him his testimony wouldn't be worth any more in that court than mine would be. I'm guilty as hell right from the start. They're all set to stand me against the wall."

"And you're all set to let them!" Lund said, so angry that his voice shook. "In heaven's name, what's wrong with defending yourself? You're worth ten times what the IWW can spend to save you, and you know it. And no woman's reputation is worth a man's life."

"I'm surprised at you," Joe said, soft and mocking.

"What kind of woman would let you sacrifice yourself that way?

If you got shot over a woman, she should have been the first one to come up and clear you."

Joe had dropped his chin on his clasped hands. "You sound more and more like my lawyers," he said. His voice had taken on an edge.

With difficulty Lund got control of himself, studying his knuckles wrapped around the bowl of the pipe, forcing his lips into a smile. "Anyway, you've got a defense and got lawyers whether you want them or not. You may have the bad luck to be acquitted in spite of yourself."

Joe shrugged, lifting his hands and dropping them again.

Not quite ready to give it up, Lund said. "Wasn't there something about the caliber of the gun? Wasn't yours a different caliber from the one that did the shooting?"

"My alert lawyers thought of that one too," Joe said, and gave Lund a wintry, indifferent smile. "They took me and the hawk-shaws down there. The guy had a record of selling the gun but not of what caliber it was. And the guy that sold it to me had left town."

His voice was so apathetic, indifferent, disinterested, and his shoulders and hands so limp and slack that Lund wanted to reach through the screen and slap him awake. He gave no handhold, his blankness and apathy were too smooth for any friendly help to catch onto. Angrily the preacher said, "What were you doing buying another gun in the first place?"

And that only got him the ironic, amused stare. "They say I wanted to kill a couple of guys."

Lund swept his hand across the little counter shelf in a gesture of disgust.

"Tell it to the cops," Joe said.

It was going badly, like a cross-examination. The steel between them was flimsy compared to the screen that Joe himself erected. Even Lund's intense desire to understand, a desire that went deeper than friendship, he knew, and rooted itself in his whole faith that right and wrong were separate and recognizable, glanced off Joe like light off a mirror. There was no confidence, little friendliness, hardly any interest in the face at the wicket, but only a closed, enigmatic, still expression that might have been either apathetic or stubborn. The eyes in their pale steadiness dominated the thin mask of a face; a little smile moved the stiff lips.

"They don't give me the papers," he said, "but the other day a trusty smuggled in a piece of the *Saturday Blade and Ledger*. I saw in there that some fellow has finally got the dope on Nebuchadnezzar. You know that yarn about how he went crazy and ate grass. Well, this bird has a theory that Nebuchadnezzar really ate alfalfa, because apparently there's all kinds of food value in alfalfa. He says you could live on it for a month." The smile pulled the lips wider. "Work and pray, live on hay. The bosses ought to get hold of that guy and put him in charge of the cookhouse."

He made himself clear. The talk was to stay away from such questions as Lund most wanted to ask. As he moved his hand sideward Lund saw the right one, the shiny patch of scar the size of a dime between the first and second knuckles, and the deformed hump on the back of the hand. Defeated in his attempts to pierce Joe's surface, he said nothing, but Joe's eyes followed his to the broken hand, and the voice beyond the screen sharpened in instant bitterness.

"That's another nice thing. I'm lying in bed with a bullet through me and just as the cops come in I reach under the pillow for a handkerchief to spit in. One of the dicks thinks I'm reaching for a gun, and he lets me have this."

He flexed his fingers, and his lips tightened and his eyes burned. "They leave you plenty," he said. "There goes the piano."

Lund sat with his head bent, feeling how everything that he could think of to say died in his mind, inadequate or inappropriate or too likely to harden Joe's protective shell. At last he said, "Joe, I can only stay about one day. There won't be visiting hours again till Friday, and I can't be here then. But I'll try to come to court tomorrow. Maybe I can see you there for a minute."

"Sure," Joe said. The fury had passed from his face; the indifferent irony was back. "Come on up and see the show. Its a three-ringed circus." A grin widened his pale eyes and forced his eyebrows upward. "Man-eating wild animals," he said. "That's me. Two clowns. Those are my lawyers." His finger made a contemptuous rattle across the screen. "They'll be in here any minute trying to pump me again."

The bell rang.

Earnestly and in haste, Lund stood up and hooked his fingers in the screen. "Listen, Joe! Don't get sore at what I say, or what your iww friends say. Let the union do all it will. Put up a fight, and quit standing on your dignity as an innocent man. You've been in this jail too long. Quit acting as if you wanted to be a spectator at your own funeral."

The upper part of Joe's face was in shadow. A sliver of dusty light came through the west window and touched his quiet broken hand. He lifted his head a little, and he seemed almost gentle.

"Okay, now *you* listen. If I'm innocent all I have to do is sit still, isn't it? I don't have to prove it. It's automatic unless they can prove the opposite. And if I'm guilty, would I let the union spend thousands of dollars getting me off? I'd sit still, wouldn't I? Either way I'd sit still. That's what I'm doing."

The policeman motioned at Lund, there was obscure scuffling beyond the screen, and then footsteps, as empty of meaning or reassurance as any of the talk, as Joe was led back to his cell.

3

The windows of the courtroom let in a view of summer sky and moving clouds. Pigeons walked the window sills and fluttered on ledges and cornices, and occasionally the breeze brought in a whiff of locust blossoms from the park below. The room, small, high-ceilinged, paneled, waited like a theater for its opening curtain.

The varnished benches were already jammed. Squeezed in with the first of the crowd, Lund sat on the center aisle and looked across a wooden rail to the table where Joe's attorneys, Scott and McDougall, laid out papers. Beyond were the witness chair, the high judicial bench. On the left side, elevated above the benches, was the jury box. In a place so severe and bare as this the most solemn and deliberate injustices could be done impartially, impersonally, without bias or ill will, because everything in the room, even the expressions on the faces of spectators and bailiffs and attorneys, made it clear that the actors here, judge and jury, prosecutor and witnesses, had ceased to be men and were for the time being mere instruments. Only the accused, in such a room, remained touched by human frailty, and he was reduced to helplessness like a child among grownups.

The jury now was in the box: a teamster, a real-estate dealer, a bill collector, a farmer, a clerk, a laborer, a coal dealer, a streetcar motorman, a salesman, another farmer, a blacksmith, a contractor. Solemnized by their position, they sat down with dignity and in silence. One or two glanced out across the room; they reminded Lund of stagehands peeking between the curtains at a filling house to estimate the crowd.

Now the district attorney, tight-jawed, preoccupied, with a smoldering look about him and an aggressiveness in his shoulders and his careful clothes. Now the bailiff and two plainclothes men coming in a side door and ranging themselves inside the rail. Unhurried, without rancor, the courtroom readied itself, and watching it as the clock crept toward ten Lund was struck not simply by the way it divested itself of human fallibility and human sympathy, but by how small this home of justice was, and how shabby with yellowed varnish and the smell of cuspidors.

The room suppressed the voices of everyone in it, but there was a steady insect-hum of whispering and low talk. Out of it the news grew: "Hillstrom. Here comes Hillstrom."

Handcuffed between two deputies, Joe came through the bailiff's door at the side. He walked with his head up, his face like something carved out of pale, flawed wood. In a gray suit, with the flowing silk tie of the Swedish Young Socialists, a poet's tie, he looked almost jaunty. His eyes touched nothing, recognized nothing, and when the deputies brought him inside the rail and unlocked the cuffs he sat down between his attorneys and gave the spectators his straight shoulders and the back of his neat head.

Around him Lund heard scraps of talk—the casual buzz, the cold dope, the shrewd speculation, the guess.

– like a ladies' man. Maybe that woman story isn't—

– bringing Judge Hilton, from Denver, the labor lawyer. Seems Hillstrom is somebody important among the radicals. They're all steamed up.

– snotty-looking cuss. How does a guy in a jam like that—

–Scott telling the newspaper boys. The person that got Judge Hilton into this is the daughter of Lorenzo Snow. How do you like that? When the daughter of the ex-president of the Mormon Church—

–Say, it'd sure be something if she turned out—

–Naw, I don't think so. Sob sister. She's been mixed up with the radicals a long time.

–Still it'd sure be—

Lund fixed his eyes on the back of Joe's head. The weight of custom and tradition and social authority in the stale courtroom, the crowd that came to feed on raw emotion as Roman crowds fed on the agonies of the martyrs, the oppressive unanimity of the forces leagued against Joe Hillstrom, were too much. He felt smothered—and if he felt so, how would the prisoner feel? How demoralizing must it be to be one pitiful little wrong-doer, or one more pitiful, wrongly accused, and sit inside the dock sensing how the quiet many-armed impersonal power closed in: the district attorney ambitious for political advancement; the jury of middle class citizens fearful of violence, scared of the taint of radicalism, hating what threatened their security; the judge an imperfect mortal cast as Omnipotence; the spectators avid for the sight of the victim's face as society struck its blow.

He could tell from the set of Joe's shoulders that he held the whole weight of it up.

Now the stage was set, the jury boxed, the prisoner at the bar, the attorneys at their tables, the evidence assembled, the witnesses summoned. The clock above the jury box said four minutes past ten. The bailiff's gavel whacked down; there was a rustle and heave as the jury, the intense district attorney, the plainclothes men, dour McDougall and pink-jowled Scott, the prisoner, the whole backward stretch of the audience, surged up in the empty ritual of respect. The door of the judge's chambers opened and a frail old figure came in and climbed to the high seat. A blood-less, thin-lipped, mottled old face looked out over the court, a bony hand and wrist stretched out of the sleeve, the gavel came down. The jammed room seated itself again, obeisance over.

He had forgotten how tedious court procedure could be, how ponderously the revenge of society moved, how legal ingenuity at splitting hairs could obscure the vital issue, divide one question into a dozen, elicit at great trouble a cloudy statement of the obvious, sift the simplest statement for hidden meanings or twist it into something incriminating. Just to think of sitting in the prisoner's box while the case against you grew by such intolerable grain-by-grain accretion, to have it confused by objections, sustainings, overrulings, exceptions, made his head ache. Simply to sit through the proceedings while they convicted or acquitted you was punishment enough for most crimes. He found his mind caught on the word "advocate," and in fantasy he stood up and asked them all why they did not lay aside all this machinery of attack and defense and put in its place some honest machinery of inquiry whose purpose was understanding and not the winning or losing of a case.

Yet he knew too that at least in the beginning these were the methods by which men had tried to correct blind vengeance into justice, and even if it came to quibbling, a quibbler was an advance over a vigilante. He knew too that the very tedium of the proceedings operated like a playwright's cunning in the building of suspense. The drama lay in the gradual approach to a life-and-death crisis by the most trivial and monotonous of means.

Here was the matter, first, of a bloodspot scraped from the sidewalk on West Temple the morning after the murder. Here was the state chemist to make his report, which was brief: the sample was mammalian blood, but it had been brought to him too late for him to say for sure that it was human. So now the district attorney in his role of Prosecutor, trying to establish the inestablishable and close a link in a desired chain of evidence:

– You say you can be sure this is mammalian blood, Mr. Harms?
– Yes.
– It could be human?
– It could, yes. It could also be the blood of a dog or cat or sheep.
– But it is not very likely to be sheep's blood, there on West Temple Street, would you say, Mr. Harms?

Perhaps at the end of ten minutes of this there would be left a little residue of belief against the defendant. There was a kind of contiguous logic involved. One of the robbers was thought to have been wounded by Arlin Morrison. One chamber of the Morrison gun had been fired. This gout of blood was found nearby on the sidewalk. Joe Hillstrom had appeared later with a bullet through his lung. Therefore this blood on the sidewalk could have been human blood shed by the robber who could have been wounded by Arlin Morrison, who might have fired the discharged chamber of his father's gun, and this robber could have been Joe Hillstrom.

The courtroom was already hot. Not paying too much attention to the circlings of the prosecutor, Lund watched Joe's head, and he saw with pain, as Joe turned to say something to his lawyers, the theatrical sneer that twisted Joe's lip. Why did he have to make it worse for himself? Why, in front of the jury in whose hands his life would be placed, did he adopt an attitude that would insult and offend everybody who watched him?

– It is true, isn't it Mr. Harms, that some chemists would have no hesitation in identifying this sample as human blood?

Joe's head jerked toward Scott again. "That's leading!" he said loudly. He threw himself back in the chair in disgust so histrionic that Lund wished for some way to shield him from the jury's eyes.

– Some chemists might, perhaps. I have had experience enough to know that a sample as old as this one . . .

Everyone, even the witness, was watching Joe and his attorneys. Scott was shaking his head, half smiling, at Joe's whispered vehemence. The room buzzed, and the gavel came down. Almost as it whacked solidly on the bench Joe was on his feet.

"Your honor, I'd like to make a few remarks!"

The thin old face looked down at him, a wedge of flesh and bone and legal precedent, the visage of judicial calm. Like an actor Joe whirled on his lawyers. His hair fell on his forehead as he struck a pose with pointing finger. "There are too many prosecuting attorneys in this case!" he said. His voice whined with tension like a bent saw. "I'm going to get rid of two of them. Mr. Scott and Mr. McDougall, do you see that door? Now you get, you're fired!"

With alarm in his heavy dark face, McDougall grabbed Joe's arm, but Joe pushed him against the table. "You can bring on buckets of blood," he shouted at the district attorney. "You bring on all the blood you like, but I intend to show a few things myself! I intend . . ."

The thundering of the gavel drowned him out, but it was at least a minute before the uproar in the courtroom quieted enough so that the judge laid down the threat of his gavel. Noise whispered and frittered away until it was still. Lund could hear the loud crackle of papers as McDougall gathered them up. The lawyer's face was hard, and dull red burned in his cheekbones. Behind him Joe Hillstrom, drawn up in a posture that Lund cringed for, a posture that was preposterously showy and arrogant, suddenly sprang forward and grabbed the papers from McDougall's hands. "Get out!" he said. "Those belong to the defense. They're paid for and I'll keep them. And you can give the defense back the money it's paid you, too."

The judge was standing, pounding again. His sagging cheeks quivered, his eyes went like swords down over the room. An irresistible pressure had forced Lund from his seat, and he realized now that the whole room was up. A young woman had sprung up from somewhere and was leaning across the rail, crying "Joe! Joe! Listen to me, Joe!"

By the time the room was again quieted the girl had slipped back to a seat near the front on the right side. For Lund she was only one more incomprehensible element in a situation already as incredible and unpredictable as a disturbed dream. That Joe Hillstrom should be in this courtroom on a charge of double murder was incredible enough. That the daughter of an ex-president of the Mormon Church should emerge as his defender, that Joe himself should base his entire defense on an unlikely story of a quarrel over a woman, that there should now be a nameless young woman leaning over the rail crying his name in the midst of the bedlam that Joe had created by firing his counsel in the middle of his trial—these were enough to compound the incredible with utter confusion. Looking again for the girl to study her face, he saw only the top of her hat among the crowded spectators.

The judge held his gavel in his hand like a weapon. His voice crackled drily over the quieting room. "Now, Mr. Scott," he said, "I warn you I will not tolerate this sort of thing in this court. You will keep your client under control, or I will have the bailiff do so."

Scott glanced sideways at Joe, and the left side of his face twitched in an irritable grimace. "Mr. Hillstrom's conduct is a complete surprise to me," he said. "Last night we were on perfectly friendly terms." With a very white fresh handkerchief he wiped the palms of his hands. "I think he is beside himself," he said.

But Joe was not yet through. He was up again like a man stabbed from behind, shouting at the judge. "Can't I conduct my own case? I did it in the preliminary hearing. Can't I examine witnesses and recall any I want to?"

"That is your legal right."

"Then I'm through with my attorneys! I want them to get out. I'll prove a lot of things without them, and I'll prove I wasn't at Morrison's grocery store that night . . ."

"I object!" the district attorney said. "Your honor, I object to the defendant's making a statement of his own case."

"Sit down, Mr. Hillstrom," the court said.

Joe remained standing. "And I won't need you to help me, Mr. Scott."

The gavel whammed the bench. "Bailiff," the judge said, "see that the order of the court is carried out."

Lund drew a deep breath and shoved himself backward from where he had been sitting on the very edge of the seat. His hands were clenched, and his mind felt like something entangled in fly-paper. That he should carry his frenzy clear to the point of being manhandled by the bailiff. . . . He must be, as Scott said, beside himself. Or was the whole outburst an act, cunningly devised to get rid of the defense he said he did not want? Did he want to conduct his own defense because he thought he could do it better or because he wanted no defense at all? And if it was an act, how ill-advised an act, calculated to prejudice everyone in the courtroom against him. And again, was that perhaps what he wanted? He seemed perversely determined to do everything backwards.

From where he had been forcibly planted Joe was still shouting at the judge. "Your honor, I want my attorneys to leave this court-room!"

The old cold face looked down; there were broken veins in the flat cheeks. "The court does not believe that it is to your best interests to be unrepresented by counsel."

"It's my legal right."

"Nevertheless," the judge said, and his lower lip thrust slightly out in decision, "it is the ruling of this court that Mr. Scott and Mr. McDougall shall remain as friends of the court, to protect the interests of the defendant. Defendant may do his own cross-examining if he desires."

Shrugging angrily, McDougall came back from the bailiff's side door, where he had been on the point of departing. Scott bowed his head, acknowledging the court's decision with a slightly ironic deference. From his chair, turned sideways so that he could watch them both, Joe regarded them with the contemptuous sneer on his mouth.

The chemist was still on the stand, a man who had given expert testimony many times on the whiff of chloroform, the taint of arsenic, the contents of stomachs, the condition of bodies. "Proceed," the court said, and nodded to the prosecutor.

"I have finished with the witness.'"

"Cross-examination," the court said.

Scott stood up and settled his coat across his shoulders. "Mr. Harms . . ."

But he was cut off by Joe Hillstrom's tight voice. "Mr. Scott, there's the door. Why don't you go?"

For the first time Scott looked annoyed. A dark flush flooded up his smooth neck and into his face. "I am here by order of the court."

And now, Lund saw with an embarrassment that approached horror, they were back at it. "Can't I discharge my attorneys?" Joe demanded.

The judge was perfectly composed, but in his clipped voice and the careful inclination of his head Lund read patience enforced with difficulty, as if the judge were addressing some incorrigible child who strained the endurance but who must be given all the outward forms of consideration. If Joe had, fantastically, been trying to show his contempt of judge and jury, and alienate them all, he couldn't have succeeded better.

"I have asked the attorneys for the defense to stay here for a while as friends of the court," the arid voice said. "They will cross-examine witnesses as before. You may take part in the proceedings if you desire."

To Lund's relief, Joe settled back in his chair and said no more. The machinery of the trial ground on. The bloodspot, still unidentified as sheep, cat, dog or human, was reluctantly passed by, and the chemist stepped down to be replaced by Mrs. Phoebe Seeley.

Because Lund had walked out her part of the drama on the corner of West Temple and Eighth South, he attended the questions and answers carefully, with an odd sense of remembering the scene himself.

Mrs. Seeley brought out her story promptly, as if she had memorized questions and answers in advance: the walk home from a show about 9:30 on the night of January 9. The slushy sidewalks, with just a path beaten along them. The two men who crowded her off into the mud, and the quick indignant look that showed her the taller one plain under the arc light.

– Were there any peculiarities about the taller of the two men you saw?

– Well, he had a mark, a scar like, on his neck, and a sharp nose.

– Such a scar, would you say, as the defendant has on the left side of his neck?

"I object," McDougall's harsh voice said. "The question is leading."

Instantly Joe was on his feet. The inopportune fury that had burst out of him twice before was so violent now that his voice cracked. "Who's counsel here, anyhow?" he shouted. "How many times do I have to fire you?"

In the momentary astounded silence Scott put his flat hands on the table and with an air of having weightily decided something stood up. "Your honor, I don't understand my status in this case, and I'm sure Mr. McDougall doesn't either. I ask for an adjournment until we can talk the situation out with the defendant."

The judge glanced briefly over the heads of the attentive jurors. "The court is recessed for three quarters of an hour," he said. "The jury is excused until eleven-thirty." The hub-bub that began among the spectators he quieted with a single peremptory rap. "I must warn the spectators. Now and hereafter, if order is not kept, I shall request the bailiff to clear the court."

Though the voices dropped again, Lund felt all around him the craning and peering to see and hear what went on inside the railing. People creaked with their desire to know. It was clear that more drama was brewing, for almost before the last juror was through the door the district attorney was leaning across the defense table. He was naturally a bristly man; now he was swollen with anger and righteousness.

"There are a few things I would like to say," he said, speaking directly to Scott. "I'm not at all surprised at this. I recall that there was a long conference in this room yesterday afternoon between the defendant and his attorneys." Leaning forward on the spread fingers of his left hand, he poked his right index finger back and forth at Scott's chest. "I just want to say that if the defense thinks it can start any insanity business in this trial it is welcome to try it. The state is ready to meet this insanity business right now!"

His head snapped around and his stern eye fixed McDougall. "Do you think the defendant is insane?"

"No," McDougall said flatly.

"Do you?" the prosecutor said, swinging back to Scott.

Scott was swelling and bridling, pulling in his neck and rolling his shoulders until his face was turkey red. "I do not," he said. "But I must say I am surprised at the district attorney's suggestion of an insanity trick by the defense."

Oh Lord, Lund thought. Now we will have hurt feelings, and expostulations, and demands for apologies, and those whose business it is to win by whatever kind of trickery will turn their incorruptible faces to the court and lay their hands on their breasts and be martyred by the cynicism of doubters. But was it possible that the whole thing *was* a defense trick, cooked up between Joe and his attorneys and played out like a memorized act? He considered the possibility and dismissed it, for though Joe's actions had had a melodramatic unreality about them, the notion of a planned act was too fantastic to bear scrutiny. He did not believe Joe was a good enough actor to do it; he did not believe their talk in the jail could have been part of an elaborate and subtle pretense.

The district attorney folded his arms and looked Scott over with a little smile. "I have nothing to retract. There is grave doubt in my mind that the conduct of the defense is in good faith." Another actor, he said his speech in the proper clear, bitten syllables.

"And in mine too," Joe Hillstrom said, and again injected his shock of surprise into the routine acts of the court characters.

Apparently the spectacle of defendant and prosecutor banding together against the defense attorneys amused the judge. With a wintry smile he said, "Bailiff, conduct the defendant into the court's chamber." To Scott, as he stepped down, he said, "You'd better go in and settle this in private."

As Scott and McDougall, closely conferring, followed Joe and the bailiff out the rear door, the court broke out into delighted clots of talk.

– This Hillstrom is crazy as a coot. Did you see him jump up there and try to yell the judge down?

– He isn't any crazier than I am. He's smart. He knows as much law as his lawyers. The D.A. had that last one figured right on the line, they're trying for an insanity verdict.

– You bet he isn't crazy. He's murderous. Have you noticed his eyes? My old man used to say you could never trust a man with those pale eyes. He'd as soon kill you as look at you.

– Are they going to put him on the stand? Have they found that woman he was supposed to be mixed up with?

– They haven't found her because she doesn't exist.

– Yes, but I heard this morning there was some jane that had come out defending him, some bigwig's wife, she got Clarence Darrow interested. Maybe that's why Hillstrom tried to can his lawyers, he's got Darrow coming in.

– What I want to know is, who's this jane that was yelling at him down there a while ago? You know who she is? She been in this before?

So I'll just sit still, Joe had said. *Either way, I'll just sit still.*

He was supremely confident, secure in his own innocence of the crime. Or he was fanatically bent on showing up the cracks in capitalist justice. Or he had some obscure motive that even his lawyers didn't know for refusing to play his scheduled part of defendant. Or he was guilty and at bay.

And what was going on in the judge's chamber now? More extravagant defiance and denunciation of his lawyers? More berserk throwing of anarchy into the orderly machinery? Was that perhaps his motive in all this, simply a delight in throwing monkey wrenches, a refusal to co-operate with any part of society's institutions? Or was he more subtle and cunning than anyone gave him credit for being, and deliberately cultivating confusion because confusion was his best defense? Or was he a little drunk on the notoriety of his trial, and trying to steal the show from the orderly character actors elected by Salt Lake County?

This last speculation, Lund admitted, was evidence of how dizzy his mind had got attempting to understand. He must keep firmly in mind, though the circumstances and the staged look of the whole trial and the histrionics of defendant and attorneys kept luring him to forget, that this was no play. Joe Hillstrom's life was at stake.

Three or four men had gathered just outside the rail on the center aisle. One of them, as he turned, showed a Wobbly button on his shirt—a massive man with very liquid black eyes, a mouth that twitched in a gritting, unreal smile, and a habit of looking beyond anyone he talked to, as if picking up meaningful hints of movement in corners of the room. He seemed to be the center of the group; it was to him that Scott came now from the inner room. On impulse Lund stood up and joined the handful of men. Scott was saying, "Once Christensen and Judge Hilton enter the case officially I'll step out if he wants, but it would be suicide to let him handle his own case even for one day."

"That doesn't seem to be the way he figures it," said a newspaper man with a pad in his hand.

The big Wobbly looked across him abstractedly, gritting his nervous smile. "Something's eating him," he said to Scott. "Can I go in and talk to him?"

The lawyer threw his hands wide. "I wish you would."

"There's a girl here I think ought to talk to him too."

Scott's eyebrows worked, but he said nothing. And Lund, to whom the whole morning had been unreal, did an uncharacteristic thing. He pushed forward to the rail and said, 'I'm an old friend of Joe's, from San Pedro. Maybe I could get him to listen."

The black eyes touched him, moved beyond him. "It's a cinch somebody has to. Wait just a minute."

He went through and up the side aisle, and the girl sitting in the third row there came out at his crooked finger. They whispered together in the aisle, the girl blushed pink, her eyes, startled, searched the Wobbly's face, her head dropped a little. Then the two of them came down and inside. The big Wobbly let his eyes cover them all. "Well, I guess we're a delegation."

The man with the pad started to come along, but the Wobbly good-naturedly put a hand against his chest and held him back. "This ain't for you," he said. "Not yet, anyway."

Four of them went on through the judge's door. Going last, Lund turned and looked back into the courtroom. He had the odd unreal shock of seeing the thing reversed, of looking out over the audience while the act was still on, as if he were someone called up from the audience to assist the magician in a trick.

Every eye in the room was on him—or on the doorway where the blonde girl had been just a moment before.

4

Joe was sitting in a chair by the fireplace, McDougall behind the desk. They were not talking. The lawyer was looking out the window, watching the clouds and the sky and whistling softly between his teeth. Joe seemed perfectly calm; he ran a comb through his hair as they came in.

"Well, Joe," the big Wobbly said. "You sort of derailed the express."

"That's sure a shame."

"What's the trouble?"

"I told you. I don't like my lawyers. I don't want you wasting money on them."

"What's wrong with them?"

Joe shrugged. His eyes flicked over to the girl, dwelt on her soberly, moved on to Lund and recognized and acknowledged him, without ever altering the watchful, sullen expression of his face. "What's right?"

Scott said, "Joe, I wish I could convince you we're both doing our best. God knows you don't give us much to work with . . ."

"That's it, isn't it?" Joe flashed. "You'd like all the details about the woman. If I'll give you the whole story and prove I'm innocent, then you can prove it to the jury and make yourself look good. But if you have to keep the D.A. from proving I'm guilty, that takes work and you don't do so well."

"Well, look at it this way," the big Wobbly began, but Joe continued without moving his stare from Scott.

"Every time a woman's name comes up, here you come gallop-
ing to snoop something out. The minute you got that wire from
Virginia Stephen saying she'd got Hilton to come into the case
you trot around to ask if maybe I got shot in her house." Again his
eyes moved to dwell somberly on the girl, who stood hanging to
the rim of her pocketbook. "Tonight you'll be around to see if Ingrid isn't the one."

Under the circumstances the words were as brutal as a blow.
Bright red flamed in the girl's face, a blush that looked so violent
it seemed it must be accompanied by physical pain.

"What you can't get through your head," Joe said, "is that I don't
have to say where I was that night. I don't have to tell anybody
how I got shot. That's not the question. The question is how
Morrison and his boy got shot. The only part of this business that
concerns you is keeping them from convincing the jury I was in
Morrison's store."

"I must say that with your attitude that's a little hard to do,"
Scott said, and spread his hands at the big Wobbly. "You see,
Ricket?" McDougall continued to look out the window across the
pigeon-messy sill.

"Joe," Ricket said, "Soren Christensen is coming in to act for
Hilton this afternoon. Couldn't you just ride it out till then?"

"Sure. Alone. Without Christensen or Hilton either, for that matter."

"You have to have somebody around that knows the law."

"I don't know," Joe said. "Maybe the new ones do. These two
don't."

Joe's expression was that of a man bored with too much discussion of the obvious. Impervious to argument, he shrugged them
all off. But Lund, having thrust himself forward, had to try. He
waited until he could catch Joe's eye, and he forced his smile,
and he said, "It's so easy to miss a trick if you're not trained to
this. Your life could depend on some petty little triviality or a
technical point. A jury can convict you because it takes a dislike
to your face."

"That shows what their justice is worth."

"It doesn't do much good to prove justice is blind and get hanged
for your pains."

"Shot," Joe said with a white grin. "In Utah they give you a choice."

Out of their reach, his back against some invisible wall, he sat and rubbed his broken knuckles with the ball of his left thumb. Scott looked at Ricket and then significantly at his watch. A pigeon fluttered onto the stone sill, and McDougall, elaborately holding himself out of the discussion, chirped at it in the silence and snapped his fingers lightly. The girl stood where she had stood since coming in, both hands on her bag, her body leaning a little, her posture awkward, and said in a voice with a faint echo of Swedish singsong, "Maybe if I talked to him alone."

Joe did not even turn his head. "You stay out of this."

Trying the faces of the others for a reflection of understanding, Lund saw that all of them were curious, none of them knew. Scott stood with his watch in hand, his legs spraddled, his brows clenched in a frown. McDougall had turned away from his contemplation of the outdoors. Ricket studied the girl with his glowing liquid eyes.

"Please," Ingrid said to them all.

Now Joe was very erect in his chair. In the strong light every mark on his bitten face showed, the scar from nose to jaw, the clipped wing of the nose, the ridged welt on his neck. His lips were thinned together. For perhaps half a minute he seemed to ponder something intense and inward. Then he said, "Maybe you all better chase out for a minute."

People were still at the rail, two reporters among them. Lund felt their curiosity as more professional but no more insistent than his own, and he felt the exact moment when the courtroom realized that the girl had not come out with the rest. From the edge of the jury box the district attorney and the judge looked on remotely.

"I don't know," Scott said, and shook his head repeatedly at the reporters. He was like a man trying to shake off a persistent fly. "Her name is Ingrid Olson, that's all I know."

"She's a musician," Ricket put in. "She helps Joe with his songs."

"What songs?"

"He's a song writer. He wrote half the iww songbook."

"Is she an iww?"

"No."

"You think she's the woman in the case?"

"No."

"How's she mixed up in it, then? What's going on in there now?"

"I don't know."

"You staying in, or is he going to act for himself?"

"Wait five minutes and we'll all know," Scott said.

"How does Hillstrom act with this girl? They seem to be pretty thick?"

McDougall said sourly, "An hour ago you fellows all thought the woman story was a pretty weak alibi."

The clock clicked at the half-hour. The judge climbed to the bench, looking a question at Scott in passing. Just as Scott put his hand to the door of the chambers, the knob turned and Ingrid Olson came out. In a breathless swallowed voice she said, "It'll be all right," and with her face held sideward and downward she hurried through the gate and to her seat. Behind her came Joe with the bailiff holding his arm.

So the entr'act was over, its ending punctuated by three measured strokes of the gavel and the bailiff's henyard gabble of invocation. It was something of a surprise to Lund to see Mrs. Seeley mount to the witness chair. He had the feeling that they should be far beyond Mrs. Seeley, into some other scene. But here she was, careful and with a prim mouth, determined to answer thoughtfully and accurately. Lund thought that as she sat holding her white gloves in her lap she looked out across the court with an air of pride.

Justice groaned on.

– Look carefully at the defendant, Mrs. Seeley. Would you be able to identify him positively as the man who passed you under the arc light at Eighth South and West Temple on the night of January 9?

– Well, not exactly. He's about the same build, and his nose . . .

– He resembles closely the taller of the two men you saw?

– Yes, I would say he . . .

– Will you describe again how this man was dressed?

– Well, he had a felt hat pulled down over his eyes, and a bandanna around his neck, cowboy fashion, and no overcoat.

– How tall would you say this man was?

– Oh, pretty tall, close to six feet, and slim.

–I will ask the defendant to stand up. Now, Mrs. Seeley . . .

Lund shut his eyes, listening carefully but with detachment. He had no faith in the district attorney's ability to extract the truth from however willing a witness. He had no faith that having committed himself as public prosecutor the district attorney was any longer interested in the truth. A conviction in the legal sense was not quite the same as intellectual conviction. And he had no faith in any human being's ability to *be* a witness, and he did not believe that anything he himself thought important could come from all the elaborate and intricate formalisms of this court. What could emerge was a barren *what* and an equally barren *how*. The elusive *who*, as the case seemed to him, was certain to be settled by implication and inference and interpretation of circumstances, without clear proofs. And if the court decided against Joe Hillstrom, if Joe Hillstrom were in fact guilty, there remained the final and wretchedly insoluble *why*.

If Joe Hillstrom were guilty, how explain it? What chain of circumstances, what dark impulse, what private fury or sudden crystallization of long impersonal hostilities, what tie-up with revolution or what need for money, what accidents and what plans and what influences, the whole web of the *why* was forever hidden, beyond the jurisdiction and beyond the capacity for inquiry of this or any other court. The answer might lie in Joe Hillstrom's mind, or Joe Hillstrom might be as ignorant of the whole action as he said he was. If it lay in his mind and memory, then how important was it that Joe's mind was a labyrinth of prejudice and devotion and idealism and half-baked revolutionary ardor and a personal hostility against fate or society or capitalism or some yeasty Enemy called the System? Lund had seen enough criminals to be impressed by their stupidity and their animalism. Joe was neither stupid nor animal. Then what could be learned, what known?

He opened his eyes and saw the back of Joe Hillstrom's head and thought how strange it was, how suddenly unbelievable, that that little round skull could contain all it contained. Like a Pandora's box, if it were opened it could overflow the world. But it remained sealed, neatly trimmed by the jail barber, dense with the things it knew, and utterly opaque even to the eyes of justice, of friendship, or of love.

That there was love involved, he needed no more looks at Ingrid

Olson's face to know. He kept his eye on her, and when, five minutes before the noon recess, she rose and went out, he followed her.

The elevator door was just closing. Dourly the one-legged elevator man—some precinct worker rewarded with a job—held it open for them. In silence they rode down the creaking old rig. Lund saw that the girl's face was drawn; her starched waist was wilted a little by the heat. At the ground floor she started toward the south entrance, and when Lund followed she stopped and turned, her face a mixture of impatience and pleading.

"Please—I haven't anything to tell you."

"You don't understand," Lund said, stopping dead still. "I'm not a reporter. I'm a friend of Joe's."

Her eyes searched his; he found them candid as well as troubled. "Even then," she said.

"I don't want to force myself on you," he said, "but I'd like to talk. Could you go with me somewhere and have lunch?"

"I'm on my way home."

"Can I come along?"

"I live clear out in Murray."

"Out where Joe lived?"

"Near there."

"All the better."

Smiling to reassure her, deliberately working the warmth that he knew people found in him, he waited. "All right," she said, and turned again toward the door.

In the hot noon the trees hung still, lush with the jungle growth of summer. Birds ducked and shook themselves under the sprinklers on the park lawn. Out by the sidewalk a fox terrier lay with its hindquarters spraddled flat in the dust. As they passed, a drop fell from its jerking pink tongue.

"Why do you come to the trial?" Lund said, and felt at once that the question sounded blunt.

Without turning her face she answered, "He should know his friends are standing by him." She led him to the corner and across the street and stopped under a tree.

"Of course," he said. "I meant . . . it's a brave thing for you to do."

"Brave?"

"Considering how people talk. You expose yourself to all kinds of guesses."

"I didn't expect to get involved," she said. "I just went there so he could see me."

Up the street he saw the yellow car coming, and he let his glance slip sideward, hoping to surprise something in her expression, but she was looking in her purse for carfare.

"He wasn't pleased to see you brought into it," he said.

She shook her head, her lips tightening. "No."

"Though you were the only one who could do anything with him."

The car started from the next corner and came rocking. They stepped down off the curb to meet it, and she surprised him with an absolutely direct look. "If I were the woman," she said, "would it be any harder for me to go and tell how he got shot than to appear in court and let everybody guess?"

He was embarrassed. "I didn't mean . . ."

"If he'd got shot over me I'd have told long ago," she said. The car passed them, slowing and grinding, with a whiff of ozone and oil and a billowing of disturbed hot air.

"Do you think he got shot over a woman?" Lund said, following her toward the front end.

The folding doors opened. "He says he did," Ingrid said over her shoulder, and mounted the steps.

They were in a seat at the rear, away from the handful of other passengers, when Lund spoke again. "You're very loyal."

"His friends should be," she said, aiming it so directly at him and his doubt that he kept silence. In the next few minutes he stole looks at her face. She was pale, and she kept her head turned to look out the window. The inconsequentialities of the trackside occupied his eyes and at least part of his brain. The car ran through a little concentration of business buildings, past the board fences of a ball park, and then into something more country than city, with only scattered houses, with big gardens, with orchards and privies. They rocked along at a clattering pace, stopping only at main intersections where the houses momentarily thickened.

"I'm sorry if I seem to keep at you," he said finally. "I'm trying to understand. Ever since I first heard, yesterday, of the trouble Joe was in, I've been trying to fit the Joe I know into this. I can't."

"Nobody can," she said.

Ingrid Olson's skull, like the skull of Joe Hillstrom, might contain some of the answers Lund craved, but he saw now, as he should have seen earlier, that there was no digging them out. His methods were the methods of the district attorney. There were no other methods available. Learning what he needed to know was like trying to weigh the impalpable air with a freight scale.

"Have you known Joe long?" he said.

"Since September."

"September. That's when I saw him last. He must have come straight up here from San Pedro."

He wondered if this decent, clean, troubled young woman knew that Joe carried a gun, and what she would make of the theory that it was for his own protection as an organizer. He wondered what she would think if he told her the story of the wad of money thrown at him frantically for hiding when the police knocked on the alley door. And yet wasn't it a demonstration of Joe's soundness that he should have been keeping company with this kind of girl, this decent clean troubled obviously good and loyal and dependable young woman? Or at least keeping part-time company with her. There was always the nameless source of his wound, if she existed.

The confusions in his mind began to communicate themselves to his body; on an empty stomach, the rocking of the car and the smells of ozone and oil and straw seats and cigar butts began to make him queasy. He sat swallowing down his uneasy gorge, making no attempt to press the conversation further, and he was glad when Ingrid Olson stood up to get off.

The two-block walk to her house quieted his stomach, but still he said nothing, because he felt there was nothing he could say. The instruments he had were inadequate for understanding or measurement. When the girl finally stopped at an unpainted wooden gate, before a house with a bow window in which stood a cardboard sign saying "Ingrid Olson, Piano Lessons," she put one hand on the gatepost and stood waiting, and he knew she was only being polite, she wanted him to say goodbye and be gone.

Opening his hand ruefully, turning it upward, he smiled. "I wish I knew what to think. It's almost as easy for me to think Joe guilty of murder as to believe this story about the woman. He just isn't the man for either one. I don't understand."

Under a catalpa tree drooping with long pods, her hand on the gate, she stood quietly, a quiet girl with her own dignity about her. Her voice was low. "Is it so necessary to understand?" she said. "Isn't it enough just to take his word and try to help?"

"I should think . . ." he began.

Massed tears had gathered in the girl's eyes, but she did not turn her face. She stared at him through the tears, it seemed to him angrily, and her mouth twisted in an uncontrollable grimace.

"Do you think *I* understand?" she said, and turned swiftly up the walk and into the house.

5

The Wobbly hall looked like every other Wobbly hall he had ever been in—a single big bare room with folding chairs piled against the wall and a "baggage room" in the back corner where migrants stacked their bindles. In the broken-down black-leather hotel chairs along the window side a half-dozen men were arguing. The room smelled of cooking and tobacco smoke and printer's ink from the old flatbed press shoved against the inside wall where a man in a canvas apron was setting up a stick of type.

At first he saw nothing of Ricket, but a second look showed him the cubbyhole office with its door half ajar, and he leaned in to see the secretary sprawled in a swivel chair before a desk tempestuous with papers and pamphlets. He was too big for the chair, the room, the overflowing desk. His movement of welcome made the chair squeal, and he lunged to keep papers from sliding off onto the floor.

"Sit down," he said. "Glad to see you."

Lund did not take the offered chair. "I've got to catch a train in a few minutes. I just dropped in to leave something for the defense fund."

"Sure thing." Pawing among papers and drawers in a half-hearted attempt to find something, Ricket said, "If I could locate the damn book I'd fix you up a receipt."

"Never mind."

"Oh sure, just as easy as not."

The forty dollars that Lund took from his wallet was more than he could spare; he would be short by the time he got home. But he would not do less. Seeing the surprise flick in Ricket's black eyes at the amount, he said, "This is a debt. This really belongs to Joe already, I owe it to him. I'll send on a contribution of my own after I get back east."

He knew that Ricket's insistence on the receipt was a recognition of his difference and his status as an outsider, a "sympathizer." Ricket would demonstrate that the iww was punctilious and that there was not the slightest chance of graft in its collection of defense funds. Though he had never believed otherwise, Lund submitted to being receipted. When the slip was in his hands he said, "How did Joe behave this afternoon?"

"Well," Ricket said, and his eyes looked beyond Lund and his mouth twitched in the phantom smile. "He didn't fire any more lawyers."

"Are Scott and McDougall as bad as he says?"

"They're all right. He never gave them anything to work with."

Ricket heaved back in the chair, found two cigars in a drawer, offered one to Lund, who refused. He bit off the end and sat absently, the smile coming and going, his brows in a webbed frown. For an aimless half-minute he tried carefully to get the cigar band onto his little finger, but could slip it only as far as the second knuckle.

"I don't know," he said, and yawned powerfully, cracking his jaws. "Scott's been on half a dozen labor cases here, he's all right. McDougall's new in town. But Joe don't even want Hilton."

"He told me he didn't want the union to bleed its treasury."

"Yeah," Ricket said. "But before he got in this jam himself he was busting a gut raising money for the defense of the Oatfield boys. No, I've watched Joe on this from the beginning. He didn't fire those two because they were doing a bad job. He fired them because he didn't want anybody defending him at all."

"Some people might take that as a sign he's guilty."

"Or extra innocent," Ricket said. He smoked thoughtfully and

watched Lund with eyes that seemed pure liquid. His voice was
gentle. "Did you ever get hauled into jail?"

"No."

The secretary dropped his head back and blew smoke at the
ceiling, and the ghostly smile like a tightening of the jaw muscles
or a gritting of the teeth came mirthlessly and went again. "I remember the first time I ever got pulled," he said. "I was just a kid,
maybe sixteen, and I was on the bum in a strange town—Denver,
if it matters any. So I was rubbering around the streets looking for
a YMCA when a cop spotted me, and finally he came up and said
he guessed he better look me over. He searched me and found a
jackknife I had, one with a button on the handle that springs the
blade out, you know? Bingo, I'm in the clink, concealed weapons.
It was that button jigger that did it. The cop booked me and
took me on down a hall and shoved me through a door, and on the
other side I kind of hesitated, you know, the way you would, not
knowing which way he wanted you to go. But I never got my
mouth open to ask, because this bull let me have it across the
face with his billy. I saw stars for about an hour, and after that I
laid all night in the tank thinking over my sins. In the morning
I was so swelled up, like a punkin all across this side, that they
finally brought in a sawbones to look me over. Busted cheekbone.
I kept wanting them to wire my folks in Sioux Falls, but they didn't
pay me any mind. They made it plenty clear how I could get a
year for that jackknife if they wanted to be tough, and they kept
inviting me to confess any robberies or anything I'd been mixed up
in. They even pretended they had me all hooked up with one
special job, but I was too dumb innocent to know what went on.
Finally I got a probation officer to wire my old man, and after three
days I got out of there."

Lund waited. "Yes?"

"I was just thinking how helpless they can make you feel,"
Ricket said. "You're minding your own business and right out of a
clear sky comes this tough mick in a blue suit and he can pull any
damn thing on you he wants. He can murder you if he feels like it,
beat you plumb to death, and the rest of them will cover up for
him like a horse blanket. You can't open your peep. Just squawk
once, or even break step going through a door, and he can bust you
with a club. If you look cross-eyed you're resisting an officer, or

trying to escape. And then they get you up before some sergeant and start firing questions at you, and there's something about a jail makes everything you say sound like a lie, even to yourself. In five minutes they got you thinking you probably *are* some gonoph. You tell 'em where to find out about you and will they do it? They'd let you rot in jail for a week before they'd even send a wire."

"Yes," Lund said again.

"I think I can figure Joe out," Ricket said. "Suppose you're him, and you get hurt—how, that's your business. You're lying in bed when the cops come and pinch you. If they can make me feel the way I did about the jackknife, how could they make Joe feel about a double murder? Would you talk for them? Even if it meant your neck, would you let them beat some alibi out of you?"

Knowing Joe, Lund admitted to himself that it could be that way. He was stubborn and he was proud.

"Even hiring a lawyer to defend him is playing their game, see?" Ricket said. "Once he got really sore he'd feel that way, wouldn't he?" With a sudden harsh movement he flapped the cigar ash onto the floor. "A working stiff like Joe hasn't got any old man in Sioux Falls to wire to. Maybe you don't know how the cops take it out on somebody they think hasn't got any friends."

"Maybe Joe doesn't want the IWW to spend its money because he thinks it isn't properly an IWW case."

"What do you mean?"

"He couldn't have been on union business when he was shot."

"Why not?" Ricket said. "That woman story could easy be something he got up on the spur of the moment. He could easy have been on union business." He batted at the smoke cloud and twisted in the chair. "What you have to keep in mind all the time is that he's a Wobbly. That's enough for the boys that are after him. Ever since Haywood tried to organize Bingham two years ago the Copper Trust has been looking for a chance. Last fall we struck the Utah Construction Company down at Soldier's Summit, on the D & RG. That puts the Utah Construction Company and the D & RG right where the Copper Trust is. This is a labor-hating state. If they can't beat us or run us out they'll frame us."

Ricket's thesis was so simple, so comforting in its directness, that for a moment Lund was tempted. It made such a close neat pattern: the bosses catching a labor organizer off balance and pinning the handiest unexplained crime on him. Sometimes the formula varied, the bosses first having the crime committed and then framing a labor man. And both variants were often enough true; it would solve a lot of questions to believe one or another of them true this time. And certainly that would be the official iww version, spread through the labor press. The printer in the canvas apron was probably setting up something of the kind now.

But there were hesitancies, impediments to belief. "I've gone through the newspapers files," he said. "They don't say a word about Joe's connection with the iww. The reporters there this morning didn't even know Joe had written any songs. He's been in jail five months, but so far as I can see they still think they've got a common laborer named Hillstrom. They don't know they've got Joe Hill."

The ghost smile became real, stretching the wide limber lips. "The newspaper boys don't tell anything they're not supposed to tell. Maybe they knew who Joe was and maybe they didn't. But the bosses did."

"What bosses?" Lund said impatiently. "Have you got any evidence of that?"

Ricket only smiled, and Lund understood him. If there was no evidence, the statement could still be made—must be made, as part of the campaign. "Anyway they know now," Ricket said after a pause. "They were around here this afternoon and I gave them an earful." With a big brass-capped advertising pencil he jabbed at the scarred desk. "Every stiff in the West knows Joe Hill from his songs. In a week or two every stiff in the West'll know he's being railroaded. You watch the support roll in."

More than ever Lund felt himself an outsider, a pale doubting Thomas. The rest of them, from Ingrid Olson and Ricket to the most nameless stiff who sent in a dollar bill in a penciled envelope, were united in a single uncomplicated act of trying to save Joe. Trying to understand (trying to judge? he wondered) he was all alone, useless, perhaps even disloyal.

"Is Mrs. Stephen part of the campaign?" he asked.

"You bet she is. She's a worker, that girl, and she's got connections."

"Her connections have already got her talked about."

Ricket's laugh was loud and full of amusement, oddly hearty after the ghostly flickering smile. "Did you see tonight's *Deseret News?*"

"Not yet."

"Not a peep," Ricket said. "Daughter of former president of Mormon Church mixed up in murder trial? Unh-uh. Not in the Church's paper."

"It'll be in the others, though."

"Oh sure."

Lund hesitated half a breath. "Anything in it?"

The big head wagged and the chair groaned. "I wish there was. She'd have come out with it and got him out of there a long time ago."

"So she's just an iww."

The secretary looked at him in amusement. When he looked directly into Lund's face his eyes were so shining that they seemed a completely transparent covering for something beyond, some hidden, alert, outward-peering life. "Just?" he said. "That's the highest office in this land of liberty."

So there was disappointment here too, in spite of all the certainty and confidence. He would find none of the answers he sought. The tiny office was layered with smoke, his legs felt as if he had walked a long way, his stomach fluttered with the queasiness that had never quite left him since noon. He said, remembering that streetcar ride and the way he had forced the girl out of her dignity and silence, "The Olson girl doesn't seem to be the one, either."

"I don't know anything," Ricket said. "I don't want to know anything. But if I was to guess I'd guess that kid had taken a beating."

Lund sighed. There was a short silence into which the accelerating argument in the other room came briefly loud: "That's a lot of crap! Look at what they did at the second national convention. If it hadn't been for De Leon we'd've . . ."

The preacher rubbed his face, very tired. He thought with cunning hidden pleasure of the Pullman, the bed, the close green-curtained darkness where he could lie down and let the motion of the train rock out of his mind the speculation and confusion, the whole war of affection and belief. To hide the treacherous evasiveness of the thought he laughed.

"The trouble with me, I was trained as a minister. I keep looking for the right and wrong in things. The motive always seemed to me more important than the act. I keep being bothered by things. Why Joe doesn't want lawyers, for instance. Why he sticks to a story like that one about protecting a woman. The only thing that seems in character at all is the way he keeps his mouth shut about what actually happened to him."

"That's a fact," Ricket said. "He's a first-class clam. Maybe Christensen and Hilton can get him talking."

"Maybe he'll fire them too."

Ricket winked. "He can't. This thing's out of his hands."

He rose, a tremendous man, a foot taller than Lund. A button of his shirt was undone, and black hair grew in a stiff curl through the opening, positive and direct as grass growing toward sunlight. He shook hands with the preacher and they wished each other luck.

The Wobblies, Lund was thinking as he went toward his hotel to get his suitcase, were as automatic as a burglar alarm. Touch any part of the mechanism, let one member be misused, anywhere, and they went off in a loud single-minded uproar. An injury to one was an injury to all. They went no further. There was one enemy, the System. No matter what happened, they knew who was to blame. They recognized one virtue, loyalty to the cause, so that their souls and stomachs were not visited by doubt and queasiness. The revolutionary faith was a flux that absorbed moral complexities and even rational doubts as limestone absorbed impurities from iron ore. Once the flux had begun to operate, there were only two possibilities, one choice. Either or, our side or theirs, iron or slag.

Joe would have support, if he would accept it; he would have a defense, if he would permit it; he would have widespread and unquestioning belief for any statement he chose to make, or any statement made in his name. He could sit still, as he had said he would, but others would move the chair he sat in. Those who would convict him because he was an iww or those who would free him unquestioned for the same reason would pick a bone over his fate. But what of those who saw with a twist of almost fatherly solicitude the broken and crippled hand, and those who wondered against their own wish if Joe Hillstrom could really have entered that grocery store masked and armed, and if he had, then *why?*

Was it disloyal to believe that almost any man was capable of almost any mistake or crime if the circumstances shoved him that way? Was it unfriendly to know that a friend was not perfect and incorruptible, but sadly human, and to like him in spite of the weaknesses he had: the profound inward hostility that made him strike out in retaliation, the fits of self-pity and self-justification, the pride and vanity, the latent violence, the great vague ambitions? Did it lessen Christ's love for Peter to know that on his last night Peter would deny him thrice? Would it change his feelings about Joe to know for certain that Joe was guilty?

He did not know. He knew only that he mistrusted the partisans who would hang or free Joe without regard for his guilt or innocence. In spite of the clumsiness and inadequacy of the court he had sat in that morning there was no solution for civilized men except to try to know, and if they could not know enough, then to know what they could. Being imperfect and human, Joe would have to put up with imperfect human justice, but it was justice that he ought to face, and not either organized vengeance or the organized clemency of friends.

He had no doubt that justice, no matter which way it decided, would be denounced by one side or the other, or perhaps both.

The Martyr

1 Salt Lake City, 1914–1915

Consider the way circumstance has of taking a man out of his own proper and recognizable character and subtly transforming him, coating him with the ions of a new personality as a lead tray is glazed with silver in an electroplating tank.

Two men are on trial before the Third District Court in Salt Lake City. One is the IWW poet and song writer Joe Hill, a name known to many, and now a face that begins to be known too, a sensitive and thoughtful and fine face, with a resolute mouth and eyes like a compassionate Christ. Folders bearing his picture are stuck up in every hall west of the Big Sioux; an indignation meeting in New York has marched with his portrait on banners; sailors have carried the story of his case over the world. Shining with firm innocence, victimized because of his organizing activities, Joe Hill rises out of the murk of the labor wars, still serving the cause even in the System's jail. More than life-size, of an immortal calmness and unshakable resolution, he takes shape in the minds of thousands, legendary, even mythical: Labor's Songster.

His origin is uncertain, for who can isolate for certain the egg and the sperm that unite to make a legend? Who can determine how much a man imposes his own myth of himself upon others and how much that myth is created by those who know him? Joe Hill began to be born in his songs and cartoons; certainly he lived, imperfectly realized, in the mind of a Swede sailor sitting on the San Pedro waterfront feeding a rat, or looking down the sad trough of Beacon Street and dreaming a dream of leading thousands. But now he acquires stature and outline through the labors of a committee; he is issued from a headquarters like news bulletins, and the headquarters is not Salt Lake County jail but the IWW hall.

Step by step, as the union fights his case against the hardening prejudices of courts and public, in an atmosphere increasingly edged and hostile, the character of Joe Hill is filled in by broadsides, pamphlets, appeals, form letters, news stories for the labor press. He emanates piecemeal from a dusty bare room where transient men sleep and cook and discuss and convene: a meager flophouse, a minimal lodge, a scanty asylum, a threadbare club, a primitive church whose symbol is the clenched fist of solidarity. It is in this cell of the new society forming within the shell of the old, this skimpy few square feet of the revolutionary future, that Joe Hill is properly born.

Throughout the course of his creation his prototype Joe Hillstrom sits waiting in the county jail. Forbidden newspapers, he can be only vaguely aware of what is happening to his identity. The little information he gets comes to him through the steel mesh of the visitors' window, or through conferences with the lawyers he has been prevailed upon to accept, or through letters that come to him from old friends, fellow workers, liberal groups, church organizations, sob-sisters, the known and the nameless who have heard his legend and wish him well. These are things which must work upon him slowly, sometimes as surprise and sometimes as reinforcement of his buried and incorrigible beliefs about himself.

As the myth begins slowly and insensibly to encroach upon the man, which is the truer part? Is it Joe Hillstrom or Joe Hill, passionate man or passionless symbol, imperfect and possibly guilty flesh or a wronged spirit, who sits through the days of testimony with his bony shoulders turned on the crowd of sympathizers and union-haters and plain emotion-suckers who pack the room?

Is it Joe Hillstrom or Joe Hill who is described in the hostile city papers as "cringing" when the prosecutor in his speech to the jury points a dramatic finger and calls him the most bloodthirsty animal in the annals of Utah crime? Does he watch with his own eyes or with the eyes of Labor's Songster while his attorneys denounce the court as unfair and the trial as a farce; and is the sneer that touches his mouth personal or abstract when the district attorney makes a ranting reply: (*My blood boils with keen resentment, gentlemen, when I hear such unwarranted attacks on American institutions—*

institutions which are the foundation stones of our glorious concepts of liberty, equality, and justice, and I tell you that when any considerable number of our fellow beings subscribe to the doctrine you heard enunciated this morning, then liberty flees the confines of our fair land and anarchy begins its sway . . .)?

Joe Hill or Joe Hillstrom, he stands before the bar of justice and hears himself convicted of murder in the first degree. Indifferently, standing straight because his body has never learned to slouch, but not respectful, not cowed, he hears the judge's dry intoning voice ask him if he has any reason why he should not be sentenced, and he shrugs off the formality: "No, let it go at that." According to the laws of Utah he is offered his choice between hanging and shooting, and his lip lifts (out of personal insolence or out of some perception of how he must look for the public at such a moment?) "I'll take shooting," Hill or Hillstrom says clearly. "I'm used to that. I've been shot at a few times before and I guess I can stand it again."

With his life already forfeit and his death sentence forming on the judge's withered lips, he ironically underlines the refusal he has made steadfastly through the trial. The bullet wound which properly explained would clear him becomes the source of an acid joke just before the words that will end his life.

That joke too goes broadcast from headquarters and adds its touch to the growing portrait of Joe Hill. The verdict has inspired a renewed burst of activity; the sentence which condemns Joe Hillstrom to be shot on September 4 doubles it again. Defense committee and lawyers sit late in the little office off the Wobbly hall. Jack Carpenter, the gimpy-legged printer, in eye shade and apron sets stick after stick of worn type. Across the country men lounging on corners or outside the doors of skid-road joints hear, among denunciations of war and the Rockefellers and the lumber trust, the story of Joe Hill's frame-up, and a few of them drop coins in the hat. From his parents' farm in Minnesota Gus Lund, ex-preacher, sends twenty dollars, and later another twenty. From the ranch crowded with lushes and hangers-on in the Valley of the Moon, Jack London sends a hundred dollars and a short note of cheer.

The man in jail, Joe Hillstrom or Joe Hill, waits, and fills his days answering his mail, and keeps his mouth shut.

Salt Lake City
Sept. 15, 1914

Dear friend and fellow worker:

Yours of Sept. 9 at hand. Glad to hear that you are still alive and kicking and back on the firing line again.

So you tried to imitate Knowles, the Nature Freak, and live the simple life. It might be all right for a little while, as you say, but I am afraid a fellow would get simple getting too much of the simple life.

Well, I guess the wholesale butchery going on in Europe is putting the kibosh on everything, even the organization work, to some extent. As a rule, a fellow don't bother his head much about unions and the class struggle when his belly is flapping up against his spine. Getting the wrinkles out is then the main issue, and everything else side issues . . .

Well, I guess Van has told you about my case, and he knows more about it than I do, because he has been around here and on the outside. I am feeling well under the circumstances and I am fortunate enough to have the ability to entertain myself and look at everything from the bright side. So there is nothing you can do for me. I know you would if you could.

With best wishes to the bunch,
Yours for the OBU,
JOE HILL

Salt Lake City
Dec. 2, 1914

Dear friend and fellow worker:

Received your letter and should have answered before, but have been busy working on some musical composition and whenever I get an "inspiration" I can't quit until it's finished.

I am glad to hear that you manage to make both ends meet, in spite of the industrial deal, but there is no use being pessimistic in this glorious land of plenty. Self-preservation is, or should be, the first law of nature. The animals, when in a natural state, are showing us the way. When they are hungry they will always try to get something to eat or else they will die in the attempt. That's natural; to starve to death is unnatural.

No, I have not heard that song about "Tipperary" but if you send it as you said you would I might try to dope something out about that Frisco fair. I am not familiar with the actual conditions of Frisco at present; and when I make a song I always try to picture things as they really are. Of course a little pepper and salt is allowed in order to bring out the facts more clearly. If you send me that sheet music and give me some of the peculiarities and ridiculous points about the conditions in general on or about the fairground, I'll try to do the best I can.

Yours for the OBU,
JOE HILL

Salt Lake City
Jan. 3, 1915

Dear Gus:

Jud Ricket was telling me the other day he had had two or three contributions from you for the defense fund. You know I never was very sold on the sky pilots, but you're one preacher I'll let into heaven whenever I happen to be tending door. Ricket tells me funds keep coming in and there is going to be enough to finance the appeal clear to the supreme court. I'm still pretty sure no man is worth that much, but if I get sore and tell them to give the money to strike relief somewhere they don't pay any attention, so I have learned to keep still. Keep still and sit still. I'd make a first class toadstool.

I was thinking the other day, when the new year rolled around, that I've been in this calaboose almost a full year, and that's a long time to live on the kind of stew they serve here. The coffee is a little better than you used to make, but not enough to get excited about. Well, when we used to sit in the kitchen and drink that turpentine we never thought that pretty soon you'd be hoeing corn and I'd be where I am. I keep myself in good spirits by reminding myself that the worst is yet to come.

No chance to read anything here. Once a month or so a missionary of some kind comes around with a basket of books, but they're all full of moral uplift and angel food, and I'd rather read old letters over again than waste my time on that. This missionary is a lot like you used to be. I think he prays for me.

Write me when you can. One thing this jail has made out of me is a good correspondent.

> Your friend
> JOE

> Salt Lake City
> Feb. 13, 1915

Dear friend and fellow worker:

Should have answered your letter before but have been busy working on a song named "The Rebel Girl" (words and music) which I hope will help to line up the women workers in the OBU, and I hope you will excuse me.

I see you made a big thing out of that Tipperary song. In fact, a whole lot more than I ever expected. I didn't suppose that it would sell very well outside of Frisco, though by the way I got a letter from Swasey in N.Y. and he told me that "Casey Jones" made quite a hit in London, and "Casey Jones," he was an Angeleno, you know, and I never expected that he would leave Los Angeles at all.

The other day the defense committee got ten bucks from a company of soldiers stationed on the Mexican line. How is that, old top? Maybe they are remembering some of the cigars in glass bottles that they smoked at the expense of the Tierra y Libertad bunch.

Don't know much about my case. The Sup. Court will "sit on" it sometime in the sweet bye and bye and that's all I know about it.

> Give my best to the bunch,
> JOE HILL

> Salt Lake City
> March 22, 1915

Dear friend and fellow worker:

Yours of March 13 at hand. I note that you have gone "back to nature" again and I must confess that it is making me a little homesick when you mention that "little cabin in the hills" stuff.

You can talk about your dances, picnics, and blowouts, and it won't affect me, but the "little cabin" stuff always gets my goat. That's the only life I know.

Yes, that Tipperary song is spreading like the smallpox they say. Sec. 69 tells me that there is a steady stream of silver from Frisco on account of it. The unemployed all over the country have adopted it as a marching song in their parades, and in New York City they changed it to some extent so as to fit the brand of soup dished out in N.Y. They are doing great work in N.Y. this year. The unemployed have been organized and have big meetings every night. Gurley Flynn, George Swasey (the human phonograph) and other live ones are there, and Gurley F. tells me things are looking favorable for the OBU.

The hearing of my case has been postponed, they say, and they are trying to make me believe that it is for my benefit, but I'll tell you that it is damn hard for me to see where the benefit comes in at; damn hard.

Well, I have about a dozen letters to answer.

Yours as ever,
JOE HILL

Salt Lake City
June 6, 1915

Dear friend and fellow worker:

Your welcome letter received, and am glad to note that you are still sticking to your "little cabin in the hills." I would like to get a little of that close to nature stuff myself for a couple of months in order to regain a little vitality, and a little flesh on my rotting bones. My case was argued on the 28th of May, and according to Judge Hilton the results were satisfactory. He says he is sure of securing a reversal, and if so, there will hardly be another trial, for the simple reason that there won't be anything to try . . .

Your friend,
JOE

P.S.—I've just found out that the Superior Court judges are getting ready to go on their vacation until next fall, so I guess there won't be anything decided on my case for some time. But "everything comes to him who waits," they say, and that's the only consolation I got now.

He had almost a month to sit and think it over between the time the Supreme Court denied his appeal and the time they came to take him back to the District Court for resentencing, but he found this waiting easier because by now he brought resignation to it. Ricket and Hilton tried to inject cheer into him day after day, but it leaked out as fast as they poured it in. He had no need for cheer. He watched them almost with pity as they wasted their time and strength in a stubborn, step-by-step retreat.

His mail increased sharply after the Supreme Court decision, and all of it was meant as encouragement. (*Don't give up. We'll fight it to the highest court in the country. The dirty plutes don't know what they started when they started trying to railroad you. We'll fill Salt Lake so full of sab cats the bulls will crawl under the beds.*) It astonished him that so many spoke to him in their letters as if they were old friends; he was surprised that so many knew his songs. More than once, reading their letters, he found himself thinking with a remote pity of Joe Hill, held in the Salt Lake jail, Joe Hill the rebel song writer. He thought of himself not as himself but as an acquaintance, a name he had heard of. But he knew in his bones they would kill him.

They came for him one day at midmorning, two deputies named Young and Raleigh, and behind them Sheriff Coues and Chief Barry of the Police Department.

"Little walk in the park," Raleigh said as he slipped the handcuff on Joe's wrist. Joe glanced down; his wrist was bare bone. He said to Raleigh, "Looks like a chicken's neck in a horse collar. You'd better tighten that up or I'll slide right through."

"Well, if you insist," Raleigh said. He was a beefy man who was a professional wrestler in his off time, and he had a purple mat-burn on one cheekbone. Beyond the gate the sheriff was relaxed, wrinkle-necked, ministerial. The police chief was a short, dew-lapped man with a mad, stubborn mouth.

"Why all the escort?" Joe said.

The chief looked at him as if he were personally furious. Sheriff Coues said, "Some of your Wobbly friends have been making threats."

"Good for them," Joe said. "What are they going to do?"

"Nothing!" the chief said, short and sudden as an explosion.

"Can't let you get away without a struggle," the sheriff said mildly. "Have to make an effort to hang onto you."

They led him out and down the corridor and out past the office and into the alley. After the cool stone jail the heat of the sun-beaten pavement was shrivelling, and the light was so strong that Joe walked the first two hundred feet with his hand cupping his eyes. Objects swam in a blind red glare, and he smelled smells he had not smelled in weeks: outside smells, asphalt and gasoline and horse manure and the moldy earth-smell of the gutter where a trickle of water ran.

They hurried him across the street and along the sidewalk under the park trees. A squirrel shot across in front of them and up the trunk of a boxelder, and people passing stared at the manacled man. He walked with his face straight ahead, the swimming dazzle gone from his eyes now, his mind on the thing he was headed toward. There was a tightness in his chest; he felt his wound. Into the cool, lofty, cuspidor-smelling tile-floored hall, then the five of them jamming shoulders in the elevator cage, staring at the back of the elevator operator's bald head and hearing the sigh of the shaft, seeing the swaying snaky cables move downward past them.

This was all as it had been many times before, and now this time the last: the cool sigh of the shaft and the bald head of the operator and the echoing tiles and the cuspidor smell of justice. He saw the hall and the offices and the sign above the door on the left that said Third District Court, Judge M. L. Ritchie.

Voices floated out the door. He heard the dry old voice of the judge and a heavy bass that replied. Then they were at the door, steel pulled at his wrist, the proceedings in the courtroom momentarily paused as they came in, and Joe, walking with his head up, met the bleak impersonal glance of the man who had condemned him once and would condemn him again. The judge nodded slightly to the party, indicating that they should sit down and wait. "The prisoners will stand forward," he said.

Two young men stood up below the high bench, a shock-headed farm boy and another with a long bony jaw and a face humped and knobbed with some skin disease. The judge sentenced them to indeterminate terms in the state prison for second-degree burglary. Joe watched their heads, wondering what they were thinking,

whether the indeterminate sentence was a relief or whether the
uncertainty left them empty and unsatisfied. He saw the shoulders
of the farm boy sway, and then the two turned away, the old
dry voice stopped, the fat bailiff left over from earlier acts of this
repetitive dream stood up at his table and read in his goose-voice.
Raleigh unlocked the handcuff.

Without being told to do so, Joe stood up. A moment ago he
had been hot, but now he felt like a fish frozen in a cake of ice.
It seemed that no sound could penetrate into where he stood; the
room and the people were outside, in another element, and he
looked up at the judge through a thick layer of almost solid air.

He was surprised when the judge's voice came through, crackly
as paper, saying the words not his own, the words also left over,
inherited from centuries of criminal courts, an echo of what hundreds and thousands and tens of thousands had heard as they
stood up for the next to the last time to face the society that hated
and feared them. It was a ritual, a remembered line in a ceremony.
Joe had heard it once already.

"Have you anything to say why the sentence of death should
not be passed upon you at this time?"

Now his own voice, and he heard it too with surprise, strong
and clear, saying words that were not his either, but formal law-
court words that he had been coached in by Hilton. "I have this to
say, your honor," his distant voice said. "I want to know why jurymen were arbitrarily appointed by the court in my case, instead
of being drawn as is the case in similar proceedings. And I want
to know how such a proceeding can be called legal in my case."

He said the words, quibbling about a technicality, because it
seemed proper to say them now and here. Something sharpened
in Judge Ritchie's eyes, the impersonal mask perceptibly wizened.
"The court is not here to answer questions, but to hear from you
any statement you may care to make regarding why you should
not be sentenced to death at this time."

"I repeat my request to be informed why I was not given a
chance in the impaneling of the jury like that given defendants in
similar cases," Joe said.

The judge leaned forward, his face and voice still impassive
but his eyes like hot little augurs boring into Joe's. "That assertion,

or intimation, is entirely false!" he said. He drew back again, and
it came: "According to the laws of the state of Utah the penalty
for murder in the first degree may be death by hanging, death by
shooting, or life imprisonment. You have been found guilty of
murder in the first degree, and have once already had the death
penalty imposed upon you. In conformity with the law, a prisoner
sentenced to death may choose the manner of his death, as between shooting and hanging. Which do you choose?"

There was a remote ringing in Joe's ears. He hated the cold
control and the utter implacable power of the man on the bench.
His voice came out louder than he intended from his stiff mouth.
"I told you before, I've been shot a number of times lately and
I'm getting used to it."

In the silence Judge Ritchie brought his gavel down lightly, for
emphasis. "Joseph Hillstrom, for the crime of first degree murder
of which you have been adjudged guilty, I sentence you to death
by shooting, the execution to take place on October first of this
year within the walls of the state penitentiary, and I call upon
the sheriff of Salt Lake County to make such arrangements as are
necessary for the carrying out of this sentence."

The judge turned his head stonily aside. A hand caught Joe's
elbow, and Hilton was there, Job's comforter, the undiscouraged,
the indefatigable. Other hands were at him, Raleigh's and Young's,
and he went out into the corridor surrounded, with Chief Barry
ahead and Sheriff Coues behind. Hilton crowded with them into
the elevator. "That pious old hypocrite!" Hilton said. The police
chief looked at him hard, but said nothing.

As they crossed the tiled hall Joe kept looking for Ricket, Carpenter, any of the boys from the hall, but there was no sign of
any of them. Either the threats Coues had spoken about were all
in the imagination of the law, or deputies and cops had scoured
the place in advance. Otherwise some of the boys should have
been in court today.

On the cement steps of the jail he stopped and said to Hilton,
"What's the date?"

"You mean today?"

"Yes."

"August second."

"August second," Joe repeated. Two months, less one day. One more month of summer and the first month of the fall.

Like a parade they went in, waited for the unlocking of the steel door, marched through. "There are some things we should settle," Hilton said. "You feel like talking them over now, Joe?"

"Sure."

The chief's huffy, sputtering voice said, "When you start planning that next move, you can tell the I-Won't-Works to stay out of it. You can tell 'em from me that blackhand notes and bomb threats and all the rest won't get you or them a god damn thing, see? We're ready for 'em and if they start anything somebody's going to get hurt."

"I haven't any control over the IWW," Hilton said. "If you want to calm them down, maybe you'd better revise Utah justice a little."

"All I want to say to you," Barry said, "is that there's enough justice in Utah to take care of any Wobbly that wants to start anything."

He turned on his heel. "Or any workingman without the means to defend himself," Hilton said after him. "He's got it bad," he said to the sheriff. The sheriff looked as if his stomach pained him.

"The governor's been getting these threatening letters," he said. "He's probably been building a fire under the Public Safety Department." His hand went into his sagging coat pocket and rattled the handcuffs there. "I know he's been building a fire under me," he said almost plaintively. "I suppose you guys have to make a noise and beat on the tubs, but if they don't behave I'll have to run the whole bunch out of town."

"I wouldn't try," Hilton told him. "Did you ever sit in on a free-speech fight?"

Waving the guard ahead of them down the corridor toward the conference room, the sheriff said, "That's what I can't figure out. What in hell do all these outsiders know about it?"

Hilton rapidly stroked the tip of his nose between thumb and finger, and blew twice to clear some tickling obstruction. He looked at the sheriff and a hint of his courtroom manner came over him. "They don't have to know anything about it but the name of the man who's been framed. You don't seem to realize even yet that you've got a great man in your bastille."

"Well," Coues said with his mild country-preacher air, "I'm willing to take your word for it. That's fair, isn't it? How about it, Joe?"

"Fair enough."

The sheriff let them into the conference room and locked them in and went away. "Well, that's that," Joe said. "Two months to live."

"Forty years to live!" Hilton said. "They can't do it to you. I honestly think that if they try to carry out this sentence there'll be ten thousand Wobs in Salt Lake to prevent it. They'd take down this town brick by brick."

He sat down and spread his briefcase open between his feet and stooped to look into it, and his easy, big-toothed smile invited Joe to confidence. "Now listen," he said. "The next step will have to be the Pardon Board. You'll be called before them for examination, probably, and there are certain things you want to hammer on . . ."

Joe listened, and tried to think the strategy important, but all during the twenty minutes of their talk he was wishing for the quiet and security of his cell.

Utah State Prison
Aug. 12, 1915

Dear friend and fellow worker:

Yours of August 5th at hand, and as you see I've been moved to the state prison. The appeal was denied and I was up in court the other day and sentenced to be shot on the first day of October. We were all very much surprised at the decision, because we thought that I would be granted a new trial anyway. But as Judge Hilton says, "The records of the lower court are so rotten they have to be covered up somehow." I wanted to drop the case right there and then, but from reports received from all parts of the country, I think it will be carried to the U. S. Supreme Court. I didn't think I'd be worth any more money. You know, human life is kind of cheap this year. But I guess the organization thinks otherwise, and majority rule goes with me.

Well, I don't know anything new. Hoping you are successful in snaring the elusive doughnut, I remain,

Yours for the OBU,
JOE HILL

2

He noticed how they all watched him: the other prisoners, trusties
in the corridors and yard with their careful voices and their
sheathed eyes, the guards whose bored watchfulness sharpened
with speculation. A kind of urgency and importunity walked with
him and dignified the guards who walked with him, made con-
temptible and unnecessary the handcuffs on either wrist. They had
him manacled like a madman, as if he were likely to spring at
the Pardon Board and tear their throats out.

Both Hilton and Soren Christensen were waiting in the outer
office. One after the other, they shook his manacled hand and
smiled hard and encouraging into his face; they appeared to be
looking for the Pardon Board's answer in his eyes.

One of the guards unlocked himself and went away. The other
motioned Joe toward one of a row of chairs and sat down beside
him. Before them Hilton planted himself with a thumb and fore-
finger in the pocket of his vest. He looked like some school-history-
book picture of Webster replying to Hayne. But a closer look
showed that his eyes were darkly bagged, his eyeballs streaked
and watery as if he had been up all night reading fine print.

"Well, Joe."

"Ninth inning," Joe said.

"Many a game's been won in the ninth."

"I suppose."

They fell silent; if there had been anything for the condemned
and his defenders to talk about the presence of the guard would
have inhibited it. With a sigh Hilton sat down and stretched his
legs. After a moment he took the folded newspaper from his pocket
and passed it across the guard toward Joe. The guard stirred,
looked questioningly at the lawyer, and then sagged back, acqui-
escing in the fiction that he wasn't there.

The paper was rolled with the back page out. Hilton's finger
tapped at a headline and Joe read.

GOVERNOR SPRY IS THREATENED

More than 300 letters and telegrams, received today, protest against Hillstrom Execution. One from Hindustan. Warnings and Arguments

More than 300 more letters from different parts of this and other countries were received at the governor's office yesterday demanding that Joseph Hillstrom be not put to death for the murder of J. G. Morrison. Some of the letters are threatening in character, and many of them bear resemblance in phraseology and arguments.

It appears that most of the letters were written . . .

The second guard came back. His eyes jumped from the paper to Joe's face. "Whose paper?"

"Mine," Hilton said.

The guard took it from Joe and tossed it in Hilton's lap. The lawyer shrugged and busied himself working at something between his teeth.

"They're ready," the guard said. He led them into the warden's office, where a group of men sat between desk and windows. Turning at the guard's tug, Joe saw that Ricket and Carpenter were there too. Carpenter shook his clenched hands at him in a boxer's gesture.

And here, as he sat down and got a chance to look quietly, were the men upon whom he depended for his life. One by one he marked them down: a shaggy man with a senatorial haircut, a solid square one with his hair parted in the middle and a womanish red mouth, a thin old man, a much younger one who sat with his hands clasped on the desk and studied Joe directly and soberly. And the chairman, the governor, complete with gavel and brief-case. A man ready with pencil and paper—apparently a stenographer—who sat just behind the governor. Joe wondered what the governor was thinking. He wondered what he thought about Joe Hill, for whom three hundred people every day wrote from countries as remote as Hindustan. When the governor's eyes touched his he sat stiff and proud, a man more widely known and more fervently admired than any of the well-fed well-educated men who would judge him.

The governor's gavel tapped the desk lightly, his eyes circled from the two iww's around defendant and attorneys and the board itself, and came back to Hilton. "Mr. Hilton, you have a plea to make before this board?"

Hilton rose, the indefatigable, the undiscourageable, as he had risen before other tribunals and other boards through all the steps of Joe Hill's fight for life, and Joe felt how all the past failures rose with him, how Hilton this time was at bay and perhaps without hope. His voice was harsh and his words angry as he went through the arguments that Joe knew now by heart. The arguments sounded to Joe's critically tuned ear like inconsequential graspings at straws, the lawyer's anger seemed general and unimportant. He was apparently denouncing the Pardon Board for the District Court's errors in selecting jurymen. He was annoyed at the whole state of Utah because his client had been left for a time without counsel and had been forced by the court to accept the services of counsel who were not to his liking. Remote as a spectator, Joe listened while one of the board questioned Hilton tartly in the matter of counsel. Hadn't Mr. Hilton's client selected Attorneys Scott and McDougall himself, or at least had not his friends of the iww defense committee selected them? And as for his being without counsel at one time during the trial, wasn't that by his own choice?

Hilton demanded a new trial. There were errors and decisions of the District Court that stank to high heaven of prejudice, there were irregularities enough to warrant ten new trials. The evidence on which Joseph Hillstrom had been convicted was entirely circumstantial, as the court records showed. And capital punishment, especially capital punishment upon purely circumstantial evidence, was a barbarity unworthy a civilized state. He asked a commutation of the death penalty against Joseph Hillstrom on grounds of a reasonable doubt of his guilt.

"Just a moment, Mr. Hilton," the square board member said. "Are you asking for a new trial, or for commutation?"

"My client would prefer a new trial," Hilton said. "If that is not your pleasure, commutation is the least that can be granted him."

He went on with his brief of the court errors, both in the District Court and in the Supreme Court, and Joe, watching the board members, most of whom were also members of the Supreme Court, saw their eyes wander, their hands cover their careful mouths.

Hilton was getting nowhere. Finally he was interrupted again by
the governor, who asked him why he had not filed a petition for
a rehearing if he felt that the Supreme Court had committed errors
of law. Hilton replied that the state of Utah would be forever
blackened if it permitted the defendant to go to his death after
a conviction on purely circumstantial evidence, and he cited a half-
dozen cases in which the innocence of the accused had been established too late. The young jurist who watched Joe like someone
trying to recognize a half-familiar face, turned his head to tell Hilton that in the opinion of the Supreme Court the evidence had been
by no means all circumstantial, and that the identification of the
accused as the man prowling under the arc light near the store
and as the man who ran from the store after the shooting was
direct and explicit.

It had begun to rain outside. Across Ricket's bulk Joe saw the
streaked air beyond the gray window. The governor's mouth was
impatient or irritated. It occurred to Joe that he might be scared,
and the thought was delicious as a cold drink to a thirsty man. He
might be thinking of his family at home right now, exposed to iww
retaliation if Joe Hill were not pardoned here this morning. He
might be scared for his own hide, and so might the rest of them.
Three hundred letters a day, thousands of them altogether—and in
the scared little bourgeois minds of people like these the iww was
a nest of dynamiters and desperate bomb throwers. Every iww
had his pockets full of blasting powder and home-made bombs. He
knew from his mail that the accomplices of the McNamara boys
were up for trial right now in L.A., and that bombs, perhaps
planted by the cops, had been confiscated in a raid on the New
York hall. No wonder the board members were sober. They were
scared stiff. They had a tiger by the tail.

A little reverie hooded him. He saw himself walking out of the
Utah State Pen into the midst of an exulting crowd that marched
with banners down Twenty-First South and jammed the streets
of Sugarhouse and roared out the songs of Joe Hill as they hoisted
him to their shoulders. He felt how their hands came grabbing
for his own, and saw their faces by the hundred.

And came out of it to hear the governor snap at Hilton, "Mr.
Hilton, you have spoken this morning in uncomplimentary terms
of the courts and justice of the state of Utah, and you have spoken

slightingly of the integrity of the gentlemen present here. For some reason, perhaps for lack of anything better, you have adopted your client's contention that he is innocent until proved guilty and that his refusal to take the stand and testify in his own behalf should not be held against him. I agree with you, it should not, and I think was not. That is the conclusion of those of us who have carefully reviewed the transcripts of the District Court. But you are acquainted with the law, as your client is not, and you should know that once a conviction has been obtained in that court, then the presumption of innocence is no longer valid. If you have evidence to establish your client's innocence we are prepared to hear it. The burden of proof is now upon the accused. And let me remind you again, the powers of this board are limited. It cannot grant the accused a new trial. It can only commute his sentence or grant him a pardon, and it can do those only upon clear evidence."

Standing thoughtful, with bent head, Hilton delayed his answer, and Joe saw that he was silent because for the moment he was utterly stumped for something to say. He had never had anything to say to the Pardon Board. The tirade he had read for a half-hour had been a last-ditch, bluff, strong-arm method applied to the law. He watched Hilton rally himself, raise his head, start all over again.

"In view of the irregularities and errors of law . . ."

"Specifically *what* errors of law?" a judge asked sharply.

"The calling of jurors instead of impaneling them in the regular way."

"The records do not show that, Mr. Hilton. The Supreme Court considered that claim carefully in reviewing your appeal."

"Nevertheless if we are granted a new trial I am confident that we shall be able to show . . ."

"Let me remind you again," the governor said icily. "You are pleading before the Board of Pardons. This board cannot grant a new trial if it wanted to. It is here to hear evidence, if you have any."

"Your excellency," Hilton said, "I think you have the good name of the state of Utah at heart. I think you would not want to see that good name blackened by a cold-blooded judicial murder."

The governor leaned across the desk with his fists tight together. His cheeks tightened until an unexpected round knob of muscle bulged at the angle of his jaws. His mouth was small and hard. "Mr. Hilton, for the last time, we are here to listen to evidence, not vilification or threats. There has been altogether too much of both in this case already. If you have no real and actual evidence to offer, please sit down."

Jud Ricket was on his feet. "Mr. Governor . . ."

The governor slammed the gavel on the desk, his jaws clamped hard, and Ricket eased himself down into his chair again. The young jurist who had been watching Joe so intently leaned and said something in a whisper. The governor listened with his eyes cold.

"Mr. McCarthy has the floor," he said.

Now it was no longer possible to be a remote and curious spectator. McCarthy's gray eyes pulled Joe into alertness, forced him to attend and concentrate. Joe braced himself against some weight of intelligence or power he felt in them, and he realized that though he had been evading McCarthy's glance, he had been aware of him all the time. Of all the board members he had been least upset by Hilton's tirade; he seemed to Joe more dangerous for that reason. And he compelled the discussion back into personal channels. It was impossible to evade him any longer, or to dream while his fate was decided.

"I want to ask a few questions directly of Mr. Hillstrom," McCarthy said. "You understand that your case has become in the public eye something more than the trial of an individual on a murder charge. Your friends have represented you as being framed by certain industrial interests because of your activity as an iww organizer."

Joe faced him, saying nothing.

"I think I speak for the other members of the board as well as myself," McCarthy said. "They will correct me if I do not. But I think the last thing any responsible official of the state of Utah wants is the death of an innocent man."

His eyes compelled such attention that Joe looked over them, at the part in McCarthy's curly dark hair.

"But no official can be moved by threats," the justice said. "Your friends are ill-advised in the campaign they have started. They have already done your cause harm."

Joe shrugged. He knew his part; he knew how the lines must go. "I can't help what other people think of Utah justice."

Something had been offered and refused. He felt in himself a kind of gathering such as he sometimes had felt before an intense physical effort. Straight as a stick, wooden-faced, he confronted the steady gray eyes.

"I am aware of that," McCarthy said, unmoved. "Despite what has been said about Utah justice, every member of this board is beyond thinking you guilty because your friends have made irresponsible threats. It is your guilt, or your innocence, that we are concerned with."

Just for an instant some obscure impatience seemed to flare in him. He drummed his fingers on the desk blotter. "Mr. Hillstrom, you have refused to testify in your own defense. If you wanted to throw doubt upon the decision of the court, I presume you have succeeded. I think you have also succeeded in embarrassing your attorneys and your friends, by asking them to defend you without the materials to make a case."

"I didn't ask them to defend me," Joe said through his teeth, holding McCarthy's eyes. It was coming out in the open now.

"Perhaps not," the justice said. "That's between you and them. What is at stake now is your life. If you are innocent, as you have persistently claimed, this is your last chance to prove it."

"I've told you all it was up to you to prove I'm guilty," Joe said. "If your law and your justice is worth anything, why doesn't it live up to its claims?" He let his hate pour out through his eyes at this one lawyer-mouthed representative of the System, but he did not, as he obscurely hoped to, force McCarthy to anger. The man looked at him coolly, with an intolerable quiet.

"Your counsel has been correct on that point. You have been convicted on evidence in a trial that the reviewing court found impartial. At this point you are guilty unless you prove your innocence." His white finger tapped the desk, he held Joe to the duel of eyes. "You doubt the integrity of this board. Here is what the board will do. If you will, in strictest confidence, tell any two members of it the circumstances under which you were shot, and to their satisfaction prove what you say, the board is ready to pardon you instantly without making the evidence public. What you tell will never go any farther, even to the other members of the board."

Joe braced himself against a feeling like slipping in loose sand. His insides twisted; with a suddenness as if something had been thrown in his face he felt himself go red. He saw the faces at the table stiffly watching him, and he saw that some of them hated and feared him and would be glad of his death, but that McCarthy did not hate him. McCarthy might demand his death, but Mc-Carthy did not hate him.

But he knew his part; he knew what words must be said. From a tight throat he said, "I don't want a pardon. I want a complete vindication or nothing. I want a new trial."

"We're past that stage," McCarthy said. "The board is giving you a chance at life, Mr. Hillstrom."

The internal shaking had worked outward until it trembled in Joe's hands and shoulders and knees; his throat was clamped as if in paralysis. For a long time he stood before them and said nothing, while Hilton and Ricket went quickly to the desk and leaned over it and talked in quick sentences with McCarthy and the governor. But when their bodies moved aside again McCarthy's eyes were on him as if nothing had interrupted their look. It was the imperturbable steadiness of the eyes that infuriated him; they could not be made angry. If there was any expression in them now aside from McCarthy's judicial calm it was pity, and the very thought that he was being pitied scalded Joe's mind.

He twisted his hard mouth. "I said I'd get a new trial or die trying. I guess I'll have to die trying."

Ricket and Hilton and Christensen pulled him aside. Their faces were anxious and he heard their anxious words: ". . . last chance. . . . couldn't do her any harm . . . think they mean it . . . wouldn't get out . . ." But he pulled away from them and turned, seeking the eyes of McCarthy. All the rest of them he ignored. It was to McCarthy that he had to justify himself, McCarthy who had to be challenged and defied.

"I won't tell you anything," he said hotly. "It's not up to me to tell you anything. If I'd had a fair trial I wouldn't have been convicted on such flimsy evidence. I won't take any offers and I don't want a pardon. I want a new trial or nothing."

Hilton's restraining hand dropped from his arm; he saw the expressive weary lift of the lawyer's shoulders as he turned away, but he saw them only from the corner of his eye. His glance was

still leveled like a spear with McCarthy's. He drew himself straighter
until he was rigid.

"I want to die a martyr," he said.

The words were like the striking of a light, for having said them
he knew that they were true, and had been true from the beginning.

So he stalemated them with his defiance, and though he was the
pawn of forces, furiously defended by one side and stubbornly and
repeatedly condemned by the other, yet he imposed his will on
them. He imposed it even on Justice McCarthy, who was not like
the others on that board. The Pardon Board met to decide his fate,
and Judge Hilton prepared a desperate contentious confused
brief, but it was Joe Hill who decided his own fate, and he left his
lawyers pleading not with the board but with him.

At a certain point they dismissed him (but he knew that even
their dismissal was an act of helplessness) and manacled him like
a maniac again, and stripped him and frisked his clothes and body
for possible weapons, possible escape tools, that might have been
slipped to him by his friends in the meeting. Just before noon,
aggrandized by his company, two guards took him back to a new
cell in the maximum-security section.

He brought his defiance and pride back with him, and he sat
with them all the rest of that day. Admiration for his own devious
cunning moved him; he felt an awed wonder at the way events
had built toward this precise and inevitable end, all the while that
he and his friends had been apparently trying to move them in
quite another direction.

In his thoughts he defied the Pardon Board and its assumptions
of power over his life, its capacity to condemn or forgive. "I don't
want a commutation or pardon, I want a complete vindication or
nothing," he had said to them. Playing the words over and over to
himself now to test them for flaws and for anything that might ring
false to the legendary resolution of Joe Hill, he found them exactly
right.

"I said I would get a new trial or die trying," he told them again,
and rubbed his closely barbered head and smiled. He thought of
writing a song or poem to express the defiant excitement he felt,
the wonderful exhilarated feeling of everything's being settled, but

he could not sit still to the job. The thought of Otto, ducking in flight from the law, filled him with contempt. He thought, That cheap yegg! but he glanced sideways in memory at the times when he himself had run, all the times when he had convinced himself that he was more useful outside a jail, and working, than inside at the mercy of the bosses and the bosses' armed men. Very sharp in his mind were nights of doubling and slinking in streets and alleys and freight yards, the watchful progress up and down the coast on the s.p., the panicked scattering in the sun and dust at Oatfield. He knew what Fuzzy Llewellyn had seen, standing on his unshaken soap box above the melee and baring his gopher teeth, staring into some vision more meaningful than the dead and the afraid. Duty and a grander opportunity lay where Fuzzy had been looking while Joe Hill fled. The shame of that flight, always with him and always repudiated, he recognized and accepted now, because here he stood where Fuzzy had stood, saying what Fuzzy had said. "I'll stick here." What a continent a man could cross with that one little step! He wondered at it and at himself, feeling in his mind for combinations of steadfast words to say for himself and others how it felt.

For supper, ignoring the meal they brought him, he ate his thoughts, and he took them to bed with him. He was used to sleeping in the light: a year and a half in jail and prison had taught him that. But he was still unused to the iron, hollow, reverberant ring of this particular prison, the empty echo that steps made, and he felt the isolation of the empty cell block. He was all alone in this section. All that ever reached him from the other prisoners was a faint drumlike hum, or the clang of their feet on the steel floor as they marched out to work or exercise or meals.

Now in the light of nighttime that he pretended was darkness, closing his eyes against the cell that was like each of the other cells they had moved him to, he heard only the sounds of his own imprisonment, the footsteps of guards, the clack of keys, the mutter of talk at the head of the stairs. In all the prison he was the only capital prisoner, the only one awaiting death. In his bed he felt his lonely distinction. This blaze of light was for him, these steps that went back and forth and the gates that grated and opened and closed again were measures against his escape. He was the man they feared and would kill, and outside thousands of people wrote angry letters in his defense, and in Australia stevedores were refusing to load American ships because of the trumped-up charges against Joe Hill.

A letter to the people of Utah began to grow in his mind—to the people of Utah and through them to the world. Craftily he assembled all the contradictory last-ditch arguments that Hilton had had to use: the irregular jurymen, the period when he was left without counsel, the prejudice in the public mind and the public press because the defendant was an IWW organizer. These were evasions and he recognized them clearly as what they were, but they belonged, no matter how widely they avoided the essential problem of his guilt or innocence. He stressed the fact that his past life must have been clean or the prosecution would have brought it up against him. He emphasized his only other time in jail, thirty days on a vag charge during a longshore strike that police and courts had co-operated to break. At some time during the night he got up and wrote for an hour, putting down thoughts that came to him. After he had lain down again he groped through a drowsy indeterminate time for some ringing conclusion, some line that would echo and be quoted and stir the admiration of people who read it.

When he finally found it, it opened his eyes abruptly onto the lighted bare familiarity of the cell, and he lay on his back trying it out with an exultant certainty that it was exactly what he wanted. He added it to the bottom of his letter to the world: "I have lived like an arist; I shall die like an artist."

Into his recollection like something seen from the corner of the eye sneaked the image of the two clerks in the music store. He turned away from it in disgust, as he would have turned upwind to head a bad smell.

Someone had to be seen, some move had to be made, some letter written, some news carried—he could not tell what, though the knowledge lay just beyond sight or reach. Frantically, tied down by a hundred cords, he struggled to stand up. Furiously he pushed against the inert bodies of thousands who hemmed him in and shut him away from where he had to be. Madly he hurried ahead of something that whipped him with anxiety, and the farther he hurried the more those who now accompanied him fell away, dropping away one by one until he went alone. The wind was at him in gusts, so that he struggled with his eyes streaming and dim, straining to see. Until all at once the wind dropped, the road ended, the urgency behind him quietly vanished. In an enormous silence he stood all by himself, and saw a ladder he must climb. It rose above him higher than a skyscraper, higher than the overhanging iron rungs that went up the stacks at Anaconda or Great Falls, a runged ladder curving upward, belling out and up and out and disappearing from his vision, a beanstalk of a ladder going up beyond the clouds. The mere thought of starting up it brought his heart like a stone to the bottom of his chest cavity. He stared upward, appalled, and the longer he looked the more a still terror overcame him. He was dwarfed by the enormous thing he had to climb. As the terror settled over him he shrank, his throat grew tight and his breath difficult, his arms were frail sticks, as helpless as if no fingers were attached. He wondered in terror how he would take hold of the rungs without fingers, and how he would get a foothold with feet that now were pegs of wood. But the thing whose name he knew and could not say was at the top of the ladder, lost far up in the dome from which came a wind as cold as if off an icefield. He saw that he was naked; the cold paralyzed his bones. And he knew that a shriek would set him free. But when he tried to scream, his voice was gone. Impotence lay on him with the weight of houses; his tongue could not move though he burst his heart in terror and strain. And now the thing whose name he knew but would not say was descending in even, untroubled spirals, the ladder weaving like a flower on its stem, its top describing circles in the sky, at first tiny as dots, but growing and looping outward, descending and toppling upon him, and he fought madly for wind, for voice.

And woke, panting, slippery with cold sweat, to look into the light in the corridor ceiling and hear the iron tick of silence. He lay breathing deeply through his mouth, telling his heart to slow down, but the empty brightness without a single sound was more terrible than the spiraling void of his dream, far more terrible than darkness. Gray-white steel, stark shadows, the stare of unrelieved and inescapable light, made a world as geometric and unarguable as the world of nightmare. Among enormous triangles and stretching rhomboids and parallels reaching to infinity across the little box of his cell, he lay, an insect caught in the heart of an insanely complex trap, and felt his little life *thud thud thud* against its cage.

It was a long time—five minutes, a half-hour—before a guard moved along the outside corridor and sent the vibration of his steps through the steel floor. Joe sat up and rubbed with the blanket along his wet arms and wrists. He felt weak and nauseated, and he hated the skinniness of his arms. He said to himself in indignation and concern, They've left me nothing but skin and bones.

The guard's steps died out, and the silence lay there, the terrible loneliness remained. More than he had ever wanted anything he wanted to talk to a friend, anyone who knew and trusted and understood him. He could talk for twenty-four hours straight; there was enough to talk about to keep him going for a week. Just to sit with somebody and drink coffee and talk and talk and talk.

When the guard's regular inspection time came round and the steps came down the corridor and the security door clanked open and the guard's face looked in through the bars, Joe was sitting up on the cot. Without hesitation he said, "Can I send a telegram?"

"In the morning."

"I want to send one now."

"You can give it to me now. I won't send it till I go off shift, though."

"Well, all right."

He grabbed up a piece of paper and a pencil and scribbled a wire to Lund in Weosha, Minnesota. It said, "If you can, I'd like you to come."

Then for a long time after the guard went away he lay wondering if Lund would do it. It was a big thing to ask. Lund was a farmer now. He'd be right in the middle of the harvest season. He wouldn't come. He'd wire or write some excuse.

But he had to come. They had to talk. Not many days were left. There had to be somebody to talk to, and Lund was the one he had always been able to talk with most freely. But suppose he did come, how would they manage it? They might not even permit visitors on regular visiting days when a man was as close to the end as he was. The way they were moving him to a different cell every day, they might keep him in close solitary the last week or ten days.

Maybe a last request. He could ask for Lund as his spiritual adviser. A condemned man had a right to that. They would let some prison chaplain come in and irritate a man all his last night with prayers and exhortations, so they ought to let in some preacher that a man could really talk to. His mind went feverish with plans and sleights and arguments and pleas. If they wouldn't let Lund come in, or give them a decent chance to talk, they were . . .

In his mind a squared calendar was posted, and he saw the clear solid week and the part of another. Eleven days. It filled him with panic to think that possibly there would not be time for Lund to get there. Perhaps he would delay, not knowing the date was so close. Sweat like the flushing sweat of sickness broke out of him again. He caught himself on the very verge of whimpering aloud.

3

Joe Hill had a week to live when Lund arrived in Salt Lake.

It was a Friday afternoon, a golden, mellow day, the sort of day that would be like ripe summer until around four o'clock, and then would haze and blur as the sun dropped, the air bluing with afternoon, sharpening toward crispness, the smell of fires hanging in the air until by six o'clock it would be an autumn dusk, with street lamps yellow at the corners and sidewalks obscure under the still-dense shadows of trees and the smells now not the peaty, moist smells of sprinkled lawns and the summer smell of wetted dust, but the cured-leaf and smoke smells of fall. Even at midday, walking up from the station with his coat on his arm and the weight of the suitcase bringing the sweat to his face, Lund saw that autumn had already come down the mountain slopes in scarlet and bronze and toned brown. He had a fancy that it lay there like a threat, though he had always held fall to be his favorite season. The sight of the slow fume of color at the city's edges, like something furtively creeping in upon the town, deepened his feeling of helplessness. He was a man come a full week early for a funeral, doomed to attend every clock tick until daybreak on October first.

From his close following of newspaper accounts, he knew that visitors were permitted at the prison only on Sunday afternoons. As before, he was here in Salt Lake with time to kill before he could see Joe. He did not assume that there were any other steps that Joe's lawyers could take, now that the Pardon Board had refused commutation. Joe was like a checker player, outnumbered and pursued by kings, who ducks and escapes into a double corner where he makes fruitless delaying moves until finally he is trapped within a barricade of pursuers. The delaying moves were all over. There would be nothing to learn from the iww hall this time, but he went there anyway.

He found Jud Ricket in the office next door, an extra room rented to take care of the Defense Committee's activities, heaved back in the chair and idly rolling his tremendous brass-capped pencil between his palms. The automatic nervous twitch had grown on him in the more than a year since Lund had last seen him. It moved the corner of his mouth twice as he sat abstractedly staring, and moved it again quickly when he looked up and saw Lund in the door.

"Yes?"

"You don't remember me," Lund said. "I'm a friend of Joe's. Lund. I was through here last year for a couple of days."

"Oh sure! We've got your contributions." He reached and shook hands and pulled Lund inside so that he saw another man in the room, a graying man, frail and pot-bellied, with a cool fighter's face oddly out of character with his sagging sedentary body. "You know Judge Hilton?" Ricket said.

Hilton's hand was narrow and fragile after Ricket's big paw. He seemed withdrawn and thoughtful. In three minutes he looked twice at his watch.

"On your way back to the coast?" Ricket asked.

"No," Lund said. "Joe sent for me."

They both gave him their instant, speculative attention.

"He did?"

"Four days ago. He wired me."

"The day he went before the Pardon Board," Hilton said. "Did he say what he wanted? Have you talked to him?"

"I haven't tried. I thought visiting hours were only on Sundays."

"They are. He didn't say what he wanted?"

"Just that he'd like me to come."

"I conferred with him yesterday," Hilton said. "It's funny he didn't say anything about wiring you."

Lund turned away from their intent eyes. He knew of no possible reason for Joe's wire except desperation. It had sounded like a cry for help, and he did not like to think of Joe so borne down that he would bend his pride that far. He looked down at his swinging shoe, and up again when Hilton spoke.

"Do you know something about Joe's case?"

"I've read the papers, that's all."

"Because if you do, you'd better tell it now. There isn't much time."

His eyes were pouched like a hound's. From above sagging lower lids the hazel irises looked out with a remote and uninterested air that matched the frowning thrust of the rest of his face no better than his face matched his body.

"I don't know anything," Lund said. "I haven't even had a letter lately."

The lawyer looked at his watch again, his attention already turned away. "You know what he did to us before the Pardon Board," he said. "Something comes over him and he goes crazy. I don't know."

"We had it all planned," Ricket said. "The judge asked for everything, new trial, pardon, commutation, the whole works at once. They've been getting letters by the thousand, they're all excited and worried, and they know damn well if they execute Joe they'll have some kind of an explosion. I think they'd give anything to get out of it whole. So we asked for everything, and hoped to get a commutation because the evidence was all circumstantial. But right when Judge McCarthy is practically begging him to give them a good excuse to turn him loose, he gets on his high horse and won't take anything but a complete whitewash. So they turn him down."

Hilton grunted. "He wants to die a martyr, he says."

In the next office Lund heard the regular sound of the press. "Is there any chance? Anything else you can do?"

The truculent face looked past him, the hound eyes staring at nothing out in the hall. "Pressure. More letters. Public indignation. Maybe we can scare 'em enough so he gets a last-minute pardon whether he wants it or not."

"I hoped the woman might speak up and clear him when she saw he wouldn't be freed otherwise."

They both moved their hands. Ricket said, "If there's a woman, she won't show now."

"Nobody knows anything!" Hilton said angrily. "He's been at cross-purposes with his counsel ever since the trial began."

"Well, cheer up," Ricket said. "Those letters are coming in twice as fast as ever. You never saw such a response. If we can get a big enough public protest, we can force Spry to grant a stay, at least."

"One thing," Hilton said. "If they shoot Joe I wouldn't want to be Spry."

"Retaliation?"

"You know how the Wobblies are. They get sore the way they are now and nobody's going to keep them in bounds."

"I wonder if all these threats don't do Joe harm, and harden the authorities against him?" Lund said.

But all he got was Ricket's obsidian glance and phantasmal one-sided smile. "Got any other suggestions?"

They were silent. Lund heard feet clattering down the brass-bound treads of the stair. Other steps came up more slowly, came up the hall and hesitated. He looked over his shoulder to the doorway and saw Ingrid Olson standing there.

A single question, an alert concentration of interest, pulled all three of them to their feet, Lund knew precisely how Ricket and Hilton had felt momentarily at the news of Joe's wire. An answer might lie behind any out-of-the-way fact. The girl's presence here now might mean something important.

Her eyes were dark, her long white hands nervous. Without greeting, she recognized and acknowledged Lund, but her eyes went back immediately to the others. "Yes?" Ricket said. "What can we do for you?"

"There didn't seem to be anything more that could be done," she said. "I thought . . ."

"Come in," Hilton said. "Sit down."

He held a chair for her at the cluttered table, and something in his face made her sit down quickly with her cheeks flaming. "My name is Ingrid Olson," she said.

"Yes, I know."

Watching her as keenly as the others, Lund saw enough in her face to be convinced that she was incapable of dishonesty and that she was unlikely to have anything important to tell. But he watched her face with the blush paling almost instantly under the transparent skin, and he wished with a hard quick brutality that she might be guiltily involved.

"Well?" Hilton said.

Impassive as a rock except for the fleeting tic at the corner of his lips, Ricket put out a foot and shoved the hall door shut. The girl shook her head at him and opened and shut her purse. Massed tears glittered suddenly in her eyes.

"It isn't what you *hope* it is," she said almost sullenly. "It's just . . . Joe and I grew up in the same town in Sweden. His mother was a friend of my mother's."

With his finger and thumb deep in his vest pocket, Hilton stood before her. "Yes?"

"Joe's father and mother weren't married," she said.

The lawyer moved his lips slightly. A shadowy frown had started to tighten between his eyes. "Yes?" he said, more sharply.

"Mother and I talked it over," Ingrid said. She had better control of her voice now; she spoke more plainly, less in a hurried breathless rush. "We thought maybe if it was known who Joe's father is. His mother was just a seamstress in Gefle, but his father is important. He's a politician now, a member of the Riksdag. We thought maybe if he knew he might do something."

Hilton's fingers tapped on the table. He looked out the window and a flatted, breathy whistle emerged from his puckered lips. Still looking out the window he said, "Is Joe still a Swedish citizen?"

"I think so, yes."

"Does he know who his father is?"

"Oh yes."

"That god damn clam!" Ricket said.

Hilton had a notebook out. "What's his father's name?"

"Hegglund."

That brought Lund leaning forward in surprise. "Sven Hegglund?"

"Yes."

"You know him?" Hilton said.

"I've heard of him," Lund said. "He's well known. He'd have weight."

Hilton was already back at Ingrid. "What's the name of this town in Sweden?"

"Gefle."

"Who'd be the head man there? What'd he be? Mayor, burgermeister, what?"

"I don't exactly know who . . ."

"That won't matter. We'll find out and get a cable to him tonight. Who's Sweden's Minister to this country?"

"Ekengren," Lund said.

Excitement had touched them all. Both Hilton and Ricket were standing. The girl looked from one to the other and moistened her lips. "Do you think something can be done?"

"Not much," Hilton said. His voice boomed and filled the office. "Not very much. This might just save Joe's life, that's all."

She went so pale that Lund was afraid she might faint, and then her skin burned a fiery red as she stood up among them. "What . . . how will you do it?"

"There's a Swedish vice-consul here," Ricket put in, but Hilton waved him impatiently down.

"We don't fool with any flunkeys. Look. We cable the burgermeister, or whatever he is, that a boy from his town has been condemned without a fair trial, and we ask him to do what he can. We wire the Minister, or better yet we wire Virginia to go see him in Washington. She's in New York, she can run down. We get the Minister to intercede. Through him we work on Wilson . . ."

"The President?" Ingrid said, with her eyes widening.

"Exactly. The President. This thing has got international implications. Wilson can't afford to overlook a frame-up that involves organized labor, and he can't permit it if it might get us in bad with a friendly foreign state. He's got to intervene. All the pressure we could apply up to now has been through working stiffs who couldn't spell. Wait till Spry starts getting letters on White House stationery or with diplomatic franks!" He took Ingrid by the shoulders and shook her with a kind of slow violence. "Thanks, many thanks! My God, imagine if we hadn't found this out till it was too late to do anything. As it is, we've only got a week. We'll have to break our necks. You go on home and if we need you we'll let you know. All right?"

"All right. Only . . ."

"What?"

"What about Joe?" she said. "He hates his father. He wouldn't take a favor from him even to save his life."

The lawyer looked at Ricket and rubbed at the thin gray hair on the back of his head. He said, suddenly soft in his manner, "You're afraid he'll be down on you for telling."

"Yes," she said directly.

Hilton walked to the window and back, moving the change in his vest pocket with thumb and finger. "What's the alternative?" he said at last. "That's the only way you can look at it. I imagine I've had as much experience with Joe's pride as anybody. But if we submit to his pride in this he'll be dead this time next week."

She nodded, gathered her purse against her, nodded again in a motion that included not only the three of them but all the inevitabilities of the situation, and went out. Halfway down the stairs they heard her footsteps become a quick hurrying patter.

Hilton had flung himself down and was already composing a cable. In the midst of an impatient scribble he looked up and said, "You're going to see Joe Sunday."

"I expect so."

"He'd better not be told what we're doing."

"Can it be kept from him?"

"For a while, maybe altogether. I don't want him throwing any tantrums and spoiling this. The best thing he can do right now is sit there in his cell and write poems."

"Well," Lund said, "I suppose he must have something to say to me or he wouldn't have wired. I'll limit myself to that."

"What about this Hegglund?" Ricket said. "How's he going to like publicity like this? He could just deny he ever heard of Joe."

"He would if it came out publicly. My God, you wouldn't go at him with a meat axe. He's going to hear this very confidentially as a whisper from the Minister or somebody, all very discreet. For all anybody needs to know, we're taking it to the Swedes because Joe's a Swedish citizen."

"We can line up the Swedish labor unions, too," Ricket said. "And

the Young Socialists. Joe used to be one, he still wears that gambler
tie of theirs. I'd better get off a cable to them too."

He clapped Lund across the back and came out in the hall with
him, and as they walked toward the stairs he swung his mallet fist
gently and knocked it on the wall at every other step. He was looking off beyond somewhere, a mile or two past the stairs, and he
said, "Can you imagine this working out any better for the union?
They try to frame a nameless worker in a backwoods burg and
bingo, they get a public uproar as if they'd collared John D. He
turns out to have friends, he turns out to be a name you can
rally support around, he's a poet, now he's the son of a Swedish bigwig." His knuckles rattled along the wainscot. "An international
stage. It couldn't have been planned prettier."

"Joe might not like it handled this way."

"He's in no position to squawk."

No, Lund thought as he went back toward his hotel. Joe was
not in a position to squawk. If he didn't want the fact of his
parentage used to save him, what could he do about it? A dozen
kinds of people wanted to save him for a dozen different reasons,
because they loved him, because they hated capital punishment,
because they thought him unjustly accused, because he was a
Swede, because he was a workingman, because he was an IWW,
because he had written songs. Every reason could be manipulated
skillfully by his defense committee and Joe could be built up as a
symbol and a martyr, and except when he was personally brought
forward, as before the Pardon Board, he was helpless to approve
or disapprove. The best thing he could do for the next week would
be to sit in his cell and write poems.

And what had been in his mind when he wired? A wish to tell
things that up to now he had kept hidden? And would he tell them
to a friend though he refused to tell them to the Pardon Board
and save his life? Or had he, simply and desperately, called for
help when he knew his last hope was gone?

In his room after dinner he spent a long time over the evening
paper. The IWW had practically taken over the front page,
crowding out the war, crowding out everything. There were
IWW-led strikes in Colorado and Montana. Railroad detectives
had dispersed a march of disgruntled harvest workers in Aberdeen,
South Dakota. In New York there had been a brush between

police and iww pickets outside the offices of John D. Rockefeller. An iww speaker in Denver had said that the blood of the innocent victims of the Ludlow massacre would stain the name of Rockefeller forever. The national guard was still out in three Colorado camps and a mass meeting in sympathy for the strikers had been refused a permit by the Denver city authorities. And there were two items on the Joe Hill case. There was a release from the governor of the text of several of the letters he had received. One said that there would be ten thousand iww marching on Salt Lake from all parts of the West if the state of Utah persisted in its bloody plan to murder Joe Hill. Another advised the governor to look to his own family; there were men who would see to it that two lives in his own immediate family would be taken if Joe Hill died.

The other item was a long statement from Joe Hill himself to the Pardon Board. Lund read it, and read it again, pondering every paragraph, trying to extract from the text some clue of wording or tone, something in or between the lines, that would unequivocally reveal Joe's state of mind. For this statement to the Pardon Board was the statement of an innocent man who wanted to live; it contained no heroics about wanting to die a martyr.

But there were too many statements that Lund could not verify, too many which contradicted the evidence of witnesses or the reports of the papers, and he had no way of telling which was the truth. He could not even tell whether Joe's logic was honest or specious, and in the end he was left wondering whether the document was really designed to convince, or whether it was an elaborate and enigmatic hoax. Its whole burden was the demand for a new trial—a demand which Joe knew was hopeless. Though he seemed to plead for his life, he took the same position he had taken before the board. He was not interested in a commutation or a pardon. Since he had already assaulted the board with a demand that was out of its jurisdiction, and been refused, why should he go to these elaborate lengths to do it over again for the press and the public?

"I want to die a martyr," he had said before the board. "The cause I represent means more than any individual's life, including my own."

But what cause? Labor's? If one could grant the premise of

a frame-up, yes, but Lund had never been able to grant that premise. He had been too close to Ricket and the forces which had created the whole myth. There was not a thread of evidence that anyone had even known who Joe Hillstrom was until Ricket himself began to go to work.

There was some deception, or self-deception, even in this final statement from the death house. Unhappily Lund bent his head and read the whole statement for the third time:

A FEW REASONS WHY I DEMAND A NEW TRIAL

When I was up before the highest authorities of the State of Utah I stated that I wanted a new trial and nothing but a new trial, and I will now try to state some reasons why I am entitled to that privilege. Being aware of the fact that my past record has nothing to do with the facts of this case, I will not dwell upon that subject beyond saying that I have worked all my life as a mechanic and at times as a musician. The mere fact that the prosecution never attempted to assail my reputation proves that it is clean. I will therefore commence at the time of my arrest.

On the night of January 14, 1914, I was lying in a bed at the Erickson house in Murray, a town located seven miles from Salt Lake City, suffering from a bullet wound in my chest. Where or why I got that wound is nobody's business but my own. I know that I was not shot in the Morrison store and all the so-called evidence that is supposed to show that I was is fabrication pure and simple. As I was lying there half asleep, I was aroused by a knock on the door. Somebody opened the door and in came four men with revolvers in their hands. A shot rang out and a bullet passed right over my chest, grazing my shoulder and penetrating my right hand through the knuckles, crippling me up for life. There was absolutely no need of shooting me at that time because I was helpless as a baby and had no weapons of any kind. The only thing that saved my life at that time was the officer's inefficiency with firearms.

I was then brought up to the county jail where I was given a bunk and went to sleep immediately. The next morning I was pretty sore on account of being shot in three places. I asked to be taken to a hospital but was instead taken upstairs to a solitary cell and told that I was charged with murder and had better confess right away. I did not know anything about any murder and told them so. They still insisted that I confess, and told me they would take me to a hospital and "treat me white" if I did. I told them I knew nothing of any murder. They called me a liar, and after that I refused to answer all questions. I grew weaker and weaker, and for three or four days I was hovering between life and death, and I remember an officer coming up and telling me that according to the doctor's statement I had only one more hour to live. I could, of course name all these officers if I wanted to, but I want it distinctly understood that I am not trying to knock any officers, because I realize that they were only doing their duty. In my opinion the officers who were in charge of the county jail then were as good officers as can be found anywhere. Well! I finally pulled through because I made up my mind not to die.

When the time came for my preliminary hearing, I decided to be my own attorney, knowing that it could be nothing against me. I thought I'd let them have it all their own way, and did not ask any questions. When the court went into session, I was asked if I objected to having the witnesses remain in the courtroom during the trial, and I replied that it was immaterial to me who remained in the courtroom. All the witnesses then remained inside, and I noted that there was a steady stream of messengers going back and forth between the witnesses and the county attorney during the whole trial, delivering their messages in a whisper. When the trial commenced, there were first some witnesses of little importance, but then a man came up that made me sit up and take notice. He put up his hand and swore that he positively recognized me and that he had seen me in the Morrison store in the afternoon of the same day that Morrison was shot. I did not say anything, but I thought something. This man was a tall lean man with a thin pale face, black hair and eyes, and a very conspicuous black shiny mustache. I don't know his name and have never been able to find it out. (Bear this man in mind, please.)

The little boy, Merlin Morrison, was the next witness that attracted my attention. He was the first one to come up and look at me in the morning of the day after my arrest. Being only a boy, he spoke his mind right out in my presence, and this is what he said: "No, that is not the man at all. The ones I saw were shorter and heavier set."

When he testified at the preliminary hearing, I asked him if he did not make that statement, but he then denied it.

I accidentally found a description of the bandit in a newspaper, however, and the description says that the bandit was 5 feet 9 inches tall and weighed about 155 pounds. That description seems to tally pretty well with Merlin Morrison's statement, "The ones I saw were shorter and heavier set." My own height is six feet, and I am of a slender build.

The next witness of importance was Mrs. Phoebe Seeley. She said she was coming home from the Empress Theater with her husband and she met two men in a back street in the vicinity of Morrison's store. One of them had "small features and light bushy hair." This description did not suit the county attorney, so he helped her along a little by saying, "You mean medium colored hair like Mr. Hillstrom's, don't you?" After leading her along that way for a while, he asked her this question: "Is the general appearance of Mr. Hillstrom anything like the man you saw?" She answered, "No, I won't . . . I can't say that."

This is the very same woman who at the district court proved to be the star witness for the prosecution. She not only described me in the smallest details, but she also told the jury that the man she saw had scars on both sides of his face, on his nose, and on his neck. I have such scars on my face, and that was practically the testimony that convicted me. Just think of it, a woman not knowing a thing about the murder passing a man in a back street in the dead of a winter night, and six months later she describes that man to the smallest details, hat and the cut and color of his clothes, height and build, color of eyes and hair, and a number of scars, and when asked, "Is the appearance of Mr. Hillstrom anything like the man you saw?" she answered, "No, I won't . . . I can't say that." Her husband, who was with her, was not even there to testify. It is true that the prosecuting attorney put his questions in such a way that all she had to say was "Yes sir," and "All the same, Sir," but she said that just the same. With a hostile judge, and attorneys who acted merely as assistant prosecuting attorneys, the prosecuting attorney had what in the parlance of the street would be called "Easy sailing."

The next witness was Mr. Zeese, detective. When I was sick in bed at the Erickson house in Murray, the lady gave me a red bandanna handkerchief to blow my nose on. At the trial she told that she had several dozen bandanna handkerchiefs that were used by her boys and brothers when they worked in the smelter. After my arrest Mr. Zeese went to the Erickson house looking for clues. He found this handkerchief, and with his keen eagle eye he soon discovered some "creases at the corners." With the intelligence of a superman, he then easily drew the conclusion that this handkerchief had been used for a mask by some "bandit." Then he capped the climax by going on the stand and telling his marvellous discovery to the judge. Mr. Zeese is well known in Salt Lake City, and comments are unnecessary.

The next witness at the preliminary hearing, Mrs. Vera Hansen, said she saw two or three men outside the Morrison store shortly after the shooting. She heard one of the men exclaim "Bob," or "O Bob," and she thought that my voice sounded the same as the voice she heard on the street. I then asked Mrs. Hansen this question: "Do you mean to tell me that you, through that single word 'Bob,' were able to recognize my voice?" Now I am coming to the point.

After the preliminary hearing I got a record of the hearings and took it to my cell in the county jail. I immediately discovered that it had been tampered with, that everything I had said had been misconstrued in a malicious way. It was a little hard to prove it at first but on page 47 I found the questions that I had put to Mrs. Vera Hansen, and there the tampering was so clumsy that a little child could see it. In the records the question reads like this, "Do you mean to tell me that you through the single word (mark, 'single word') 'O Bob, I'm shot,'" etc. Four or five words. Here anyone can see that the official court records were altered for the express purpose of "proving" that someone was shot in the Morrison store. I then started to look for testimony of a man with a black shiny mustache but to my great surprise I could not find it anywhere in the records in spite of the fact that this man had positively recognized me at the preliminary hearing. No wonder this very dignified stenographer, Mr. Rollo, who is also stenographer for the supreme court, was shaking like a leaf when he put up his hand and swore that the records were "correct" in every detail.

The strange part of it is that the state supreme court in a statement prepared by them for the press are, so my attorney told me (I am not allowed to see any papers) making the very same mistake. They say that Mrs. Vera Hansen said in her testimony, "O Bob, I'm shot," which is not correct.

At the time when I was shot I was unarmed. I threw my hands up in the air just before the bullet struck me. That accounts for the fact that the bullet hole in my coat is four inches and a half below the bullet hole in my body. The prosecuting attorney endeavors to explain that fact by saying "that the bandit would throw one hand up in surprise when Arlin Morrison got hold of his father's pistol." He also states that the bandit might have been leaning over the counter when he was shot. Very well. If the bandit "threw up his hands in surprise," as he said, that would of course raise the coat some, but it would not raise it four inches and a half. "Leaning over the counter" would not raise it at all. Justice McCarthy agrees with the prosecuting attorney and says that throwing his hands up would be just the very thing that the bandit would do if the boy Arlin made an attempt to shoot him. Let me ask Mr. McCarthy a question. Suppose that you would some dark night discover that there was a burglar crawling around in your home, then suppose that you would get your gun and surprise that burglar right in the act. If the burglar should then reach for his gun, would you throw up your hands and let the burglar take a shot at you and then shoot the burglar afterward? Or would you shoot the burglar before he had a chance to reach for his gun? Think it over. It is not a question of law but of human nature. I also wish Mr. McCarthy would try to find if it is possible to raise a coat on a person four and a half inches in the manner described by the prosecuting attorney.

We will now go back to the bullet. After the bullet had penetrated the bandit, the prosecuting attorney says that it "dropped to the floor" and then disappeared. It left no mark anywhere as an ordinary bullet would. It just disappeared, that's all. Now gentlemen, I don't know a thing about this bullet, but I will say this, that if I should sit down and write a novel, I certainly would have to think up something more realistic than that, otherwise I would never be able to sell it. The story of a bullet that first makes an upshoot of four inches and a half at an angle of 90 degrees, then cuts around another corner and penetrates a bandit and finally makes a drop like a spit ball and disappears forever, would not be very well received in the twentieth century. And just think that the greatest brains in Utah can sit and listen to such rot as that and then say that "Hillstrom" got a fair and impartial trial.

I have heard this case rehashed many times and I wish to state that I have formed my own opinion about this shooting. My opinion is this: Two or three bandits entered the Morrison store for the express purpose of killing Mr. Morrison. As they entered, both of them shouted "We've got you now!" and started to blaze away with automatic Colt pistols caliber .38, and having the advantage of surprise it does not seem reasonable that they would allow a boy to shoot them. The story about that remarkable disappearing bullet; the fact that the official records were changed for the purpose of proving that someone was shot in that store; all that goes to show that there is a decided lack of evidence to prove that anybody was shot in that store outside the two victims. Nobody saw the Morrison gun fired. Merlin Morrison ran in deadly fright into some back room and hid himself. In spite of the fact that he was almost scared to death he "counted seven shots" and that is supposed to be some more proof that the Morrison gun was discharged. Six shots were fired by the bandits and all the bullets found. But there had to be seven shots fired, otherwise there would be no case against me. The boy "counted seven shots" and that "evidence" is introduced by the state as "proof" that the Morrison gun was discharged. Any sensible person can readily see what chance a frightened boy, or anybody else for that matter, would have to count the shots when two bandits are blazing away with automatic pistols. There were some officers there who claimed that they smelled the end of the gun and that thereby they could tell that the gun had been recently discharged, but the gun expert from the Western Arms Company exploded that argument. He stated that it was a physical impossibility to determine with any degree of certainty at what time a gun had been discharged, in a case where smokeless powder is used, on account of the fact that the odor of powder is always there. Then there was that empty chamber in the Morrison gun. An officer testified that it was customary among police officers to keep an empty chamber under the hammer of their guns. Morrison used to be a sergeant of police, I was told.

Then there was a "pool of blood" found two or three blocks away from the Morrison store and the prosecution made a whole ocean out of it in spite of the fact that the Utah state chemist would not say that it was human blood. He said that the blood was of "mammalian origin."

Then there is Miss Mahan, who is supposed to have heard somebody say "I'm shot." At the preliminary hearing she was very uncertain about it. She said she thought she heard somebody say those words but she was not by any means sure about it.

Now, that's all there is, to my knowledge, and I am positively sure that all this so-called "evidence" which is supposed to prove that the Morrison gun was discharged on the night of January 10, 1914, would not stand the acid test of a capable attorney, such as I am now in a position to get. At the time of my arrest I did not have money enough to employ an attorney. Thinking that there was nothing to my case, and always being willing to try anything once, I decided to go it alone and be my own attorney, which I did at the preliminary hearing.

A few days after that hearing an attorney by the name of McDougall came to see me at the county jail. He said he was a stranger in town and had heard about my case and would be willing to take the case for nothing. Seeing that the proposition was in perfect harmony with my bankroll, I accepted his offer. I will say for McDougall, though, that he was honest and sincere about it and would no doubt have carried the case to a successful finish if he had not got mixed up with that miserable shyster Mr. Scott. Before my trial, I pointed out the fact that the preliminary hearing records had been altered, but they said that the said record did not amount to anything anyway, and that it would do no good to make a holler about it.

Then the trial commenced. The first day went by with the usual questioning of jurors. The second day, however, something happened that did not look right to me. There was a jury of eight men entered the courtroom. They had been serving on some other case and came in to deliver their verdict, which was one of "guilty." Then the court discharged all the jurors and they started to go home, but for some reason Judge Ritchie changed his mind and told three of them to come back and go up in the jury box and be examined for my case. I noted that these three men were very surprised and that they did not expect to be retained for jury service. I have therefore good reason to believe that they were never sub-poenaed for the case, but just simply appointed by the court. One of these men, a very old man by the name of Kimball, was later on made "foreman" of the jury. During the course of the trial I was surprised to see that some of the witnesses were telling entirely different stories from the ones told by them at the preliminary hearing and I asked my attorneys why they did not use the records of the preliminary hearing and pin the witnesses down to their former statements. They then told me that the preliminary hearing had nothing to do with the district court hearing and that the record did not amount to anything. They did, however, use said records a little, but only for a bluff. After I had watched this ridiculous grandstand play for a while I came to the conclusion that I had to get rid of these attorneys and either conduct the case myself or else get some other attorney. I therefore stood up the first thing in the morning one day and showed them the door. Being the defendant in the case, I naturally thought I should have the right to say who I wanted to represent me, but to my surprise I discovered that the presiding judge had the power to compel me to have these attorneys in spite of all my protests. He ruled that they remain as "friends of the court" and that settled it. Mr. Scott went after one of the state witnesses in a way that convinced me he really could do good work when he wanted to. After he got through with this witness (Mrs. Seeley) he came up to me and said, "Now then, how did you like that?" I said, "That's good, but why didn't you do some of that before?" "Well, er . . ." he hesitated. "This was the first witness we had marked for cross-examination." If that is not a dead give-away, then I don't know anything. It will be noted that Mrs. Seeley is one of the last witnesses for the state.

I will now say something about the pistol which I had in my possession when I called at Dr. McHugh's office to have my wound dressed. That pistol was a Luger caliber .30, a pistol of German make. I laid my pistol on the table while the doctor dressed my wound and I thought that he would be able to tell it from other pistols on account of its peculiar construction. He said he did not know, however, what kind of pistol mine was. That was an even break, and whenever I get an even break I am not complaining. He did not, like most of the state witnesses, commit perjury, and is therefore in my opinion a gentleman. There was another doctor, however, by the name of Bird, who dropped in while Dr. McHugh was dressing my wound. He only saw the pistol as I put it in my pocket, and he said so at the preliminary hearing, but at the district court hearing he came up and deliberately swore that my pistol was exactly the same kind of pistol as the one that Morrison and his son were killed with.

As I said before, my pistol was a Luger .30. It was bought a couple of months before my arrest in a second hand store on West South Temple street, near the depot. I was brought down there in an automobile by three officers and the record of the sale was found on the books: price, date of sale, and everything just as I had stated. The books did not show what kind of a gun it was, however, and as the clerk who had sold it was in Chicago at the time a telegram was sent to him to which he sent this answer: "Remember selling Luger gun at that time. What's the trouble?" I bought the pistol on Sept. 15, 1913, for $16.50. Anybody may go to the store and see the books.

Now anyone can readily understand that I am not in a position where I could afford to make any false statements. I have stated the facts as I know them in my own simple way. I think I shall be able to convince every fair-minded man and woman who reads these lines that I did not have a fair and impartial trial in spite of what the learned jurists may say to the contrary. If you don't like to see perjurors and dignified crooks go unpunished, if you don't like to see human life being sold like a commodity on the market, then give me a hand. I am going to stick to my principles no matter what may come. I am going to have a new trial or die trying.

Yours for Fair Play,
JOE HILL

Under Lund's window the street lights had come up. Across an acreage of roofs and chimneys he saw the sky die swiftly from blood-red to rust to slate gray. There were gaps in Joe's argument, sophistries, substitutions of plausibilities for fact, a jesuitical seizing of technicalities, a profound and perhaps significant silence about the crucial circumstances of his wound, his throwing away of the

gun, his sharp whistles outside the Erickson house before Dr.
Bird took him in, the suspicious flight of Otto Applequist. Yet the
statement was plausible too; it had, even in its sophistries, the
ring of a man who believed what he said. The gaps could easily
be there because he was honorably hiding something, woman business or union business, that prevented frankness. Despite the gaps,
Lund believed. Whatever Joe was hiding it was not guilt, or at
least the guilt for the crime he was charged with.

One statement could clear him, if he would make it. But instead
of that he would go to his death arguing technicalities and plausibilities, either because he hoped they would save him or for some
enigmatic reason that was like a bad joke persisted in. Or he might
be freed by the under-cover, confidential manipulation of a relation-
ship and a connection that Joe himself would scorn to acknowledge
and refuse to use.

To a simple man with a moral view, the differences between
guilt and conviction, innocence and freedom, were a trouble to the
mind.

4

The visiting room at the State Prison. In the center a rectangular
steel cage, a room within a room. On three sides of the cage, inside
and outside of the screen, a scarred table, and on inside and outside continuous benches. Visitors and prisoners sit on the benches,
their arms on the table, and talk through the net of steel. On the
fourth side the cage opens into the prison yard by a barred door.
Prisoners are brought in here, visitors come through the office from
the front entrance. At both entrances stand uniformed guards. The
walls of the visiting room are plaster painted a robin's-egg blue
except for a wainscot strip of pebbled metal painted a poisonous
and angry green.

At the entrance from the office a little group stands uneasily
quiet—Ingrid Olson and her mother, Jud Ricket and Jack Carpenter of the defense committee, Gustave Lund. In a few minutes

Joe Hillstrom enters the cage from the prison yard, handcuffed between two guards, one of whom detaches himself. The other comes along and sits down beside Joe on the inside bench.

Ricket says something under his breath and Carpenter lurches on his crooked leg. The two women look uncertainly at the men, the men look back. There is only a half-hour altogether; someone must go first. And with the guard there it will be hurried, public, dismal. The prison does not leave a guard with anyone but Joe. In the cage two other prisoners are talking with visitors in a freedom that seems extravagant by comparison.

At last Ricket, with a last questioning look at the others, shrugs and starts forward. At the screen, still standing, he puts out his hand to touch Joe's fingers in the parody of a handshake, but the guard warns him off. Beside Lund Jack Carpenter jerks with anger, muttering.

Joe looks wasted and pale from sickness and imprisonment, his scarred face is wedge-thin, but he sits erectly with the guard like an enormous manacle on his left wrist, and he smiles. Even from forty feet away Lund sees his eyes, how passionate and troubling a blue.

The group by the door cannot hear what Ricket says. He talks earnestly, his head close to the wire, and Joe listens, nods, nods again, smiles. He says something and Ricket replies.

Abruptly Ricket is on his feet. Contemptuously he raises his hand, turns it around several times before the face of the guard to show that he has nothing concealed in it, and touches the tips of his fingers to Joe's. For a moment he is bent, concentratedly bowed toward the prisoner; then he breaks away and comes back toward them massive and grim. Jack Carpenter starts, half turns in question of the unspoken order they follow, and goes on.

Carpenter does not sit down, and his voice is loud enough to be heard. He ignores the guard; to him the man is not there. He looks through the screen, his bad leg bent, his body twisted to balance his weight, and he says, "This isn't goodbye, Joe. I want you to know that. I'm not sayin' goodbye. All I want to say is keep your chin up in here, keep fightin'. That's what we're doin' outside, and we'll win yet. You'll be out of here a free man."

He stops. His throat works. With a harsh violence he raises his hands and shakes them fiercely before his face. "Okay, boy!" he says, and swings and comes limping back. Lund looks away, not to watch his face.

The remaining three hang, hesitating. "Next?" the guard at the door says. "Who's next?"

Ingrid pushes her mother forward, and Lund feels a pang of fierce jealousy, thinking that next time she will try to shove him ahead, keep the final minutes for herself. Lover or friend, who has the most right? Joe has wired him to come. He glances again at Ingrid and sees unexpected lines in her face and neck; she looks strained, prudish, a vinegarish old maid, waving her mother on.

The woman comes up slowly to the wire net. Her hands start to come up and fall again quickly as she glances at the guard. With her hands like dead birds on the table she slumps to the bench and leans forward. Lund hears only her first words, "Oh, Joseph!" and then murmurs and the sound of her crying. He sees Joe's stiff head nod, he sees the long look Mrs. Olson gives him, and then she too comes stumbling back.

Lund feels unclean, watching her face twisted with crying, and he wonders what the guards are made of, to sit impassively handcuffed to scenes like this. If the girl goes now he doesn't want to watch. He knows her face will crumble as it crumbled at the gate when they talked the first time. It would have been better if none of them had come. They all pretend hope, they all carry in their minds the possibility that Hilton's efforts will bring a last-minute reprieve, but they all come too with the knowledge that this may be their last look at Joe and their last word. He knows the girl will collapse.

He will not quarrel with her over precedence or time. She may go now or he will. For a moment their eyes met, Lund makes a gesture, a motion indicating that she may choose. She has her arm around the shaking shoulders of her mother, and her face is raised. A nod, and she has taken her arm away and is walking firmly toward the cage.

So far as Lund can hear or see—and he watches painfully, unable to look away—she says nothing, and neither does Joe. He cannot see Ingrid's face, only her stiff back, but he can see Joe's pale cheek and the almost luminous even blue stare.

Ingrid bends and puts her face against the screen, holding it there until Joe bends awkwardly to meet her, pulling at the handcuff that tethers him to the guard. They kiss through the steel net, and Ingrid's hands come up to press through the wires against his cheeks. Directly from the kiss, moving stiffly, she steps back and comes to her mother. Her face is like paper. Looking neither right nor left, their necks rigid against looking back, the two women leave.

Lund rubs his sweating hands on his sleeves. "How much time?" he asks the guard.

"Five-six minutes."

Five or six minutes to say and hear everything that might be said. He feels his own face gray and inflexible as he comes up and slides onto the bench.

They face each other, friends and antagonists, the preacher and the slave, and what they find to say is trivial, a thousandth part of what they might say, or a deliberate avoidance of that. Joe speaks first.

– I was afraid you couldn't come.

– I was glad to come.

A pause while they smile almost in embarrassment at each other. Between them now, Lund feels, there is no room for complaints, sympathies, attack or defense or contention. They are old friends and one will die in five days. He has his own consolations, so that the consolations his friend can offer him are probably unwanted. Yet there has been a telegram; a kind of desperation has arranged this meeting. Lund searches the sharp face for the despair he has half expected to find in it, and he does not find it. Even after that unbearable minute with the girl, Joe Hill is serene, or seems so. He sweeps the backs of his fingers across the steel mesh.

– Seems as if all our talking is through one of these strainers lately.

– It's good to talk to you, even through this.

– I guess so.

His eyes wander to the corner of the cage, where an old Greek with a face like a bird of prey talks vehemently to a little pock-marked man behind the wire. His voice is loud and harsh; he pays no attention to other visitors or to the guards; he has the confidence that the tongue he speaks is unknown; his anger or whatever is bothering him can be private even when he airs it at the top of his lungs. Joe looks from the old Greek to Lund, his eyebrows

waggle humorously, but under them his eyes for a moment are
bleak.

Lund waits (for you did send a wire, there was some reason.
When the last chance failed and you were sure you had to die,
you did send. Why? What did you want to say?).

– Well, anyway this will be the last time I have to look at this
joint.

– Don't give up hope. You'll be saved yet.

– That's a pipedream.

– Hilton is still working. Everybody is.

– They've spent too much on me now.

– Why do you keep saying that?

– Because it's true. If the state of Utah wants to kill me, I'm
ready.

– I can't imagine it.

– I am, just the same.

There is a momentary duel of eyes, and Lund looks away in
shame, feeling almost as if he has been trying to argue Joe out
of his resignation. Now he looks back, forcing his smile, trying
to project his friendship and his goodwill, even his love, through
the mesh to the remote man inside.

– Joe, why did you send for me?

– I guess I wanted to talk.

– So do I. That's why I came. But how can we?

The thin hands, shrunken from long idleness, go sideward in
an impatient gesture.

– Pretty bum place for it.

– There isn't any other place, and not much time.

His own words bring to Lund a panicky sense of urgency and
hopelessness. He cannot stand to hold Joe's glance, and he looks
away, but within three feet of his face is the square, putty-colored
face of the guard, a pair of flat streaked eyes with a roll of skin
like a welt all around the lids. Joe's voice brings him back.

– I want to ask a favor.

– Anything.

– The night I wired you I got to dreaming, just the woolliest
kind of old dreams. I woke up scared to death and I wanted to
talk to somebody. So I wired you.

– I'm glad you thought of me that way.

—But this is no good, through this strainer, with Fido on my
arm. I want to talk all night.

—I wish there was some way.

—Maybe there is. When the law murders somebody it does it
politely. They give a man a chance to kiss the hand that kills
him. That's what they have these "spiritual counselors" for.

—But the prison . . .

—How do you know? They're all scared of the iww, but you're
no iww, and can prove it. You're an ordained preacher. You're the
only spiritual counselor I'll have. Except for all this security business they haven't been making it tough for me. They give me
pencil and paper, why wouldn't they give me the preacher I
want?

—But there's a regular prison chaplain.

—I wouldn't let him inside the same cell with me. Look . . .

His eyes widen with a compulsive, insistent stare. He takes
hold of the mesh with his crippled hand and his face is so tight
the scars whiten along his jaw. He shakes the screen a little in
his excitement.

—They always give you a big feed. They always let you have
your little last-minute requests. Well, this is mine. I'm going
to . . .

A bell rings. The putty face of the guard rises as he stands up,
and Joe is tugged to his feet.

—I'm going to write the warden. You go see him. Tell him he
has to.

—Joe! Suppose it doesn't work, this is the last time.

—No goodbyes. See the warden. He's got to. Don't let him say no.
The guard leads him away.

See the warden. With the authorities so upset they kept Joe
handcuffed even inside the prison, what chance was there of an
irregularity so extreme as the one Joe asked? But he had to try.

Behind the steel grill in the main hall a guard sat a high desk
with the switchboard of an alarm system on the wall at his side.
He looked down on Lund aloofly, a man of immeasurable restric-
tive power. Across the hall in the anteroom to the warden's office
two trusties worked at typewriters.

"I'd like to see the warden," Lund said to the guard.

The guard looked down. "I think he's out of town."

"When will he be back?"

"Ask in there."

Tiny and impotent, he stood in the anteroom before a counter, enclosed within the implacable institution. Even the man who came forward, a prisoner himself, was part of the granite structure of rules, regulations, routines, precedents. A man's life could get lost in this maze without a trace. A man's death could be brought about by the invocation of these routines and never cause a stir. Procedures would be put in motion, duties assigned and performed, entries made. The thought of Joe being led back deep into the interior of the place put him forever out of reach.

"When will it be possible to see the warden?" he asked the trusty, a man who wore a patch of cotton under one lens of his glasses and looked like an undernourished clerk with a scraggly chicken-neck.

"He's out of town."

"When will he be back?"

"I couldn't say."

"Didn't he leave any word?"

"None that I know of."

"Is there anybody who would know?"

"I'm afraid not."

"Well, is there somebody in charge while he's gone? Is there a deputy warden, or somebody?"

"In charge of what? What did you want to see him about?"

"A matter of prison rules."

The skinny trusty looked worried and baffled. "Oh no, you'd have to talk to him personally."

He turned away, but Lund put his hands on the counter and leaned anxiously, remembering the futile two or three minutes through the screen, the imperturbable guard. No goodbyes. See the warden. "Listen, this is terribly important!" he said. "I've got to see the warden."

The trusty turned, waiting patiently, making no sign.

"Tell me this," Lund said. "Isn't he required to be here for the execution Friday morning?"

He was watching the patched and sunken face closely, and he

saw something change there, some movement of the eyes or set of the muscles. "Isn't he?"

"Yes," the trusty said. "I expect he is."

"But you don't have any idea how much before then he'll be back."

"No."

Lund knocked his fist lightly on the counter. He caught the trusty's one shy eye again. It occurred to him that the trusty might have been on the brink of what Joe faced himself. He might be a lifer, condemned and commuted, or he might have known men who had waited out their last hours in the maximum-security cell block. He couldn't be as wooden as the guards.

"Maybe you can help me," he said. "I'm a friend of Joe Hillstrom's."

"Yes," the trusty said, without expression.

"I'm a minister, a Lutheran minister. I've been running a seamen's mission. Joe wired me to come. He wants me for his spiritual adviser on the last night. That's why I have to see the warden."

The trusty shook his head.

"You don't think there's a chance?"

"I wouldn't know anything about it."

"If he's scared I might be an iww, I can prove I'm not. I can prove anything the warden wants me to. But it's Joe's last request, do you see? He's depending on me to arrange it."

"Yes," the trusty said. "Well, you'd have to talk to Mr. Webster."

Lund subsided. It was hopeless, as he had known all along it was. And there was no help to be had from this man. Looking at him, he wondered if he were the kind of trusty who had sympathy for other prisoners or the kind who preyed on them more brutally than the guards. Where had he read about trusties who were grafters and sadists and takers of bribes? Jack London, probably. It occurred to him that he might get help by offering this man a bribe, but his mind revolted. He felt defeated and sad, and he said, "Will you do something for me?"

The man looked at him silently with his one careful eye.

"Do you answer the telephone?"

"Generally."

"I'll be calling every few hours until I find the warden in. Will you connect me, if he *is* in? I know he may be hiding out to avoid cranks, but believe me, I'm not a crank. Get me through to him when you can, will you? My name is Lund. Will you remember that?"

The trusty took out a handkerchief and blew into it and folded the handkerchief carefully. His eye came back to Lund's as if trying to surprise something. "You're a minister, you say?"

"Yes."

"Just a second," the trusty said. He seemed to have thought of something, or remembered something. His eye wandered past Lund; he seemed to listen to a voice in his head. "There's a chance he might've come back," he said vaguely. "Hold it a minute, I'll see if I can find out anything for you."

There was an elaborate pretense about him that brought a flicker of hope to Lund. He waited, listening to the dry click of the typewriter operated by the other trusty-clerk, and hearing the routine noises from outside the anteroom. A guard looked in and went away again. An official voice informed someone who had just come in that visiting hours were over.

It was several minutes before the inner door opened and the one-eyed trusty slipped quietly out. Lund could tell nothing from his face, though he searched it for hope. Puny and pale, he went in squeaky heavy shoes across the office space and sat down at his desk. Just when Lund's heart had fallen like a stone and he was turning away in angry defeat, the little man looked up across his typewriter and said mildly, "You can go in."

Galvanized, Lund went through the gate and tapped on the door. He looked at the clerk and the clerk nodded, so Lund pushed the door open. A bald, Napoleon-browed man sat behind a long desk under the windows and watched him enter. He was as immovable as the walls, the guards, the steel gates and the elaborate security regulations. He did not look friendly or receptive; there was a hard pinched frown between his eyes.

"Mr. Webster?" Lund said. "My name is Gustave Lund."

The warden shook his hand one perfunctory shake and nodded to a chair. With the light in his face, Lund saw the other as a haloed silhouette. "Did your clerk tell you . . . ?"

The warden gave him a short shake of the head, the merest fraction of a no.

"I've just been talking to Joe Hillstrom," Lund said, and took a deep breath, for he felt that his words were lost as soon as uttered, smothered and absorbed in the warden's unfriendly silence. He plunged desperately, talking too fast, knowing he should be cunning and persuasive but unable to halt the rush of his babbling speech. "Joe is writing you, or will be. You can check all this with the guard that brought him into the visiting cage. Joe has a last request. He'd like me to be his spiritual adviser the last night. I'm a minister, I've known him for years. He's a boy I . . . There's a good deal to him, I'm very fond of him, do you see, I . . . It seems something you might be able to grant, even it it is a little irregular."

There was absolutely no light in the warden's opaque eyes. His hands were quietly folded on the desk. Lund stumbled on, in despair at his own ineptitude, but watching the warden's face for a wavering or softening of the granite. "I know a lot of people have been making threats, you have to be exceptionally careful. But I can prove I'm who I say I am, I have plenty of identifications, you could wire the synod, or I can give you any number of references."

The warden spoke, and his voice was as impersonal as crackling paper. "Where did you know Hillstrom?"

"In San Pedro. I conducted a seamen's mission there until last year."

He was terrified that the warden would catch that up, ask why he no longer conducted it, drag out the fact of his dismissal and make it into a demonstration of his fraudulent intentions, but the warden glowered at him across the gleaming scratched surface of the desk with the window's bars dimly reflected in it, and spoke as if filling out some form.

"What denomination?"

"Lutheran."

"Is Hillstrom a Lutheran?"

"I think he was baptized a Lutheran."

"Is he a religious man?"

"No," Lund said honestly. "I'm afraid he isn't."

"Then what do you expect to do for him?"

"Anything I can. He wants very much to talk to me."

"As a minister?"

"No. More as a friend. He's a strange, bottled-up boy. I don't think he's ever been able to talk to most people . . ."

"If we started opening the death cell to the friends of prisoners, where would we be?"

"He wired me," Lund said earnestly. At least it was easier to answer specific objections, it was better than trying to be persuasive in the face of stony silence and suspicion. He leaned against the desk and held the opaque eyes. "He wired me to come on clear from Minnesota because he wanted to talk to me. Is that so different from the service a chaplain could perform? I was in there just now to see him, maybe for the last time. There were four or five people saying goodbye, and he sat there in that cage with a guard on his wrist. How could he talk?"

"It isn't our function to see that he gets opportunities for conversation," the warden said. "Our function is to hold him until justice can take its course."

"But there's real doubt in his guilt!" Lund said. He looked past the warden at the pouring light from the window. A bare tree swayed its twigs in the wind beyond the bars. "It may be you're holding an innocent man who is too honorable to save himself at someone else's expense."

"Do you believe he's capable of that?"

"He's capable of anything."

The warden looked away, drawing down the corners of his lips. When he looked back the frown was pinched deeper between his eyes and his voice was heavier, deeper in his throat, like a growl. "So are his friends, evidently. How do I know you're not one of the ones who have threatened to murder the governor and the prosecutor and me and a half-dozen other people, or storm this prison and take Hillstrom by force, or blow up every business building in Salt Lake?"

"Those are not Joe's threats, or mine either."

"They're his friends'."

"His friends are extreme because they value him," Lund said. "He's become a symbol for them. They think they can save him that way."

"And they're very much mistaken!"

"Yes," Lund conceded. His shakiness had passed as he found the warden capable of speech, capable of anger. He sat alertly, waiting, feeling that if the warden would argue it he could be convinced. The warden drummed his fingers on the desk as if impatience had come upon him abruptly. His eyes were hard and unfriendly.

"What precisely is it that you think you could do in Hillstrom's cell if you were permitted in?"

"I don't know. He wants me there. I think it might calm him to talk."

"Confession?"

"I don't think he has anything to confess. But maybe some of the things he has refused to tell."

The warden drummed again, rose and went to the door. "Bring me the register," he said, and waited there until one of the clerks put it in his hand. Back at the desk he opened it, thumbed the pages. Lund, looking at the upside-down sheets, saw long tabulations, and at the top of each page two pictures, Bertillon photographs, full face and profile. When the warden stopped turning and sat studying a page, he could recognize, even in reverse, the thin face of Joe Hillstrom.

"What denomination, did you say?" the warden asked.

"Lutheran."

"Do you think the Lutheran God is any better than any other?"

"You mean for Joe? No," Lund said. "I'll be honest with you. I wouldn't try to pray with Joe. He wouldn't have it. He's a religious nature, I'm sure of it, and he's sensitive, and moral ideas mean something to him. But his religious impulses have all gone toward rebellion. He's politically religious, if you know what I mean. Even so, I'm sure I can bring him some kind of consolation that no prison chaplain could, because I'm his friend. In a big inhuman institution it must be hard to hang onto your identity. I think I might reassure him."

The warden brooded a moment, holding his jaws in his hand. Then he swung the ledger around so that Lund could read it. "There's what he is to us," he said, and in his voice Lund heard something like humor or bitterness, some irony evasive and unacknowledged. He looked at the photographs: the profile that of a workingman with a tough, scarred face, a cold and almost repellent face; the front view of a workingman with the eyes of a

seeker or a saint. The warden was silent while Lund read the
entries down the page:

Hillstrom, Jos.	*Alias #3256*	*S.L. Co.*

WHAT COURT *3rd Dist.*		CRIME *Murder, first degree*	
DATE OF SENTENCE *July 6, 1915*		TERM OF SENTENCE *Death*	
DATE OF CONFINEMENT *July 6, 1915*	PREVIOUS CONVICTIONS		
OCCUPATION	NATIVITY *Sweden*	MARRIED? *S*	
COMPLEXION *Sallow*	AGE *33*	HEIGHT *5' 10½"*	WEIGHT *146*
SHOE *9*	HAT *7⅛*	COLOR OF EYES *Blue*	COLOR OF HAIR *Brown*

OTHER DESCRIPTIVE MARKS

* *Three blue dots between thumb and first finger of left hand.*
* *Gun shot scar 2" below left nipple.*
* *Gun shot scar below left shoulder blade.*
* *Gun shot scar through right hand.*
* *Gun shot scar through 3rd finger of right hand.*

* *Large scar "operation" on left side of neck extending under chin.*
* *Two scars on right side of face.*
* *Large scar on right side of neck.*
* *Large scar on back of right forearm.*
* *Wing on left side of nose missing.*
* *Mole on left ribs.*
* *Teeth — good.*

WHEN DISCHARGED	EDUCATION *Read*.. √ .. *Write* .. √ ..	
HABITS OF LIFE *Temperate* . √ . *Intemperate*	RELIGION *Lutheran*	

"A bundle of scars," the warden said, watching Lund with an
odd fixed brightness in the eyes that had up to now seemed dull
and opaque. "A bundle of scars, a temperate habit of living, a
physical description, a number, a date, and a sentence. They
sound a lot alike by the time they come to us."

"Joe's different. He has a quality. He could have been something."

"Most of them could."

Rising, the warden leaned on the window sill and looked out into
the enclosed patch of garden. For a moment he watched something, bird or gardener or animal, intently, following some motion
with his eyes. Then he turned his eyes almost absently toward
Lund and said, "All right, Bestor. You can come out."

The door of a closet near the outer door opened and a guard
came out. Lund stared from him to the warden, and the slow red
rose in his face. The guard looked at the warden questioningly,
and went on out of the office at the warden's nod.

"That was hardly necessary," Lund said.

"If you read my mail," the warden said, "you'd think maybe it was."

Still angry, Lund rose and looked across the desk. "I'm sorry I bothered you. I thought there might be a chance."

The warden had closed the register, and now stood with his fingers on it. "Have you some sure way of identifying yourself?"

"I could get the synod rolls, they would show me as a missionary. And things like these." He emptied his pockets and wallet and found a library card on the San Pedro Public Library, two letters addressed to the Rev. Gustave Lund, an old calling card, one of a batch he had had made years ago for formal church purposes. "I can get you more," he said. "Any sort you suggest."

Leaning until his weight bent the fingers backward, the warden seemed not to have heard. His eyes had barely glanced at the papers Lund showed. "There's been a lot of loose talk about Utah justice," he said. "I don't know whether Utah justice is any different from justice in other places. It's not my business to question the decisions of the courts. I'm here to take care of people after the courts have decided." He chewed his lip briefly; his voice was a drone. "Justice is a complicated maneuver," he said. "It takes a hundred different kinds of men doing a hundred different things, and any of them can be wrong. But you can't throw it out or blow it up because of the chance of error, or even because of some particular error. You can't obstruct the operation of the due process of law by vigilantism and bomb threats and half-baked nonsense like these threats to storm the prison. You have to go ahead and do the best you know how, doing your own part of the job, or there's no security for anyone anywhere."

"Yes," Lund said, wondering if the identification had been not enough, wondering if even yet there was a chance the warden would yield. He thought he heard a strain of self-justification in the warden's voice, as if the storm over Joe Hill had made him examine the foundations of his own job. He watched the warden shake his thick shoulders irritably, and he met the sudden eyes.

"You're a minister," the warden said. "You deal in life and death, you ought to know something about it."

He came around the desk. "Get some more identification from your synod," he said. "Come around here prepared to be searched clear down to your skin, and bear in mind that you're dealing with a man who's up against his last hours on earth. Strength is what he needs, not sob-sister sympathy. You can come in Thursday night after supper and you can stay through to the end if he wants you."

Angrily he walked to the door with the prison register under his arm. Lund's gratitude could find no words, but he could not go without saying something. He thought ruefully how all through this interview both he and the warden had been assuming the worst. As he went through the door at the warden's curt gesture he said, "Maybe none of this will be necessary. There's still a chance something will happen."

"And if you value your peace of mind, and don't want the permission rescinded," the warden said, "you will keep this whole transaction to yourself."

He nodded stiffly and Lund went past him and out through office and hall and court, where a guard opened a narrow pedestrian gate and let him into the street. He was exultant about the permission he had gained, and yet it struck him as a sad cause for exultation, and the prospect of the night-long vigil with Joe made him flinch as if at a vivid imagining of physical pain. More and more, as he rode home on the rocking streetcar, he felt depressed and hopeless. It would take more than Hilton's manipulation of Swedish officials to halt the forces that closed in upon Joe.

He sent two telegrams and called on a local Lutheran pastor for identifications, knowing that he would need them.

But he underestimated Hilton's ingenuity and Ricket's vigor and the devotedness of the agents they had set to work across the world.

By the time he had dressed the next morning and gone to the hotel newsstand for his paper, word of the unjust conviction of Joseph Hillstrom had been cabled to Gefle and the burgermeister had cabled back to the Swedish Minister in Washington. Virginia Stephen had called upon the Minister, Ekengren, and talked with him privately for an hour. Ekengren had wired the Swedish vice-consul in Salt Lake to investigate the case, and he had telephoned Secretary of State Polk and made an official request. The Secretary of State, after consulting with President Wilson, had wired Governor Spry asking for a stay of execution pending more complete investigation. Two professors at the University of

Utah had made public statements denouncing the proposed judicial murder of Joe Hill, and the Pardon Board had called them to come before it the next day and state their position.

In the crowded front page of the Salt Lake *Tribune* all of Lund's fatalistic certainty was wiped away. The forces closing in on Joe Hill might be ponderous, but forces even more ponderous were rallying to his defense.

He waited, and he bought every edition of every newspaper, and he hung around the hive of the Wobbly hall. Swept up and carried along by the tide of jubilant, intense activity, Lund was reminded of a party headquarters during a bitter election, or of that moment in a tug-of-war when after a long wavering stalemate one side begins to surge and haul the opposition off balance, forcing them to give a step, to slip, to brace and give again, bringing them in by hard weight and strength.

Ricket was in the office eighteen hours a day, Hilton was in and out, the exultation grew while they waited for the inevitable cracking of the opposition. But on the morning of September 29 when Lund went over the jubilation was gone, faces were grim, Ricket's phantom smile was jerking his cheek three times a minute. The vice-consul had reported to his Minister that in his opinion Joe Hillstrom had had a fair trial. The Pardon Board, questioning the two professors, had found them both ignorant of key facts in the case and had dismissed them as moved more by partisan zeal than by considered evidence. Governor Spry had told the press that unless the State Department specifically requested a reprieve, none would be granted.

A fury like battle-fury possessed the Wobbly hall. A fight broke out and Ricket plowed out of his office like a locomotive to break it up, yanking the two battlers apart and throwing them halfway across the room. Lund stayed in the separate office, his own temper frayed, irritably wishing the Wobblies had more sense and less courage, more capacity to think and less to swing a blow. But he waited there because in this one day that remained anything that happened would have to happen through Hilton and Ricket. Hilton had been on the telephone to Washington three times during the morning and was trying again now.

Nothing happened, no word came through. Eventually Lund straggled back to his hotel room and lay on the bed, hearing in the

street below the passage of people free to move around and go
and come. He thought of Joe deep in the steel and stone of the
prison, and wondered if he knew of the breakdown of this last
chance after the high and exultant hope. It occurred to him too
to wonder if Joe really would want a reprieve, or if the stiff
serenity of the last Sunday still armored him.

One more night. Tomorrow night at this time he would have
to enter that deep cell and try to give hollow comfort from a
hollow heart. The thought made him turn in impotence and
anger on his bed.

But again he reckoned without the tenacity of those who had
gone to war in Joe's name. The morning paper reported a telegram from Woodrow Wilson himself, requesting a reprieve while
reports of prejudice and irregularities in the trial could be in-
vestigated.

Without comment, Governor Spry had granted a stay until
October 16.

5

The case of the State of Utah versus Joseph Hillstrom brightens
and darkens like a day when wind brings clouds across the sky
and the threat of rain thickens only to be burned away again. In
the Wobbly hall there is a week of something almost like relaxation,
almost like confidence. Hilton has gone to Washington to confer
with Minister Ekengren; the moguls who have interested themselves in labor's singer go about their ponderous inspection of the
records. Still dredging in an attempt to strengthen the conviction,
the police dig up the arrest of Joseph Hillstrom in San Pedro in
connection with some streetcar robberies, but since they can prove
only that the police held Joe for a few hours for questioning, their
net gain from the maneuver is a hornet's nest of counterattack from
the Wobblies who resent the attempt to smear Joe's character.

The letters still pour in upon the governor and warden and the
Supreme Court judges, but the threatening tone of many of them

diminishes somewhat, as if their authors were waiting to see what happened. Lund, waiting too, moves to a less expensive hotel and measures out the days that for him tighten and grow tenser as the reprieve wears away. He has not seen Joe; by now Joe is allowed no visitors at all.

He is troubled by the inconclusiveness of the reprieve and the thought of what will come after it. "What evidence can we get?" he keeps asking Ricket. "What is there to show Wilson and Ekengren? Has Hilton got anything new, or do we have to depend on technicalities again?"

All he gets is a shrug, an intense black stare, a twitch of the nervous cheek. "The records of the stinking District Court ought to be enough."

"Those have already been reviewed three times."

"Sure, but not with the whole United States including the President looking over their shoulders. They know they can't get away with this cover-up now. They'll find some way to crawl and save their faces, but they'll have to let Joe loose eventually."

"I wish I could believe that."

"Wait and see," Ricket says. "If they try to push this legal murder through they'll get the surprise of their life. This thing grows like a snowball. Look at that!"

He waves his hand at the desk heaped high with letters and papers. It seems to Lund that the contemplation of how big the thing has become brings a glitter to his eyes. The state may finally execute Joe Hill, but a wonderful and world-wide protest will have been stirred up. From this little iww local have gone out appeals and denunciations and cables that have brought out a solid front of support from Melbourne to London, and pulled in the unexpected great of the world. Lund suspects that Ricket looks with awe on the thing he has started. For that matter, Lund does too.

But he waits uneasily, because it is clear that there is no new evidence, no fresh approach, and he is afraid that the investigation by the Minister and the President will only corroborate the investigations by the Superior Court and the Supreme Court and the Pardon Board and the vice-consul. There is nothing new; there is only the plea, made in spite of Joe Hill's own expressed wishes, for clemency and pardon, and the insistent threat of violence.

He waits, and on October 16 the Pardon Board meets again, and again it finds no ground for clemency. Joe Hill is sentenced for the third time, and the execution set for November 19. When Lund tries to obtain permission to see him, the warden is abrupt.

"I told you you could come in the last night. But until then nobody sees him, and he can thank his friends for it."

So the preacher goes back to his hotel and counts his money and thinks out his personal problems and writes his father asking for a loan. Having come this far with Joe, he will stay to the end, for the end is now inevitable.

Once, sometime during the days and weeks of waiting, Lund was stopped on the street by a crowd that overflowed the sidewalk and spread out across the car tracks. The eyes of the crowd were turned upward to the stone face of the Salt Lake *Tribune* building, and looking up with them Lund saw outside the second-story windows a great board, like a child's game but of enormous size, shaped like a baseball diamond. All around the board were little tabulations, a scoreboard marked off by innings, places for the indication of balls and strikes, outs, hits, runs, errors, sacrifices, and an opening past which rolled one by one the names of players as they came to bat. The scoreboard read

Red Sox 0 0 0 1 2
Phillies 1 0 0 0 1

He had forgotten. The World Series.

Streetcar bells clanged, and cars pushed through the crowd that moved and packed and ebbed back again onto the tracks. Up on the ingenious board, by some intricate system of telegraphic reports and electromagnets and a sweating crew of technicians, the newspaper brought the game across twenty-five hundred miles and replayed it in the Salt Lake City street. Every player's position was marked by a red and a white light; the pitcher's mound was bald in the center of a green acreage, as in a real diamond; rows of small white lights ran along the baselines. At home plate a swiveled bat waited; on the pitcher's mound a magnetized iron ball wavered and started toward home.

The bat swung, a light went on, *strike*, in the balls-and-strikes tally. The count was one strike and two balls. The ball rolled back to the mound, hesitated, started again for the plate. Again the bat swung, and the steel ball rolled with dignity out past first base into right field, and in right field the red light blinked. A fly to the outfield. In the corner of the board yet another light went on. One out.

Lund watched through half an inning, then another half, then through the sixth and seventh innings. The crowd stood good-naturedly in the street and good-naturedly got out of the way of streetcars and took its seventh-inning stretch and passed remarks and watched intently every time the ball moved, every time the bat swung, every time one of the intricate system of lights blinked on. If the white light went on at any position when the ball rolled that way, it was a hit. Then there was the delighted suspense of seeing the runner blink down the baseline, past first, on to second while the ball rolled around in center field, then past second and on toward third to an outbreak of yips and groans. A triple. Now he's in the hole. Only one away. Let's see him get out of this without a score.

They talked to the hitter, advised the manager, rode the pitcher. With great nimbleness, with an instant and infallible understanding, they kept all the complex lights in their eyes and minds. Excitement went with the frantic serial blinking when the next batter hit a fly to left and the baseline lights, hesitating for a moment, started toward the plate from third. The ball rolled in in a straight unhurried line, the runner was paralyzingly slow, there were eight lights, seven, six, and the ball already past the third baseman on its way in, and five and four and three and the ball almost home, and then the white light at the plate and a new light in the scoreboard under "Runs." He had beaten the throw. Still another light burned steadily a moment: Sacrifice.

Standing in the street with the sun on them they cheered and booed and groaned and laughed, awaiting the outcome of a game that seesawed and fluctuated and was tied up in the seventh and went on into the eighth and ninth still tied, and on into extra innings.

Lund waited with them. The noise of the crowd was like the noise of a real bleachers; he followed the lights like real players, real base hits. He even had a favorite: for some reason he was rooting for Philadelphia, though he had no notion why unless from pure under-dog sympathy. He assumed that the favoritism of others in the crowd was based on things just as trivial: a onetime residence in Philadelphia or Boston, a liking for an individual player, a prejudice against New England. He himself intensely wanted Philadelphia to win.

And why? Here, twenty-five hundred miles from a ballgame between teams not ten of the crowd had ever seen play, men stood for hours in the street and for trivial reasons heated themselves with partisanship and delighted themselves with suspense. They threw their voices at the board, trying to influence it, and obscured the afternoon traffic with their planted bodies. And behind the board were technicians who worked like Fate but who took their orders from a telegraph wire.

Everybody he knew was taking his orders from a telegraph wire, even the ones who appeared as unchangeable as Fate. And the score of that game would not be affected by his partisanship, the technicians would not refuse to record runs when runs were scored, his bleacher enthusiasm could not make a fly ball fall out of the reach of an outfielder. The game was in the hands of the players; the rest of them were recorders and spectators. The events that ground their way along the magnetized board were events that the players themselves would shape.

Though it seemed to him somehow a shameful thing to remain a spectator he knew of no other thing that he could be.

But some were not content to be simply spectators. They wanted to influence the magnetic board, throw pop bottles and cushions, kill the umpire.

Ten days after Joe Hill was resentenced and his execution set for November 19, an "Open Letter to the Board of Pardons" appeared on trees and poles around Salt Lake City. It attacked Utah justice, the Copper Trust, the Mormon Church, the prejudiced public, all who had conspired to bring about the legal murder of Joe Hill, and it was signed by Judge Hilton. Chief Barry sent out a special detail which tore all the posters down. Next night more went up. Next day they came down.

Police and special deputies were now guarding every bank and public building in the city to forestall iww dynamiters. Special guards were posted around the capitol and the governor's home. One of these deputies was startled one afternoon by an explosion on the next corner. He ran down, found that somebody had set off a cannon cracker, and came back to his post. Beside the sidewalk was a paving brick he did not remember seeing before. With his foot he pushed it over. It looked peculiar, as if it had been sawed in two and cemented together again.

A powder company expert took it apart later. It contained a nitro charge big enough to blow up the whole capitol, with an arrangement of sulphuric acid which was supposed to eat down through to detonate some giant caps. The deputy's kick had spilled the sulphuric and spoiled the bomb.

After that the governor called in Ricket and was locked in with him for an hour. To reporters, when he came out, Ricket said nothing about what the governor had talked about. But the bomb, he said, was a phony, a dud, a plant set out there by the deputies themselves in order to make their jobs last.

There was a fifty-fifty chance that he was right. But the fear of dynamiters was by now even beginning to keep people away from shows. In secure parlors there was talk of vigilante action to clear the town of red agitators, and there were letters to the papers asking why the authorities permitted a whole city to be terrorized.

The Swedish Minister engaged a lawyer to go over the Hillstrom case (because of pressure behind the scenes from Joe's father, or only because he would do his best for a Swedish citizen?). President Wilson was called on by Gurley Flynn and promised to make a complete investigation. In San Francisco Samuel Gompers presided over an AFL convention which memorialized the Utah authorities asking clemency or a new trial for Joe Hill. (Ricket was ribald and delighted over that triumph. Now, he said, the heat was really on Wilson. Gompers had to be listened to.)

By grapevine among the rank and file of the Wobblies the word was out that the Wobs were gathering in Salt Lake to free Joe Hill by force, if necessary. In Oakland, eight men grabbed a freight and started eastward. In Denver, stopped by ordinances against IWW street meetings, Wobblies crossed the street to a Salvation Army meeting where they sang Wobbly songs to Army tunes and later passed the hat for the Joe Hill defense. There were a half-dozen men reckless enough to march on Salt Lake. By now, an IWW street meeting in Salt Lake drew hundreds, and there was always bad feeling, heckling, a street full of cops, fights and arguments. In the hall the baggage room was jammed with stiffs who had drifted in quietly, looking for trouble.

The game dragged on through the extra innings, the perfect autumnal weather darkened, the days shortened, the nights were cold. From any high point the smoke was like a dark gray quilt over the valley in the mornings, and on the mountains there was snow.

The city was in a state of siege. "Aren't you afraid they'll raid you and close the hall?" Lund asked Ricket. "I'm surprised they never raided you long ago. They certainly hate you enough."

"They're scared," Ricket said. "The whole damn world has got its eye on what they do. They're scared to make a pass."

But one night Lund was reading in his room, wearing out another few hours of the waiting. The room was stuffy, the radiators knocking with pressured heat, and he opened the window an inch or two to clear away the smoke of his pipe. He sat half stupefied, despondent and tired and confused in his mind, thinking that his presence here, his whole involvement in the case, was absurd and useless, a sentimental concession to himself rather than any help to Joe. He had his own life to untangle. With the fundamentalists in control, there was no chance of his getting another missionary assignment. He might as well admit that he was out of the ministry. But instead of making decisions for himself, he sat bewitched in Salt Lake City waiting for a death that was postponed and postponed and postponed but never called off.

Through the crack in the window he heard street sounds, voices, steps, and then a sudden clamor of angry shouts. Someone yelled above all the noise, a cracking yell. Someone ran hard down the sidewalk; further up a police whistle shrilled. These days, a fight couldn't start anywhere without a cop's showing up in thirty seconds. But now a silence, a wild shout full of fear or warning that went up into a scream and was blown away by a shot.

Lund threw open the window and leaned out. The night was so smoky that he could see little except vague shapes of men running, halfway up the block. There was no more yelling, but a murmur of crowd sound began to grow, and within minutes a patrol wagon careened around the corner and clanged to a stop.

By the time Lund got outside, the wagon was coming back, forcing its way through the crowd. The crowd, Lund with it,

moved aside and then curved back behind, trying to see into the
rear end, but the view was blocked by the body of a policeman
hanging to the handrails.

It was an hour before Lund could find out exactly what had
happened: a standing feud between two men had culminated in
a shooting and a death. The one was now in jail, the other in the
morgue. But the one in the morgue, a man named Roy Horton,
was an IWW.

Lund made his way back to his room filled with a sick, resistant
certitude that what had happened would lead to worse and worse
things. The violence that began this, the remote and ambiguous
murder on West Temple Street almost two years ago, and the
unexplained shot that somewhere, that same night, had torn
through Joe Hill's chest, led by an inevitable course through greater
and greater violences.

What had been passion before would be murderous hatred now.
Tomorrow there would be even more special deputies patrolling
the streets. The desperate talk of storming the prison and liberating
Joe Hill by force would spread. The fingers of policemen would
be nervous on their guns; citizens would check the locks on their
doors; no IWW would think it safe to go abroad unarmed. It was
utterly mad, and the shooting of Roy Horton might have no
connection whatever with the IWW—no more, perhaps, than the
shooting of John Morrison or Joe Hill had—but this killing would
be sucked into the general vortex and made to do service as a hate
breeder.

At the center of all this, generating lines of force that went
through the whole world, was a sailor friend of his, a Swede with
a knack for drawing pictures and writing poems, a man with little
education but with a strong inclination toward the arts, a man
who used to drop in and drink coffee and argue social rebellion
in the mission kitchen. He was as remote now as a vague great name
in the papers. The errand Lund had come on was an arrogance
for which he could hardly forgive himself.

Involved in this whirlwind of violence, and hating violence as
the father of all evil, wanting only to speak humbly and with
understanding to a friend, he felt sad and incapable, and he shrank
from the thought of going to Joe's cell, as he would certainly have
to unless the President chose to intervene a second time.

Wilson tried. His second telegram, sent on the morning of November 17, asked what his first had asked: a stay pending further investigation of the case. All that day the governor was in a close meeting with the Pardon Board and the warden of the prison. By the time the afternoon papers went to press he still had made no statement. Lund, waiting in the halls of the capitol with a handful of iww's and newspapermen, was put out with the others when the building closed.

He slept badly and was up before six, but the hotel newsstand was not open and no paper boys were on the streets. It was seven o'clock before he got a *Tribune* and saw the headlines.

Governor Spry's telegram in reply to the President's was long, more than a column. It reviewed the case and the interventions in the case, and it withheld its decisive meaning until the final paragraph:

It is a significant fact that those only are appealed to who have no knowledge of the facts and those only demand clemency who are either prejudiced in Hillstrom's favor or who demand his release regardless of his guilt. I am fully convinced that your request must be based on a misconception of the facts or that there is some reason of an international nature that you have not disclosed. With a full knowledge of all the facts and circumstances submitted, I feel that a further postponement at this time would be an unwarranted interference with the course of justice. Mindful of the obligations of my oath of office to see to it that the laws are enforced, I cannot and will not lend myself or my office to such interference. Tangible facts must be presented before I will further interfere in this case.

6

There was a period when they sat on the two ends of the prison cot and said nothing at all. If there were things to be said of the soul and of the peace that passeth understanding and of the possibilities of a blessed Beulah Land or a perhaps more blessed obliteration, they were not things that Lund could introduce. He was here at Joe's insistence; he had his mind locked against the thought of daylight tomorrow morning; he was waiting for Joe to say the things that he had apparently wanted Lund to hear. He wanted to know what lay on Joe's mind, but he would not for a fortune have tried to pry. He wanted to hear Joe say for sure that he was innocent, but he would not ask. And he wanted to touch Joe's hand or shoulder in brotherhood and somehow communicate pity and sympathy and a shared terror of what would come, but there was no way to begin.

Joe had been alone and a prisoner for almost two years. It was not being sentimental to guess that the mere presence of a friend, without a word spoken, might be enough for him. It did not matter, really. Lund was eager to be used in any way he could be helpful. He stole glances at Joe from under his thoughtful hand, appraising the silence between them, trying to guess if what only made him uneasy were comforting to Joe.

Joe looked as if he saw visions. His eyes were a little glazed; muscles worked in his lean jaw. His face under the hard light was pale, ascetic, absolutely expressionless except for the air of seeing that it wore. Lund thought in surprise, watching him, that even with the scars it was an almost beautiful face.

Joe's head turned; his eyes, wide in the blue stare, touched Lund as if without recognition, wandered past him, came back. "Quiet night on Skid Road," he said, and stood up abruptly to take one long step toward the door, then two shorter ones back to the cot. He stood above Lund and said, "We ought to have some coffee. They give you comfort for your soul but not for your belly."

Before Lund could answer, he was back tapping with a pencil between the bars. Steps came down the empty steel corridor, the key rasped in the security door, the steps came on and a moon-faced guard stood outside.

"We'd like some coffee," Joe said. "Don't you suppose at a time like this they'd think of that themselves? I've got Reverend Lund in here and we'd both like coffee."

His voice was loud and peremptory. For a second or two the guard stared into the cell. "Okay, Joe," he said. "I'll see what we can do."

"Bring plenty. Tell 'em to bring a pot full."

As the guard went back up the corridor Joe sat on the cot's end. "They're trotting out the best in this old hotel now," he said. Learning on one elbow, he looked away from Lund and talked jerkily as if he had been running. "I went through this once before, just before the President wired the first time. They had me all fixed—that time too. Steak dinner, baked potato—big slab of pie. Same tonight. It's the special firing-squad blue plate."

Opening and closing the hand, he rubbed at the bumpy knuckles where the policeman's bullet had gone through. "It's a fright how polite they can get just before they shoot you full of holes. This guard—runs errands for me as if he was my gunsel. If I asked for a hot-water bottle I bet he'd try to rustle it somewhere."

"I expect he's had orders."

"Yeah," Joe said. Something went out of his face, some artificial animation. The nervous rubbing of his hands stopped, and he held both hands flat against his thighs. "I expect they've all had orders."

Lund put out a hand and shook Joe's knee slowly, and as if to acknowledge a joke Joe turned his head and smiled. The silence came back, broken only by a faint, reverberatory hum as if they were inside a great barrel; across the hum went the unmeaning steps of a guard. The toilet five feet from Lund gave off a strong smell of disinfectant; he had a moment's mad illusion that he was in a pool hall on Beacon Street in San Pedro with the ventilator dragging at the thick air and the smoke. Here the smell and the big humming emptiness were the same.

"You've had a long wait," Joe said. "Over a month and a half."

"That's all right. I wish I . . ."

He caught Joe's eye, stopped. Joe stood up again.

"I expect there are a hundred things I ought to be doing," he said, and his eyes went from corner to corner, from cot to toilet to door.

"Can I do anything?"

"I don't know," Joe said, still looking around as if trying to remember something he had lost. His voice was as jerky as his eyes. Restlessness or excitement was in his limbs. He sat down and almost immediately stood up again, feeling for the pencil in his shirt pocket. "Maybe there isn't anything to do, at that. Maybe everything's done."

"Any letters?"

"Maybe one or two. There's plenty of time."

Plenty of time.

In the outer corridor steps again, and after a moment the direc-tioned hollow noises of the guard coming. Joe went to the door to look. "Aha! He got that coffee, at that."

The guard set down the tray and unlocked the door and shoved the tray with its pot and two cups into the cell with his foot. Joe stooped for it.

"The very best in their crummy old hotel," he said. "They even asked me last night if I wanted a stimulant. I told them I wasn't a drinking man. I bet they'd let you get stiff drunk. It'd suit them fine if you went out there in the morning too sopped to know what was going on. But I'm not taking any of their stimulants. I'm going out there sober."

His voice was high and brittle. Pouring two mugs of coffee, he slopped some on the tray. "Here," he said, and held one toward Lund. He ignored the guard, who watched for a few seconds and went away again.

Looking at Lund over the rim of his cup, Joe made a short, harsh gesture with his free hand, cutting sideward at the air. Lund felt how since he had come in here the flesh had shrunk on his fingers. He was bloodless from the shoulders down, though it was not cold in the cell. For a while he warmed his hands around the mug, and then he could stand to keep still no longer. He had been with Joe an hour, and there had been nothing but pretense or silence.

"Don't be sore at me, Joe," he said. "But why don't you speak and save yourself?"

Everything about Joe's face, nose and lips and cheeks and chin, was pinched and sharp. It seemed that his skin had tight-ened across his bones. Carefully his hand reached down the empty cup and set it between his feet, but hardly had he straightened before he had stooped to pick it up again. Concentrating on the motions of his hands, he poured the cup full.

"Maybe I don't feel like speaking," he said at last in a silky whisper. He seemed to nurse some fierce thought. His palely beautiful face was expressionless, but even in profile the eyes seemed to Lund to glow and burn.

"But it's such a miserable waste!" Lund cried. "Why must you throw yourself away?"

He found it impossible to read the stare that Joe turned on him. "Waste?" Joe said. "Throw myself away? You don't know what you're talking about."

"What else can you call it?"

The grin that grew over Joe's pinched face was of an incredible impudence. "You might call it an organizing job," Joe said.

"I'm glad you can joke about it."

"It's no joke. The union stands to gain more if they shoot me than if they turn me loose." Bending, he set the cup on the floor again, and suddenly he was very excited. A faint pink jumped into his cheeks, the unmutilated side of his nose flared, in his neck a vein stood out rigidly, parallel with the rigid scar. "Here's the President of the United States after them to free me! Here's the Swedish Minister sticking his nose in. Here's even old Sam Gompers the union scab-master, people all over the world writing and wiring in here. You think that doesn't do anything for solidarity? You're supposed to be an educated man. What do you think the Mormons would have amounted to if they hadn't shot Joe Smith? How would Christianity have got along in Rome if the Romans hadn't liked throwing them to the lions? They'd have been just another little sect about as big as the Holy Rollers are now." He barked out a laugh. "For that matter, what if nobody had hung Jesus Christ on a cross?"

Lund looked down. It embarrassed him to watch Joe's violence, because he could not rid himself of the feeling that the violence was faked. The sudden brief tirade had the artificiality of an act, like his tirade in court when he fired his lawyers. It wasn't like Joe; right now Joe was breathing harder and faster than he needed to, working himself up to a passion for some obscure reason.

And how could it be said to him now, a few hours before his death, that his martyrdom was tainted by the dubious methods his friends had used in advertising or—concede the suspicion— promoting it? Joe Hill as he lived in the minds of well-wishers around the world was a fiction, the product of deliberate manufacture.

He said at last, "Of course. A martyr catches the imagination.

You can build a church on one martyrdom. But why should you
be the one?"

"I think it was kind of predetermined," Joe said. To Lund's
amazed glance he appeared now to be entirely sincere. His lips
firmed until the outline of his teeth was molded under them,
and he said, "When I first came into this burg I had a cold
hunch, and I kept having it. Something was due to happen to
me in this place. I could feel it."

"And you think this is what it was."

"Yes."

Lund shook his head and studied his hands. Without raising his
head he said, "But you could have stopped the whole trial at
any point by telling your story. That doesn't make it look predetermined. It makes it look as if *you* had determined it."

He caught Joe's lips curving, his eyes wide in the look of lamb-
like innocence. "Suppose I never had any story to tell?" Joe said
softly.

For three breaths Lund was conscious of how the air sucked
into his lungs and was forced out again. He breathed as if by
conscious effort, and he felt the blood drain and gather in a
painful clot under his ribs. He had always been afraid of this;
he had always half believed it.

"Suppose I really was in Morrison's store," Joe said in the same
soft monotone. "It didn't have to happen the way they said it
happened. All those dicks and lawyers were guessing. My own
lawyers were guessing too, but they had a different guess. It didn't
have to be the way any of them said. Suppose it was. Suppose
I was in there with Otto, the way they said I was, and we were
going to collect a contribution from Morrison. Suppose the boy
grabbed in the icebox for the gun and I had to shoot in self-
defense. Or suppose Otto did the shooting. Then suppose I'm
wounded and feeling ashamed of myself for getting in a jam
like that, and sorry about the boy and his father. There isn't
anything I can do. It's all finished. But keep on supposing. Suppose
the union insists on defending me even when I don't especially
want to be defended. They figure an injury to one is an injury
to all, and they're ready to give it everything they've got. But
with them in it I've got to be innocent, don't I? I can conduct a
silent defense, but I've got to be innocent, and say so, or the union

can look bad. And if the union is going to get the most for its money I've got to be shot."

Lund did not trust himself to speak, but he watched Joe walk to the end of the cell, turn, stoop to shake the coffeepot, pour a little lukewarm coffee into his cup. At last, when it appeared that Joe was going to say no more, Lund said, "Is that the way it happened, Joe?"

"That's a suppose story," Joe said. "You can think up a lot of interesting yarns sitting around a jail."

"Then you really weren't in Morrison's store."

"Does it matter whether I was or not, so long as the union is able to make people think I wasn't?"

"It might matter to you, personally."

"How?"

"It might be on your conscience."

"What's on my conscience won't matter to anybody this time tomorrow," Joe said. Already his mind seemed to be on something else. He jumped up from the cot and snatched the pencil from his shirt pocket. He seemed ready to do enormous labors. With his thumbnail he broke away the wood from the tip of the pencil to improve the point, and he squeezed in past Lund and sat down and wet the pencil with his tongue. His concentration, like his passion, struck Lund as manufactured. He was like a man playing charades, acting out words for others to guess. Though he was within two feet, Lund felt that he wanted to appear unaware that he was not alone.

A sad discomfort, a rankle of hurt feelings that he instantly diagnosed and repudiated, made the preacher stir on the cot. Joe spread his paper on the seat of the chair and wrote carefully for a minute. From above the toilet he reached down the stamp pad and the rubber stamp with which he signed his name, and he inked the stamp and impressed it under what he had written. As if Lund were furniture, he moved around him to the door and rattled his pencil between the bars. As the guard's steps came near, Joe turned and held the paper so that Lund could read it. It was a telegram addressed to Bill Haywood in Chicago; it read, "Goodbye, Bill. I'll die like a true-blue rebel. Don't waste any time mourning. Organize. Yours for the OBU. Joe Hill."

Waiting for the guard, he was drawn up like a prince. The

light falling from above poured over his fair hair and his slim rigid shoulders. He was limned with light as he thrust the paper through the bars. Every slightest motion was exaggerated, theatrical, posed—or was it kingly? Inscrutable, wrapped in dignity or clothed in affectation and an actor's sense of his own conspicuousness, he stood alone under the floodlights of a stage watched by hundreds of thousands, and he spoke his curtain line and it rang like a blow on iron.

What was on his conscience would not matter.

For a long time Lund had felt that he was in Joe's cell more to watch than to do anything else. Joe did not want to talk. He wrote, or he walked the three steps of the cell back and forth, or he stood in attitudes of thought until he seemed to have fallen asleep on his feet.

A compulsion for oracular utterance was upon him. Once, when Lund asked if he didn't want to lie down and get some sleep, he stopped pacing and chopped out a laugh and said, "There'll be plenty of time for that later." Around nine-thirty he rattled his pencil in the bars and ordered another pot of coffee, but when it came he was sitting at the chair with the tablet before him and he did not even notice that the guard had come. Lund poured him a cup and he let it sit at his elbow and grow cold. He was full of electric energy even when he sat still; he wrote a furious sentence and crumpled the paper and threw it on the floor and sat thinking again.

At ten he sent another telegram, again to Bill Haywood. Again he showed it to Lund and again he stood under the drench of light like a general in his headquarters and gave a message to the world. This time it was no battle-cry but a mordant joke, a play on words. "It is a hundred miles from here to Wyoming," he wrote. "Could you arrange to have my body hauled to the state line to be buried? Don't want to be found dead in Utah."

In two hours he had said hardly fifty words to Lund, who sat feeling helpless and out of place and watched Joe burn with an incandescent energy into his last hours. Only once did Lund try to break through to him, and then he spoke only because he felt his obligation as friend and counselor heavy upon him.

"Joe, have you got any family that I could write to? Anyone you'd want to hear?"

"No. No family."

"Isn't your father living?"

That made Joe turn half around, his neck corded from the strained position. "I don't know," he said. "I guess so. It doesn't make any difference to me whether he is or not."

So there was no point in pressing or discussing that. If the small-town baron had bequeathed anything to his bastard son it was nothing but an encysted hate. If he had done anything in the last few weeks to save him, he had done it weakly and under cover, not to hurt his own career with publicity. Joe didn't even know that the iww had appealed to him; he would never forgive them if he found out.

Lund's legs were asleep from long cramped sitting on the cot. It seemed dismally late. He stood up and looked quickly at his watch, but the wide alert eyes raised up and caught him. Joe flung down his pencil—whether in anger at him or petulance at some thought that was hard to phrase Lund didn't know. He stood looking at the narrow head and the prison-shrunken figure: a bundle of scars, a temperate way of life, a name, a number, a sentence. But he could not bring himself to believe that he was doing Joe any good, or could ever again do him any good. Joe's mind was outside himself; he had no need now for human talk or the arm of a friend.

"Joe," he said, "I don't think you really need me or want me here. I'll stay as long as you like, but wouldn't you rather I left you alone?"

Joe chewed his upper lip, regarding him steadily. "What time is it?"

"Ten thirty-five."

He saw the computation go through Joe's mind; momentarily the eyes were vacant and dull.

"I've got quite a lot to do," Joe said.

Wanting to cry with the futility of his attempt, Lund reached the rolled-up overcoat from the head of the cot, and Joe watched him without moving to stop him. But when Lund stood at the bars and tapped for the attention of the guard, Joe caught his arm in a hard grip.

"Messages," he said. "Not much time. But come back. Get some sleep and come back. I'll be through then."

"I don't know whether I can arrange this at all," Lund said. "The warden may insist that I stay, now I'm here. He might not let me back in in the morning."

"Well, call him up," Joe said. "There's no use you losing a whole night's sleep."

"I'd gladly lose a hundred times that if you wanted it."

But he got no answer, and now the guard was outside. Lund turned, feeling sick, from Joe's face, which seemed suddenly ghastly. "Joe'd rather I went away a while, and came back in the morning," he said. "Could I talk to the warden on the phone, or get a message to him, to make sure it's all right?"

"I don't know if he's still up."

"Could you see?"

Before the guard could answer, steps sounded in the outer corridor, turned into their cell block, stopped while the key clanked in the security door midway down. Then the warden himself, with another guard, was looking in through the bars. He looked at Joe and Lund but he spoke to the moon-faced guard.

"How's he been?"

"Okay. Writes. You saw the telegrams."

With his head sunken and thrust forward, his frown pinched in, his bald head shining under the light, the warden looked steadily at Joe. "Everything all right with you?"

"I could use some hot coffee."

"You'd better lay off the coffee and give your nerves a rest."

"Coffee never hurt my nerves."

"All right," the warden said, hardly moving his lips. "You can have coffee if you want it."

"I was just asking the guard if I could talk to you," Lund said. "Joe and I seem to have about talked it out. He'd like to be alone a while to write some letters."

"I thought he wanted you here all night."

"I did too. But I think I bother him. He wants to get some things written."

"He could come back early in the morning," Joe said.

The warden stared in silence. Then he grunted at the guard. "Let him out."

The door grated and swung, and Lund went out. Through the bars he shook Joe's lumpy hand.

"You don't mind, Gus," Joe said.

"Of course not. Whatever you like," Lund said. "You're your own best judge." Gripping the hand harder, he said ineffectively, "Try to stand right with yourself, Joe," and was led out. Before he left the prison the warden gave him a spectator's pass that would admit him in the morning.

Near midnight, walking the block and a half from the streetcar stop to his hotel, he saw the armed guards slowly patrolling, their breath steaming and their shoulders muffled in sheepskin coats, before the doors of downtown office buildings.

Sick, confused, a failure both as preacher and as friend, torn between morality and compassion, and bewildered at the way Joe had gone beyond him, Lund left a call for four-thirty and crawled up to bed in the stuffy steam-heated room. He was tired out; merely sitting in Joe's cell had been grinding labor. But it was a long time before he slept, a long time before he could rid his mind of the image of Joe Hillstrom, full of some ecstatic vision, living out in his last hours not his own life but his forming legend.

7

The city was cold-dark as they came through it. The streets were empty and silent; intersections under the mortuary shine of the arc lights looked so cold and forgotten that he shivered under the heavy coat. He could see his breath in the side-curtained gloom.

The taxi turned left up Twenty-First South and climbed the hill around a curve, bouncing in the rutted gravel. Lund peered out, and abruptly the high stone walls were there, alert lights on the towers, an automobile's lights flaring as it pulled through the gate between two guards with rifles on their arms. That car could contain the firing squad. He tried to follow it, but the wall shut it off and its lights vanished somewhere inside. Beyond the walls and the guard towers the sky over the Wasatch was just paling toward dawn. The air was dry, bitter with smoke, perfectly still, cold as iron.

"Say!" his driver said, rousing from a chilled torpor. "They're shooting a guy out here this morning."

Lund opened the door and groped his way out, reached under his overcoat and with difficulty got at his wallet. The guards at the gate forty feet away were watching him closely. Down the street under the nearest arc light a handful of men clustered, also watching. As Lund put the wallet away and turned toward the gate one of them left the group, came a few steps peering, and then came on at a limping run. Another guard appeared promptly beside the two at the gate.

"Wait!" the running man called, and Lund recognized Carpenter. The printer's face was gray, as if he had been standing in the cold a long time. The light from the gate shone bright on a drop at the end of his nose. He laid his hands on Lund's arm and said breathily, "Can you see Joe? Will they let you in?"

"I don't know," Lund said. "I hope so." His own lips were stiff, but somehow the coldness in his mind rather than in the air had made them so.

"You can get inside, though," Carpenter said. His breath blew in quick spurts of steam as he turned his head toward the watchful guards behind the gates. "They won't even let us close," he said bitterly. "We can't even walk on the sidewalk in front of the god damn place. It's against their law to walk on the sidewalk."

His gray mouth twitched, and he hung onto Lund's arm. "Listen! If you get to see Joe, tell him not to give up, hear? There's still hope, tell him. Some guy in Seattle has wired the governor that he was with Joe the night Joe got shot, and can tell the whole story. The whole Pardon Board is up there meeting with the governor right now. Tell him we'll get him loose yet."

"Is that true?" Lund said. "Are they meeting?"

In spite of himself, in spite of his disbelief, he felt the hope awaken in him like a sleeper rising on an elbow to listen. There had been a dozen stories, a dozen sleights, a thousand threats, but this was the real crisis now. This wire from Seattle, whether true or faked, might get Joe another reprieve. If the board took it seriously enough to meet about it . . .

His mind was running ahead, and he brought it back to Carpenter. "I was up there. I seen Straup and two or three others go in, about two-thirty this morning. Tell Joe that. There won't be any shooting, tell him. They wouldn't dare."

"I'll tell him if I get the chance," Lund said. "I'll try."

He left Carpenter on the sidewalk and went up to the smaller pedestrian gate at the side of the big double steel ones. The guards stared at him hard-eyed, and even when he presented his pass they made no move to unlock and let him in. "Come back at six-forty-five," they said. "Spectators and witnesses at six-forty-five."

"But I'm Hillstrom's spiritual adviser!" Lund said. "The warden told me late last night it would be all right to come in."

"What's your name?"

"Lund."

"Go in and ask Bestor," the guard said to his companion. Lund was left standing outside, like someone caught trying to sneak into a show without a ticket. Farther out, on the sidewalk, Carpenter stood where he had intercepted Lund. From his little sentry-box window a guard called to him: "All right, you, move on down there."

"Go screw yourself," Carpenter said, and stayed where he was.

The guard came out of his box and made a threatening motion with his gun. In a frenzy of defiance Carpenter yanked his coat open over his chest and faced him. The gate lights fell on his working face. Coat still held open, jaw thrust out, he came two steps closer. At the arc light below, the little group of Wobblies moved uneasily. One of them called something to Carpenter.

The third guard returned from the main building, and his chief, tense at the steel grill, said over his shoulder, "Okay?"

"Okay."

The lock of the small gate clicked swiftly. "All right, come in here." Lund was pushed on toward the building. Over his shoulder he saw the head guard and one companion open the gate and walk out to Carpenter, who came to meet them with his frantic chest bared. Even when a rifle barrel jammed into his belly he held the coat wide. There was not a word spoken that Lund could hear. The second guard frisked Carpenter and then the two of them crowded and pushed him backward to the little group

under the light. There the head guard held his rifle on them
and the other frisked them one after the other. When the last
one had passed under his slapping hands the two bulky uniforms
with rifles held flat across their chests used the guns to push
the whole group off the sidewalk and clear across the street.
It was like pushing snow off a sidewalk with a scraper.

The guards were coming back when Lund reached the steps.
Over the wall the crest of the mountains was sharp against the
empty lightening sky. A silhouette with a rifle came out on the
wall and stretched, spreading its arms.

The first thing Lund saw as he stepped inside was a clock with
its hands at ten minutes past six. The numbness that had fastened
upon his senses during the tumbril-like ride from his hotel, the
somnambulist muffling of his mind so that even the guards and
the sullen Wobblies moved silently and stiffly like images on a
screen, departed from him as if the floor had given way, and he
stood in the doorway shaken by absolute terror, staring at the
face of the clock. He was a sleeper shaken awake by shouting
and a stridency of bells; a confused stander in a passageway while
panic streamed past.

Slowly the room filled in and he took his eyes off the clock
that said there was almost no time left, no more than sixty minutes
more before it would be too late forever. If any reprieve came,
it would have to come before the minute hand of the clock went
once more around.

The guard in the cage and another against the wall, the one
who had come out of the closet in the warden's office, were
watching him. Big with blue and brass, belted with broad leather
and hung with guns, they let their eyes feed on him. He hardly
heard his own voice saying good morning, and he cleared his
throat, getting himself together. The guard Bestor examined his
pass and handed it back. "You'll have about an hour to wait."

"But I saw the warden last night about eleven. He said it would
be all right to go back in with Joe."

"You the fellow that was in his cell, the YMCA fellow?"

"I'm a minister, yes. I was there last night."

Both guards were regarding him steadily, and he saw that their
resistance, their uniformed dull opportunity to stand in his way,

was a pleasure to them. They enjoyed seeing him push and try to get by. His tongue stumbled in his mouth. "The warden said this pass would let me back in this morning—before they come for Joe."

Bestor shifted, still leaning against the wall. He creaked softly like a saddle when he moved. "I couldn't let you in on that. It don't say anything about letting you into his cell."

Lund put his hands in his overcoat pockets to hide their shaking. "A man is going to die this morning," he said sharply. "He has a right to whatever consolation can be given him. Is the warden in?"

"He isn't seeing anybody."

Lund made one step toward the warden's office door, and Bestor made one step as if to intercept him. They confronted one another, crouching a little, like wrestlers feinting for a hold. In Bestor's face Lund saw every habit of restraint, every lust for domination and denial, that could ever have been bred even in a prison. The man was a walking cell block, with a lock for a mind. In his passion Lund even estimated the chances of beating him to the warden's door, jerking it open before the guard could lay hands on him, but the very thought of himself in that position, possibly getting himself shot and appearing in the paper as a desperate IWW intent on murdering the warden. . . .

The outside door opened and Sheriff Coues came in. He nodded around and started in toward the warden's office, but Lund stopped him. "Things have got mixed up. Last night the warden told me I could spend the last hour with Joe. He gave me this pass. But this man can't let me past, and he has orders to keep everybody away from the warden."

The guard had relaxed, easing himself upward to erectness with padded muscles. The sheriff eyed Lund a moment, looked at the pass. "Let's see," he said, and turned the knob of the warden's door.

Warden Webster pivoted at his desk; he had evidently been sitting looking out the window into the darkness. "What's it look like out there?"

"It'll be all right," Coues said. "I posted eighteen deputies around outside, with shot guns. Those guys are all wind. They won't start anything."

"Everything ready?"

The sheriff sighed as if he were tired to the bone, and sat down on the edge of the desk. He yawned artificially, inducing the yawn with widened jaws, and rubbed a hand up his cheek and over his brows and eyes. "I wish to Christ it was done."

Lund had been standing back uneasily. The clock was the most important thing in his mind; he felt how it had moved even since he came in here. "Mr. Webster," he said, "the pass you gave me won't get me past the gate out here. Could you pass me through?"

The warden turned a cheap alarm clock that sat on a file beside his desk. It said six-twenty-two. "Boench given Hillstrom a hypo?"

"He wouldn't have one," the sheriff said.

"How's he acting?"

"Quiet. I went up about one and he was writing a song."

Irritably the warden swiveled in his chair, confronting Lund abruptly. "If he's ready by himself he'd better be left alone."

"He asked me to come back," Lund said. "You heard him."

The warden put his two flat hands on the desk as if about to push himself to his feet. His sleepless eyes were streaked and pouched. It occurred to Lund that he was a sad man, and that the sheriff was another. The more responsible instruments of society's revenge were not so much vindictive as sad and tired.

"Mr. Lund," Webster said, "my whole feeling in this business is that Joe ought to be allowed to die as quietly as possible. If you're going up there to exhort him and stir him up and shed tears over him you can't go."

Clenching and unclenching his hands in the big linty pockets of his coat Lund said softly, "Do you think I *want* to go? He asked me to come."

"All right," Webster said. "At ten minutes to seven Sheriff Coues will come to get him. You can stay until then. When he's led down, you join the witnesses."

He went to the door. "Bestor."

The guard came smartly forward.

"Search Mr. Lund carefully and then take him up to Hillstrom's cell."

For a moment Lund looked into Bestor's still hazel eyes. The man with the lock for a mind would have the satisfaction at least of frisking him.

In five minutes the prison yard, the bleak spread of gravel just growing visible, and a trusty who crossed on some early errand and looked at them and said "Good morning, Mr. Bestor," in the soft, careful prison voice. Now the door and the prison smell, the faintly stale smell of paint, hot radiators, disinfectants, many men, a smell that would have been like the smell of a gymnasium except that a gymnasium always had the odor of sweat and activity and bodily heat in it, and here the smell was cold in spite of the warmth of the building. Now the iron stairs, two angled flights, to Number One cell block on the third tier, and the faces of impassive guards, a new shift.

He stood while Bestor explained to the guard on duty at the gate. Down the aisle he saw the steel door locking off the maximum-security section. He wished Bestor would not talk so loud: the man's voice thumped and echoed like a voice in a barrel. Lund dreaded another voice from the one occupied cell, telling them all to go away.

As if bucking an invisible current, he followed down the corridor through the inner door and along the row of cells to the one that held Joe. Joe was sitting on the cot reading. Somehow Lund had the impression that he had jumped there just a moment before. The floor all around him was strewn with balled-up papers. The mere sight of him sitting there, and the moment's contact with the wide blue stare that could mask anger, contempt, a joke, fake innocence, interest, set Lund's heart to pounding with painful heaviness. He slipped in the door and spoke, finding his voice hoarse. "Hello, Joe."

He was amazed that Joe could smile. "Don't be so downhearted, Gus," he said. "Take off your coat and sit down."

"You're all right," Lund said gratefully. "You've got courage."

"Cheer up," Joe said. "This dying business isn't as bad as it's cracked up to be."

Struggling out of the overcoat he had the feeling that the cell was too small for the task; it was like trying to take it off in a telephone booth. But it give him a moment of something to do, and it let him make the routine offer of assistance that was always the easiest thing. "Anything I can do?"

"Everything's taken care of," Joe said. "I wrote some letters but the guard'll take care of those."

"I heard you wrote a song last night after I left."

"Yeah. Want to see it?"

"I'd like to."

He sat down on the cot to read the carefully copied sheet that Joe handed him. His mind was pulling against itself, one part of it cunningly estimating what time the clocks said now, another part alert for signs of cracking in Joe's surface calm, still another trying to focus upon the words of the song. The song was entitled "Don't Take My Papa Away from Me," and it was a tissue of shopworn sentiment and threadbare clichés, a lugubriously bad song:

A little girl with her father stayed, in a cabin across the sea,
Her mother dear in the cold grave lay; with her father she'll always be—
But then one day the great war broke out and the father was told to go;
The little girl pleaded—her father she needed
She begged, cried and pleaded so.

Don't take my papa away from me, don't leave me there all alone.
He has cared for me so tenderly, ever since mother was gone . . .

While he read, Lund's mind was wrenched with unhappy amazement that this song should have been written, seriously and on the last night of his life, by the same man who a few hours before had sent out that austere telegram to Bill Haywood and the embattled iww throughout the world. Spartan and sentimentalist lay side by side in Joe Hillstrom. Like a spit of rain flicking across a lighted window the image came and passed: Joe's stiff and posed and light-drenched figure as he thrust the telegram out through the bars at the guard. He looked up from his reading into Joe's eyes, and the eyes were asking for praise.

"It's good," he said miserably. "They'll have it in the songbook."

For a moment Joe's eyes were dead and blank, as if there were some wandering of his attention, an interest in something remote and inward and inaccessibly private. Then he forced light back into them—it seemed to Lund to grow by a visible act of will—and he said, "I wrote something else. Look at this."

The sheet he handed Lund had three stanzas written on it in the neat copybook hand, and it was signed with the rubber stamp slantingly across the bottom. The verses were entitled "Joe Hill's Last Will."

"Read it aloud," Joe said urgently, and Lund read.

> My will is easy to decide,
> For there is nothing to divide.
> My kin don't need to fuss and moan—
> "Moss does not cling to a rolling stone."
>
> My body? Ah, if I could choose,
> I would to ashes it reduce,
> And let the merry breezes blow
> My dust to where some flowers grow.
>
> Perhaps some fading flower then
> Would come to life and bloom again.
> This is my last and final will.
> Good luck to all of you.
>
> JOE HILL

Not trusting himself to speak, Lund nodded and handed the paper back. In a moment he saw that Joe's attention was wandering again, the inward resolution wavering. Already many minutes had passed. It must be at least a quarter to seven.

Abruptly Joe swung around. "I thought something might happen," he said in a high, tight voice. "It did before."

"Resign yourself, Joe," Lund said. "It's the only way. Please, boy!"

He put his hand on Joe's arm and saw the stretched lines from the corner of the thin mouth. "I've never preached at you, and I won't now," he said. "In the end we answer to ourselves. If you can come before yourself with a clean conscience they can't hurt you, Joe. They can't touch you."

Joe's head jerked, a strange pecking motion as if he were recovering from being pushed, and his lips parted to show the even clenched teeth. "I can answer to myself all right!" he said shrilly. "They've had plenty of chances to change their minds. Thousands of people have put in a word for me. President Wilson has wired them twice. They still want to shoot a man because he's an enemy

of their filthy capitalist system. All right, let them shoot me! I'm
ready for them. What are they waiting for? Why don't they come
on?"

Lund grabbed Joe's shaking hands and hung on to them both.
He wished he hadn't come. It was unbearable, and he did not
help Joe. In the face of Joe's cracking control he wavered, thinking
of what Carpenter had panted at him by the gate. Which was
better, to take the last walk resigned to your death, or to walk
out still believing the miracle might free you before the firing
squad took aim? He did not know, he miserably did not know.

"Joe," he said, "listen, Joe! It isn't final yet. The Pardon Board
has been meeting all night. Somebody wired from Seattle that
he could prove an alibi. There might be . . ."

Joe's lips flattened across his teeth, and his breath wheezed.
His eyes darted around the cell as if in search of a door. "Then
there's still a chance!" he said.

"I don't know," Lund said. "Don't bank on it too much. There
isn't much time. You've got to be ready, you've got to be resigned."

Joe pulled away. "I'm all right. Don't worry about me. I'm
ready for them." His eyes were moving constantly around the
cell, and he kicked the balled-up papers with his feet. Words
came out of him in bursts, jerkily.

"Messed the place all up. Writing all night. Ought to clean
the joint out." He smiled a strained, ghastly smile. "Brought up
to be neat. Sailors always neat. Ought to sweep out here."

Before Lund knew what he was about, he was at the door,
calling to the guard. "Hey, Hutton. Hutton!"

The steps came fast, almost at a run.

"I've only got a few minutes," Joe said. "They'll be here any
time. I never had any last requests of anybody, but I've been
a neat man all my life. I'd like to clean this place up before I
go. Can I have a broom?"

"That'll be all right, Joe. You don't need to worry about that."

"Just the same, I'd like to clean it up. I haven't got much time."

The guard went up the corridor and came back very quickly
with a broom, which he shoved handle first through the bars.
Joe started sweeping, his head bent, his jaw set so hard that
the scars on cheek and neck stood out like welts. Sitting on
the cot, Lund pulled his feet up while Joe swept under them.

The papers were just gathered into a neat pile when they heard the slow crowded footsteps on the stairs.

Lund crossed the cell in two steps, took the broom handle from Joe's hands and set the broom against the wall. There were no voices coming with the steps, only the sound of somehow laboring feet, and sharp and clean in Lund's mind flashed the picture of the first funeral he had ever preached at, the funeral of a very big man in a lodge hall in Minneapolis: his mind echoed with the unpadded bare silence of that hall, and the way the pall-bearers' feet had labored under the weight of the dead, going out.

He wrung Joe's hand, but the hand was flaccid, and he stared in anguish into Joe's eyes, but the eyes were fixed on something far off. Joe's nose was sharp as a pencil; the tight lines were deep from nostrils to lip. He did not turn when the steps halted outside, but the unmutilated wing of his nose fluttered, and his chest swelled. Over his shoulder Lund looked into the eyes of Sheriff Coues, and with Coues, crowding the corridor, he saw Bestor, three deputies, a smooth-faced white-haired man with a doctor's black satchel.

"All ready, Joe?" the sheriff's deep sad voice said.

Joe stood with his back to them. The cell lock clacked, and Lund after one last hopeless wringing of the slack hand, squeezed out the narrow door. "He all right?" the sheriff asked, and gestured with his eyebrows at the doctor, obviously asking if Joe needed a hypo.

"He's all right," Lund said from a choked throat, and even while he spoke he was shoved headlong into the sheriff by the guard behind him. He turned, half falling, his mind full of the incredible belief that it was a last-minute rescue, that the Wobblies had succeeded somehow in forcing their way in, that the guards, Bestor, the doctor, might be Wobblies in disguise—his mind was an explosion of thoughts even while he struggled for balance.

He turned in time to see the cell door slam shut. Joe's stooping body leaped and bent, and the cot skidded across the cell, barricading the door, just as the sheriff and the recovering guard threw their weight against it. With a crack like a shot Joe broke the broom handle across his knee and lunged. The guard yelped like a dog, the sheriff leaped aside. Then the guard was back in the corridor holding his wrist, from which blood welled up swiftly along a jagged tear. Deputies with guns in their hands were ranged along the front of the cell. Inside, behind the cot, Joe couched with the broken broom handle, holding them off as if with a sword.

"Go on, shoot!" he screeched. "You're going to shoot me anyway, save your paid murderers the trouble! Why don't you shoot me?"

Two deputies rushed the door, but the broom handle darted and drove them back. Sheriff Coues moved them aside and stood before the door. He was the only man there who was not furiously excited. "Joe," he said, "what do you think this is going to get you?"

"Never mind. Just try coming in here after me."

"You're going to die, Joe," the sheriff said, and his voice boomed in the hollow cell block sad and slow. "You're paying a debt, and you can't beat it. You're just making it hard for yourself and everybody else."

"Just try coming in!"

"I thought you'd die like a man, Joe."

"I'll die like a man. Come in and see."

"You and I always got along," Coues said. "I think we respect each other. But when I come in after you it won't be me coming, Joe. It'll be the law, and you can't buck it. Now I'm coming in."

He put his shoulder against the door and pushed, paying no attention to the threatening stick. He pushed the cot angling across the cell and squeezed past it and went up to Joe and held out his hand. After an unspeakable moment Joe laid the broom handle in it.

"Now I know I was right about you," Coues said. He beckoned the doctor, who took his bag inside. "Roll up your sleeve, Joe," the sheriff said. "This'll make it easier."

They read the warrant to him from the corridor while he stood with his arm bared to the doctor's needle. Five minutes later Joe Hill came out of his cell with a fixed, gritted smile on his face, his shoulders back, his head up. His eyes were fixed, staring far-off, blue and milky as the stare of a cataract-blinded man, and his head was tipped slightly sidewise, as though he listened.

The sheriff handcuffed his hands in front of him, and a deputy took each arm. Bestor, the doctor, the two guards, Lund, all stepped back against the corridor bars and the deputies started forward.

Lurching, yielding to their hands, Joe walked ahead stiffly. Sheriff Coues and the third deputy fell in behind, and Lund came like a sleepwalker beside the doctor.

He walked like a blind man, as stiffly and as blindly as Joe Hillstrom walked. Like a blind man he felt the iron corridor turn into the landing above the stairs, and like a blind man he set his feet carefully one after the other on the iron treads: eleven steps, then a landing and a turn, then eleven more steps and the solider landing of the second tier; than eleven more, and another landing, and eleven more and the solid cement. Fear came up through his legs at that change: no more stairs; that much of the journey done.

Fear came in with the bitter morning air at the opened door, too, and as the cold rushed to meet them Joe Hill said loudly, as if he were truly blind and could not see those he spoke to, "You're killing an innocent man. I could be a free man now if I'd wanted to compromise. My trial wasn't a fair trial and I wouldn't take anything but a complete vindication. I said I'd get a new trial or die trying. Well, I haven't stopped yet."

Lund saw that gray light had flooded up over the mountains. The whole prison yard lay bare and open to the little procession. He saw Joe Hill's erect back marching slowly between the shuffling, usherlike deputies. Joe's had remained bent slightly as if he listened for something, and he looked in a quick half-circle when they were halfway across the yard. There was not a movement from the guards in doorways and on the walls. The sound of shoes on cement was a slow dry shuffle.

Fifty feet or more of cement sidewalk—and Lund's feet knew how Joe's were feeling it out step by step. He felt how the terror came one swift stride closer as the feet left the cement and crunched in cinders at the beginning of an alley between buildings. Now against the outer wall, crowded between that and one of the buildings, the spectators came in sight, twenty-five or thirty men huddled under the thin vanishing steam of their breath. The fear came a step closer and took him harshly by the throat as the procession turned left around a corner into the rough alley, and there was the chair.

The sheriff turned and motioned; he had to wave twice before Lund realized that he was the one being signaled. He stumbled out of the hypnotic procession and over to the group of witnesses. Some malady was on his eyes. He saw the little file move up the alley like a distant caravan toiling across a plain, and at the end he saw the execution frame, crude and rough as the cross of Calvary—a raw plank backstop backed with steel, and in the planks that masked the steel back a hole as big as a man's two fists chewed out by the bullets of past executions. Bolted to the frame in front of the backstop was an ordinary office armchair.

The chair faced a stone building across the alley. Directly across, in the double doors of what looked like a machine shop, Lund saw a green curtain that moved a little in a breath of wind. Through the curtain, three at kneeling height and two at standing, jutted the barrels of five rifles.

They stopped Joe Hill in front of the chair, and Lund saw his head move as he looked toward the curtain and the screened source of his death, the hidden men whose names only the sheriff knew, who came in a closed car and left the same way, with the faint consoling possibility that the rifle they had fired might have contained the one blank cartridge of the five.

It seemed to Lund that when he looked sidelong at his death Joe jerked in the deputies' hands. And when the sheriff moved slowly up and tied a black handkerchief across Joe's eyes, the listening tilt of the condemned man's head was so pronounced that Lund looked around wildly in the hope that what Joe listened for might still come. A messenger from the Pardon Board which had been meeting all night might yet make unnecessary the splintered backstop and the casual chair, the rifles and the hidden sweating executioners, the waiting chaplain and the three doctors lined up with warden and sheriff beyond the place of execution. Like a sleeper groaning in nightmare he moved, trying to struggle back out of the danger and horror he had fallen into, but when he opened his eyes wide and breathed deeply, steadying himself, the prison yard and the alley were the same.

They removed the handcuffs from Joe Hill's wrists and put him in the armchair. Not a sound came from them. They stood as silently and watchfully as he knew the Wobblies were standing outside the prison walls.

As if he were to die himself, and had passed beyond hope

or fear, Lund felt quite suddenly calm. He looked with clear eyes at his friend who was really about to die and saw the deputies strapping his shoulders back to hold him erect in the chair. As the white-haired doctor bent forward with his stethoscope to his ears to examine the heart of Joe Hill, workman and singer and rebel, hero now in a hundred rww halls, either a martyr to law's blindness or a double murderer, Lund examined that heart in another way, and could not find the answer he searched for.

The doctor pinned a heart-shaped target on Joe Hill's breast, and Lund's throat tightened till the constriction was hard pain. He bent his head and said a swift prayer, but the substance of his prayer was incoherent to himself, and he might, for all he knew, have said it aloud, "God help you, God help us both, God help us all."

"I die with a clear conscience!" Joe said suddenly, loudly. "I die fighting, not like a coward. But mark my words, the day of my vindication is coming!"

Beyond the execution platform the sheriff stepped out one step and raised his hand. His face was graven with deep, anguished lines. "Aim!" the deep preacher-voice said.

Joe struggled against the straps that held him. His fury pulled him to a strained half crouch, and he screamed toward the curtained doorway. "Yes, aim! Let her go! Fire!"

Lund turned his face, blinded with a rush of tears. He heard the deep voice of the sheriff and the hot slam of the rifles. The man next to him let out his breath in a slow, whinnying sob.

The preacher turned and stumbled across the yard toward the front gate. The sun was red over the guard towers and the tops of the inner buildings. As he crossed the yard he heard the wild, savage ululation from outside the walls, the cry as direct as the roar of an angered animal.

For them, at least, there were no complications, no querying of the demands of vengeance, and justice, and love.

May Day, 1916

It was perhaps a minute after the pinch of white dust had blown
upward and dissipated itself among the leaves before any sound
came from the crowd. Then a single voice, hoarse and untuneful,
insistent, full of a bawling ardor, started to sing. The song was
"There Is Power in a Union"—one of Joe Hill's.

Other voices joined in instantly. The song spread like a grassfire,
so that within seconds the whole great crowd was singing.

No one proposed it, no one had had the idea before, but now
all had it together. In an orderly column, six or eight abreast,
holding up their red One Big Union pennants like the banners
of an army, they fell in line by the hundreds until they were
massed in a column half a mile long, and singing as they went,
they marched out of the cemetery and down the streets of Seattle.
When they came to the King County jail they spread out all
around it, still singing.

Police appeared; during lulls in the singing we could hear the
sirens as reinforcements came hurrying. But the crowd gave the
police no cause to disperse it. Orderly, quiet, confident, almost
carefree, they stayed massed outside the jail for two hours, singing
to the IWW prisoners inside. Late in the afternoon, when they
had sung themselves hoarse, they passed the hat and took up a
collection for Tom Mooney and Warren Billings, awaiting trial in
San Francisco on a charge of bombing the Preparedness Day
parade.

The song they sang last, the one that groups of them were

still singing as the crowd broke up into groups and couples, was
the one they had begun with:

> There is pow'r, there is pow'r
> In a band of workingmen,
> When they stand hand in hand,
> That's a pow'r, that's a pow'r.